He was still recognizably Paul Norris at that point,
but no longer recognizably human.

Inside his open mouth, Andy could see two rows of what looked like razor-sharp teeth. His tongue was distended, his eyes blazing red, and his fingernails, gripping the edge, looked like gnarled claws.

Andy was willing to attribute the sight to a stress-related hallucination . . .

But then Paul spoke again, and even his voice had changed. It was deeper, more gravelly, and froze the blood in Andy's veins, goose bumps breaking out all over his skin as Paul Norris's words carried a sibilant undercurrent Andy was sure would be the last thing he would ever hear.

I'm dead I'm dead I'm dead I'm dead I'm dead

"Say hello to the wife and kids for me, will you, Andy?" he asked. "And when you see mine, tell 'em Papa's got a brand new bag. And he *reeeeeally* likes it!"

Andy tried to reply, to use some semblance of that moment's humanity to anchor Paul somehow, but it was so hard to even breathe. The unholy thing that used to be Andy's best friend and partner sprang from the hole in the wall—on the fourth floor of the building—and was gone.

Enter the terrifying world of

30 DAYS OF NIGHT

Available from Pocket Books

30 Days of Night: Rumors of the Undead

Graphic Novels/Comic Books
available from IDW Publishing

30 Days of Night

Dark Days

30 Days of Night: Return to Barrow

30 Days of Night: Bloodsucker Tales

30 Days of Night Annual 2004 (featuring "The Book Club," "The Hand That Feeds," "Agent Norris: MIA," "The Trapper")

30 Days of Night: "Picking Up the Pieces" (featured in *IDW's Tales of Terror*)

30 Days of Night: "The Lady in Black" (prose fiction featured in *The Complete Dark Days*)

30 DAYS OF NIGHT™

RUMORS OF THE UNDEAD

STEVE NILES & JEFF MARIOTTE

Based on the graphic novels
from IDW Publishing

POCKET STAR BOOKS
New York London Toronto Sydney

An *Original* Publication of POCKET BOOKS

A Pocket Star Book published by
POCKET BOOKS, a division of Simon & Schuster, Inc.
1230 Avenue of the Americas, New York, NY 10020

ISBN-13: 978-0-7434-9651-3
ISBN-10: 0-7434-9651-5

This Pocket Star Books paperback edition March 2006

10 9 8 7 6 5 4 3 2

Manufactured in the United States of America

Authors' Note

In the *30 Days of Night* mythos, *Rumors of the Undead* takes place following the events of the graphic novel short story "Agent Norris, MIA" (which itself takes place immediately following the events of the graphic novel *Dark Days*) originally published in *30 Days of Night Annual #1* (August 2003). However, it should be noted that one does not need to be intimately familiar with that particular story in order to enjoy this work.

30 DAYS OF NIGHT™

RUMORS OF THE UNDEAD

Excerpted from *30 Days of Night* by Stella Olemaun

I can't be absolutely accurate when it all began. When my life changed forever.

Maybe it was just a day before the sun set on Barrow, Alaska, for the winter dark.

My husband, Eben Olemaun, and I were the sheriff and deputy of Barrow, this remote, northernmost Alaskan town, population four hundred sixty-two after most folks left for the winter. Eben was a native Alaskan, a full-blooded Inuit. He loved Barrow in a way I never quite could, but he helped me learn. I moved on north to here when I left college and my home state of Michigan.

I was avoiding facing my parents. Eben was avoiding growing up. We fell in love the second we met.

He was already a deputy and managed to get me into the law enforcement game as well. I thought initially it was because he was selfish and didn't want to be away from me, but once he saw I could handle myself, it worked out and eventually we became the first husband/wife sheriff and deputy team in the state of Alaska.

Believe it or not, it could have been a dream life in so many ways. I look back now and I look at the things I complained about: the cold—I thought *Michigan* winters could be brutal—the extreme time periods of sunlight and darkness, the locals, even Eben's reluctance to have a child. . . .

Then of course, somewhere very far from us, it seemed like the entire world was on the fast track straight to hell. . . . What happened two months earlier clear across the country, where the remains of two skyscrapers were being sifted through as part of the largest crime scene on the face of the earth, and the bombs were dropping in retaliation half a world away, locals all jumpy to begin with, some remarking that those responsible could now come scuttling across the tundra to fuck up the pipeline, just you wait and see . . .

I look back at everything with such different eyes now, and I'd give anything to relive the time before our own little world crashed down around me.

Before darkness came in human form. Before I saw most of the people I knew killed, murdered right before my eyes.

We started getting the calls on the day before the sun was to go down for the next thirty days . . . sunset until sometime in mid-December.

It seemed to be an annoying but harmless string of vandalism and theft calls. Primarily people began calling the Barrow Sheriff's Station to report missing cell and satellite phones. At first it all appeared so benign, so odd, but it was also our first big clue that something in Barrow wasn't right.

Then the citizenry's computers went missing and, in some

cases, smashed. Phone lines were cut. Finally, reports of damaged snowmobiles and other all-terrain vehicles began to pour in.

It seemed like we were under attack ourselves, not by terrorists but by pranksters, kids, maybe dopers. It was so sudden and strange that neither Eben nor I could make any sense of it. But then it hit me—all the signs were there.

We were systematically being cut off from the outside world.

As it turned out, the thefts were (mostly) being perpetrated by a stranger who Eben and I arrested at Sam's Place, the local eat-and-drink.

The stranger, this straggly biker type with a stench like a rotting corpse, was our first glimpse at what we were up against, our first look into a world I wish we'd never had to witness. This mystery man had been causing some kind of uproar at Sam's Place, so Eben went down to have a chat.

It seemed it would be like any other arrest. We were fairly used to the ranting and raving of the drunks and drug users. Alcohol was prohibited in Barrow that winter and several before due to the alarming suicide rate incurred by the days and weeks of darkness. All the law did was cause folks to get the drinks and drugs from outside town. As if the cold wasn't numbing enough . . . Plus you never knew who it was trying to get in their last fix—someone working the pipeline deciding to venture on the one last bender for a month.

Either way, Eben would straighten him out. That was my

husband's style after all: he'd charm you, and then if that didn't work, he'd pound you into the ground.

Evidently the man, whose name we never learned, had been yelling obscenities, and making a general nuisance of himself. He was even insisting on having his hamburger served super-rare, still uncooked and dripping with beef blood. Oh yes—drunk *and* high. Those are the worst ones.

After a heated exchange between Eben and the stranger, I assisted my husband bringing the man into custody. Swearing an oath to uphold the law usually means that confrontations with such characters cannot be avoided, but man, did this one give me the creeps.

This stranger, this horrible man, seemed more than just addled as he sat in the holding cell back at the station.

He openly admitted to the thefts of the phones and townspeople's personal property ("Great!" Eben had remarked, grinning. "Open-and-shut case then. Thanks for ignoring that 'can and will be used against you' thing I mentioned before.") . . . and hinted at some grand plan by some unnamed person or people.

Eben and I did our best to ignore him.

He went on and on in his cell, warning us about a coming threat that he would not name, then started referring to himself as a "scout."

I was thinking, *Scout? For what? A movie shoot?*

Finally, Eben had had enough. He and the stranger barked at one another through the cell bars—

The power went out. Jesus. *That* was creepy.

Now the "scout" laughed, warning us that the time had come for *something*—something we would be helpless against.

While he threatened and the lights stayed out, all I could think was what I had already begun to fear—we were being cut off from the outside world. All of our lines of communication and travel were being severed one by one; first the cell and satellite phones, then the snowmobiles and snowcats . . . and finally the lights.

Gus Lambert—a likeable but secretive guy who didn't come into town very often—was in charge of Barrow's power station, which sat on the crest of a hill just south of town. If there was trouble with the lights, Gus was the man to check on.

When Eben and I discussed this amongst ourselves, it was like adding gasoline to the fire. The scout went absolutely wild.

"Now you're catching on. Check on Gus! Board the windows! Sandbag the doors! You'll try it all! But one by one THEY'LL *pick you off and strip the meat from your bones!"*

The scout became more and more agitated with every passing moment, screaming, tearing at his greasy hair, throwing himself around the cell, but it was one of the final things he said that will forever haunt me, the first hint of what we would soon be up against.

"It's gonna be beautiful! And then I get to be with them!"

Them.

Such a simple, innocuous word, and yet it carried so much weight.

Who the hell did he mean?

I wanted to write him off as a nut, we got lots of them up

north, but crazy people don't carry out such elaborate plans . . . or do they?

What was happening to my town?

With the lights out and the citizens of Barrow coming into the streets wondering what was going on, Eben and I decided then and there to drive out to the power station . . . but not before the scout decided to throw us one more unexpected twist.

Right before our eyes, he grabbed hold of the reinforced steel bars of the cell, pulling them apart with his bare hands as if they were made of rubber.

His shoved his manic face through the widening opening, hissing:

"You are so FUCKED."

Utterly horrified, I reeled backwards away from the scout, fumbling for my service revolver even as I wondered how much PCP one needed to ingest in order to pull apart the holding cell's bars.

The madman started crawling through the substantial hole he'd created. Eben stood his ground, stood in the path of the scout, at the same time pulling his own weapon.

Eben gave the scout one warning, which of course went unheeded, and fired a round into the stranger's head.

To my utter shock, the man didn't fall right away, but remained on his feet for two more steps and then fell, twitching and what appeared to be clawing at the floor.

I stood over him and saw the exit wound in the back of his head, the sticky matter blown out and clinging to the jagged edges.

And still he moved.

Eben stared down in shock. "Is he dead?"

Without even thinking about it, I unloaded my clip into the stranger until his head was all but gone. "He is now."

I had never done such a thing in my life . . . and yet I felt no remorse—I knew I'd killed . . . a monster, something unnatural.

As I fired the last bullets into the head, pulping flesh and bone into one, the stranger still managed to grab my ankle.

Now, looking back though, I must have been in shock as well. Even in that state, I knew this was all impossible, the sickness rising in my belly, the kind of sickness that only comes with fear. . . .

It would only get worse when Eben and I drove out to the power station and found Gus Lambert.

The station was destroyed.

Gus's severed head—eyes permanently frozen in a rictus of wide-eyed confusion and horror, mouth open as if silently protesting the situation—was left on a pike, gore splattering the snow around it, like a twisted message for us of our impending doom.

The destruction to the power station was thorough. Satellite dishes in pieces, wiring torn and burned, the generator broken into a battered iron hulk. Repairs would take months. But there would be no repairing Gus.

The rest of him was in parts, scattered in the snow.

The sickness brewing in my stomach finally won out, shooting into my throat and bringing me to my knees. In the course of only a few hours, my life in Barrow with Eben was being turned on its head.

Eben and I drove back toward town, freaking out, wondering what the fuck was going on. There had been only three violent deaths, possible homicides, in Barrow in the time I'd served as deputy.

Gus and the stranger in the cell were two of them.

Eben was openly speculating: Some kind of gang? Escaped prisoners? Terrorists trying to get at the pipeline?

Neither he nor I had any way to temper the terrible fear rising in each of us, a fear with no name, and no reason.

"Eben, stop the truck!" I yelled as we came around the southernmost slope of Barrow.

I saw movement through the trees, something out beyond the frozen paths of trees and frozen hills.

Shapes.

Eben pulled the truck over.

The sun was long gone now—the skies above Alaska and the entire top of the world had gone dark. Eben and I had taken time earlier, before the chaos, to sit on a hill and watch that big yellow ball disappear for the next thirty-plus days. We said, as we did often, how much we loved each other. It is a moment that will drive me for years, if not the rest of my existence.

But right then, there was no light to comfort us, and wouldn't be for a long time.

We stepped from the vehicle, Eben looking through his pair of well-worn night-vision binoculars to where I was pointing.

I looked out into the darkness with my naked eye. Small shapes were moving in the distance.

When Eben slowly lowered the binoculars, I could see by his expression what he saw.

And for some reason, a line from the play I studied back in college, *Macbeth,* immediately leapt to mind, crystal clear:

By the pricking of my thumbs, something wicked this way comes.

Eben didn't even look at me. "Get in the car." he said. "We have to warn the others."

I

MORNING SUN, diffused by the yellow brown haze that snugged over the Los Angeles basin like a toxic cap slowly strangling the life out of its citizens, eliminated the Slumber Motel's only advantage: neon so old it looked retro. It was one of those typical Hollywood joints that tourists sometimes accidentally picked off the Internet. Usually they realized the error of their choice before checking in, and switched to one of the national chains. If they didn't, then their first night's lullaby was dealers and hookers plying their trades, the shopping cart people collecting bottles from the trash cans around the vending machines, junkies hitting up guests for smokes and spare change. The cops came around once in a while, but they preferred to stay away if at all possible. Even the scrawny palms shed their fronds and stood bare, jaundiced and sickly, as if they'd rather die than live too close to the faded pastel box.

Andy Gray knew that crime was a given at a place like this. Only the presence of yellow crime scene tape wound around the trunks of the spindly palms and tied to the rusty iron banister and the squad car sitting at the curb with two uniforms inside it were unusual.

Andy left his Bureau ride, a standard gray Crown Vic, and walked up to the black-and-white, waving his ID at the two young cops.

They emerged from their car, stretched out the kinks. "Help you?" the male cop asked.

Andy scanned the man's brass nameplate. "Special Agent Andrew Gray, FBI," he said, passing over the leather folder with his shield and ID card. "I need a closer look at the crime scene, Officer Ybarra."

Ybarra checked out Andy's identification, then smiled broadly. His teeth were white and straight, accentuated by his dark olive skin. His partner, a woman named Coggins, was almost a foot shorter, but solid. She kept her lips pressed together in a thin line as she handed him a clipboard. Andy added his signature to the list of those who had come before him. "CSIs have been here all night," Ybarra told him. "But they're gone now, so I guess it's all yours."

A rookie, then. LA cops had never routinely referred to the criminalists who examined crime scenes as CSIs until the TV show came along. There were too many specialties—medical examiners, latent print examiners, forensic anthropologists, photographers, trace evidence examiners. A cop with more experience might have said, "The CSIU has been here all night." The crime scene investigation unit covered all bases, and cops—forever going up against criminal defense attorneys who'd grasp at any straw they were offered—needed to learn to speak precisely. Andy guessed that the CSIU had, in fact, spent the night here, with the possible exception of the medical examiner. MEs only came out when there were dead bodies on hand.

Trouble was, Andy was pretty sure there had been a dead body in that hotel room.

The fact that nobody knew the body was dead was the whole problem.

He turned away from the cops and looked over the scene, trying to take it in as it was now without remembering what he'd been told about the events of the night before. What he'd seen when he got to the LA office.

Jacob Paul Norris. Andy's partner. Dead man walking.

The science of modern crime scene examination had pretty much been invented by the FBI. He remembered what he had learned at Quantico, that approaching a crime scene with preconceptions blinded you to the reality of the situation. Andy Gray emptied his mind and opened his senses.

The stink of rush hour traffic fumes along Sunset.

Glass on the parking lot surface, glittering in the morning light. Some of it tinged with red.

Blood—pools of it, almost black on the macadam. More splashed against the pale yellow stucco walls.

Small puddles of something else, on the sidewalk that ran along in front of the rooms. A housekeeper's cart had been caught in the crossfire. The puddles were probably shampoo, cleansers, solvents, something like that. Forensics would confirm that for him.

Chips out of the stucco. Bullet holes. At least a hundred, he guessed.

Motel room windows shattered. Curtains swaying gently in the breeze that also fluttered the crime scene tape, making a noise like a kid with a playing card in his bicycle spokes.

Another smell, metallic, underlying the exhaust fumes. Copper. Blood.

And a third, fainter still. Familiar. Andy searched his memory and came up with it.

Rotting meat.

Staying where he was, Andy turned slowly, taking in the surroundings. A block wall at the end of the parking lot—part of a liquor store. Sunset Boulevard—cars slowing so their occupants could gape at the wreckage of the motel. Like traffic didn't already suck bad enough. Across the street, a tattoo parlor, then a trendy bar, then the Standard Hotel with its upside-down sign. Cute.

Andy lived in Sacramento with his wife and two daughters, but he'd been spending so much time in LA, he was beginning to hate it as only a native could.

Only days ago, there had been yellow tape around the Standard, too, but the hotel's owners carried more weight with the city than the Pakistani family that owned the cleverly named Slumber Motel. A woman had been murdered at the Standard. Shot. Didn't even make the evening news. The Olemaun woman had been checked into the next room, but she'd vanished.

She was, officially, a "Person of Interest" to the LAPD. She had already been that to the Bureau.

Andy shrugged. He'd seen enough out here. He would demand copies of all the CSIU's reports and fill in any blanks that way. Time to look at what he had really come here for.

Paul's room.

He returned to the Crown Vic. From a kit in the trunk he took some plastic booties and tied them on around his ankles, covering his shoes. The CSIU had already taken their pictures and measurements and samples, so he wasn't concerned about Locard's principle of exchange. Andy wasn't going to contaminate the crime scene by looking at it, but if the stories he'd heard were true, he had no interest in contaminating his own shoes by stepping into that room unprotected. For the same reason, he tugged on latex gloves. The dark suit was off the rack from JC Penney, and if he got anything on it he could expense the dry cleaning. But the shoes were Bally, a gift from his wife. Not cheap—not on his salary.

So outfitted, he crossed the parking lot to the door of Room 7. The door was closed but not locked. He turned the knob, pushed it open.

Even though the window facing onto the parking lot had been blown out, fresh air still hadn't cleansed the stench inside. This was where the meat smell had come from, and a lot of the blood. It looked like Paul had been moonlighting as a butcher, running his own slaughterhouse from the room.

The blood was everywhere. Some of it was fresh, still liquid, some brown and crusted on surfaces as if it had been there for days. Spatter on the walls and pictures and mirrors, drip patterns on the ugly gray carpeting and the once white bedspread. Puddles drying on the fake wood veneer of the dresser and the little round dining table.

He continued into the bathroom. A sink with a mirror over it, a toilet, a bathtub with a shower, and a small opaque glass window that probably opened onto the alley. A towel rack that had probably held cheap white hotel towels. The CSIU had taken those. Andy could see spots where they'd swabbed the blood in here, but plenty was left behind. If he had to guess, and Andy Gray didn't like guessing, he'd say there had been multiple violent deaths in this small, dank room.

The mirror was filmed with red as though somebody had feebly attempted cleaning the gore. Through the crimson screen, Andy caught a glimpse of a man as bland as his name. Short, graying hair; sallow skin; the look of a man who spent too much of his time inside or in the dark. He didn't want to examine himself any closer and looked away.

The sink looked like a painter had been cleaning brushes in it—a monochromatic painter, at that. *Paul's red period.* Even—Andy felt his gorge rise, fought to keep down his coffee-shop breakfast—the sides of the toilet were coated with the stuff. Chips in the porcelain showed bone fragments as well.

Good Lord, what had gone on in here?

Something on the tile floor. Andy bent over, afraid to kneel in this place. Pulled a pen from his pocket and used it to nudge the tiny object. A tuft of fur. He scanned the rest of the floor, still bent over. A tiny tooth in one spot, something else that might have been a cockroach's carapace. He had been told that they had actually recovered animal parts from here—rats, insects, lizards. All of them ripped open, desiccated.

All of them drained of blood.

Andy stood up again, too fast. The room tilted and he had to catch himself on the edge of the sink. *Thank God for the latex gloves,* he thought. Would there be any shower long enough and hot enough to scorch him clean after this? It was the oldest cliché in the book, but Andy would never get used to seeing scenes like this. He would worry when his stomach *didn't* tighten up.

He had to get out of here. His pores felt clogged with grime, his nose packed with blood. He tasted it. He knew the evidence technicians had taken all of Paul's belongings—clothing, laptop, briefcase, any notes he might have made. Local cops hated it when the Bureau swept in demanding their evidence, their casework. He didn't blame them a bit, but he had done it himself and would do it again today. They didn't know what they were looking at, had no clue what the big picture was, and they could not be allowed to know. LA's Assistant Director in Charge himself had made that abundantly clear.

So Andy would supplement his walk-through with everything the LAPD's Hollywood Division had collected, and he would make enemies of the Hollywood cops in the bargain. Cementing the Bureau's reputation as a bunch of hard-nosed assholes who didn't care about the cops on the beat. Andy wasn't really that way, but there was nothing he could do about the perception.

Outside, he peeled off the gloves and booties, wadded them together and shoved them into one of the motel's outdoor garbage cans. He felt bad for the next homeless person who would reach in there, but not bad enough to want to carry the stuff away with him. The sooner he could put this all behind him, the better he'd like it.

It would not be behind him any time in the near future, he knew.

He still had to find Paul. Now, at least he had a better sense of what he was looking for.

Paul had never come right out and used the word to describe himself. But he and Andy had been on the Stella Olemaun case long enough to know what the word was. What Olemaun claimed it was, anyway, even though Andy had never been willing to accept her terminology.

The phrase Paul preferred, just because of who he was, had been "fuckin' bloodsuckers." To Stella Olemaun, a little more refined—and who wasn't, compared to Paul Norris?—the word was . . . no.

No way. I can't even go there or I'll just lose my mind.

Special Agent Andrew Gray didn't believe in anything of the sort.

Some of his colleagues may have been slightly more open-minded, but as far as Andy was concerned, *Creature Features* stopped running on TV a long time ago, so that was that. Life wasn't made up of rubber masks, campfire ghost stories, and dimly lit movie theaters; it was all the product of someone else's overactive imagination. He even hated bringing the girls to see Santa Claus, for Christ's sake.

Uh-uh. Beyond the garden-variety nutjobs, Bela Lugosi's dead, Herman Munster's on Nick at Nite, *and everything else is bullshit,* he had thought once upon a time.

But . . . that was before he had seen Paul last night at the local Bureau office.

They'd been partnered up for years. Paul was a lot of things, many of them unpleasant, but he had never been the . . . the *thing* that Andy had talked to yesterday.

He had been, in some undeniable, awful fashion, changed.

Recalling the encounter made Andy feel sick. Confused. Frightened. But he had to do it. He had to fill in all the impossible blanks with logic and reason or he would never rest. That was the way Andy was. Everything had to fit somewhere, with a label and clear definition. Andy Gray had no room in his logical brain for anything filed under supernatural . . . or unnatural.

He waved to the cops, Ybarra and Coggins, started the Crown Vic, pushed down the blinker arm, pulled out into the frantic traffic on Sunset. From here it wasn't far to Runyon Canyon Park. He could ignore the junkies, look at some patches of real grass and genuine trees, imagine for a minute that he was a long way from the city. He needed that right now, needed dirt under his shoes and the calls of birds other than pigeons and a glimpse of blue sky somewhere in the oppressive LA smog. He needed things that were *real*. Christ, he'd settle for anything this side of a nightmare.

What he really needed was a hug from Monica, and the laughter of his kids, Sara and Lisa, but he was too unclean even to talk to them. The park would just have to do for now.

As if that could somehow dispel the panic festering deep within him—the kind that would fill his world, seize him up as he drowned in the icy darkness growing inside his head.

Over and over he kept telling himself:

This is not happening.

This is not happening.

This is not happening.

2

The Bureau had pioneered the use of psychiatry in criminal investigations. Every graduate of the Academy had courses in behavioral sciences, abnormal psychology, and the criminal mind. Andy was no exception. He had read, in those courses, about many cases over the years of people who *believed* themselves to be . . . those things. These people shunned daylight and drank blood. Some of them had filed their canines into sharp fangs. Some of them had even killed.

Ironically, the problem they all ran up against was that they couldn't handle the nasty side effects of what they craved. Blood wreaks havoc on the human digestive system. Drinking your own is slightly less harmful, but drinking that of others can lead to a wide array of unpleasant reactions. So their guts protested, their stomachs erupted. Most who tried blood wound up in the hospital. They hated it—the light, the sterility. But at least their lives could be saved, albeit through intravenous feedings.

Eventually, with the help of long hours of therapy, or jail time, most of them were convinced that they were not, in fact, creatures of the night, nocturnal drinkers of blood. Even a little trolling about on the Internet revealed that most of them were just misguided outsiders desperate for attention and a way in, or around, a world that had otherwise rejected them.

But even worse, and Andy had learned this the hard way, for every dozen or so freaks who believed themselves to be the real deal, there was one who thought he or she was the hero of the picture, a hunter of some kind.

On the basis of the evidence the Bureau had seen so far, Stella Olemaun seemed to be a charter member of this category; a hunter, or vigilante, depending on where you stood. And unlike most of the other wannabes, a trail of death and destruction followed Stella around.

At first, she had been observed meeting with some of the arms dealers in and around Alaska and the Pacific Northwest—the ones that the FBI kept tabs on, anyway—in the wake of Ruby Ridge, Oklahoma City, and 9/11.

Then in Los Angeles, a riot had broken out at a university appearance where she'd been promoting her book, *30 Days of Night*. There had been gunfire and explosions, and a lot of strange rumors and incomplete reports about the evening; fights, bloodshed . . . even a report of a man burning to ash onstage. *That* part had to be just a story though—no physical evidence was found to support that zinger.

The LAPD, not knowing what to make of it and with too much on its hands already, had wisely downplayed the whole thing and had not pressed charges against Olemaun.

Pressing charges meant a lot of the wrong kind of attention.

Stella Olemaun had been active enough, and vocal enough, to have attracted the interest of the FBI even before her book—purporting to tell the "true, inside story" of the incident in Barrow, Alaska—had been published.

Special Agents Andy Gray and Paul Norris had been assigned to find out what she was really up to.

But with all this mass hysteria around, Andy had never heard of an FBI agent who had come to believe that *he* was caught up in it as well.

Until last night.

Andy sat on the park bench and took a sip from a bottle of Coke. The grass and trees were at the full green of late spring, before summer's heat and dry air sucked it out of them.

He had to clear his head, to straighten out the tangle of impressions he'd taken away from Norris's hotel room, and from his encounter with Norris during the night. Doing so would mean sorting out who Paul had been, what had happened to him, and what he had become. Because something had *definitely* happened to him—the Paul Norris he'd seen last night was not the man Andy had known for the better part of his adult life.

Not by a long shot.

* * *

Close friends since their Academy days in Quantico, Andy Gray and Paul Norris were eventually partnered on the job, working out of the Sacramento field office. Partnering the two men bore immediate, fruitful results. Both had distinguished themselves in the line of duty, but together they proved to be an unstoppable conviction machine. Bank robbers, kidnappers, drug kingpins, and white-collar criminals fell before their combined efforts. Andy noticed that Paul had become even more outrageous during the intervening years—he drank more, smoked more, swore more, and generally carried on. But when he focused on a crime, he was like a laser, burning through anything in his path until the bad guy was in jail. Andy was as straight as his friend was freewheeling, and figured the two of them balanced each other out. *Like some TV police drama from the seventies.*

Three weeks after Paul's sudden transfer to Los Angeles (an admittedly difficult time for Andy as he missed working with his good friend), the two agents were teamed up on another case, in spite of the fact that they worked out of different offices in different cities. Together, they got the goods on a state legislator from LA who was using his position to extort money from a variety of businesses, domestic and international. The Assistant Director in Charge at Los Angeles and the Special Agent in Charge at Sacramento both knew a good thing when they saw it and looked for ways to keep the two partners working together.

When the Stella Olemaun situation came up—especially when it became clear that she would kick off her book tour in LA—they were assigned to keep an eye on her and her strange entourage. Instead of being in the audience when she gave the speech that turned into a riot, Andy and Paul were in the parking lot watching her car and shooting the breeze. Neither had any idea of the fireworks that would take place inside, nor did they expect she'd use, inside a college auditorium, any of the weaponry she had acquired.

Hearing the commotion, the agents rushed to the scene, but campus cops and LAPD were closer. Once they had moved in, Andy and Paul held off, letting the locals calm things down. LAPD took Stella into custody but kicked her loose almost immediately when she said that the gunfire and explosives had only been used against the subject of her book. The whole thing was presumed to be just another LA publicity stunt.

That was when things fell apart.

Andy had gone into downtown LA to start the paperwork necessary to take Stella off the LAPD's hands. Before he even got there, Paul called on his cell to let him know that she'd already been released. Stuck in LA traffic, it was more than an hour before Andy made it back to Hollywood.

By then, Paul Norris had vanished.

Andy tried his cell. No answer. Called his house, but Sally hadn't heard from him. He walked through the Standard, looking for his partner. Nothing. Paul was simply gone. *Poof.* Andy called the Assistant Director in Charge and let him know what had happened.

When an FBI agent disappears, the Bureau mobilizes—within an hour they had agents canvassing Sunset and the surrounding streets. They had feelers out for his credit cards. His photo had been sent around to every LAPD division, every LA sheriff's office, the California Highway Patrol and the Border Patrol.

But he was nowhere to be found.

Officially, Special Agent Jacob Paul Norris was MIA, but off the record, the Bureau assumed he was dead, as did Andy, because while Paul had plenty of faults, he wasn't the kind of guy who would just walk away from the job. Until there was a body, though, Andy wasn't willing to believe it, period. He stayed on the scene day and night, looking for his partner.

Then in the Standard, a woman named Judith Ali was shot in the face at close range, blowing a fist-sized hole out of the back of her head and splattering the hotel room with blood and brains. Because Ali had been seen around town talking to Stella Olemaun, and what a coincidence, her room was right next to Stella's, the FBI took a keen interest in the case. But not Andy. To him, it was just a distraction from the real issue at hand: Where was Paul?

For Andy, the mystery and desperation surrounding Paul's disappearance were quickly giving way to borderline-obsessive behavior. Andy Gray would have been the last to claim that his marriage was completely sound. The time he'd been spending in Los Angeles hadn't been helping things any, nor had Monica's perception—not altogether unfounded—that he'd rather spend time with Paul Norris than with her and their children. But during the time that Paul was missing, Andy didn't want to talk to anyone who couldn't help find his partner. That included Monica. After the third time he hung up on her, she stopped calling.

Finally, on the third recanvassing of Sunset, an agent found the Slumber Motel employee who had checked an apparently not-quite-dead Paul Norris into Room 7. The motel employee hadn't noticed anything particularly strange about the guest, but the agent talked to a housekeeper who said the guest had refused to let her in to clean or change linens, and that every time she went past the room, the stench grew more and more horrific.

A night clerk had seen Paul going in and out of the room, only after dark, and sometimes returning with what looked like squirming bundles. The clerk had knocked on the door once to tell the guest that pets were not allowed in the motel, but the guest—who had checked in under the name Fred Savage—replied that if he didn't mind his own business, he'd severely regret it.

The Bureau converged on the Slumber Motel. They listened through the windows and heard Paul Norris ranting quietly to himself, and also heard the squealing and shrieking of small animals being killed. In Judith Ali's room at the Standard, half a cockroach had been found, and later on, at Andy's suggestion, it was tested for DNA. Paul Norris's was found. His fingerprints were all over the room.

When he first heard the news, Andy sat in his rental car—Paul's car having been returned to the Bureau to be combed for evidence—and buried his face in his hands. He thought he was going to weep, but tears wouldn't come. Instead he felt a deep hollowness.

His best friend in life had become a murderer, some kind of savage beast.

Andy found himself looking to the past, looking for clues to Paul's apparent breakdown. But it was too sudden. Inexplicable.

Knowing how close the two men were, the ADIC called Andy into the LA office while the Bureau and the LAPD's SWAT team moved on the motel. No one expected Paul Norris to come through unscathed, and they didn't want Andy to see his partner wounded or killed. While Andy was driving across the city once again, the agent in charge at the scene called Paul's room. Paul confessed to the murder of Judith Ali, but insisted that he'd been ordered to do it by "his mistress." The agent told him that the motel was surrounded and that they'd like Paul to surrender himself.

Paul came out, all right.

But he carried a pistol in one hand and a shotgun in the other. According to reports from the scene, before he started firing, he shouted, *"All right, which one of you fuckheads wants their ass kicked first?"*

Dozens of weapons were pointed at Paul Norris. The

agents and SWAT team—to a man and woman wanting to give Paul every chance—waited until his finger was tightening on the shotgun's trigger before opening fire.

Once they did, it was a massacre.

The first bullet slammed into Norris's chest, a perfectly placed heart shot. The next one couldn't be definitively identified as at least twenty rounds struck him simultaneously. Before the roar of gunfire died down, seventy-eight bullets had hit Paul, and another fifty-two had missed their target. Paul lay in a pool of his own blood on the edge of the parking lot, under a thick cloud of bitter black smoke.

But that wasn't the end of it.

In fact, the real fun was only just revving up.

3

INCREDIBLY, Paul Norris wasn't dead.

Not entirely.

Andy was still at the Bureau when he was brought in. Paul was on a stretcher, banded down with ripstop nylon straps. The ADIC had tried to prepare Andy for what he'd see, but it was still far worse than Andy could have imagined. Open, bleeding bullet wounds by the score. Wounds that should have killed him a dozen times over. And yet . . .

"Good to see you again, Andy," Paul said. "How are the kids?"

My God, he's still breathing . . . let alone asking about my family.

Andy had convinced ADIC Flores to let him interrogate Paul alone, and the paramedic team that had brought Norris in wheeled the stretcher to a special containment unit that had been prepared for him. There, they stood the stretcher upright so that what was left of Jacob Paul Norris could look Andy Gray in the eye.

Between them were a row of steel bars and a panel of six-inch-thick glass. They could hear each other because of a sound system built into the special cell. On Andy's side of the glass there was a single desk and a chair, so he pulled the chair out, placing it in front of the glass pane.

"This looks much worse than it is," Paul remarked.

Andy sat down with a cup of coffee in his hand and looked at his friend, trying to puzzle out what had happened to him.

He couldn't escape the obvious conclusion. This had to have something to do with the Stella Olemaun case. The things that had attacked Barrow, Alaska, staying for the entire month of deepest winter, when the sun never rose.

No. Goddammit, no. I can't believe a word of it. Sure, it might be one way to explain what had happened to Paul—presumably, something like that could survive being shot seventy-something times. *Remotely possible, maybe.*

But I just can't accept it. No way.

He stared at Paul, sipped his coffee, and tried to come up with some other plausible explanation. The staring contest drew out for several agonizing seconds.

"The paramedics ran vitals on you," Andy said after a while.

"And?"

"You're dead."

"Actually," Paul countered, "I'm somewhere in the middle. My missus disappeared before I could get a taste of her blood."

"Blood?" Andy echoed reflexively.

"Yes," Paul answered. "Blood. I'm turning into something that needs blood to survive."

Andy remembered the stories from Abnormal Psych. *People who took it as far as killing small animals and drinking their blood. Sometimes, in rare cases, killing people. Fucknuts.*

Was that what had happened to Paul? Had something inside him snapped? Over the days he'd been missing, had he been convincing himself that he was one of the undead, requiring blood to keep going? What in the name of God would compel him to do that all of a sudden?

Finally, he came right out and asked him. "What the hell happened to you out there, Paul?"

Paul answered matter-of-factly. "I tailed the Olemaun woman. But then another woman, one with a taste for blood, came along and made me her . . . servant. Her Renfield, I guess. She took me, Andy. I had no choice."

Yeah, sure. Paul had been "taken" by women before, sometimes while they'd been on the job. He'd never disappeared for more than an hour or so, though, and the fluid he'd been drained of those times hadn't been blood. *But this . . . this is something different, more extreme.* The blood running and drying from Paul's numerous wounds demonstrated that. And the stink that came off him—more than just the fact that he hadn't bathed in days, more than the blood on him—it was repulsive, foul, rancid. It was the stench of the dead . . . only worse.

For the first time in ages, more than anything at this moment, Andy Gray needed a cigarette.

"So what do we do now?" Andy asked. It was Paul's psychosis, after all. Maybe he would have a way to deal with it.

But his answer was unnerving.

"You'd better figure out a way to kill me, or get the fuck out of here."

"What's that supposed to mean?" Andy asked him.

The response was a malevolent glare.

Whatever disorder possessed Paul, it was getting worse by the minute. In spite of his wounds and his mental state, Paul had been talking to Andy like the old friends they were. His answers had been insane, and yet lucid, all making sense within the mental construct he'd built for himself. And the height of the insanity was that Paul had sucked Andy completely into this mindset, detaching himself from a situation that any causal observer could see had already descended into madness.

The most frightening part about it, though, was that Andy had never seen Paul look at anyone, not even the crooks and scumbags he hated so much, with anything like the disdain he showed Andy at that moment.

What happened next was even more surprising. Start to finish, it took only a few seconds, but when Andy rewound it in his head, trying to examine it piece by piece, it took him hours.

Because what happened next should have been impossible.

Paul flexed, almost like a man shrugging on a jacket, and the nylon bands simply exploded off him.

Unbound, he grabbed the steel bars, bending them apart wide enough to step through.

With his fists, he punched right through the supposedly unbreakable glass.

Andy was cut by flying shards, but in his horror he never even felt them.

Paul, impossibly strong, was coming for him.

And then he lifted Andy off the ground by the collar of his cheap suit. Andy kicked at the air helplessly. He opened his mouth but couldn't force any sound out.

Andy had had guns pointed at him, two-bit drug lords screaming, as they were led away, that they'd cut his family's throats while he'd be forced to watch . . . but right now, he had never been so terrified in his life.

"I could have taken *a thousand more shots,* outside the motel!" Paul roared in his face. "But the head . . . nothing can live without a head."

He lowered Andy, who was paralyzed with fright, unable to fight back. "Think about that next time we meet," Paul whispered in his ear. Before Andy could respond, Paul slammed him against the wall. "But for now," he continued, "I seem to be changed, and the sun is coming up in a few hours."

Changed? My God, the strength he had exhibited had been nothing short of superhuman. Andy knew all the theories about adrenaline, the stories that under extreme stress people could do amazing things. A father had once lifted an entire automobile off the ground because his son had been trapped underneath it—was Paul experiencing some sort of adrenaline overdose?

Then of course, it got even worse.

While Andy tried to shove himself to a sitting position, back against the wall, Paul hoisted the metal desk above his head without even struggling. "So I have to say good-bye," he said, "before I do something delicious to you that I might regret."

With that, he threw the heavy desk through the exterior wall. The wall simply blew out as if struck by a missile—brick, plaster, and studs gave way before it, and there came from below a crashing sound of crumpled metal and glass smashing as the debris hit the vehicles parked in the lot, car alarms now blaring. Paul leapt like some kind of enormous toad into the hole he'd made. He paused, just inside the building, and glanced back at Andy.

He was still recognizably Paul Norris at that point, but no longer recognizably human.

Inside his open mouth, Andy could see two rows of what looked like razor-sharp teeth. His tongue was distended, his eyes blazing red, and his fingernails, gripping the edge, looked like gnarled claws.

Andy was willing to attribute the sight to a stress-related hallucination . . .

But then Paul spoke again, and even his voice had changed. It was deeper, more gravelly, and froze the blood in Andy's veins, goose bumps breaking out all over his skin as Paul Norris's words carried a sibilant undercurrent Andy was sure would be the last thing he would ever hear.

I'm dead I'm dead I'm dead I'm dead I'm dead

"Say hello to the wife and kids for me, will you, Andy?" he asked. "And when you see mine, tell 'em Papa's got a brand new bag. And he *reeeeeally* likes it!"

Andy tried to reply, to use some semblance of that moment's humanity to anchor Paul somehow, but it was so hard to even breathe. The unholy thing that used to be Andy's best friend and partner sprang from the hole in the wall—on the fourth floor of the building—and was gone.

Andy lurched to his feet and instinctively ran to the hole, half expecting Paul to still be there somehow, a malevolent spider ready to drag the hapless insect away. Nothing. Just the clamor of the ceaseless, shrieking car alarms. He couldn't see Paul or much of anything else anywhere down below. Nothing but the darkness, even though down there was still lighter than the shadows that were gathering inside his head.

What . . . what . . .

The primal scream nearly escaped his throat when the room filled with people.

"Obviously, this can't get out."

Assistant Director in Charge Hector Flores's eyes bored into Andy. They were sitting in his office forty minutes after literally all hell had broken loose. Andy had been checked over by paramedics—the cuts from the flying glass had been bandaged, his back and ribs ached from having Paul throw him around, and exhaustion from staying awake for the past few days was starting to catch up to him. He'd been offered a sedative, but turned it down.

Right now he needed to get on Paul's trail, and he didn't want anything that would hamper his reaction time or fog his mind.

"Out?" Andy echoed, not quite understanding.

"An FBI agent who somehow acquires incredible strength and a thirst for blood?" ADIC Flores said. He was a Hispanic man in his fifties, stocky, neatly groomed. His suit had probably cost as much as Andy's car. "Come on, Agent Gray. That kind of thing would make us a laughingstock. We're already having enough turf trouble with the CIA, and there are plenty of others who are no fans of the Bureau. If we want to keep any kind of profile at all, we've got to keep this in-house. Completely. Understand?"

"I understand," Andy said, finally catching on. *He means cover-up. Something like this happens, something unprece-*

dented, and a powerful, dangerous madman is loose in one of America's largest cities, and instead of devoting all available resources, he just wants to bury it, pretend like nothing happened.

All because Flores was concerned about the Bureau's place in the intelligence pecking order, worried about their funding in the next budget.

That's just fucking great.

"What about his family?" Andy asked. "Have they been notified?"

"We'll take care of it," Flores promised. His attitude was laid back, but his dark eyes were quick and intense, and Andy had seen him in action, sizing a man up as swiftly and accurately as a lifelong butcher eyeballing a pound of ground chuck. "We'll tell them Norris died heroically. We'll set them up for life, financially . . . but you've got to keep away from them, Gray. I mean, I know you guys were friends, but you'll see them all at the funeral. Act normal. Just don't say anything that could compromise us."

"And Paul?" Andy pressed. "What about him?"

"We're looking for him, but we're doing it under the radar," Flores said. "No one knew him better than you, though." Flores leaned forward. "What we need you to do is to get out there and eliminate any trace of this whole mess."

"Sir, I don't understand—"

"Yes, you do," the ADIC clarified. "Scrub that motel room. The police reports. The Judith Ali homicide. All of it. As far as we're concerned, it never existed."

"Like Paul never existed?"

Flores shrugged and scratched at his silvery temple. "Have it your way," he said. "Just take care of it before it bites us in the ass."

"What about the hole in the wall?" Andy pressed. "All the agents who were at the motel, or here in the building when Agent Norris escaped?"

"We're taking care of internal matters," Flores answered. "And I've talked to the Special Agent in Charge in Sacramento. He's willing to have you assigned down here for as long as it takes."

Terrific. Monica will be thrilled to hear that. As if I haven't been gone enough lately.

But he kept his mouth shut. He didn't want to head home yet.

The Bureau wanted Special Agent Gray to hide the truth about Paul Norris from the world? Fine. As long as they'd pay him and give him the flexibility he needed, he was happy to let them think he would do that.

What Andy would really be doing was trying to uncover the truth. At this point, all he had was a head full of questions and a few aches and pains for his trouble.

You'd better figure out a way to kill me, or get the fuck out of here.

Paul Norris—the old Paul—would have wanted an answer. It was always about catching the bad guy, bringing him down.

The new Paul was some kind of monster. Now it looked like he *was* the bad guy. Andy wanted a concrete explanation. Wanted to understand.

Think about that next time we meet.

And all of a sudden, Andy Gray found himself very, very afraid of the answers he was trying to seek.

4

"MONICA?"

"Andy? Are you—"

"I'm okay, Monica. Listen—Paul's dead." It wasn't the whole truth, but it wasn't a lie. He was, according to the paramedics, clinically dead.

Stronger than ever, but dead.

"Oh my God!" Shock in her voice, as expected. She'd never learned to like Paul, but she had tolerated him for Andy's sake. "What happened, Andy? Were you there?"

"I'm fine, Monica, don't worry about me. It was a line of duty thing, something I'm not really supposed to talk about. Just know—" This part was a lie, and it caught in his throat like a fish bone. "—just know that he died a hero."

Andy listened to his wife, breathing hard, trying to control her emotions. She was frail. Like a baby bird, he sometimes thought, physically and emotionally—Monica was stick-thin and as light as if her bones were hollow. Where Paul's wife fought a constant battle against her weight and was all curves and bosom and rounded flesh, Monica was the exact opposite. Her body seemed diminutive, a tall child's, no fat on it. Her skin hung loose on the bones and was wrinkled as an old woman's at thirty-four. She had beautiful, thick brown hair, the healthiest thing on her, but people sometimes thought it was a wig and she a cancer patient.

As if in response to her physical self, Monica's emotions also seemed to be lacking a crucial protective layer. She wept easily. When she did cry, it was quietly, like she pushed everything down underneath that thin layer of skin and the tears that shone on her cheeks were only the few that managed to escape. She could also be easily pleased—Andy remembered making her weep tears of joy once by simply bringing flowers home for no reason one Saturday morning when he'd gone to the hardware store for some plumbing supplies. He was amazed that she'd survived childbirth twice, but their daughters seemed to bring the most happiness into her life.

He wondered what it said about him that he didn't feel the same way.

"Anyway, this is why I haven't been—"

"Andy, how is Sally taking it?"

"—talking to you, and—I haven't talked to her yet. I mean, a few days ago when we were looking for him, but not since . . . since we've known. The Bureau is taking care of telling her."

"Because she just dotes on that man, God knows why, and you're his closest friend, you really should be there, and—"

"Monica, the Bureau wants to handle it. They told

me to let them take care of it. Don't worry about Sally, she'll be all right. They'll make sure she gets Paul's full pension and probably more on top of that."

"It's not just about the money, Andy. I mean, it always seems to be that with you guys, but it's not."

"I know it's not, Monica," he said. It was just that the money stuff was easiest to talk about. "Just . . . don't worry about her. She'll be okay. And I'm sorry I haven't been talking to you these last few days, but I've been trying to find him, you know, and it's been . . . it's been hard."

He was calling her from a motel room—not the one he'd been staying in before while keeping Stella Olemaun under surveillance, and for damn sure not the Slumber Motel. This one was cleaner than that pit. Here, Andy wasn't afraid to touch the bedspread or to walk on the carpet with his bare feet. And there were no signs of insect life or rat droppings in the bathroom—although, to be fair, in Paul's room those could well have been his own additions.

Besides those advantages, this room—inside the oddly named Swiss Chalet Motel, in a building that resembled a Berlin apartment building more than a Swiss chalet—had a working TV with a working remote and a telephone that could make outgoing calls. Scanning through the Bible in the nightstand, Andy had seen that there were call girls' phone numbers scrawled in the margins, but then this was still LA, and some things were inescapable.

"It just . . . it hurts when you hang up on me, Andy."

"I know, Monica. I said I'm sorry." He found himself beginning to panic, afraid she was going to want to talk about the state of their relationship. *Not right now,* he thought. *I have too many other things on my mind.* "Listen," he said quickly. "I have to get going. I'll let you know after I talk to Sally, in case you want to call her. But don't do it till I tell you the Bureau has told her about Paul."

She rushed through an abbreviated good-bye and Andy hung up. He blew out a sigh of relief. The discussion would have to come sometime, but today was not the day for it.

Monica Gray hung up the phone and dabbed at her eyes with the tissue she had tucked up her sleeve. She usually had one there, ready for any emergency. No matter how many tissue boxes you kept in the house there was never one handy enough when a child had a nosebleed, or you spilled a little coffee.

Or somebody died. Even somebody you didn't particularly like.

A noise behind her. She turned in her chair, tucking away the tissue. No sense advertising that something was wrong.

Sara stood there looking at her with her hands clasped together in front of her. Seven years old, ponytailed, chipmunk-cheeked. She had her mother's lustrous brown hair, thank God—Lisa, the older one, had inherited Andy's. It was blond now, but thin, and would lighten to almost white in the sun. She'd probably be gray by the time she was thirty, like her dad had been.

"Lisa got in a fight at school today."

And that was just the capper she needed. "I'll talk to her about it, Sara," Monica said. "You shouldn't be a tattletale, you know."

"I thought you should know is all."

"Thank you." Monica sniffled a little, but she was finished crying, for now. She left the cordless on the table, where she had been paying bills, trying to stretch Andy's salary and what she could make part-time at a nearby dry cleaner's now that both girls were in school all day, and went to look for Lisa. The same school bus had dropped off both kids, but if Lisa had come inside she had slipped away somewhere.

Monica found her in her room, where she had already settled at her desk and started her math homework. Fractions, which Monica had always had trouble with herself. She knelt beside the small desk and waited until Lisa looked her way.

"Want to tell me what happened?"

"Nothing happened."

"That's not what I heard."

"Sara's a rat."

Monica held back a snicker. "All right, maybe so. But that doesn't change the facts. Are you okay?"

A big sigh. "I'm fine, Mom." Her father's daughter.

"I'm fine" would be engraved on Andy's tombstone, if Monica had her way. She couldn't remember the last time he'd voluntarily been to a doctor.

"What happened?" she asked again.

This was met with a smaller sigh, and then Lisa's blue eyes clouded. "Chloe said the FBI sucks," she said. "She said they let America get attacked because they don't know what they're doing and they can't use computers. So I pushed her on the playground, and then she hit me."

Monica enveloped her daughter in her arms. "You don't need to fight to defend the Bureau," she said. "You know your daddy can use a computer, because you've seen him, right? It's true that the Bureau has had some computer problems in Washington, at the headquarters. You remember when we went there a couple of summers ago?"

"We went twice, Mommy," Lisa corrected. "When I was little, and then again when Sara was little. Every time we go someplace it's Washington. I want to go to the Grand Canyon. Or New York."

"I know, honey. Daddy loves the FBI. The point is, just because they had problems there, that doesn't mean that individual agents like your dad are stupid. And it was a lot of people who messed up and let terrorists attack us. They're all working hard to fix things. Fighting is wrong and it's just going to end badly, right?"

Lisa backed out of the hug, held her mother's gaze.

She was often, like her father, dour. More apt to frown than to smile. Monica often wished her daughter could experience the happy-go-lucky naiveté of youth, but that seemed to be Sara's exclusive province. She smiled readily and laughed hard at the silliest things. Lisa, on the other hand, seemed to have been born depressed and gone downhill from there. "I guess so," she said.

"You know I'm right," Monica said, smiling enough for both of them. She wanted to let Lisa know that she wasn't really in trouble—that sticking up for her dad was never a bad thing, but there were acceptable ways to do it. "Anyway, I have some bad news to tell you, and it's more important than some foolish thing Chloe said. Something has happened to . . . to your daddy's friend Paul." To Andy and the girls, Paul Norris was Uncle Paul, but she had never been able to call him that. To Monica, Paul Norris was nothing but a foul-mouthed, unpleasant man, and she thought it was pretty heroic of her just to allow him near her kids.

"What happened?" Lisa's eyes were already shiny, as if she knew what was coming.

"Some bad people killed him."

Lisa swallowed and looked away, toward a display of Kim Possible action figures on her dresser.

"Daddy's going to find them and put them in jail," Monica added.

"When is Daddy coming home?"

Monica couldn't restrain her sigh. "I'm not sure, honey. As soon as he can. He just has some things to do first." She gave Lisa another hug, holding her for a long time, feeling the girl's thin arms tremble as they reached around her mother's back.

On her way to tell Sara, she wondered if Andy had the first idea how much effort it took to hold a family together. Sure, there were men who did it. But not *her* man, and, she suspected, not a lot of others. Andy thought she was weak, but in his world, people had to be summed up quickly and simply. Dangerous, recidivist, harmless, strong. He had no clue about the strength required to bend with the winds that threatened to tear a family apart day after day, and to which so many people succumbed. Money, anger, sorrow, all the stresses of day-to-day life, exacerbated by every emergency, big or small. One had to be a willow to stand against it. Rigid wouldn't do the job.

And Monica Schwann Gray was a willow. She had stood against gale force turbulence in the past and was sure she would again. But she would never let her family be torn asunder, no matter what. She had seen it happen too many times, to too many others. Not her. She sniffed once, determined not to let Sara know that she had been upset.

A willow . . .

Andy had encountered Angelica Foster numerous times, working on cases with Paul. She was a forensic pathology technician for the Los Angeles office of the FBI. Paul thought she was hot and had tried to bed her on a few occasions. Andy was pretty sure he'd never succeeded.

Now Andy wanted her, but for something else entirely.

He had killed a few hours in the motel room, talking to Monica, watching a brainless movie on TV, finally getting some uneasy, dreamless sleep. When he woke up, he'd drenched the sheets in cold sweat and he felt like buses had been running over his skull.

But churning over things in his mind, he had at least arrived at a plan of attack. The first step was to find out everything he could about Paul Norris. There had to be a way—a scientifically valid and logical way—of determining what had really happened to him. Andy needed the answer to that question. Once he had that, it would help point to where Paul might have gone.

And Angelica, who had been analyzing the physical evidence, was the place to start.

He found her in the lab, as usual. She wore a pale blue lab coat, cut, like all such garments, in the most unflattering way possible. Even through that, though, the various bulges of her figure strained it in promising fashion. Her shoulder-length, jet-black hair was kept in a net—any stray strands could compromise criminal cases, so she took no chances with it in the lab. Andy had never seen her away from here, but he imagined when she let it loose it was quite a sight. Her skin was an olive hue, her dark eyes shining like black pearls above prominent cheekbones. Andy didn't know what her racial background was but guessed there was an interesting genetic stew making up her DNA.

"Special Agent Gray," she said when she saw him. She backed away from her equipment, lowered her face mask, and tossed him a smile that could brighten anyone's day. "Here about your partner? I'm so sorry to hear what happened to him."

The official line, Andy had been told, would be that he had been found dead in the Slumber Motel, murdered by terrorists whose organization he'd been trying to infiltrate. That dovetailed well enough with the Olemaun case, which had officially become a terrorism case when she'd been observed acquiring large quantities of explosives from a dealer in Valdez, Alaska.

There were plenty of people who wouldn't buy it, including everyone who'd been on the scene of the shootout and everyone who'd seen the huge hole in the wall—or whose cars the desk Paul had thrown through it had landed on. But ADIC Flores was dealing with those people one on one, trying to convince them that it was in the national interest to remember it the way he wanted it remembered.

Angelica hadn't been around that night and had only been assigned the serology workup when she'd come on duty this morning. Now, toward the end of her shift, Andy hoped she had made some headway.

"Thanks," he said, feeling like a fraud for accepting her condolences. The only thing that made it okay was that Paul really was lost to him, genuinely dead or not. "Have you come up with anything?"

She twitched her nose and frowned, which made deep dimples carve her cheeks. "It's really strange," she said. "I've been running and rerunning the tests, especially with the erythrocytes—those are the red blood cells—because I keep coming up with . . . well, stuff in the blood that shouldn't be in the blood. I've double- and triple-checked, too, because some of the serum samples I had seemed to be older than they should have been, even though the chain of custody shows that the blood came from Special Agent Norris just last night. And do you know why they're not doing an autopsy? Greg won't tell me."

Andy shrugged. "I don't get involved in that stuff. What do you think the blood is telling you?"

"I just don't know yet," Angelica said with a shake of her head. "Off the cuff, it looks like he was sick or something. But I don't know with what. What's even stranger, this isn't the first time I've encountered this sort of thing lately. I pulled the file to be sure my memory wasn't playing tricks on me, but I was right. There was an arson-homicide over on Westholme recently."

"That's near UCLA?" Andy asked.

"That's right. The home belonged to a Dr. Amos Saxon, a professor there. Dr. Saxon also had a research contract with the Department of Defense, which was why the Bureau was brought in. As far as I've heard, there are no suspects yet, and no one seems to know if the murder was related to his DoD work."

"I heard something about that," Andy said casually. In fact, he'd more than heard about it; he had stopped at the scene. The bodies of two police officers had been found at the burned-out house as well as that of the deceased Dr. Saxon. All three bodies had extensive dental disfigurement—as if someone had taken a hammer to their teeth. The LAPD's assumption was that the killer was trying to hinder identification of the victims. Andy didn't buy that for a second—the cops were in uniform, with name tags on, and Dr. Saxon was inside his own house. But he didn't have any better theories.

The reason he'd been to the house, though, was that Dr. Saxon had also been the sponsor of Stella Olemaun's campus visit.

"It's been in the news," Angelica said. "Anyway, blood taken from the scene had the same strange properties. I haven't yet been able to identify it, but I'm still working on it."

"Okay, Angelica, that's great," Andy said. "Let me know if you come up with anything, okay?"

"I will, Andy." She gave him a pouty look. "I know I said it before, but I'm really sorry about Paul."

"Yeah," Andy answered. "Me too."

5

Carol Hino rode the train from Manhattan home to Connecticut every day at six-fifteen. She had been doing so for years, almost always carrying a manuscript along in a leather Gucci bag to read on the trip. This evening, she almost dreaded fishing the rubber-banded stack of papers from the bag.

The book would almost surely be a big hit, but it was the latest entry in the my-parents-treated-me-so-awful-but-I-turned-out-okay sweepstakes, and Carol was just weary of it all. In this particular case, the author's parents had been con artists, moving around the country one step ahead of the law and the wrath of their victims. The parents had been consumed with finding the perfect score, with angles and percentages, which had ended up leaving their single daughter pretty good at math but a little deficient when it came to everything else. Like, human contact, social skills, any kind of stability. The author's mother wound up in jail from time to time—a fate her father escaped only by going missing for months, or even years, at a stretch.

The story was interesting and well written, and the author had come through relatively unscathed, with a few years of psychiatric help and the occasional application of modern pharmacology. In fact she, like Carol herself, had graduated from Sarah Lawrence with honors. So the ending was upbeat enough. Carol just couldn't bring herself to feel enthusiastic about it.

Just now, Carol had another problem. As the year ground on, spring giving way to summer, the days were getting longer. It was customary in New York publishing to close early on Friday afternoons in summer. Kingston House, the company Carol worked for, followed that tradition. But her boss responded to the approach of that season by expecting longer hours put in during the week, and Carol had been at her desk until seven-thirty. By the time she reached the station in Connecticut where her Honda was parked, it would be full dark.

Knowledge was supposed to open doors, tear away blinders, enhance one's understanding of the world and one's place in it. It was meant to be a positive thing. Or so she had always thought.

No more. Because what she had come to know had convinced her that the world was really a terrifying place, far more so than she had ever imagined. Now, Carol Hino kept her doors locked and her alarm set and slept lightly, when she slept at all, and she made up for the lack of sleep with pills and caffeine. She was vigilant at all times.

Especially in the dark.

Carol had learned to hate the dark.

* * *

Andy made the rounds of the other labs in the building. He ordered tests, unless they were already in progress, of samples of tissue Paul Norris had left behind when he'd broken through the glass, of Paul's voice as recorded in the conversation they'd had, of the structural integrity of the glass itself and the bars and the desk and the wall. He left his cell number with people in each case and asked to be called as soon as there was any breakthrough. The day shift was ending, and in a couple of cases he talked to night shift techs instead.

Finally, Greg Sugarbaker, the bureaucrat who ran the lab, collared him near the elevator. "Special Agent Gray," he said grimly. "My condolences on your partner."

Sugarbaker, of all people, knew that there had been no autopsy ordered because Paul's body wasn't here to slice up, knew further that he had escaped his bonds and broken through the wall. So his sympathy was nothing more than an act. One that Andy was willing to go along with.

"Thanks," he said. "I'll miss the ornery bastard." That much was true, regardless.

"From what I hear, you've got my lab technicians in a bit of a tizzy," Sugarbaker continued. "Sounds like you're running things around here instead of me. Ordering up tests, demanding quick results, that kind of thing."

"I'm just trying to find out what happened to my partner," Andy assured him.

"I understand that," Sugarbaker said. "I'd do the same thing. And trust me, we're working on it. It's our top priority right now."

"Thanks."

"But *I* have to be the one to set the priorities," Sugarbaker added. "If it was any other way, then every agent who had a case would be in here saying his results needed to be in first. Nothing would ever get done."

"I understand," Andy said, knowing that the murder of an agent would always top the heap no matter what.

Greg Sugarbaker leaned close and lowered his voice conspiratorially. "You've been on people so hard, some of them think you're up to something. Like you and Norris got mixed up in something . . . unsavory, and now that it's cost him his life you're trying to hush it up."

"I just want to know what happened," Andy said again.

"I know that, and I respect it, Agent Gray. Believe me. But you've got to understand how things look. You don't work out of this office, so these people don't know you that well. Even if they did . . . well, you know what it's like. Post-9/11, post-Department of Homeland Security. Everybody's on edge and no one really trusts anyone else. All I'm saying is take it a little easy, all right? We'll make sure you know everything we do as soon as possible."

Andy stuck out his hand and Sugarbaker took it. "Thanks," Andy said with sincerity. "I appreciate everything you're doing for Paul."

"No problem," Sugarbaker replied. "Glad we had this talk."

At the Swiss Chalet, Andy left the TV running on low volume, just to provide some background noise. He sat at the desk and wrote on motel stationery. He was brainstorming, doodling, jotting notes, trying to let his subconscious make the connections he hadn't been able to.

He looked at some words he'd scrawled. *Rats. Bugs. Blood. Strange blood. Saxon? Teeth gone. Renfield.* That last word had three underlines. What the hell did Paul mean by that?

He'd brought a copy of the tape from his interrogation of Paul and a tape recorder back to the motel with him. He played that part back again.

"I tailed the Olemaun woman. But then another woman, one with a taste for blood, came along and made me her . . . servant. Her Renfield, I guess. She took me, Andy. I had no choice."

She made me her Renfield. A weapon? There was a British rifle, but that was an Enfield. How did someone make you her Renfield?

He unplugged the room phone from the wall jack and plugged his laptop in its place. All the taxpayer money that went into the Bureau's coffers, and sometimes the best tool an agent could use was Google.

No use, though. Too many hits. A punk band, a record label, various references to Scotland, people whose screen names or websites included the word but with no apparent reason why.

To narrow the search, he put in some of the other words he'd jotted down. *Renfield blood rats bugs,* he typed, then hit the search button.

And it all came into immediate focus.

The common thread was Bram Stoker's *Dracula.*

Apparently, Renfield was a character in the original novel and the filmed adaptations. Andy scanned through some of the descriptions of the character—a mortal man who did Dracula's bidding. Obsessed with the consumption of life, he ate all the vermin he could find in Dr. Seward's sanitarium, before Dracula gave him a purpose in life.

Perhaps more to the point, Andy found references to a psychological condition called Vampire Personality Disorder, or VPD, and nicknamed Renfield's Syndrome. This was the condition he had recalled earlier, although he hadn't been able to remember the name or the nickname.

Renfield. Paul had fallen under the sway—or believed he had—of some woman. *His mistress.* She commanded him, and he simply obeyed. *She took me, Andy,* Paul had said. *I had no choice.*

Must be handy if you've snapped, gone over the edge, start murdering people and pointing guns at your own fellow agents, to be able to blame some unnamed "other."

This didn't tell him where to look for Paul, or really what had happened to him. But it pointed in a certain direction—the same direction a lot of the other circumstantial evidence pointed.

Just not toward a destination he wanted to let himself arrive at.

Paul had been holed up in that motel room, eating bugs and rodents, because he had become someone's Renfield. He was already changing, becoming something else, something terribly strong.

Something undeniably evil.

The murder of Judith Ali must have been done at the behest of his mistress, whoever that was.

Andy rubbed his face. He was getting off track, the logical track, at least.

He hadn't shaved in a couple of days. He had taken a quick shower this morning, but he could stand a real one, and a shampoo. He remembered feeling nasty, unclean, in Paul's room at the Slumber Motel, but he still hadn't really done anything about it. Now, however, he felt it again—a crawling sensation, like a million maggots moving about just under his skin. His stomach lurched and he dove to his feet, ran for the bathroom, got the toilet seat raised just in time.

When he was empty of what little he'd eaten in the past few days, Andy turned on the shower, as hot as he could stand. He yanked off his dirty suit and threw it onto the floor, in a corner. He'd have to see if it could be dry-cleaned adequately, otherwise he would just throw it away. Naked, he stepped underneath the stinging water and tried to let it scald away the filth, the nightmare memory of his friend's unholy transformation. He closed his eyes and let the spray pummel his face. Grabbing the thin bar of motel soap, he peeled away the paper wrapper and used up most of the cake lathering himself over and over, attempting to purge the uncleanliness. In between lathers, he emptied most of a bottle of motel shampoo.

Finally, he shut off the water, stepped out of the tub, toweled himself until his overheated skin was raw. He ran an electric razor over cheeks and chin, combed his short gray hair. Fortunately, he kept a second suit in his travel bag, and although it was wrinkled, at least it was clean. He put on a fresh white shirt, zipped up his slacks, tugged the jacket over it. No tie, which was unusual for him. But then, he wasn't working tonight.

Decently groomed for the first time since Paul had disappeared, Andy realized that he needed some solid food. As soon as he thought about it, he was starving.

He left the motel and drove until he spotted a steak house. But Andy liked his steak medium rare . . . a little bloody . . . and suddenly his stomach started to twitch again.

Driving past it, he kept going until he found a salad bar restaurant instead. The place was pretty dead. He loaded up a plate of salad, supplemented with some bread and potato soup. He didn't think he could handle any kind of meat though—he couldn't even put artificial bacon bits on the salad.

Sitting down to a regular meal now felt odd. When

he was at home, Andy tried to have dinner with the family every night. Lisa and Sara were usually happy to share what they'd been up to at school, although he suspected that within a year or so he'd start getting the "nothing" response he had usually given as a boy, when his own parents asked about his day. He had actually come to enjoy the evening meal, prodding the girls to eat their vegetables, holding out hopes of dessert in exchange for cleaning their plates.

While running surveillance on Stella Olemaun, Andy and Paul had eaten a lot of fast food, usually in the car, because it seemed that she was almost always on the go. Every now and then, when they had her staked out somewhere, one of them would go to a restaurant and get take-out, which they consumed wherever they were holed up. Now, Andy ate and watched the people around him: families with kids, young couples on dates, the players from a touch football game with friends and supporters. Normal people with normal lives. Darkness had fallen; they could have been *them,* he supposed.

Andy's persevering logic still suspected that it was too late for Paul. He had gone too far over the cliff, and there was no way back up. The best he could probably look forward to was a long stretch in a facility for the criminally insane, followed—if he survived at all—by an old age on lithium or some other psychoactive drug that would keep his madness under control.

Unless, of course, he really *had* become one of them.

The thought struck Andy as a horrible certainty, startling him so much he sloshed coffee onto his plate. He set the cup down with trembling hands. It was all true—*had* to be true. Stella's book. Her tale of the attack on Barrow. Paul had somehow run across one of them and been changed. Madness couldn't account for that incredible strength, for the ability to survive all those bullets. It could explain the mental and psychological transformation, but not the physical. Not the fact that he'd had no heartbeat, no respiration, when the paramedics checked him out.

Paul Norris was dead, and yet he moved, he talked, he functioned. In some ways, better than he had been when he was alive. There had to be a scientific explanation, because everything in the world, however bizarre, ultimately could be explained by facts and logic. Maybe it was some kind of illness, a virus. Andy didn't know enough advanced medical theory to figure it out for himself, but he was convinced that such an explanation existed.

He had dished himself up a bowl of fruit with whipped cream for dessert, but no longer hungry, he left it on the table and went back to the motel. There, he took off his suit and brushed his teeth. Downing three sleeping pills, he climbed into bed and turned on the TV, not caring what was on.

I know what I have to do.

Half an hour later, he was dead to the world.

* * *

"Paul Norris is a vampire," Andy said.

"Andy, you've been under a lot of stress—" ADIC Flores began.

"No, sir—believe me, I know how absurd it sounds. But let me lay it out for you."

The ADIC waved his hand like he was signaling a runaway train. "Don't bother, Andy. Please. We're the FBI, not the fucking Ghostbusters. Or the, what was it—the *X-Files*. The FBI doesn't look for Bigfoot or *chupacabras* or UFOs. We don't investigate haunted houses. And we sure as hell *don't* do vampires."

Andy looked at the photos on the wall behind Hector Flores. Presidents, senators, every director since Hoover. Serious people. Morning light flooded in through the office window.

Andy was serious, too. "Sir, we can't just rule it out without looking at it."

"We can't?" Flores echoed. "We *can't?*" He laughed. "We sure as shit can, son."

Hoover hadn't approved of swearing—at one time, Flores would have found himself back in the field. But then, Andy remembered, Hoover had a taste for crinoline and lace and the occasional cashmere shawl, so nobody was perfect.

"He was dead, sir," Andy pressed. "The paramedics couldn't find any sign of life. He took seventy shots, including some to the heart and skull. He was in our most secure cell, lashed to a stretcher with nylon straps.

And he just . . . he just broke out. Through the straps, the bars, the glass, and the wall. Who can do that, sir?"

"Andy, let's not make this any worse than it is," the ADIC said.

But Andy had wound himself up. He stood. *"Who?"* He was shouting now. "Paul Norris couldn't! I worked with him for decades, sir! He was strong enough for a middle-aged guy, but there's no way he could have done that stuff. It's impossible. Not even including the fact that it's impossible for someone who's been shot up like that to be walking around and talking anyway. It just could not happen.

"But it did. I saw it. He picked me up like I was nothing and tossed me aside. He lifted that desk over his head like you'd lift a basketball. That cell is wired, sir, so I know you've seen the tape. You can't deny that."

"I can deny anything I want when it's absolutely fucking lunatic, Special Agent Gray!" Flores seethed. "Which, in this case, *it is!*"

Flores stopped himself, ears burning red, then exhaled slowly before saying: "Andy, don't make me call your Special Agent in Charge and have you spending the next six months on some headshrinker's couch. You've suffered a terrible loss, your partner and friend is gone, and we all understand what that can do to a man. Paul's funeral is this afternoon. Go to it, then take a few days off, get your head straight. When you feel better you can come back to work and get busy on that thing I asked you to do."

Andy, steamed, shoved his fists into his pants pockets. "The cover-up, you mean."

"I wouldn't use that term around here," Flores said.

"That's what it is."

"Take a few days, Andy. Go home, if you want. Get laid. Something, I don't care. Just don't show up here again until you're ready to be rational."

Nothing else he could say, no way he could make the ADIC admit the truth.

Andy turned and stalked out, slamming the glass office door behind him as he left.

But the door had an electronic closing mechanism, which caught it and brought it to as gently as a baby's sigh.

Figures. Even the inanimate is against me now.

6

ANDY DIDN'T LISTEN MUCH to the minister's words. Paul's funeral was held in the Presbyterian church that the Norris family irregularly attended. No one there seemed to know him very well, and another FBI agent who sat near Andy told him that in the church, God, not the deceased, was the object of worship, so eulogizing the departed was discouraged. The minister spoke about God's will and His love, and Andy found it all a bit weary and platitudinous.

As the man droned on, Andy looked around at the building, at the coffin in front of the altar that allegedly contained the mortal remains of Jacob Paul Norris: loving husband, adoring father, loyal government employee . . . and now, something else entirely?

Crosses all over the place. He couldn't believe that Paul would pass up a chance to observe his own funeral, if it was at all possible. But if he had really become a vampire, could he enter a place devoted to God? With all these crosses around? There was so much Andy didn't know. If they were real, as he was coming to accept, how much of the movie stuff was really true? He couldn't picture Paul turning into a bat—and certainly he hadn't when he'd escaped the other night.

Or had he? Paul leaped, but I didn't see what happened next. I never saw or heard Paul land. Maybe he sprouted wings and flew away? Bullshit. But wasn't the whole thing bullshit? When dealing with the impossible, it made sense not to rule anything out simply because it was improbable.

Occam's razor was a way of life for Andy Gray.

And never more so than when it came to Paul Norris, from the moment they met.

The first time he could remember having seen Paul was in a classroom at the FBI Academy in Quantico, Virginia. The room was as bureaucratically bland as most such spaces, with metal desks and plastic chairs arranged in neat rows and the instructor standing at the front of the room behind a wooden podium. The instructor had been babbling on about the rehabilitative benefits of federal penitentiaries and blah blah blah when someone sitting behind Andy interrupted him. Andy was surprised that the student—or New Agent Trainee, as they were called—had not raised his hand and waited to be called on.

"Um, excuse me, sir," the NAT said. "But that's bullshit. Some scumbag who rapes a grandmother isn't going to be turned into a solid citizen by being forced to hang out with other rapists and murderers."

As one, the entire class turned to look at just who the hell was about to be thrown out of class.

Andy was almost as surprised by the young man's appearance as by his willful ignorance of Academy policies. For years, the Bureau had stressed hiring people who were average looking in every respect. Finally, it had occurred to them—coincidentally at the same time that the civil rights movement was gaining ground—that "average" in Harlem or the barrio or a NOW meeting was different from "average" at an Elk's Club in Iowa. Looking at the NAT who had spoken out of turn, Andy Gray had to wonder if they were now trying to infiltrate some subversive organization of ugly people.

Because if ever there was a single word that could describe Paul Norris, it was homely. He had, if anything, gotten better looking over the years, but to look at Norris recently one would never guess that. Young Paul Norris had an enormous nose and ears that stuck out on both sides of his head like car doors. His hair was blond, but greasy and already thinning on top. His lips were thick and red and twitched as if each had independent will. While Andy watched, Paul's pasty cheeks flushed as if he'd just realized what he had done.

"You are quite possibly correct, Mr. Norris," the instructor had said, miraculously unperturbed. "However, it is not the FBI's place to determine the validity of any particular punishment. Our job is to bring in the perpetrators, and from there it's up to the state."

Paul nodded in acknowledgment to the instructor, then noticed Andy gaping at him. He stared back for a second, then gave a wink and a wicked little smile.

From that time, Andy Gray had made a point of paying attention to Paul Norris.

Andy had been drawn to law enforcement under unusual circumstances: as a child, he had been subject to terrible fears—nightmares that recurred for weeks at a time, phobias and worries about just about everything—and he thought, from an early age, that people who carried badges and guns could face any danger, and the philosophy stuck. He'd felt a strange fascination with this fellow NAT, someone who was willing to say anything to anyone when it struck him as important and who seemed afraid of nothing at all. Paul Norris had an obscene streak and a disdain for traditional rules of conduct. But he also—perhaps more significantly—had a deep-seated, abiding respect for the law and for "justice" as *he* understood it. He hated anyone who preyed on the innocent—drug dealers, scam artists, criminals of every sort.

And the conversations! After Academy hours, sitting in one of the Quantico taverns frequented by NATs and jarheads from the Marine base, Paul would expound at length about his concepts of honor and decency and the FBI's role in promoting both. Andy was happy to buy the pitchers for them both. He felt drawn to the odd young Agent Trainee, and over the remaining fifteen weeks at the Academy, they became fast friends. They trained together, went to the firing range together, studied together after class. At the end of the program, Andy graduated in the top ten of his class.

Somehow, although he was rarely observed studying, Paul was in the top five.

After the Academy, they were separated for a few years while Andy was assigned to the Chicago field office and Paul to Boston. But the two stayed in close contact, writing and calling and later, emailing with regularity. Andy met and married one Monica Schwann, who worked at the dry cleaners to which he took his suits. Paul was so unimpressed with Monica and dismissive of the idea of marriage in general, that for a wedding gift he gave Andy a Swiss Army knife with a card that said, "For when you need to cut the strings."

Andy had laughed at that. For some, that would have been the end of the friendship, but Andy knew it was only par for the course with Paul Norris (although he didn't dare share the incident with Monica).

A couple years after that, Paul met and married Sally Winston, a voluptuous blond executive assistant in an office he was investigating on suspicion of fraud. Andy couldn't help but give Paul hell over *that*. By the time the two men were partnered in the FBI's Sacramento field office, both couples had two daughters around the same ages, and their friendship was stronger than ever.

So he was sorry when Paul was transferred again, this time to Los Angeles. The two families had one last farewell bash, a pool party at the Gray house to which most of their co-workers were invited. In spite of Andy's nagging fear, Paul got only a little drunk and didn't embarrass himself too thoroughly. Then Paul threw an arm around Andy's neck and clanged his Heineken bottle against the metal outdoor table to draw everyone's attention. Paul's Hawaiian shirt was open, exposing his flabby chest and a gut that hung off his skinny frame like some kind of alien appendage.

When all eyes were on him, Paul raised his bottle into the air. "I want to thank my pal Andy Gray for this bash," he announced. "And for more than that—for being the best friend a guy could have. We've been through it all together. Quantico, the bachelor life, the married life, fatherhood. And through everything, there's been one constant, one thing that never changes, no matter what." He paused, took a swig of beer, lowered the bottle with a small belch, and added, "Andy's got the littlest dick in the FBI, at least since Hoover died. And no matter how black things got for me, that knowledge has always pulled me through."

The partygoers laughed—some with enthusiasm, some uneasily, since the pool was full of their kids and many of them went to the Presbyterian church together. Andy felt his face crimson, but he chuckled and made a gun out of his fingers, shooting Paul in the head.

"All I can say is, thank God you're leaving," Andy deadpanned.

"Hear, hear!" someone shouted to roars of laughter.

Thank God we're leaving, Andy thought.

The mourners were filing out of the building. Sally Norris took Andy's hand, then drew him into a crushing hug. "Ride over with us, Andy," she said. "I need you around right now."

Andy looked at her, eye make-up smeared by tears, nose red. She wore black, of course, a snug-fitting dress with a little jacket, and a small hat with a dark veil that draped over her blue eyes. Behind her, the kids, Nicole and Debra, looked on. He wasn't comfortable with mourning—had always hated to have to inform next of kin of someone's death and was glad that was usually the province of local cops. But how the hell could he turn down his best friend's wife? So he waited with her and the girls until everyone else had left the church and expressed their sympathies to the grieving family.

The limousine was long and black and cooled inside to an almost Arctic degree. Andy sat in the rear-facing seat, so through the back tinted window he could see where they'd been, but not where they were going. That was okay. As he talked to Sally, he tried to scan the cars behind them. *To see if Paul's following.*

"Were you with him, Andy? At the end? I couldn't

get much detail out of Hector or anyone from the Bureau."

"I wish I had been," Andy said. He hated to lie to the "widow" Norris, but there was really no choice. "Maybe I could have done something. I was looking for him—I don't know how much you were really told."

"Like I said, not much. Apparently he was captured by the people you were following, and they killed him."

"That's pretty much what there is to know," Andy said. They were being followed, all right—a long line of cars pulled into the lane behind them, directed there by a motorcycle cop. Their headlights were on. "We tried to find him in time—you know we were all out there looking."

"I know." She rubbed her nose. Andy was afraid she'd start crying again, but she didn't. "I wish they'd let me see the body, though." She leaned over the space between seats and whispered so the girls couldn't hear. "Was he . . . tortured?"

Andy nodded grimly. This was the story he'd agreed on with ADIC Flores. "It's better if you don't hear the details."

Sally attempted a smile. Her eyes were a lovely blue, like fading denim, and the veil gave them a smoky, mysterious aspect. But the smile didn't make it that far. "Thanks for taking care of me, Andy," she said. She nodded toward the girls. "Of us."

The gravesite was on a grassy slope from which, if you looked hard enough through a screen of trees and the haze of Los Angeles air, you could see a thin wedge of the Pacific Ocean. The cemetery itself spanned two slopes, arcing down toward one another into a deep V, the center of which made a line pointing toward the sea. It called itself Restful Acres, although Andy doubted anyone was fooled into thinking its inhabitants were merely resting.

He certainly hoped they weren't. Then again, his perception of such things was undergoing a radical change.

The crowd had thinned since the church. Most of Paul's brother agents were there, appropriately and typically clad in dark suits and sunglasses. Other mourners Andy didn't recognize, mostly women. He guessed they were friends of Sally, and some young children with parents were probably friends and schoolmates of the girls.

He found his attention drawn to the trees at the edge of the cemetery. Beneath their canopies the shadows were full and dark.

That's where Paul would be, if he was here.

With no one paying attention to him, Andy wandered away from the grave—the box that would go in there was empty anyway—toward the trees. He reached under his jacket, almost by instinct, and touched the Glock .22 resting in his belt holster. *If Paul was there . . .*

He let the thought die. If Paul was there, the weapon would be as useless against him as the hundreds of rounds fired at him outside the motel. He was probably better off looking for a sharp stick in the downed branches under the trees.

The grass underfoot was soft and springy. At the tree line, it gave way to jagged oak leaves with a thin scrim of taller, weedy grass at its edge, where the mowers didn't reach.

Andy's stomach crawled in anticipation.

Nothing.

No one lurking back here, although scattered bottles and other trash indicated that people sometimes passed their hours under the shade. *Probably homeless people.* Beyond the shield of trees, down a rock-strewn slope, was the 405, the freeway noise masked by the breeze rustling the oaks.

Satisfied that Paul wasn't hiding out here after all, Andy turned and made the hike back up to the grave where the short ceremony was just coming to a close. He had to wait for Sally again, since his car was back at the church. And here, beside what everyone believed to be Paul's final resting place, the mourners who had come were effusive in their grief, weeping and wailing and threatening to crack Sally's ribs with great hugs. Andy stood off to the side with Debra and Nicole, who had both sobbed earlier but now simply observed, struck more or less dumb by the behavior of the adults.

When they were back in the limo, Andy holding Sally's hand across the space between seats, he asked her the question he'd been saving for the right time, whatever that might be. "Can I come over to the house,

Sal? I'd like to paw through Paul's office, see if I can rustle up any notes or anything that might help me find whoever did this to him." He smiled. "That's a pretty mixed metaphor, isn't it?"

Sally laughed for the first time all day, and when she did, Andy could see what it was about her that kept Paul coming back. She was a very attractive woman. Her smile was infectious and her laugh was a bright spark on a gloomy afternoon. "Isn't a metaphor supposed to clarify things?" she asked.

"English was never my best subject," Andy admitted. "Come to think of it, I don't think I had a best subject. Just some that were less worse than others."

She laughed again. "Of course you can come over. You know what his office is like, but if you think you can find anything in there that will help, be my guest."

"Great. I'll be over a little later this evening, if that's okay. I have some other stuff to take care of first."

"We'll be home," Sally said. "Probably eating ourselves sick on all the stuff friends and neighbors have been bringing over."

Back in his own car, Andy turned on his cell phone and discovered a message. *"Special Agent Gray, this is Angelica Foster in the serology lab. I think you'll want to take a look at the Hollywood Motel, Room 23. DNA from blood found there is a positive match for Stella Olemaun. Let me know if you have any questions."*

In the fading light, Andy found himself fighting the

traffic to yet another run-down Hollywood joint. This one was a three-story brick building on Gower, a couple of blocks off Hollywood Boulevard. The Boulevard was its typical mix of tourists, Goths, punks, and whores, but after he turned onto Gower the tourist element disappeared. As he climbed the three steps to the door of the motel, a black LAPD robbery-homicide detective in an expensive cream-colored suit was coming out. "Taylor," Andy said, recognizing the man. "Andy Gray, FBI."

Taylor gave a fake smile. "Long time, man," he said, offering his hand. Taylor had been a UCLA running back, decades before. He still had the broad shoulders, deep chest, and crushing grip, but his short hair was as much salt as pepper now. "What brings you here?"

"I'm not entirely sure," Andy confessed. "Got a message from our lab that there's blood up in Room 23 matching someone I've been surveilling, a lady named Stella Olemaun. What's the situation? There a body?"

"Enough blood for one," Taylor said. "But no, no body. Room was rented to a woman, described as having short red hair, kind of pretty but otherwise average. She paid cash, wrote down Betty Ford in the register. No one called her on it. Ask me, the clerk don't know who Betty Ford is. No visitors seen. She paid for a week. Week's up, management knocks on the door. No answer. They go in. Blood all over the floor, but old Betty's gone. You think she's your Stella?"

"Sounds like her," Andy said. "She has a habit of

moving on quickly, under the radar. Usually we've been able to pick up her trail again. Last we knew, she was over at the Standard, under her own name, using a credit card. Then she was gone and we haven't been able to find her since. It looks like this is where she came, but she might have left that same night for all I know."

"You're welcome to look at the room," Taylor said. "I think it's a dead end, though. We combed it. Not so much as a loose pube left behind—just the blood that soaked into the carpet. No luggage. We could pull the tub drain, but we'd just find skin and hair and fluids from the last fifty years of guests, since I doubt they ever clean it. Towels were dry and folded, though, so it didn't look like old Betty took a shower during her visit."

"So you're not going to call it a homicide?" Andy asked him.

"No body. Who's dead? We don't know. Somebody turns up, we'll reconsider, but at this point the only law broken I can see is someone paid for seven nights and didn't check out on the eighth day. Even making a mess on the carpet isn't illegal. Yet. Hospitality industry gets its way, maybe it will be someday."

"All right, thanks," Andy said. He had no interest in looking at yet another bloody motel room—the rooms of Judith Ali and Paul Norris had been plenty for right now. If Taylor said there was nothing left behind, he was probably right. Andy knew him as an ambitious cop with an eye toward politics, and if he thought there was a case here he'd have been all over it.

Which left Andy at loose ends. He had told Sally that he had things to do, but that had been another lie since he hadn't known about the phone message at the time. He just had wanted some time away from her and the kids. He was trying to think of Paul as changed, not dead—some kind of monster. Being around Sally made it more difficult to make the mental leap. She reminded him of Paul the family man, the guy who sometimes slept around but always went home eventually.

The Swiss Chalet wasn't far, though. He drove back there, kicked off his shoes, unknotted his tie and draped it over his jacket on the back of a chair. A short nap before he went over to see Sally. He didn't need dinner—the food Sally had mentioned would be more than sufficient. He stretched out on top of the blanket, closed his eyes. Just a few minutes . . .

The stink of blood filled his nostrils, coppery and thick. Shadows coagulating into shapes: faces, open-mouthed in soundless screams. Teeth, tongues, lips caked in blood, scarlet smears on chins and cheeks.

His own father, scarred and slack-jawed like he'd been in his last years.

Andy woke up sweating hard, breathing fast, his heart pounding. The dream had been diffuse, lacking in specificity and fading fast, unlike the persistent nightmares of his childhood. But for those few moments of sleep-panic, the terror of the last few days had been driven home in an undeniable way. His friend, he was convinced, had somehow gone over that impossible barrier, become one of the blood-feasting undead. He had only half-believed it until now.

But sitting on the edge of his bed, still trembling slightly, he knew that if he didn't believe, he never would have had such a dream.

Like it or not, Andy Gray had become a believer.

7

THE NORRIS HOUSE CONTAINED a curious mix of furniture old enough to be called antique, including a faded orange armchair that Andy remembered from Paul's first apartment after the Academy, and Crate & Barrel-provided updates and accessories. Andy had never really talked to Paul about it, but guessed that he'd insisted on hanging onto some of his old things, while letting Sally take care of replacing any that wore out or fell apart. Andy sat on a couch where he had rested many times over the years, a brown cloth-covered job with strings of light and dark green woven through. A spring jabbed at his butt.

Sally sat across from him in a more modern forest green wing chair. Between them was a contemporary maple coffee table, with two cups of herbal tea cooling on it. Sally's *Cosmo* graced the tabletop, a veritable wonderland of cleavage smiling up at Andy. Sally had changed out of her mourning clothes into one of Paul's white shirts with jeans and fuzzy socks. The shirt was buttoned only halfway up; when she leaned forward for her tea, Andy got a pretty good look at things.

Andy tried to keep his gaze focused on her face as he

launched into the interrogation. "How much did Paul tell you about his cases, Sally?"

She shifted in the chair. The shirt gapped, but she demurely smoothed it shut. "You spent more time with him than me, these past few months," she replied. "He told me that you were keeping an eye on a potential terrorist, trying to gather enough evidence to bring her in before she pulled some big attack. But that was it."

"I know we were away a lot," Andy said. "Either out of town or on stakeouts. Monica complains like hell about it as well, but it's just life in the Bureau, I guess. I'm sorry he wasn't here with you more."

"I could never understand why he couldn't at least sleep at home when he was here in town on a job," she said.

"We had to take odd shifts sometimes," Andy tried to explain. "One of us catching a few hours' sleep while the other watched, then switching. Even though the woman we were tailing often slept all night, she didn't always—sometimes she'd get up and walk the streets at two A.M., and we had to be on her when she did. Other times, she slept all day and was active all night. So Paul couldn't take a chance on coming home, even though he wasn't that far away."

Sally sighed. "I guess so. I mean, I get the idea, I just didn't like it. Especially now that he's gone, and I think about all those nights I slept alone . . . and all the ones from now on."

"Did he get in touch at all, or try to, during the time

that he was missing?" Andy asked, wanting to direct the conversation back to more pertinent areas.

Sally looked at her teacup, bent forward and took a sip before answering. *Classic evasive maneuvers. The kind of thing a witness does to put off replying to a question she really didn't want to address.* "I don't know," she said finally, setting the teacup back on the table. "There were a couple of phone calls where nobody was on the line when I answered. Or nobody spoke, anyway—you know, how when you pick up the phone and you can hear that hollow silence, like there's someone there but they're just listening, holding their breath? Once I was so sure it was Paul I actually said his name."

"What happened?"

"Nothing. A click, then the dial tone."

"So whoever it was hung up when you said the name."

"I guess so," Sally said. "I told myself it was just a wrong number, and when I called the person Paul, he realized the mistake."

"But now . . . ?"

Sally hesitated again. "Now, I'm not so sure. What if it really was him? What if he was hurt and couldn't speak, or was afraid that whoever was holding him would hear? What if he was trying to send me some kind of message, to tell me how I could help him?"

"But you didn't think that at the time?"

Another sigh, another shift in her chair. "I don't know, Andy. I . . . I'm so scared by all this."

"Scared of what, Sally?"

She held his gaze this time, her blue eyes steady, unblinking. "I don't know that, either. Something. The Bureau's not telling me everything, and neither are you. That much I can figure out on my own. And I understand that you can't—that's part of life at the Bureau, too. But I get this . . . I don't know, this vibe, you know, in the dead of night. I guess it's just the three o'clock blues, the dark night of the soul or something. I just find myself waking up with this creepy sensation, and it scares me to death."

Andy was the first to look away. He couldn't tell her what he believed. If he did, ADIC Flores would have his head. Anyway, what he wanted was to puzzle out on his own what had happened to Paul and find a way to make it right again. Involving Sally would be counterproductive, and maybe even dangerous to her and the girls.

"It'll pass, Sally," he said at last. "It's probably just anxiety because he was gone, and then . . . you have every right to be frightened and upset, believe me. But I'm here for you guys."

The ghost of a smile flitted across Sally's face, gone as quickly as it had come. "Thanks, Andy."

"I miss him too, Sally. You know that, right?"

She leaned forward, the shirt falling open. He tried to keep looking at her eyes, tried not to let his gaze drift down her neck, into the open shirt. She brushed his knee with her left hand. "I know you do, Andy. You've known him longer than anyone."

"Yeah," he said, his voice suddenly tight. "Can I take a look in his office now, Sally?"

"Sure," she said, straightening up again. "You know where it is. Let me know if you need anything."

Andy rose and left the room without looking back.

Paul's office was in the back of the house, through the kitchen. It was on a corner with two windows, but Paul had never, to Andy's knowledge, opened the blinds on either one. He flicked on the light switch as he walked in, turning on an overhead fixture. On the desk was a green-shaded banker's lamp, and Andy switched that on, too. Even with both lights on, the office was a gloomy place, dark shadows filling the corners.

A big old wooden desk, two black metal filing cabinets, a wooden credenza with yet more files. A rolling leather desk chair and two straight-backed wooden chairs for visitors. One of those was piled high with manila folders.

Not many people bothered to visit Paul in his home office, and he didn't really spend a lot of time in here, Andy knew. Enough time to dump things onto the desk or stuff papers into a cabinet, but not enough time to organize or straighten anything. But Paul had been a closemouthed guy. If he had an idea, he'd niggle with it until it was in presentable form, backed up by some kind of evidence, before he'd share it. Even with his partner or his wife.

If there was a lead to whatever had put Paul into the path of his "mistress," this was where it'd be.

Andy started with the desk, which looked like it was the most recent dumping ground. Sitting in the leather chair, he flipped through the files on top one by one. Taxes, receipts, insurance—mostly household stuff, unrelated to the job. He pulled open the shallow center drawer. Pens and pencils, a calculator, paper clips, letter opener. In the middle of it, a leather datebook. Andy opened it, turning the pages rapidly until he found the most recent entries. Some he recognized, appointments the two of them had kept together.

But in the margins on the page showing the week during which Paul had disappeared was a notation he did not recognize.

It said simply "Bar." Plus an address on an alley off Sunset. Andy couldn't recall Paul ever mentioning the place, and if it had been one of his regular watering holes he wouldn't have had to write down the address. So what was it? Andy knew the general neighborhood—low-rent strip clubs, liquor stores, dives.

He jotted down the address on a piece of blank paper from a note pad on the desk, and moved to the next drawer, top right. Right on top was a copy of Stella Olemaun's book, *30 Days of Night*. Andy took it out and started thumbing through it. The book hadn't been available very long, only a couple of weeks. But this copy was already worn. The dust jacket was scuffed and torn at the bottom. Pages were thumbed down, earmarked. Paul had underlined passages in blue ball point, written quick notes—sometimes as little as an exclamation point or a question mark—in the margins. He'd never even told Andy he was reading it. Obviously there had been some angle to the Olemaun case that he had been chewing on for a while without mentioning anything to Andy.

On the other hand, if Paul had been reading this and taking it seriously . . .

Was Andy's entire worldview wrong?

This was what everything hinged on—was the world what Andy Gray had always believed it to be, or was it a much darker place? Was it a world of life in cycles beginning and ending in patterns set when organisms crawled from the murky pits, or was it a world where death was an option? A world where the dead could rise again and feed upon the living?

He put the book down on the desk, determined to take it away with him so he could review what Paul had been reading. Even as Andy drew his hand away from it, he knew that his belief had just been reinforced. The rest of the facts—most notably, Paul's survival under the barrage of fire, but also his impossible strength, the unknown characteristic of his blood—could not be denied. Nor could they be explained by a purely psychological condition.

Paul Norris is a vampire. Might as well get used to the idea because it's not going away.

A hand on his shoulder startled him and he almost screamed.

Heart hammering, he spun around and saw Sally

standing behind him. "I'm sorry," she said quickly. "I didn't mean to startle you, Andy. I just wanted to see if you needed anything."

He took her hand, already beginning to calm, heart rate dropping closer to normal. "It's okay, Sal," he said. "I guess I just didn't hear you come in."

Her hand was warm and soft and she returned his grip instead of letting go. She didn't say anything, just looked at him with her full lips slightly parted. Sally Norris was a beautiful woman, always had been. Andy remembered feeling a rush of jealousy when Paul had married her, because she was so flamboyantly attractive, while his own wife's beauty was much harder to find. Sally was a decade younger than Monica but looked like she was right out of college, and when the two went out together they were sometimes taken for mother and daughter. Much to Monica's chagrin. And, Andy had to admit in the deepest recesses of his heart, to his own.

But now Sally was holding his hand and tugging on it, and he came up out of the chair. She stepped back a pace, pulling him toward her. He could see that the white shirt was open a couple more buttons and there was no bra beneath it, just her breasts swaying freely beneath the thin cotton. His breath caught and he felt an unexpected stirring at his groin. "Sally, I—"

"Shhh." She let go of one of his hands, pressed her fingers against his lips to silence him. "I don't want to talk right now," she said, her voice husky, unfamiliar. But she held her fingers where they were, wiggled one between his lips. He felt her fingernail tap against his teeth and he opened his mouth, drawing her fingers inside. He tongued them, sucked on them. Sally let out a low moan, pulled her fingers free, brought them to her own mouth. Then she lowered her hand and moved into Andy, her lips seeking his, tongue darting from between them and exploring his mouth. With his free left hand, Andy reached around her, pressing her against him. His hand roamed up her spine, then around her ribs, finding the swell of her right breast. Her kiss became more urgent, and then she broke it off.

"Upstairs," she whispered.

It wasn't him, he knew, had nothing to do with him being Andy Gray. It was all about Sally. She had needed someone, anyone. Needed human contact, and physical release, and he was the easiest route to both of those. He was here, handy. She knew he wouldn't turn her down.

They shed their clothes within seconds. Sally lay back in the center of the bed, spreading her legs. There would be no foreplay. Andy didn't wait for further invitation but moved toward her. Taking him in her hands, she guided him inside and pressed up against him urgently. She was wet and warm and smooth and soft and hungry.

This was her scene, Andy realized, her thing. She had wanted it, had set it up from the beginning, and now she would have things her way. Not that he objected—

he'd been away from home for weeks, and even when he was there, sex was almost mechanical, habitual more than passionate. But Sally Norris was a woman who radiated sex, and he was helpless to resist even if he'd wanted to.

They lay still, his head resting on the pillow of her breast, while their breathing slowed to normal. Both were covered in sweat. The sex had been the most intensely physical Andy could remember for a long time, and even though it hadn't been particularly long lasting he was spent, utterly drained. "Are you okay, Sally?" he asked quietly after a time. "Do you need anything—"

"I'm good, Andy," she murmured sleepily. "I'm fine, really. Just . . . just lay with me for a while."

He moved off her and snuggled in beside her, pulling covers up over both of them. She smiled at him, then turned on her side. Within a few minutes, he heard the regular, deep breathing that indicated sleep. His mind had already kicked back into high gear, though. *Should I tell her the truth about Paul? It might help her.* But it also might give her false hope that he would return someday. And how would she take the idea that he was still functional, still sentient, but had not come back to her? That could hurt worse than just believing him dead.

After Sally had been asleep for about ten minutes, Andy rolled out of bed. He looked at her, sleeping soundly already, lips parted. A beautiful, sexual being, sated for now. He walked to the window and looked out at the yard beyond, and the street, silvery in the moonlight.

But as he stood by the window, he had that uncomfortable, familiar sensation that he was being watched. A peeping tom, in this neighborhood? Could be. Or just some concerned neighbor, worried about Sally, looking up and seeing a naked man in her bedroom on the night of her husband's funeral? That or something else; either way, the feeling unnerved him. He backed away from the window, into the shadows where moonlight couldn't penetrate.

As if touched off by the embrace of darkness, a wave of guilt and revulsion washed over Andy. He reached for his underwear, his pants. He couldn't stay here, couldn't face Sally when she woke up.

Dressing quickly, he left her room, heading for the stairs. But before he made it down, another door opened and Sally's oldest, Nicole, came onto the landing. She rubbed her eyes with little fists. *Okay . . . now* this *is awkward. I've gotta get out of here.* Andy stopped on the stairs and looked at her. "What's wrong, Nicole?" he asked. "Can't you sleep?"

"The moon is too bright, Uncle Andy. It shines in my window, and while I was awake and looking out the window, I saw a man jumping."

"Jumping?" Andy echoed.

"On the roofs, across the street," she said. "Jumping from roof to roof. I thought it was Santa Claus for a minute, but then I remembered that there is no Santa, I only pretend there is because Debra still believes in him. She's only six."

"I know."

"So it wasn't him. I thought maybe it was Daddy, visiting from heaven. I couldn't see him very good but it looked sort of like Daddy. But if it was, he would come and see me, right?"

"I'm sure he would, if he could." A sudden chill gripped Andy and he shivered. "You know what, Nic, I know your daddy is up in heaven, watching you from up there. What you saw outside—what you thought you saw—that was probably just a dream."

She shook her head, her long blond hair flailing. "I know if I'm asleep or not, Uncle Andy," she said. "I wasn't asleep."

Andy was running out of ideas. "Maybe it was an angel."

"Angels have wings, they don't hop. And they wear white dresses, not suits and ties." She stifled a yawn. "I think I'll try to go back to sleep," she said. "If you see my daddy outside, tell him to come back home."

"I will," Andy said, unconvincingly.

Nicole went back into her room, and Andy made a quick pit stop to Paul's office for the copy of *30 Days of Night*. Having retrieved that, he fled the Norris house. The Bureau car waited in the driveway.

Andy scanned the rooftops, the trees, the shadows. Nothing. If there had been someone out there, he was gone now.

He quickly opened the car, tossing the book onto the passenger seat. Cranking the engine, he turned on the headlights and backed out of the driveway.

But the guilt didn't stay behind. No sir. He had never had sex with another woman since marrying Monica, hardly ever even flirted. He just wasn't that kind of guy, not like Paul or Sally, for both of whom sex had always seemed as important as eating or breathing.

Now, he had not only slept with someone else, but she was the widow of his partner, on the day of his funeral.

And to make it worse, the guy wasn't even really dead.

Paul Norris watched his own funeral through binoculars stolen from a sporting goods store on Alvarado. There was a vantage point on top of a self-storage warehouse across the freeway from the cemetery, and he crouched there under some ductwork, keeping out of the direct sunlight, swaddled completely in protective clothing (one couldn't be too careful, after all), training the glasses on his wife and daughters.

And Andy, of course. That fucker. His ex-partner and alleged best friend, who arrived in the limo with Sally and stayed so close to her for most of the graveside service that people might start to wonder just who was the husband here. Except for the time he wandered away altogether, off into a little stand of oaks by the freeway.

Paul thought maybe Andy needed to piss or vomit and couldn't wait for a bathroom. But he did neither, just looked around for a few minutes. At one point, he stared out across the freeway. Paul started—it felt like Andy was looking straight into his eyes, although of course, without binoculars there was no way Andy could see Paul. Still, it was a bit disconcerting.

As if that wasn't bad enough, later on Andy had gone to Paul's house. Paul had seen the lights in his office come on—*my own private office, on the day of my fucking funeral!* What was up with that? Didn't Sally respect anything? The office light stayed on for the rest of the night, even after the girls went to bed and Sally's bedroom light went on, and then off again.

Andy didn't leave until quite a while after that, and even when he did take off, the office light continued to burn. Paul didn't quite know what to make of it all. Sure, Sally liked men—sometimes six or seven at a time, an occasional kink Paul was happy to indulge because he loved to see his hot wife push her limits.

But with sexless Andy Gray? And on the very day she buried her own husband? That was just beyond good taste.

Paul's first impulse was to go in through the window and rip her throat out. The thought of those glorious crimson plumes covering her gave him a charge every bit as sexual as watching her in action with other men. He could imagine the surprise in her wide dying eyes as he bent to drink it up.

Still . . . she was his wife, though, his Sally, and while he seemed to have become . . . something else . . . he couldn't bring himself to kill her.

Or Andy.

Not yet, anyway.

There was enough of the human Paul Norris left in him that he remembered the two people he had loved the most during his life.

No telling if it would last—all this was too new, too strange, to him. He didn't have a roadmap, no useful guidebook beyond Stella Olemaun's—and the amount that she didn't know could have filled a volume at least as thick. She had seen a lot and lived to tell about it. But she had also theorized much, mere guesswork at best, and her book contained huge swaths of misinformation.

There was nothing Paul hated more than someone who couldn't get their facts straight.

So Paul was on his own. Whether his empathy for Sally and Andy would last, he couldn't say.

For now, though, he would let them live.

Guess it's your lucky night, motherfuckers.

Wallowing in grief and guilt, Andy braked suddenly and pulled into the liquor store parking lot. He wasn't a big drinker anymore, and had finally quit smoking several years ago. But right now those things were minor details, lacking in import. He snatched a big bottle of Jim Beam off the shelf because he recognized the brand.

At the counter he asked the bored-looking clerk for a pack of Camels. "Filtered or un?" the guy said.

"Unfiltered," he said. He didn't know quite why he was doing this, what he expected to accomplish. Punishing himself? Seeking oblivion in booze and smoke? Whatever—he didn't want to analyze anymore tonight.

Walking out of the store with his purchases in a small brown paper bag, he stopped short.

A motion, on the rooftops opposite?

He looked.

Closed shops, their signs off, windows dark.

Above, empty roofs and a blank gray sky. The sky was never really black here; the city's lights bounced off it and kept it a kind of flat not-black. The moon was visible through it, and a random handful of stars.

If he'd seen anything on the roofs, though, it was gone now.

He shrugged, opened the car, put the bag on the seat next to Stella Olemaun's book.

Gunning the engine, he headed back toward his motel. He could almost taste the Jim Beam.

Excerpted from *30 Days of Night* by Stella Olemaun

Eben and I tore off back to town as soon as we saw the invaders walking across the open tundra.

They alarmed us on such a primal level. Maybe it was everything that had led up to it; the stolen phones, and damaged communications satellite, the stranger we were forced to kill . . . or maybe it was just the sight of them.

There were dozens of them, scattered in an almost organized fashion, like an invading army. But they were more than that.

Later I would see them up close for myself—their eyes shimmered in the moonlight, their teeth were like razors, but it was their absolute normalcy that chilled me the most, I think. They wore street clothes; jeans and t-shirts, several in suits, others in dresses.

If they had really been human, considering what part of the world they were in, they would have frozen to death dressed like that.

I remember looking at my husband, normally courageous in the face of trouble, and seeing real terror in his eyes. That was as disturbing as anything that was happening. Eben wasn't afraid when he was supposed to be—he was just one of those people. No fear.

But as we drove back towards Barrow proper, slipping and fishtailing in possibly the last working vehicle, I saw his eyes wide, darting, looking for answers, his hands shaking as he gripped the wheel.

"What should we do?" I asked.

I was numb, couldn't think, my law enforcement training unfocused—I remember how stupid I felt asking what needed to be done.

We had to get back to town. But then what?

Eben swerved again on the icy road. He was driving too fast. Icy shards of snow were falling, obscuring what little we could see through the darkness and iced-over windshield. I stared into the night as we raced by and had the most absurd thought: the invaders were *right there,* keeping pace, just outside our vision.

I placed my hand on Eben's leg and caught his attention. He looked at me and, for that one moment, I had my husband back. His eyes softened and that familiar confidence I relied on returned, however fleeting.

I repeated my question. "What should we do?"

Eben shook his head apologetically and repeated what he'd said outside. "We should warn the others."

"And tell them what?" I asserted.

"I don't know," he stammered and then he laughed nervously. "I really don't know."

I saw them first this time.

* * *

I had my hand on Eben's shoulder and glanced back through the snow-peppered rear window. Between the stripes of ice melted by the defroster strips, I saw shapes on the road—not a vehicle, but human shapes.

Running after us.

"They're following," I remarked.

Eben glanced in the rearview then quickly down at the speedometer. It read forty-five miles per hour.

"Impossible."

It wasn't. They were closing in, six or seven human figures. The one in the lead was near enough that I could see his leather jacket, his head shaved bald, the numerous silver-hoop piercings in both ears.

Eben stepped on the gas. I looked behind. Only the bald man stayed with us. The others suddenly swerved left into the darkness.

Eben struggled to keep the truck on the icy road and I could offer little help, so I crawled over the seat into the rear cab and removed my sidearm.

"What are you doing?" Eben barked from the driver's seat.

"Running interference," I yelled back. "Roll the back window down!"

As the glass lowered, I could see the bald man clearly. He was less than twenty yards behind and gaining fast. His eyes were shimmering black and for a moment, I thought he was grinning. But no—it was a mouthful of the largest, sharpest teeth I'd ever seen.

I pointed my pistol out the window, trying to steady my aim despite the rattling vehicle and the frigid wind swirling around the cab. The bald man swerved in and out of my sight. I couldn't get a steady shot, so I fired four rounds right at his chest. The first two missed, but the other two caught his shoulder and spun him like a top.

The slugs didn't kill him—they hardly drew blood near as I could see—but it gave us the precious time we needed to get away.

Eben and I were silent for the remainder of the short trip into town. Several times, while Eben negotiated the rough terrain, I thought I saw other figures outside in the darkness. Running with us, toward town.

We were traveling over fifty miles an hour.

My memory flashed to the stranger in our jail bending the bars, the teeth of the chaser, and now the human figures keeping pace with our truck. I think it was at that point I allowed the word that had been creeping in the back of my mind to finally surface.

Vampires.

I didn't say it out loud. I didn't say anything. I just looked over at Eben and I could see his mind was racing as fast as the truck. I wondered if he thought like I did, already contemplating the same impossibility.

8

ANDY GRAY'S HOME OFFICE was neater than Paul Norris's. But then, just like Paul's office, Andy was hardly ever there. The house, a traditional suburban ranch, was big enough for each girl to have her own room, Monica to have a sewing room/office of her own, and Andy to keep an office. Monica called it a den, but to Andy that term implied casual pursuits, hunting trophies, pleasure reading in a big leather club chair. He called it an office because when he brought work home, this was where he sat to do it. His desk was secondhand and had come with the uncomfortable wooden rolling chair he still used. Like Paul, he had filing cabinets, but his were pine, scarred, and stained.

He didn't have a leather club chair, either. He did have a fake-leather easy chair that had once reclined smoothly with the crank of a lever. Now the recline mechanism was broken, but if he leaned back hard enough he could wrench the chair into a slightly inclined position. He did so now, positioning it under a floor lamp. A tumbler of Beam rested on the corner of the desk, within easy reach, and he'd balanced an ashtray on the chair's arm. Sitting back, Andy opened

Paul's copy of *30 Days of Night.* He had come home to read it, wanting to be away from Los Angeles, away from Paul and Sally and everything else. He had been drinking hard ever since buying that first bottle, and if he was going on the extended bender he foresaw, he wanted to do it in the safety and comfort of his own home.

Before he read cover to cover, he decided to skim the sections that Paul had underlined or otherwise noted. These were obviously the passages that had meant the most to his partner, so he hoped in them he might be able to find some clue to Paul's fate. He had been back in Sacramento less than twelve hours—long enough to take a short nap, to say hello to the girls, long enough for Monica to complain about him being gone, to berate him for reeking of tobacco, and to wonder why he was being so cold and distant now that he was back.

"My partner's dead," he had said, closing the door to his office. "I have to figure out who did it." The facile answer, if not necessarily the honest one. Monica muttered something in reply, but he hadn't heard her through the closed door.

"Their strength is unbelievable," one underlined passage read. *"I have seen feats of strength that I would have considered impossible by any human. Steel-walled sheds torn through as if they were paper. Cars tossed around like trash bags at the dump. People literally ripped in half, arms yanked from sockets. The word 'preternatural' comes to mind when I try to think of how to describe what they can do, because no natural*

human who ever walked the earth has displayed such raw power."

No kidding, Andy thought, remembering the way Paul had held him off the ground in one fist and then hurled him aside. Paul had been grinning at the time, too, as if enjoying himself immensely. If, as he'd said, he had been in the process of changing, then the immense strength had probably been new to him, a wonder.

Had Paul allowed himself to be captured?

He'd always been a bit of a show-off. He had never liked to work hard, but much came easily to him, and he wasn't one to, as they said, hide his light under a bushel. Even back in their Academy days, when he excelled at something, he liked to make sure others knew it. He'd been one of the best marksmen in their class, and had pointed it out to one and all, even going to the range at odd hours so he could demonstrate his skills to new groups of NATs and the other law enforcement officers who trained at Quantico.

Maybe he knew the strength was coming—could probably feel its onset when the rain of lead hadn't killed him—and decided he wanted it to happen someplace where he could impress others with it.

Hell, he probably knew Andy would be there. That would be the ultimate—showing the guy who knew him best that he was no longer the man he'd once been. Paul would be all over that.

Andy shook his head sadly and returned to the book.

Another underlined passage spoke of the mouths of

the vampires, the rows of sharp, uneven teeth, the stench of their breath, the long, flicking tongues. That was Paul, too. Andy hadn't noticed the teeth and tongue until the very end, although Paul's breath had been foul from the start. That was probably a natural effect of drinking the blood of rats and bugs, though. The teeth and tongue were a physical change that may well have been among the last to take place. The sight had been horrible: Paul's mouth coming open, revealing rows of teeth like razor wire, and that bright red tongue uncoiling from between them.

In only a few pages, Andy had confirmed that the changes that had come over Paul mirrored the physical attributes of the creatures Stella Olemaun wrote about. He dipped into the book again, finding a vivid description of a murderous spree. He only read a few lines, stopped, took a sip of the Jim Beam, then drained the glass.

If Paul could survive on vermin blood while he was changing, would that still work once the change was complete? Did these things *need* human blood to stay alive, or was that just a preference? The question was important—crucial, because it went to the question of whether or not Paul had necessarily become a killer after he changed. He had chosen not to kill Andy, even when he could have. If he really *had* been watching his old house, then he'd also chosen not to kill Sally and the girls.

In life, Paul had often been rude, coarse, unsubtle.

Monica called him the classic boor. Diplomacy was often needed on the job, but that had been hard for Paul. He was the kind who'd rather bust someone's head than try to persuade him to turn himself in. The two partners complemented one another that way. Andy was the opposite, turning to violence only as a last resort, concerned for the feelings of others. Paul called him a squishy liberal, even though he knew it wasn't accurate politically, because Andy would always look for a way to avoid having to hurt someone.

In death, or un-life or whatever it was, what would Paul be? Would he automatically become like those who had invaded Barrow, ruthless killing machines interested only in fresh meat? Or would he have free will? And if so, how would he choose to exercise that will? It was a stretch to assume that because someone was often a jerk in life, he would, at the first opportunity, become a serial murderer.

But on the other hand, if Stella's account was to be believed, the vampires in Barrow were killers one and all. It was hardly possible that they had all been killers during their lives as well. There must have been something inherent in becoming a vampire, then, that made them drop their inhibitions against killing. They were far enough outside human society that the old rules no longer applied to them. They were simply exercising their survival instincts, because they really did need human blood to survive. They were trying to propagate their species by turning Barrow's citizens into vampires.

Wait . . . that last point didn't seem to be the case. Andy flipped ahead in the book, and couldn't find a specific reference. But if everyone killed by vampires became vampires, it shouldn't have taken long for Barrow to be completely overpopulated with them, to the point that some would have to leave, or they'd all run out of food. But that didn't seem likely here. Andy sighed. There was still so much he didn't know. This book was a starting point, but he guessed there was a lot more information to be had, if he could separate the fact from the fiction.

He turned back to page one and started to read.

Angelica Foster had been putting in such long hours at the lab she was afraid her apartment would attack her, like antibodies going after an invading virus, when she went in. It was a chance she was willing to take. She had actually left work twenty minutes early for a change. She'd stopped at a market, bought fixings for salad, a box of bowtie pasta, a baguette, and a bottle of white wine. She wasn't having company—just wanted to relish eating at home for a change instead of grabbing another cellophane-wrapped sandwich in the break room at the Bureau. She tried to remember the last time she'd brought someone home—male or female; she liked either—for anything resembling pleasure. A long, long time. Months. She'd burned through a lot of batteries in the meantime.

Of course, she had brought work home with her.

She turned on some soft jazz and unloaded her purchases in the kitchen. She clicked the oven on to 350 and started the water boiling in an old Revere Ware copper-bottomed pot she'd inherited from her mother. Added a dash of salt and a little olive oil. While the oven warmed, she cut off a quarter of the baguette and sliced into it, smearing butter on each slice and dusting them with garlic, rosemary, and a little oregano. This she wrapped in foil. When the oven had preheated, she put the bread onto the center rack and set a timer for fifteen minutes. By this time, the water had come to a strong boil, so she shook some of the pasta out of the box into it, stirring as she did. She brought it back to a boil and then turned it down to simmer.

This part under control, she went into the other room and booted up her desktop computer. Candlelight might have been more appropriate, she figured. But this was not a date—of which she'd had precious few lately. Not that she wouldn't have liked some, but work consumed her time and attention.

Back to the kitchen, where she tore apart lettuce, sliced tomatoes and baby carrots and celery. She scraped all the ingredients into a bowl, tossed them with some roasted garlic dressing and Parmesan cheese. By now the kitchen smelled heavenly, and in her dining room-slash-office the computer screen glowed. She left the kitchen for a minute, went to the computer, and logged online.

Angelica kept her apartment nearly as immaculate as

her lab. Although she worked long hours, she usually tried to dust and run the vacuum two or three mornings a week before she went in. Everything had a place, from the cubbies for mail and bills to the antique brass wall hooks on which she hung her keys. Her desk and dining table were also antique. A black faux leather sofa and some bookcases finished off the room, and a short hallway led to a bedroom and bath.

Back to the business at hand—eating. She took a bite of the pasta—*aahh. Ain't nothing like the real thing, baby.*

While she ate, Angelica thumbed through printouts she had brought home from the lab. The samples of Paul Norris's blood showed strange irregularities that she had, so far, been unable to explain. Cells were present that shouldn't have been—cells whose origin and purpose were a complete puzzlement. They seemed to replicate quickly, as if blood was a favorable environment. As far as she'd been able to tell, they acted like . . . cancer cells, although no cancer that she could find referenced in any of the usual literature.

Angelica had hoped that looking the papers over in a different environment would allow her to bring a fresh eye to the problem. So far, no luck. She shoved the printouts aside, frustrated, and tackled the garlic bread instead.

Doing her dishes, a memory flitted past her consciousness like a butterfly over a field, and she snatched at it. An article she had read in the *Journal of Serology.*

The author had discussed a newly discovered type of cell, and had a particular name for it. *What the hell was it now, though?* Angelica had thought the name would stick with her, but now it seemed determined to evade her attempts to recall it. Finally, as she dried her wine glass, it came to her.

The Immortal Cell.

Angelica hurriedly put away the dry dishes and went to the computer. Email had downloaded and waited for her, but she skipped over that and went straight for a search engine. She plugged in the phrase, clicked on SUBMIT, and waited.

Thousands of pages were returned in response to her search. Articles and books on cancer, on immortalization of cells as a way of avoiding the normal process of aging and death. She couldn't remember the author of the original article, so wasn't able to reduce the number of hits that way, and her journals were back at the lab. She resigned herself to scanning hundreds of listings to see if anything jumped out at her.

On the third page, something did.

Felicia Reisner. That, Angelica remembered the moment she saw it, was the author's name. She typed that into the search field and narrowed the results considerably. She went from listing to listing, reading enough of each to know whether or not she needed to keep going. When her wall clock chimed ten, she was still less than halfway through. She was beginning to feel drowsy, though, and another glass of wine would put her right to sleep. Instead, she brewed a pot of black tea and kept going.

She was on the second cup when she found the message board. She almost spewed tea all over her keyboard when she read the name of one of the message posters.

Dr. Amos Saxon of UCLA. The biology professor who had invited Stella Olemaun to speak on campus and whose body was found in his own burned-out house. Blood from that scene had contained similar properties to Norris's blood.

The board was a university medical discussion group. On it, several months before, Dr. Saxon had posted some questions about Felicia Reisner's "immortal cell" hypothesis. Part of Reisner's answer read, "The disease begins with a single cell in the body, one which mutates, essentially destroying the failsafe mechanisms of cellular replication, causing the cell to reproduce indefinitely. The cell and its direct descendants are therefore 'immortal,' and proceed, replicating out of control, eventually spreading throughout the body and disrupting all its normal processes."

Dr. Saxon's response was succinct.

<<Maybe they should call it the VAMPIRE cell.>>

Reisner did not reply, and the thread had died.

Angelica shuddered, chilled to the bone for no discernible reason. She left the computer on and went back to the printouts. Norris's blood was Type O negative. It was thick with the strange cells—the seeming cancer cells that didn't look or act like any cancer cells she'd heard of. There were so many of them, as if they were being fueled by some unknown process. She wasn't absolutely sure, but it appeared that they had even continued to replicate after the blood had been removed from Norris and stored at the lab.

More confusingly—and ominously, considering Dr. Saxon's parting remark—blood taken from inside Norris's stomach had the same mixture of his normal blood and the "immortal" cells. Blood he *ingested*. Why would it match blood from his circulatory system? Sure, when a person ate, that food was eventually converted to energy and would reach the bloodstream in the form of various sugars and so on. But you didn't find Snickers bars or hamburgers or tofu floating around in the arteries in their original, undigested state.

The VAMPIRE cell . . .

She hurried back to the computer. Found Special Agent Andrew Gray's email address and typed a quick note to him, outlining what she had found and promising to keep working on it.

Once that was sent, the weariness that had sent her to caffeine was upon her again. She could have another cup, but she'd be up all night for sure if she did that. Better to knock off for the night, try to get in six or seven hours. In the morning she could come back to this. Maybe by then she'd know the right questions to ask, the right avenues to explore. She shut down the computer, rinsed out her teacup.

On her way to the bathroom to brush her teeth, Angelica heard a soft knock at the front door.

Gray?

Impossible. He couldn't have already received the email and come over here.

She crossed the darkened living/dining room to the door, peered out through the fish-eye peephole.

The hall looked empty.

Making sure the chain-lock was on, she opened it.

No one there.

Had she imagined it? She *was* pretty tired.

Shutting the door again, she locked the knob lock and set the dead bolt. Turned to try for the bathroom again.

And stopped dead.

A man, in front of her. Light hair, dark suit, tie. Tall.

And teeth.

She worked for the Bureau. Never a field agent, but still, you picked up some stuff. She had to get a good look at the guy, memorize the face, measure the height against some known object, estimate the weight. If he robbed or raped her, he would not get away with it.

But she couldn't get past all those teeth, small and sharp, like rows of needles. And between them, snaking toward her, a long red tongue.

"Sorry to interrupt the nightly beauty regimen,

Angel," he said. His voice was soft, almost a whisper, inhuman yet somehow familiar. His breath was foul, like spoiled meat. "But it's time for you to die."

Angelica opened her mouth to scream then, and tensed her body, ready to fight. Knives in the kitchen, a heavy vase about ten steps away on the table. She'd find something—

He moved faster than she could believe, faster than her eye could follow. She almost felt the snap of her neck, but then her spine was broken and all feeling was gone. At the same time, the apartment went black.

9

ANDY READ *30 DAYS OF NIGHT*, front to back, and then he started over. Like his partner before him, he found himself making margin notes and highlighting certain sections. When that was no longer sufficient, he found an old legal pad and started scribbling down thoughts on that.

Stella Olemaun was onto something, he had decided.

This book, labeled fiction, was anything but. She really had lost her husband and most of her friends—hell, most of her entire town—to a vampire attack during the long Alaskan winter.

He even thought he understood her motivation for writing the book. The world needed to be warned, to be convinced that vampires were real, and dangerous. He knew now that Stella was no terrorist. She was the opposite—a lonely hero, crying out for sanity in a world that wanted more than anything to ignore her. He didn't blame her for stocking up on weapons and explosives—anything to blow the heads off those bloodsuckers. As the days wore on he started to feel under-armed in his own house and took to wearing his Glock during all his waking hours, stuffing it under his pillow at night. He hardly left the house at all, except for one trip into town for a shotgun and a few boxes of shells.

Monica complained, but he found he was becoming extremely adept at tuning her out.

He had startled Sara one night, when she had padded to the bathroom in her little nightie and found him sitting there in the dark with the gun clutched in his hands, unshaven and bleary eyed.

He sat locked in his office, his phone unplugged, turning the book over in his hands. Why was it called fiction? That seemed an odd choice—certainly, it didn't read like a novel, and he'd seen enough of the truth, through Paul, to know that it was an inaccurate label. Worse, it took away the book's power, its ability to persuade. Calling it a novel made it too easily dismissed. As nonfiction, it had a certain power, but as fiction it was schlock, certain to be ignored by every reviewer, every talk show host. The book might have had a shot at the bestseller list if it had been handled correctly. It was juicy enough, full of violence and gore and raw, naked emotion. Andy could picture Stella as a guest on the morning network news shows, covered in *The New York Times*.

Instead, she was an afterthought on the American scene, with nothing more than a few web pages devoted to her work. And those seemed to have been put together by the kind of paranoid nutjobs who made Art Bell seem convincing.

Stella must have been furious when they'd told her,

he guessed. It was clear that she'd poured heart and soul into this project. Kingston House, the publishing company, had obviously paid her and put some money into the thing—why would they intentionally sabotage their own release?

Andy plugged in his phone. With three calls, he was able to identify the book's editor, a woman named Carol Hino, and get her number. He dialed it and waited.

"Carol Hino's office," a chipper young feminine voice said.

"This is Special Agent Andrew Gray of the Federal Bureau of Investigation, for Ms. Hino," Andy said.

"Ummm . . . just a second." The line clicked as Andy was put on hold. Less than thirty seconds later, someone picked up.

"This is Carol Hino." Her voice was more mature. Something else. A little bit of a quake. Nervous, maybe.

Andy identified himself again. "I'm calling about the book *30 Days of Night,*" he added.

"I really have nothing to say about that," she replied. That quake again. "And I'm really very busy."

"This won't take long, and it's extremely important, Ms. Hino."

"I'm sure I don't know anything that would be of interest to the FBI."

"You'd be surprised, ma'am," he said. "Everybody thinks that, but sometimes private citizens prove very helpful."

"Like I said, I'm very busy, Mr. Gray." She was more

than nervous. He could hear her dry swallowing, her throat clicking. She was scared. "And how do I know you're really FBI?"

"If you'd like, you can call the main switchboard in Washington and ask about me," he assured her. "I work out of the Sacramento, California, field office. I can give you my ID number. You can get the phone number from Washington information, or online at FBI-dot-gov. Once they've confirmed my identity, you can call me back or I can call you again."

"Thank you, Mr. Gray. That won't be necessary. Now, please—"

"I'm afraid I have to insist, Ms. Hino. I only have a couple of questions, won't take more than five minutes of your time. If that. What I was wondering was, since it's obvious that Stella Olemaun put a lot of work into this book, and described her own experiences in some det—"

"Not just her," Carol Hino interrupted.

"Excuse me?"

"Stella didn't write the book alone. We only used her name, but since you're FBI you might as well know. I had her work with a ghostwriter to make sure we'd end up with a publishable manuscript. Stella's a smart woman, but she's a small-town sheriff's wife, you know, and not really a professional quality writer."

Andy was astonished. "A ghostwriter?" he repeated.

"That's right. It's really done all the time, especially with celebrity books. People want to think their favorite movie star wrote that novel or autobiography all alone, but it's rarely the case."

"Who was this ghostwriter?" Andy asked.

"We have a nondisclosure agreement with him, but . . . I'm sure you could get around that with a warrant or a court judgment." She seemed to be thawing a little now that she was talking about things she knew about. "His name is Donald Gross. He's well known in the business as what we call a work-for-hire writer. Sometimes he does ghostwriting, sometimes novels based on licensed properties, like movies or TV shows. Under his own name, he writes true crime books—the really bloody kind you can find in supermarkets sometimes? He's a pro, he writes well, and he gets his manuscripts in on time. If I had a dozen like him I'd be a happy woman."

"Where can I find him?" Andy asked. "I'd like to ask him some questions as well."

"I wish I could tell you," Carol said. "He seems to have vanished. After he turned in the book with Stella, he seemed to be frightened of something. Not that I blame him. He insisted that his name not appear anywhere on the book—it wouldn't have anyway, and he knew that. Then he just . . . I don't know. He stopped answering phone calls, emails. We even had a royalty check that was mailed to him come back to us. No forwarding address. No writer in the history of the world has ever dodged a royalty check, that I'm aware of."

"That does seem strange," Andy said. "Does he work with an agent?"

"No," Carol said. "He does all his own deals. He told me once he'd rather keep the extra fifteen percent than put some parasite's kids through college."

"He sounds like a character," Andy observed.

"The kind of man the word 'curmudgeonly' was coined to describe."

"Well, I'll look for him," Andy promised. "See if we can't get that check to him after all. Thanks for telling me about him. But my real question was this—after all the work that Stella and this Donald Gross put into the book, and the money that Kingston House put into it, why call it fiction? Wouldn't that guarantee that nobody would pay any real attention to it?"

Another dry swallow. When she spoke again, it was barely above a whisper, the quake back in her voice, only worse this time.

It was the sound of pure terror.

"They made us, Mr. Gray. They made us change it to fiction."

A moment of silence made Andy wonder if she had hung up. But then her voice came back, catching, as if she was fighting back tears.

"They said they would be watching."

A click, a dial tone. Carol Hino had hung up on him after all.

"Andy? Andy!"

Boomboomboomboomboomboomboomboom

"Andy!"

Monica, outside the office door. Pounding on it. He reached over, turned the radio up louder. Went back to his reading.

The Internet was an amazing resource. Trouble was, there were no filters, nothing to say if anything he was reading there was true, or made up, or hallucinations. But it connected him to primary sources—newspaper accounts, family journals, and the like, from all over, and those proved helpful.

He focused his attention initially on the communities around and above the Arctic Circle, like Barrow. There was plenty there to occupy him.

In 1953, the population of the town of Tiksi, in the former USSR, had seemingly vanished over a particularly harsh winter. Americans—those who heard about it at all—attributed the event to Soviet atomic testing and speculated that the people had simply been relocated to allow for underground tests in their region. Others, more cynically minded, just assumed the Soviets had tested with the people in place, and the resulting radiation had wiped them out.

A similar event had occurred on the small Soviet island of October Revolution, but in 1968. American technology was able, by that time, to determine if there had been any kind of weapons testing. None had been recorded. But once again, the population was simply gone, over the timespan of winter's darkest weeks.

Nord, Greenland, 1911.

Mould Bay, Canada, 1879.

Tromso, Norway, 1842.

The Kola Peninsula, Russia, 1799.

In each of these places, thriving populations had mysteriously vanished. All during the winter, all around the Arctic Circle. All places where the sun set and stayed down for weeks at a time.

Reading these accounts chilled Andy to the bone. They were unlike Stella's account of Barrow in one important particular—in none of them had the kind of mass slaughter she had described been observed. When the sun rose again, the people in these towns were simply gone, disappeared.

One plausible reason for that came immediately to Andy's mind—unlike in Barrow, no witnesses had survived.

He glanced at the clock, then regretted having done so. Middle of the night. No wonder Monica had stopped knocking—she'd gone to bed hours ago, he was sure. He wasn't ready for sleep yet. He'd been nipping from a new bottle of Jim Beam, and a haze of smoke hung over the room. His mind reeled from the things he'd been reading about. He knew he couldn't sleep even if he tried—too many connections clicking in his fevered brain for that.

This had been going on for weeks. He hadn't been keeping track of the calendar, had just been working in here until sleep overtook him, then waking and working some more. Monica made meals for him and he ate them when he was hungry, never mind that they were cold and sometimes beginning to congeal a little. Between the Beam and the Camels he couldn't taste much anyway.

He turned back to the computer. Forget the Arctic Circle for a minute—what about other vanishing populations? Roanoke, Virginia, where an entire colony had disappeared in 1590, leaving behind the single word "Croatan." He'd had a vague memory of that, and reading an online account brought it back. There were a number of theories to explain where those early settlers had gone, but none of them was definitive. The Anasazi people of the American Southwest, who seemingly disappeared without a trace around 1519. They were assumed to have been assimilated into neighboring tribes, but that was just theory, unproven. Recent archaeological evidence pointed to cannibalism among them, too, which may have been a misreading of proof of vampiric activity. The population of Easter Island, who vanished after building their monolithic stone heads. Everywhere he looked, there were more examples, large and small.

Certainly all of those disappearances couldn't be blamed on vampires. It was likely, however, that some could have been. Andy tugged aside the blinds on his office window and gazed out into the darkness beyond. That was where they dwelled, he knew, where they thrived. Humans had always sought out the light. Obviously, Andy had not been around in the earliest days of the protohumans, but he could picture them taking cover in caves or trees as darkness fell, only emerging with the dawn. Then when they learned to tame fire—certainly one of the most urgent goals of those early humans—they could keep the night at bay.

Were there vampires even then, lurking in the shadows, ruling the night? Or were they some more recent evolution? There had to be some scientific basis for their existence—Andy could not bring himself to believe that they were supernatural in origin, the work of the devil or some such nonsense. He'd had a hard enough time accepting the idea of real vampires at all. Asking him to accept some sort of dark magic was just too much.

As he watched the sky, the eastern edge began to tinge with gray. Dawn soon. He blew out a sigh of relief. Every night that passed was one more small victory.

He unlocked the office door and went out. The nearest bathroom was the half bath on the other side of the kitchen. He was in there for a couple of minutes, and when he came out Monica was in the hallway, glaring at him, wearing an old green bathrobe of fluffy cotton over nondescript cotton pajamas.

"Sally Norris just called for you," she said. "Actually, she called several times last night, a couple of times during the day yesterday, and at least once a day since you got home. Which you wouldn't know, of course, since you've spent just about every waking hour locked away in that office, avoiding your family. Any particular reason she'd be calling you so much? Something I should know?"

Andy didn't try to understand the rage that came

over him. It blew up as if from nowhere, a hurricane-force gale of fury at the unimaginable gall it must have taken for her to ask such a thing. "How about her husband was just murdered?!" he screamed at her. "How about I'm the guy who's trying to find out who did it?! Jesus Christ, Sally is a friend of yours, or at least I thought she was. Now you're, what, having a little jealous fit because she dares to call me about the case? Why didn't you just tell me she was on the goddamn phone?"

Monica's vaguely birdlike face registered shock, as if she'd been physically struck. "I did," she said, her lips beginning to tremble. "I knocked on the door and told you."

"Bullshit!" Andy roared. "I would have taken Sally's call!"

"You told me to fuck off," Monica said. The word was startling, coming from her mouth. Monica never used strong language, never swore. Andy didn't either, for the most part, but in his anger he didn't question the things he'd been saying. "Sally's been calling so much, I've been wondering just who's doing the fucking."

Andy's hand bunched into a fist. Before he threw the punch, though, the wave of anger started to pass and he realized what he'd nearly done. He shoved the hand into his pocket, as if he could simply put away the action. He didn't trust himself to talk, though. He knew this conversation had to come to an end before he did or said something from which there would be no coming back. Turning away from Monica, he returned to his office and locked the door again. Behind him, he could hear her appealing to him in a voice that was shaken and weepy.

He ignored it.

Something else was nagging at him, something he'd been thinking about before the overwhelming need to piss had driven him from the safety of his office. He felt like he'd become a bundle of such urges—a bizarre combination of questioning intellect and base animal desires. Every now and then he had to eat, sleep, defecate. Maybe sex with Sally Norris had been as much about his own urges as hers, after all. But those were physical demands: attributes of a body that was, after all, only human. The rest of him was consumed with the puzzle. What had happened to Paul Norris, how could he deal with it, and where was Paul now? After the survival urges, those were the only things that mattered.

Which reminded him of why he'd returned to the office in the first place. The email from Angelica Foster.

Amos Saxon.

10

Dr. Amos Saxon had been one of those professors who taught for the love of it, not for the money. He never could have afforded his place on Westholme, just blocks from campus in Westwood, on his salary. It had set him back a couple million, easy, and according to the research Andy had done before driving back to LA, he'd paid cash.

But then, teaching was only part of Saxon's life. He had a medical degree and still saw a select few patients. He wrote books, including a pop-science book on the physiology of romance that had hit the bestseller lists, and several more scholarly works that had been adopted by college courses across the country. He had government research grants and contracts. He was also paid by private companies for consulting work. He had led what looked to Andy Gray like a charmed life.

Just not charmed enough. Some firebug had charred him to the point where the good doctor had to be identified through his dental records.

After rereading the email from Angelica Foster that detailed the similarities in blood taken from Norris with blood from the Saxon house, Andy had settled into his chair to do some more fact-finding about the professor. Rich, of course. Divorced, but sometimes seen with glamorous ladies, including the occasional starlet. There seemed to be some whiff of scandal, involving a student. The story died quickly, but not without imparting a certain roguish edge to Saxon.

Andy had fallen asleep then. He'd crashed for a couple of hours, awakened, changed clothes. Avoiding Monica and the girls, he'd climbed into his own car, a six-year-old Toyota Camry, and made the long drive down to Los Angeles. The short sleep had helped refresh him, and coffee and No-Doz from a variety of gas stations and truck stops fueled the rest of the trip. Now he stood once more among the ashes of Saxon's house, horribly aware that dusk was not far off.

The first time he'd been here had been right after the fire. Saxon had been the one who had brought Stella Olemaun to the campus, and that had put the professor on the Bureau's radar. Two LAPD officers had also been found dead at the scene, however, and the Bureau had let the LAPD handle the investigation. They had generated the reports that had eventually landed on Andy's borrowed desk at the Los Angeles field office.

Now he'd thoroughly digested those reports. With the addition of what he knew about Paul Norris and Stella Olemaun, he looked at the crime scene with a different eye. He walked through the rubble, comparing it to floor plans and photos he'd seen of the house before the fire. He could tell that he was in the wing of Dr.

Saxon's home that was devoted to his work. The place had contained a home lab, an exam room, a waiting room for his wealthy patients, a records room, and more. The sharp stink that the fire left behind was fading as wind whistled through parts of the house opened to the air. The house next door, grounds and one end partially burned in the blaze, was covered in tarps that flapped like sails in the wind. Miraculously, a towering jacaranda tree on the property line littered the scorched lawns with its purple blossoms, completely undamaged.

Inside the records room, files had been stored in fireproof metal cabinets, but the cabinets had been opened, their contents incinerated. This had been one of the first clues that the fire had been intentionally set, since someone had to have opened those cabinets to allow the fire access. Andy tucked his flashlight between cheek and shoulder and rummaged around in the ashes, but there wasn't enough left of any single file to offer the first clue as to what Saxon had been up to. Desktop computers were melted lumps of plastic and wire. According to the reports, none of their contents had been salvaged, and back-up CDs were either destroyed or missing.

He passed through an arched doorway—the house had been the kind of modern Tuscan style that made the pages of the architectural magazines—and into what had been Saxon's medical offices. Ash drifted on the marble floors of the waiting room. What looked in the photos like plush leather couches were burned, with only blackened metal frames remaining. A table of chrome and glass was relatively intact. The police remains had been found in this room. The captain of the two officers' squad had been unable to explain what they'd been doing here. Andy couldn't hazard a guess, not without a lot more information. And that did not appear to be forthcoming.

He moved into the next room, an examination room separated from the waiting room by a steel door. The heat had been so intense here that the door had melted slightly, becoming misshapen, and it hung open but refused to swing on its hinges in either direction. The door had kept out some of the fire's fury, though, leaving the room more intact than most. Steel cabinets contained barely charred medical equipment—syringes had melted plastic tubes but the metal parts remained, along with stainless steel bowls and other items Andy couldn't name that were still whole. Even the examination table was in relatively good shape, with its leather scorched and curling away from the cushion, but the rest of the table was mostly undamaged. Andy's flashlight illuminated a strange texture below the leather surface, and he opened a pocketknife and scraped at it. Reddish brown shavings curled away from the knife's blade.

From the looks of it, the table had been soaked with blood, so drenched that it had seeped through the leather and dried inside the cushion. He sniffed it but the scent of blood was gone, covered up by the burned smell. Still, someone, he thought, had bled profusely on this exam table.

He moved on to the next room, which didn't look like any doctor's office he'd ever seen. Affixed to the walls were metal D-rings. The steel of the rings was chipped and dented, as if other metal objects, presumably chains or the ends of straps, had been attached to them. The whole effect was more like a dungeon than a doctor's office, causing Andy to wonder if the student in the hushed-up scandal had spent some time as Saxon's prisoner or willing slave.

Much of the paint had flaked off the walls, but there was still some, pale green with a band of darker green, left behind. Looking closer, Andy could see some odd markings on the walls, between the D-rings. He held the light at an angle, studying the markings. They went from a couple feet off the floor to about six feet high, a little less in some cases. There were four of them, darker smudges against what remained of the paint.

The image flashed into his mind as soon as he realized what must have happened. *Four people, bound in standing positions against the wall. Fire booming in, through the exam room, through the connecting door. Heat sapping all the moisture from the air, boiling the fluids in their bodies. Eyeballs popping, brains exploding against skulls, merciful unconsciousness preceding the incineration of the corpses.*

No. Not complete incineration. There had been enough remaining of the cops to identify the bodies.

But the report hadn't mentioned any bodies found in here, even though this room was farther from the fire's source, and its stone walls and ceiling and marble floor had provided little to fuel the flames.

So someone had removed the remains of whoever had burned to death in this chamber. Andy shone his flashlight around, trying to disprove his own theory. If there had been some other fuel load in here, the fire might have flared hotter. Bookshelves, heavy wood furniture, anything like that. In one corner a thick pile of ash had settled. He sifted through it with his foot, encountering something hard deep inside it. He toed the object out of the ashes, squatted over it. It was black and familiar. He picked it up, tapped it against a cleaner part of the floor to knock some of the soot away.

A human jawbone, teeth still attached.

Whoever had cleaned up the scene had missed this, and the LAPD's investigators hadn't found it yet. Or had passed it by intentionally.

Something was wrong with it.

Andy trained his light on the thing. He'd thought it human at first, and it still looked like it. But the teeth . . . they weren't human.

There were two rows of them, not one. Sharp as tiny razors. Smaller than most human teeth, except for two at the sides, near the front—just below where the canines would be. These two were twice the size of normal teeth, and ended in arrowhead points.

Fangs, jutting up like tusks.

Andy almost threw the thing aside in horror, but caught himself before he did. This was proof—solid, undeniable.

This could only have come from a vampire.

Andy turned off Sunset and pulled the Camry into a parking spot halfway down the next block. He had put the jawbone into the glove compartment with the flashlight, but now he fished the flashlight out again, pocketed it. Checked his Glock to make sure all sixteen rounds were in. Patted his jacket pocket to confirm the second clip.

He couldn't come back to LA without checking out the bar Paul Norris had noted in his datebook, but night had fallen while he was still at the Saxon place. Even before he'd been aware of vampires, he wouldn't have walked into some Sunset alley dive without carrying. Now he just wished he had a bazooka or something to back up the Glock.

He hiked back up to Sunset. Cars flashed by, human life continuing in spite of the horrors that waited in the dark, horrors they could never suspect. Andy had spent his adult life trying to keep the rest of his countrymen safe from the nightmares they couldn't know—criminals and terrorists, con artists and hustlers, killers and kidnappers and thugs. The life of an FBI agent wasn't for everyone, but he had thought he was pretty well suited to it. Paul Norris, even more so, because Paul understood the darkness in the human soul better than Andy did. Better than most. Andy could only reach it on the intellectual level, but Paul could feel it intuitively, could tap into it without having to try.

Andy found the alley, between a closed insurance office and a massage parlor, and he turned his back on the street. The massage parlor's entrance was off the alley, on the right, so customers could come and go without being observed from the street. A couple of curtained windows and a neon sign were the only things visible from Sunset. Farther down the alley, on the left, was another door, tucked beneath a fire escape.

Here was the entrance to the unnamed bar. Andy went straight to it, paused outside, pressed his ear against the door. Nothing. Either it was closed or abandoned or . . .

He didn't want to think about the other possibility.

The door was locked, but gave easily when he forced it, the rotted wood of the jamb crumbling beneath his weight. An awful charnel-house stench assaulted him when he went inside. He had smelled so much blood since Paul's disappearance, he was afraid his nose would be permanently crusted with it. He tried a light switch, but it flipped uselessly. Pulled the flashlight out and turned it on.

The place was a disaster. It looked like the aftermath of the biggest barroom brawl in history. Tables and chairs were overturned and strewn randomly about the space. At the back was the bar proper, but shattered multicolor glass was all that remained of its bottles.

Inset behind the bar was a flat surface with glue marks on it—a mirror had hung there, once. It was probably more of the broken glass now.

And blood.

Blood, everywhere.

Spatter marks on the walls. Spray all the way up on the ceiling, almost invisible among the exposed ductwork and wiring. Dry pools of it on the floor. Dried, flaking like old paint.

A massacre? Or something worse?

A feedlot.

Andy stood in the center of the room and shivered, causing the light's beam to wobble uncontrollably.

How many had died here? He felt death's presence, haunting the place as it had other mass murder scenes he'd experienced over his career. He had never believed in ghosts, but was willing to accept that so much carnage left behind some sort of negative energy.

Paul noted this place in his datebook. Had he actually been here? Wouldn't he have told me about it if he had?

Unless this had been the end . . . the last place he went before he changed. Was this where he'd met the "mistress," the one whose orders he had to obey? The one who had left him before completing his transformation?

Andy wanted out of here.

The choices seemed to be to go over the place inch by inch, like a real crime scene, or just get the general sense of it and leave. He was pretty sure that taking the crime scene approach would leave him physically ill. Maybe worse than that—what if the vampire disease was viral? He could catch it from all the blood in here. And who knew what other sicknesses might be lurking in it, or what other bodily fluids were present that he couldn't detect with nothing more sophisticated than a flashlight?

Fuck this.

He was starting for the door when he heard the noise.

A kind of scuffling sound, like when he'd had rats in the attic in the Sacramento house.

He swiveled, training the light toward the bar. *Wouldn't be surprising to find rats here, or any other kind of vermin.* But when he shone the light that way, he spotted something he'd missed the first time—a heavy black door blocking a passageway to a space behind the bar.

Swearing under his breath, Andy crossed to the door. He really wanted to get back to his car and away from this place. He'd only had a couple hours of sleep. It was night in LA, he was beat, and he'd been punishing his body mercilessly. He didn't know how long he could keep driving himself like this before he collapsed. He drew his weapon and tugged the big door open.

Behind the bar was a cavernous dark space. *When this was a going concern, they probably held concerts or dances back here.* The light's beam barely penetrated to the far walls, where furniture and equipment had been shoved to the side. Above, more exposed ductwork and wiring and shadowed rafters.

The gun was almost back in its holster when he heard the noise again, coming from the shadows at the extreme far end of the huge space.

He pointed weapon and flashlight there but saw nothing more than stacked tables and chairs covered with a film of dust.

"FBI!" he said commandingly, sounding a little silly to himself in the empty room. "Who's there?"

The scuttling sound again, moving left along the far wall. Andy tried to track it with the light. Nothing.

"FBI!" he shouted again. "Show yourself!"

The sound stopped suddenly. Andy held his breath, fought to keep the Glock steady. Moved the light in ever-widening circles, looking for the rat or whatever it was. Sweat dampened the hair at his temples, dotted his upper lip. His heart sounded loud in his ears.

And then it was back, the same dry scraping skittering noise, but not down where it had been against the far wall.

This time it came from *above* him.

Andy swung the light up in time to catch a human figure, a man, moving among the steel rafters. It stopped—*he* stopped—as if pinned by the circle of light, and turned his head to look down at Andy.

He was gaunt, almost spiderlike with his long, rail-thin arms and legs spread, clinging impossibly to the ceiling.

In the glow of the flashlight Andy could see him in

horrible detail, could see his gnarled fingers release their grip.

He dropped, straight at Andy.

His fanged mouth opened as he plummeted, and old blood stained the creases around it, drawing lines down his chin. Eyes black as hollow pits, fingernails jagged claws caked with dirt and blood, hair black and matted, as filthy as the rat Andy had expected to see, and he fell toward Andy, who raised his weapon

head shot head shot head shot

and squeezed the trigger twice before the thing landed on him, aiming right into the thing's open mouth. The muzzle burst was blindingly bright in the dark space. The creature spun madly in the air. A flailing limb slammed into Andy's head and they both fell sprawling to the filthy floor. The Glock flew from Andy's hand.

As he scrambled after it, the creature took off. By the time Andy had the gun in hand and had rolled to his knees, the thing was gone. The door he'd come in through swung on rusted hinges.

Andy put his hand down to help push himself to his feet, and it slipped in a slick puddle. He went down again, cracking his knee hard on the concrete floor. Pawing for traction, his hand hit something else. He grabbed the flashlight and aimed it at the ground. He'd fallen in a pool of fresh blood, but there was more—bits of bone, teeth, and wrinkled gray and pink tissue that could only be brain matter. Disgusted, Andy lurched to his feet, shaking the crap from his hand as best he could. He'd need sterilization after this.

He got to the door, passed through with gun and flashlight in unsteady hands. The smaller room on the other side was empty, as far as he could tell. The door to the outside stood ajar, though he'd pushed it to when he came in.

Which meant that he had shot the thing in the head, doing enough damage to spray himself with bone and brain. But the creature had run away in spite of the wound.

All the way back to the car, on legs that threatened to give way at any moment, Andy watched and listened, ready to fire again at the slightest unusual movement. He walked down Sunset with light on and gun in hand and no one even slowed to give him a second look. After he left Sunset the street was darker, the rush of traffic behind him. His car was where he had left it. He beamed the light inside the door before climbing in, and as soon as he was behind the wheel all strength left him, the adrenaline surge leaving him weak and shivering in its wake. He managed to lock the door, then put his hands on the wheel and rested his head on them.

He stayed that way for long minutes, not moving except for the uncontrolled shaking of his limbs. Finally he was able to calm that, but he still felt drained and hollow. Exhausted. He hoped he could stay awake long enough to find a motel room—one far enough away from here that the creature couldn't follow on foot, but not so far that he'd have to drive all night to get there. He hoped he would be able to sleep, that nerves wouldn't keep him up despite the bone weariness he felt.

He opened the glove compartment to toss the flashlight back in.

The vampire jawbone was gone.

Andy realized that he had locked the car before going inside, but it had been unlocked when he returned. No sign of who had broken in, but the incontrovertible proof he had discovered, just an hour before, had been taken.

When he finally felt that he'd regained enough strength to control the vehicle, he found the keys where he'd thrown them on the passenger seat and inserted the ignition key. Before he could turn it, his cell phone chirped at him. Fishing it from his pocket, he glanced at the caller ID. A Bureau number.

"Gray," he whispered into the phone.

"Andy, it's ADIC Flores," the familiar voice said. "I know you've been working with Angelica Foster in the forensic lab, so I wanted to let you know right away."

"Know what?" Andy asked. Dreading the response, knowing it couldn't be good news, not for Flores to be calling himself at such a late hour.

"She's been killed, Andy. Her throat cut open, or torn open with some weapon we haven't identified yet. Raped, probably postmortem. It's a sick one, Andy. Special Unit's taking care of it, so don't feel like you've got to worry about it. She's one of our own, and we won't let this one go until we've fried the bastard."

Wearily, Andy nodded his head, then remembered Hector Flores couldn't see that. "Thank you, sir. I'm sorry to hear about Foster. She was good at her job."

The ADIC made some additional sympathetic noises and then disconnected. Andy folded his phone and shoved it back in his pocket.

The Bureau could think whatever it chose to about Foster's death, but Andy knew it had been no random sex crime. Angelica Foster was the linchpin connecting Paul Norris, Amos Saxon, and Stella Olemaun. Her death now wasn't coincidental.

It was a message—a warning—from an old friend.

And its meaning couldn't have been clearer if it had taken one of those huge billboards facing onto Sunset to send it.

II

ANDY MANAGED four hours of sleep.

When he woke up he found a nearby liquor store and bought a fifth of Jim Beam and a tall Styrofoam cup of coffee. He carried both back to the motel room, poured out some of the coffee and dumped about a quarter of the bottle in. Sat on the edge of the bed, his mind blank, staring at a bad reproduction of a Georgia O'Keeffe painting on the wall opposite, and swallowed the brew down.

When it was gone he crushed the cup and tossed it toward the trashcan, missing it. He left it there and went into the bathroom. Stripped off the stained suit he'd been wearing since the morning before. He cranked the shower as hot as he could stand and climbed in. Once again, he used the soap and shampoo provided by the motel to try to cleanse himself, but no matter how hard he rubbed he couldn't shake the memory of sitting down in that muck of blood and brain.

Andy turned off the shower and walked, still dripping, back into the bedroom. The bottle stood on the nightstand. He unscrewed the lid, raised it to his lips, tilted his head back and let the liquid burn his throat as he swallowed it down. When it was gone, he shook his head savagely and returned to the bathroom for a towel. He wiped himself dry and pulled his dirty clothes back on. He hadn't brought any luggage with him from Sacramento. He ran hot water on his finger and brushed his teeth with it. He realized he didn't meet the Bureau's grooming standards, but at this point he was beyond caring about that.

In his own way, he was nearly as transformed as Paul. A stranger even to himself. And not one, he reflected, that he liked a whole hell of a lot.

In the car on the way to the LA office, he called the Special Unit and grilled the agent who'd caught Angelica's case, finding out everything he could about the circumstances of her death. Everything he heard made him angrier and angrier.

Once he reached the office, he showed his ID and ignored the curious and horrified looks of the agents around him. He went straight to Angelica Foster's office and started rifling through her files and papers, looking for any notes pertaining to her research on Norris or Saxon.

He was only in there a few minutes, still empty-handed, when Hector Flores burst in flanked by two bruisers Andy didn't recognize. "Special Agent Gray," the ADIC barked, letting Andy know right off that he was in trouble. "What are you doing in here?"

"Trying to figure out what happened to my partner," Andy said. "And to Angelica."

"I told you that the Foster case was being handled," ADIC Flores said. "And I gave you specific instructions about how to handle the Norris case."

"And if you don't mind my saying so, sir, those instructions are bullshit," Andy shot back. "And your take on the Foster case is bullshit, too. She was not the victim of some random pervert. She got too close to the truth about the vampires, and Paul killed her for it."

"Gray, you're out of line!" he shouted. The ADIC's face was red, spittle bursting from his lips as he replied. "I want you in my office . . . *now!*"

"I'm not going anywhere," Andy countered. "I'm staying right here until I find what I need to close this case."

"You are not *on* the Foster case!" Flores insisted.

"It's all one case, *Hector,* and since you've decided not to put anyone on it, I've assigned myself. How can you say that Angelica's death was a sex crime? The blood was drained from her body. Drained! Where was it? Did you find a convenient bathtub full of blood? Some plastic jugs? No? Of course not. But you continue to claim that some rapist did this?"

"Gray, you're drunk—" Flores interrupted.

"That's got nothing to do with it," Andy said. "Where's the blood? If this wasn't a vampire attack, then where's the blood? And Hastings told me the penetration was postmortem, even the slash wounds on the neck were postmortem. Did you try to reason that one out, Hector? Did you try to stretch your tiny pea brain a little to figure out why that might be?" Andy's hands closed into fists and he had to fight to keep from pummeling the ADIC. "How about because the killer was trying to cover up the *bite wounds?*"

Hector Flores turned to one of the giants standing behind him. "Cuff him," he said, jerking a thumb toward Andy.

Andy lost it then. He hurled himself at the self-important prick, fists battering the ADIC's trunk and arms. He wanted to claw the guy's eyes out, but the two goons grabbed his arms and dragged him off Hector. "Cool down, Gray," one of them said. He looked like a steroid case, with a bull neck and arms almost as big around as Andy's waist and dull, blunt features. His lips barely seemed to move when he spoke. This one had short blond hair; the only thing that distinguished him from the other guy was that the other one's short hair was dark brown.

Andy gave up the struggle when he realized he couldn't budge these guys, and their grips on his upper arms were crushing. ADIC Flores took advantage of his situation to jab a finger in Andy's chest as he straightened his own tie and suit jacket. "You're out of here, Gray," he said. "Out of the building, and on indefinite leave pending the results of the disciplinary hearing you're going to have. I can already guarantee what those results will be. You'll be charged with assaulting a superior. You'll lose your job and your pension and you'll be damn lucky if you don't serve time."

"You mean I won't be taking orders from scumbags like you?" Andy asked with a snarl. "Break my heart."

ADIC Flores looked away from him, addressing the bruisers instead. "Get him out of my sight."

The bruisers complied.

Back in his office, ADIC Flores poured coffee into a navy blue cup with the Bureau seal stamped in gold on the side. He glanced at himself in a small mirror he kept in his center desk drawer, made sure he was put back together, and then called Special Agent Dan Bradstreet into his office. Dan appeared two minutes later. His pin-striped gray trousers were creased, his club tie knotted in a perfect Windsor, his shoes shined, his conservative brown hair neatly combed. He looked like a cross between a college football hero, circa 1960, and an artist's rendition of the ideal FBI agent.

As far as Hector Flores was concerned, he *was* the ideal FBI agent. He did what he was told. He didn't ask difficult questions or try to rock the boat. So many agents these days thought they had to be whistleblowers, had to clean up the agency and make sure no more 9/11s happened on "their watch." Hector had little patience for reformers. He liked agents who let their superiors worry about such things while they did their jobs.

Dan Bradstreet was that kind of agent, and Hector had trusted him on a number of different occasions. A crew of bank robbers had terrorized LA, killing seven people, including the father of one of Hector's friends who had been working as a bank guard. Hector had been able to find out who the leader of the crew was—to his own satisfaction, though he couldn't turn up the evidence to prove it in court. Still, he'd promised his friend justice, so he turned Dan Bradstreet loose on the crew. Justice had been served.

Another time he'd sicced Dan on a colleague who had threatened Hector's promotion to ADIC. Hector had convinced Dan that the nation's interests would be best served if Hector had the job. Dan listened with polite disinterest and said he'd make sure it wasn't a problem. Two days later, the other guy not only withdrew his application, but quit the Bureau and moved to a ranch in Wyoming.

So Hector knew he could count on Dan to take care of things with a minimum of fuss. He waited for Dan to sit in one of his guest chairs. "I just threw Andy Gray out of the building," he said. "Or had Bunson and McClary do it, anyway. Gray's off the reservation, Dan. He physically attacked me. He's been drinking, and he's got a bug up his ass about Foster and Norris, his ex-partner."

"What do you want done?" Dan's voice was like melted butter. Hector loved listening to it, and if Dan had been a radio personality or a recorder of books on tape, he would keep one playing whenever he was tense or irritated.

"I want you to ride his ass," Hector said. "See where he goes, who he talks to. If he starts spreading nonsense about vampires, I want to know about it. If he takes it any further than that, punch his ticket."

Dan simply nodded, as casually as if Hector had asked him to return somebody's phone call. Hector knew full well the trouble he'd be in if it was disclosed that he had ordered the execution of an FBI agent, even one as seemingly rogue as Andy Gray. He was confident, however, that Dan would take the secret to the grave.

Andy was past the Grapevine by noon, with the long, flat stretch of Interstate 5 unspooling up the center of the San Joaquin Valley before him. The road cut through the middle of California's agricultural region, with nothing on either side but flat fields stretching away toward distant slopes at each horizon. At midday, the valley was hot and dry and still, except for the traffic racing up and down the ribbon of highway as if in a desperate hurry to get to either northern or southern California.

He had paused in LA only long enough to swing by the downtown branch of the public library. Citing the Patriot Act and flashing his ID, he had demanded all the books they had on vampires and vampirism, fiction or not. When he saw the cartfuls they wheeled toward him, he recoiled and went through them, picking enough volumes to fill two large shopping bags. He focused on history and biography, though he also included some fictional works he recognized the titles of, such as

Bram Stoker's *Dracula,* Stephen King's *'Salem's Lot,* Anne Rice's *Interview with the Vampire,* Richard Matheson's *I Am Legend,* and *The Vampire Tapestry* by Suzy McKee Charnas. The nonfiction books varied from pop occult books to ancient tomes from the library's special collections. They filled the trunk of the Camry as he sped north.

Stubbing a Camel out in the car's ashtray, Andy recognized that his obsession with this investigation was sending the rest of his life swirling down the porcelain bowl. He was running on caffeine and nicotine and booze. He'd sworn like the proverbial sailor at his wife. He had almost never raised his voice to Monica, and he'd almost punched her. He had shut his daughters entirely out of his life. Oh yeah, and he had just attacked the head of the LA FBI office and might wind up in jail.

He needed to get a grip on things and get his life straightened out. Yes, what had happened to Paul was important, and not just because Paul was his oldest friend.

It could be more than life-changing—it could be world-changing.

Proof positive of the existence of vampires—proof like the jawbone he had briefly possessed—would impact every country, every culture. Armies would be mobilized to fight the threat. Law enforcement would be pressed into service. Some would die so that many, many more would live.

It's more than that, though. As Andy drove, one hand

resting lightly on the wheel to keep the car moving up the long, straight blacktop, new cigarette balanced on the edge of his lip, he tried to figure out just why he'd jumped so far off the ledge.

He kept flashing on a long-ago image of his father, who spent six years in a coma back in Minnesota. He was brain dead, kept alive by an assortment of machines and devices that made his lungs work, kept his kidneys going, fed him, and dealt with his waste. He had never wanted to be kept alive through what were, somewhat absurdly, called "heroic" means, a fact he'd imparted to his only son on numerous occasions. Usually with a couple of beers in him, during a commercial break before a football game started up again. Football games on TV were what passed for father/son bonding in Benjamin Gray's household during Andy's early adulthood.

A dozen years before, however, a rainy-night collision with a sixteen-wheeler had wiped out all of Ben Gray's higher bodily functions. His cerebral cortex, Andy was told, had been destroyed by damage to the skull and brain. According to every test that could be done, the brain's electrical activity was flat. Ben Gray could sit up if he was propped in a bed, and his face showed a range of expressions, but the doctors insisted that they bore no relation to external stimuli or to anything that Andy's father was thinking about. He wasn't thinking at all. He wasn't aware that he was in the world. He was, for every practical purpose, a dead man.

And yet Ruthann, Andy's mother, had insisted on

keeping him alive, on hooking him up to the machines, tubes, and wires that could prolong his existence. It wasn't a life, Andy had come to believe. He wasn't in pain, but he didn't feel anything else either. He was set up for visitors, and he smiled and farted and drooled and frowned, and then they left and he was laid back down and his sores treated.

Andy reminded his mother what Ben had always said. It made no impression on her. She was determined to be a martyr to the cause of Benjamin Gray, and she devoted her life, and what little money she had in the bank or could borrow on credit cards, to keeping his cause alive even though he was not. She would declare that he was, that he grew despondent if Andy didn't visit regularly, and that regular visitors left him overjoyed. Of course, she was deluding herself. Andy could have been hitting his dad in the face with bricks, for all Ben Gray knew or cared.

Finally, sick of watching his father's not-life perpetually extended, Andy had enlisted lawyers and fought his mother in court. It had been a tough battle, because there was no living will or medical power of attorney in effect when the truck had claimed him, but Andy had eventually prevailed. The machines were shut down, the tubes removed, and Ben's body caught up to where his brain had been for years.

The struggle had cost Andy what was left of his relationship with his mother, which had been souring for years anyway. The last words Andy had said to her were,

"Why can't the dead rest? Just let the dead be dead!" She had started weeping huge crocodile tears and hurried from the room. What little they had to say to each other after that, for the four years she had left before she drank herself to death, was relayed through attorneys.

Andy's daughters had never met their paternal grandparents, and that was just fine with him.

Thinking of it now, and making the connection to Paul's case, it hit home with a ferocity it hadn't in years. Andy's hand on the wheel shivered, so he brought the other hand up and gripped it, white-knuckled, until the quake passed.

Let the dead be dead.

Some people just couldn't be trusted to do the right thing.

Paul Norris had known that Andy would be told about Angelica's death. Hector Flores would be sure to let him know, because the Los Angeles ADIC was the consummate bureaucrat, with charts and lists and notebooks detailing everything that went on around him, and he would be aware that Angelica was working on matters of interest to Special Agent Gray.

It had been a little more complicated than sending Andy an email or calling him on the phone, but a hell of a lot more fun. Angelica, after all, was a bit of a babe. Better than that, she'd thrown some attitude at Paul in the past, just because of some comments he'd made and that one time when she was backing away from a microscope and he'd wound up with a handful of ass cheek.

So he had thoroughly enjoyed ripping into her flesh with his teeth. The slightly rubbery texture of the skin just below her jaw, the layer of salt from the long, hard day she'd put in at the lab, a hint of seasoning from the cooking she had been doing, all washed down with a chaser of blood. The terror that registered in her eyes at the very last moment, when she finally recognized him in spite of the physical changes he'd been through, had sweetened the pot that much more.

Thing of it was, though, Andy had received the message and then declined to heed it.

Stupid fucker.

Paul had known Andy long enough to predict what his former partner's response would be. Andy would want to understand what had happened to Paul. He was a guy who liked to make things right if he could—that urge was the main reason he'd joined the Bureau—so he would search for some kind of cure or treatment for Paul's condition.

Paul still didn't know a whole lot about what had happened, except that it wreaked havoc with one's dental situation, elongated fingers into gnarled claws, gave him amazing strength and stamina, and induced a craving for fresh blood. But he was pretty sure there was no such thing as a cure, unless you counted bright direct sunlight or decapitation. Which meant Andy's quest was doomed to failure.

More precisely, if Andy succeeded, Paul was doomed.

Just as bad, Andy would never keep quiet about the whole thing. Bad enough that Stella Olemaun had written her fucking book and had it published. Sure, it had been labeled fiction, but that hadn't stopped people who had some small bits of awareness from recognizing the truths it contained and enlarging on them. There were websites now, about Barrow, and the whispers, the rumors of the undead.

This new species that Paul Norris had been unceremoniously inducted into clung to the darkness, and that worked on a metaphorical level as well as a literal one. Paul didn't have access to the woman who had made him, who should have shown him the ropes, but in place of that he seemed to have some kind of racial consciousness. One of the things he understood, almost instinctively, was that his new kind had survived over the centuries by keeping their existence secret. Everyone had heard of vampires, but modern society considered them amusing stories and entertaining (if not horrific) distractions, not a real threat. More primitive cultures, in which stories of vampirism were handed down orally instead of relayed through movies, TV, comic books, and pulp novels, either still believed or considered them creatures of history, relegated to the distant past. Either way, the same forces that kept them isolated from Western pop culture also prevented their stories from impacting the global stage.

The danger was in someone bridging the gap—convincing enough of the world that there was truth mixed in with the obvious fiction.

Which was where someone like Andy, a respected FBI agent with a clean record, could be a problem. If he was able to figure out what Paul was only just learning—just how prevalent vampires were—and could disseminate that information, he could cause big problems for them everywhere.

Which was why he had needed to be warned off.

Paul didn't want to kill his best friend. He would if he had to, of course, but things weren't at that stage yet.

So he had sent the message, via Angelica Foster. Andy wasn't stupid enough to misinterpret its meaning.

But then, instead of dropping the whole thing, wouldn't you know that Andy had gone to a Los Angeles library and loaded up on books about vampires.

Paul had his own business to attend to; he couldn't keep an eye on Andy indefinitely. He had, however, managed to follow him from the Bureau office to the library—Paul could be out in the car for brief periods during the day, because he'd had the foresight to steal one with heavily tinted windows and windshield, as well as keeping his body completely covered from head to toe in protective clothing. It was a somewhat dangerous move, given how direct sunlight affected his kind, but a risk that seemed to pay off for him nonetheless.

Once the sun had set, at the library he had identified himself as an FBI agent, hot on the trail of a man posing as an agent, and been handed a complete list of the books Andy had taken.

Just about their entire vampire library, it seemed.

Only one conclusion presented itself.

Andy was determined to ignore Paul's warning.

Paul sighed. This sucked on so many levels.

After leaving the library, Andy had headed north. Now, maybe he was just going back to Hollywood, or to the Valley, or something like that. But maybe he was heading home to Sacramento. Which would mean a long trip in the car, or worse yet, an airplane.

One of the real drawbacks of this whole bloodsucker thing was that Paul's mobility was severely cramped. If Andy continued to be a problem, and especially if he moved around much, Paul was going to have to deal with him in a more definitive fashion.

It was all up to Andy. So far, he had made all the wrong moves.

Paul hoped he wised up, and soon.

Excerpted from *30 Days of Night* by Stella Olemaun

I wish I had a story of victory to tell, but that would not be an accurate account of the events that transpired in Barrow that winter.

Eben and I made it back to town, but we weren't alone.

The invaders had come as well, and they were attacking.

At first, we could only hear distant screams and gunfire mixed with a strange shrieking roar of the undead as they killed.

I cannot describe accurately enough the feeling of absolute helplessness that Eben and I experienced. Not only were we the sworn legal protectors of Barrow, but also fellow residents. These were our friends, our family! We tried to fight the attackers . . . but weapons were useless against them except to slow them down a beat or two.

I watched a family, the Sullivans—Brandy, Mark, and their daughter Sally—dragged from their car as they tried to escape. The marauders were spindly, dark shapes who moved more like spiders than humans.

They tore the family apart, figuratively and literally.

First, they separated them from each other, ripping Sally from her mother's arms. They beat Mark down into the snow, tearing his clothing and skin at once as if they both offered the same resistance. They stripped Mark, five or six of these terrible creatures, and then, while his wife and child cried, they bit into him, savagely at his wrists, his throat, and one beneath the thigh.

I tried to help. I fired shots. I screamed, but all I did was draw attention to us, and Eben had to drag me to safety in a storm cellar beneath the sheriff's station. Surviving was our only hope; saving was not in the cards. It was a horrible truth to come to.

Four hours after Eben had spotted them walking across the open terrain surrounding Barrow, those things had come to Barrow and turned our home into a burning bloodbath. We had no way to call for help, and no reason to believe anybody would come.

We were on our own against an invading force we could hardly comprehend let alone combat.

And this was only the first day.

There would be many days and nights to come, us hiding in the darkness, listening to the constant tortured screams of townspeople being murdered for the blood in their veins.

12

VIRTUALLY EVERY CULTURE ON EARTH had vampire stories.

Andy learned the Tartars of Central Asia believed that solar eclipses were the work of vampires sneaking out of distant stars to suck the life from the sun. In one of the oldest books he'd obtained at the library, an English tome from 1851 entitled *Mysteries from Beneath Our Feet,* he read a story of a bloodsucker who emerged from holes in the ground to prey on shepherds sleeping out in the fields with their flocks, leaving the victim just as white as his sheep. Andean legends told of *condenados,* souls refused entrance to heaven because of earthly sins, who sustained themselves by sucking the life force from victims after tricking them into sex. Other Andean stories went further, describing another class who mesmerized its victims and drained their body fat. The Warao people of South America believed that vampires drained blood from humans to be imbibed by dark spirits of the Underworld.

He read in *Pagan Races of the Malay Peninsula* that vampires were not really demons, but flesh-and-blood monsters, heads with attached entrails that drank the blood of the living. As far back as he could find, there were tales of vampires—all the way to the sacrifice of live animals, or humans, to gods who would then consume their flesh or blood.

It seemed unlikely, as he pawed through *The Vampire in Fact and Fiction* and *Vampires from Around the Globe* and *I, Vampire* and *Feasters from the Grave,* that such a specific sort of story would have roots in so many different places and that such a diverse assortment of people would fear the beings who came in the night.

Unlikely, unless those people all understood something that modern Western civilization, in its limitless "wisdom" and sophistication, had decided to pretend was nothing more than a story.

Vampires were real.

Andy had seen that for himself on numerous occasions, even if he no longer had the physical proof.

"Andy!"

It was Monica once again, outside his office.

He'd been home for days, locked in here most of the time, avoiding her and the girls. He ignored the pounding on the door, slid the window open, pissed out into the backyard. What the hell—no one could see with the fence surrounding the house anyway.

"Andy," she said, her voice weary. "I know what's going on. I talked to Sally Norris. I'm no idiot, Andy, and I'm not the prude you think I am. You fucked her. You know what? It doesn't matter to me. We can work through this, Andy. We just have to talk."

He zipped up and closed the window. His office had

been redecorated, hurricane style. He couldn't suppress a smile, thinking about how much Monica would enjoy that metaphor. She was a pretty conservative lady, the perfect Bureau wife in many respects, but she had an inexplicable love of natural disaster movies. Earthquakes, forest fires, volcanoes, tidal waves, tornadoes. The cheesier the better; anything made pre-1980 or for basic cable went immediately to the top of her list. It was one of those things, like her passion for sugary Hostess treats, cupcakes and Twinkies and the rest (except those coconut-covered snowball monstrosities), that had endeared her to him in the first place and kept things fresh over the years.

Andy had left the stuff in the filing cabinets alone but otherwise, anything that wasn't pertinent to the vampire case had been thrown out the window. He supposed it was being ruined by the sun and weather and urine, but he didn't care.

In its place was the information he was amassing on vampires. A map of Alaska was stuck to one wall with sixteen-penny nails, the only ones he'd been able to find quickly in the garage. Barrow was circled in red Sharpie ink. Articles he'd found online and printed out were taped all over the place. Books covered every surface, some open to particular pages and others stacked up, either waiting or already read and set aside.

The dinner plate he had been using as an ashtray was overflowing onto the desk, and cigarette butts had burned spots into the room's carpeting, left wherever they'd fallen. Empty bottles circled the wastebasket. On the way up from Los Angeles he had stopped at a gas station with a mini-mart and stocked up—ten cartons of Camels, and all the Beam the kid had in stock. Kid was pale and skinny, with hair dyed black, long on one side and skin-short on the other. Piercing in his lower lip and three in his right eyebrow. He looked like he hadn't seen the sun in months, maybe years, and working late shift in a place like this, he probably had no real reason to. Andy loosened the Glock in its holster when he walked into the store—kid looked like one of them, he thought. But when the kid opened his mouth, Andy checked his teeth, and he was okay.

Before he checked out he tossed in a couple boxes of candy bars right off the rack—Kit-Kats, Heath Bars, Milky Way, Three Musketeers. He'd been supplementing his meals with these and brewing coffee right on his desk. He figured Monica would stop cooking for him soon, and then he'd have to order in pizza or Chinese. At any rate, she'd already started leaving his meals on paper plates, because he wasn't returning the china ones.

"Andy, let me in," she pled. "For our daughters, if not for me." She had threatened earlier to call a clergyman, or his boss. Andy didn't know if she had done either. No one had come calling, though, so he guessed it was a bluff.

He twisted the volume knob on the ministereo he had always kept on the credenza. A distorted guitar wailed against a thunderous bass line. Andy hated heavy metal, but it made a good noise filter.

Paul Norris. Angelica Foster. The rest of the victims. They were what mattered, not Andy's little life, his family. Had he not taken an oath to protect people and uphold the law?

Monica knocked a couple more times, barely audible above the music. Andy opened a book and started to read, concentrating to tune her out. Next time he looked up, she seemed to be gone. He turned the music down and plugged the phone back in. Dialing LA information, he got the number for the police division serving Westwood. Called that number, identified himself as FBI, and got through to one of the detectives working the Saxon fire and the deaths of the two police officers.

That detective didn't have much to say, but he revealed that the cops were off duty, and the last person who'd seen them alive was another uniformed police officer named Goodis. Paydirt. Andy pushed a little and got Goodis's home number—the guy had been calling in sick all week.

Goodis answered the phone with a tentative "Yeah?"

"Officer Goodis," Andy said, trying to sound more like a Fed than the wired-up lunatic he knew he was becoming. "Special Agent Andrew Gray, FBI. I work out of the Sacramento office, although I've done special assignment stuff through LA, so if you want to check up on me I recommend you call up to Sac."

"No, that's okay," Goodis said. *He sounds depressed. Morose.* He wondered if the guy had been calling suicide hotlines, and pictured him sitting in an empty house in a bathrobe and boxers, with his service weapon in his lap, trying to screw up the courage to swallow it. "What do you want?"

"Dr. Amos Saxon," Andy said. He heard Goodis swear under his breath, but kept on. "He's associated with a figure from a terrorism case we've been working on, one Stella Olemaun. I believe she was brought in over a disturbance on the UCLA campus, at an event Saxon set up."

"I heard something like that," Goodis said. Noncommittal.

"And now Saxon's dead," Andy continued. "And his house torched, and two cops killed at the same time."

"Yeah."

"I want to know what happened," Andy said.

"Can't help you."

"Try. It's important."

"Sorry. I don't know."

"You were the last one to see those cops alive. You must know something about where they were going, what they were doing at Saxon's."

"I don't know anything," Goodis insisted. "I already told you that."

"Yes, and I don't believe you. What's your first name? Alan, isn't it?"

"Look, I have to go," the cop said.

"It's very important," Andy reiterated.

"I'm hanging up now," Goodis said. "And I won't be answering anymore, so don't even try."

"But—"

"You want to know what I know?" Goodis asked suddenly, angrily. "Here it is. I hope it helps."

"What is it?"

A pause.

"It's all true."

There was a click and then a dial tone. Alan Goodis was gone.

What he'd told Andy was chilling. But it was nothing he didn't already know.

The undead stalked the unwary, ruling the dark, and had for . . . well, centuries, at least. Maybe as long as there were human beings. Maybe before that.

Andy unscrewed another bottle, took a long swig. Wasn't even hot anymore, going down. Just like water.

Didn't get him drunk anymore, either. Didn't dull the images. He needed more.

A knock on the door woke him. His face was pressed flat against the desk, resting in a puddle of his own drool. He sat up.

"Daddy?" It was Lisa. He still knew his daughters' voices. "Daddy, I need to talk to you."

He didn't respond. She'd go away in a couple minutes. Then Sara would come. Her voice was more plaintive, higher pitched, harder to ignore.

But ignore he would. He didn't want them to see him, not like this. Anyway, he had work to do. He glanced at the clock, realized he'd slept for almost two hours.

How many people could they kill in two hours? He couldn't imagine. A lot.

They don't all turn their victims. Somehow they were selective. If they didn't turn any victims, then the species would die off. He doubted if they reproduced the old-fashioned way.

At the same time, if they turned all of them, then their numbers would grow geometrically. One bloodsucker feeding once a day would turn seven people in a week. Say it took those seven a week to become full-fledged vampires, about what it had taken Paul. By the end of the second week, that would be fourteen. The next week those fourteen would turn a hundred and ninety-six, plus the seven new ones from the first. Two hundred and three. The next week they'd turn more than fourteen hundred. The following week, almost ten thousand. Almost seventy thousand in the week after that.

From one vampire. Andy had no clue how many there were, but a damn sight more than one. So they couldn't turn all their victims, because in at most a couple of months, the human race would be all vampires, and then what would they feed on?

So they had to pace themselves.

Plus they'd been smart for all these centuries, or

they'd already have been identified and probably eliminated.

The one that had attacked Andy in the deserted bar had seemed bestial, barely more than a ravening animal. But they had to use their brains or they never would have survived. Which meant they had some degree of free will, deciding who to turn and who to kill, how to hide, how to travel and not get caught.

In Stella's book, it was theorized that they could live forever if they had a blood supply and didn't have their heads removed. They were immortal, but they had to feed on humans, which meant they were also evil.

But then again, maybe not. Did vampirism simply change people into beings who needed human blood to survive? Was the rest of it, the evil part, merely a response to that? After all, the constant need to murder would warp even the most decent person, in time.

If they truly needed human blood. Paul had survived for a while on the blood of rats and insects, it seemed. But he'd been in a transitional phase then, not yet a full vampire.

So many questions. Did these creatures—did Paul Norris—have free will? Had he run away from custody, and from Andy, because he was afraid of how he'd be perceived, or because he really did want to embark on a postlife of murder? Would he become like that pathetic creature Andy had shot in the bar? And would Angelica Foster become one of them next?

Andy turned back to the books. The novels themselves contained so much nonsense. Wooden stakes to the heart. Turning into bats and fluttering away. Garlic, for God's sake. Having to sleep in a bed of their native earth—there was a provincial belief for you. These days few people reached adulthood anywhere near their native earth, it seemed, so anyone who became a vampire would be immediately doomed.

The only sure things Stella Olemaun described in her book were decapitation and sunlight. Andy was determined to find any common enough threads in the other nonfiction accounts to suggest more possibilities.

The most pervasive vampire stories, of course, came from Eastern Europe. Albania, Romania. Transylvania, the home of the fictional Dracula as well as the historical Vlad Tepes, who bathed in the blood of the Turks slaughtered by his armies.

"Andy!"

Monica again. Her voice sounded shrill, but there was a hoarseness to it, too, as if she'd been shouting her throat raw. Andy turned up the radio again. Shrieking vocals competed with her persistent calls. He tried to tune her out again and kept reading. Lit another cigarette and dragged smoke down into his lungs, held it there. Unscrewed the lid from a new bottle of Beam. *Running low,* he thought, raising the bottle to his lips.

The words swam. Blood. Deep forests of night. Familiars. Fangs.

Immortality.

It all sounded too magical. Andy thought there was some scientific validity to it, but not the way the old legends from the Balkans talked about it. To them it was all about devils and angels. The idea of immortality played into that, because only magic could make someone truly immortal.

What happened to Paul could possibly extend life expectancy, because with it came the ability to survive major injuries that would kill anyone else. But tissue aged no matter what. An ancient vampire couldn't count on his body to respond the way a younger body would.

Unless, Andy reasoned, blowing a cloud of smoke at the ceiling, *the body survived those horrible wounds by regenerating tissue at some otherwise unimaginable speed.* That kind of regeneration might also provide a kind of immortality, if all the body's tissue—veins and marrow and flesh and muscle, in addition to bones, teeth, and so on—could be replaced as it wore out.

He was no scientist, and his knowledge of anatomy was only that of a functional adult with a college degree. He could only speculate based on what sounded reasonable to him. Which led back to the idea that it was a virus, transmitted by the exchange of blood between biter and bitee. The question that raised was how a bloodsucker could decide, if that was the case, who would be turned and who would just be . . .

Andy tried to puzzle it out, but there were too many

unknowns, too many variables, and he was suddenly so tired that the thoughts seemed to smash into each other in his brain like bumper cars. He shoved a bunch of books onto the floor, put his feet up on the desk, tilted back in his swivel chair, and closed his eyes.

Dead to the world.

13

ANDY WOKE UP with his head feeling like a malevolent invader determined to do him in. Turning it either right or left more than about a millimeter sent white-hot bolts of pain shooting into his temples. His mouth was dry and he knew he should drink some water, but just the thought of consuming anything made his stomach do flips.

I'm just not a hard-drinking man, and the sooner I figure that out the better it'll be for all concerned.

The last bottle he'd emptied was on its side on the floor. Noticing it made Andy realize that his bladder was urgently full, and he considered opening the window to take care of it, or maybe trying to use the bottle. He didn't trust his hand not to shake too much for that, though, and wasn't sure that he had the strength to open the window. Anyway, the house seemed quiet—maybe everyone had gone to sleep. The clock said it was almost seven, but he wasn't sure if that was morning or evening.

He forced himself to his feet, his head throbbing with every motion, every breath. Worked his way over to the door and managed to turn the knob. He put a hand against the jamb, steadying himself so he didn't fall over from the wave of dizziness that washed over him. When it had mostly passed, he continued, tugging the door open and walking out into the hall. Across the kitchen. The bathroom door was open, and he didn't bother to close it behind him. The toilet seat was down. Bending over to flip it up almost made him vomit, but at least he was in the right place.

He pissed for a long time. Didn't bother to flush since that would require bending again. In the hall, he thought again how quiet it was—the quiet of an empty house, which had a different quality than a house in which the inhabitants were just keeping silent.

All he could hear was the steady *chukk-chukk-chukk-chukk* of a lawn sprinkler, which might have been his own or a neighbor's.

Golden sunlight washed in through the windows in the living room. Daytime, then, but the sun would be setting in a while. He'd slept for hours—some of the night and all day long. Where was everybody? Maybe they had finally wised up and left him.

He had not wanted to interact with his wife or daughters, but he needed to resupply the office if he was going to stay in there much longer. He was nearly out of matches, and he was pretty sure that bottle of Beam had been the last one. If his family was away somewhere, it'd be a good time to make a quick trip to the store.

Except for the pounding headache and the nausea, of

course. Those would have been worse, however, if Monica had been yelling at him. He started across the living room, glancing up the stairs as he went.

Lisa was there. Her blond ponytail dangled over a stair near the top. Her head was turned up toward the ceiling, neck bent at an odd angle.

Blood had run down two more steps, like spilled paint. Andy could see fat, languid flies walking in it.

"Lisa!" His head nearly exploded, but he ran for the stairs in spite of it, clawing the Glock from its holster. "Lisa!"

No response. Except for the position of her body and the blood running from her, she could have been sleeping there. Andy took the steps two at a time, his own discomfort forgotten.

Lisa's eyes were open, staring at the ceiling. She died frightened. Thick dried blood partially obscured a gash at her throat. She had soiled her pants, and the smell of blood and shit and death made Andy's stomach churn. Her skin was pale, like porcelain, and although there was blood on her and on the stairs, Andy could see no lividity on her back when he lifted her up by the shoulders. He pressed near the wound, but no blood came forth. It was as if she had been drained—the stain on the stairs was nowhere near all the blood that her body had contained.

How . . . ?

Sara.

Monica.

He stepped over his daughter and continued up the stairs, heart thudding dully in his chest.

Every agent—every cop, probably, of any sort—woke sweating from 3:00 A.M. nightmares of something happening to his family. Some thug he put away who came out still holding a grudge, or the friend of one going away for a long stretch, who figures the best way to even the score is to fuck with the lawman's wife and kids.

But it was like the nightmares of his childhood. Just bad dreams, nothing he really thought would ever happen.

It had.

He swallowed down bile.

He found Sara in her room. Dead. Like Lisa. Lying on her own bed, which was soaked with blood. Throat ripped open. Also like her sister, she seemed to have been drained of blood, except for what had spilled onto the bed.

He clenched his fists, closed his eyes to keep the tears from falling. "Monica!" he called. *"Monica!"*

No answer. The house was utterly silent except for the rustle of a breeze shifting the curtains. Was this how the killer had entered? Andy went to the window, looked down.

Below, in the backyard, a blouse and pants that belonged to Monica were sprawled on the grass. Even from here Andy could see the bloodstains on the clothing. His sprinkler pivoted on its axis, sending water arcing across the yard. "Monica!" he shouted again.

Swallowing hard, he ran downstairs and out the back door. The clothes had not just fallen there, but had been arranged—pants with the legs spread, blouse above them with the sleeves pointing toward the far corner of the yard, past the swing set and a big oak. Some kind of signal. Andy hurried around the tree, the sprinkler catching him full on, soaking him.

There, against the fence. Monica.

Andy stopped in his tracks. Forced his feet to move, to continue toward his wife. Even as he looked at her, though, knowing she was dead, his professionalism began to take over. He stopped short of her and cast a critical eye at the crime scene. Every few seconds the sprinkler's water cascaded into him, but he ignored it.

Uneven drag marks cut across the grass toward where she ended up. So she had been killed there, and had fought all the way. The clothing must have been placed after she was dead.

Monica's corpse, like those of the girls, was bone white. Blood spatter on the grass around her and the fence behind her, but not an adult body's worth. Throat savagely torn open by multiple cuts, blood around the wound and splashed onto her chest, stomach, thighs, diluted by the lawn sprinkler's spray. Her eyes were open; water ran down her cheeks like tears and drooled out from between slightly parted lips.

She had been posed in the corner of the wooden fence. Her head was up, eyes open as if she was looking at him. Her hands were raised, nailed over her head to the fence. Her legs were spread wide, knees up, as if inviting him.

With the fence surrounding the house, obstructing the view from prying eyes, apparently no nosy neighbors had witnessed this violent display and called the police.

Andy moved closer. Whoever had done this—and he already thought he knew who that was—would have left prints or some sort of contact evidence, unless he'd worn gloves and a latex bodysuit. This had been a very close-up, physical assault. From here, he couldn't even rule out sexual assault. And the killer had roamed through the house—more opportunity for trace evidence left behind.

Then his mask of professionalism broke—Andy let out a choking sob.

He ran across the yard, dropped the gun and took Monica in his arms. He tried to free her hands from the fence, but they were nailed on too well. He pressed his face, damp with tears, against her cold flesh. "Monica," he said between sobs. "Don't be gone, Monica. I'm sorry I shut you out, only please, just don't be gone. I don't think I can . . . I can . . ."

He choked on the words and stopped trying to speak. Monica was beyond hearing anyway. It was too late to beg forgiveness. The dead could not forgive or offer comfort to the living.

Let the dead be dead.

"Andy?"

A male voice, from behind.

Not Paul Norris.

Andy turned, scooping up his weapon.

He knew the man who stood there, trim in his neatly tailored gray suit.

Special Agent Dan Bradstreet. Hector Flores's errand boy. Or at least, that was his rep.

Andy watched Dan's face, his eyes. They widened, twitched, taking in the scene.

Seeing Andy on his knees, holding Monica, covered in her blood. Soaking wet, unshaven, hair uncombed, no doubt looking like hell.

Andy felt utterly sober now, but knew he didn't look it.

Dan tried to hold his gaze steady as he reached for his gun.

Andy did the same.

"Dan . . . Dan . . . seriously . . . I didn't do this, Dan. You've got to believe me. I just now found her here. My daughters are inside."

His gun was in his hand, pointed at Dan. Dan's was pointed at him. "I believe you, Andy," Dan said. He didn't sound very convincing. "I've been keeping an eye on you, Andy. I know you didn't do this."

"Then put away the gun, Dan."

"You know I can't do that . . . but you need to lower yours, Andy. Now. We can work this all out, but only if you put your weapon on the ground. You know the drill."

"I know how it goes, Dan. But I also know that if I put mine down, you'll take me into custody. You'll let me tell my side of the story, but by then it'll be too late."

Dan shrugged. "It looks like it's already too late, Andy."

Andy had been with the Bureau long enough to know how it would go down. Especially since he'd already assaulted ADIC Flores. He would be locked up. He'd get a public defender who wouldn't be able to do anything to help him, because the evidence would show that Andy had been home alone with his family, that he had his wife's blood on him, that he was armed, that he had been drinking heavily, and had gone crazy and slaughtered them.

He would spend the rest of his life in jail. Maybe appealing a death penalty, maybe just in a maximum-security lockup with a bunch of people he had put into the system in the first place. Every time he went to sleep, every time he stepped into the shower or the yard, he would expect a shiv in the back, or a strong arm or a length of clothesline looped around his throat.

Meanwhile, the real killer would be free. No one would believe Andy's version of what had happened here. If they did, they'd still railroad Andy, to cover it up.

Some things just couldn't be talked about.

"Put it *down*, Andy." Dan motioned with his weapon. "I'm not going to tell you again."

Mexican standoff.

"Fuck you, Dan."

Andy fired the Glock.

The shot hit Dan's hand. Chunks of flesh flew and blood spurted, and his gun went sailing. Flores's little helper screamed in agony. *"Shit!* Andy, God—"

"Sorry, Dan."

Dan scrambled for the gun, groping toward it with his left hand. Andy fired again, this time hitting Dan's left thigh. Dan swore again as the leg collapsed beneath his weight.

"Jesus . . . Andy . . . why did you—?"

"I could have killed you, Dan. If I'd done what you think I did, I wouldn't have hesitated. But I'm not going to kill you. After I'm gone, I'll call nine-one-one, get you some medical help."

Dan writhed on the ground near the oak tree. Andy went to him, kicked Dan's gun farther away and shoved his own deep into its holster. He took Dan's cuffs from his belt, wrapped the agent's arms around the oak, and cuffed them together. Dan, weak from shock and blood loss, could barely fight back.

"I didn't kill them, Dan. I know you don't care but I want you to know that."

"Then who did, Andy?" Dan sputtered through clenched teeth, breathing heavily. "You were the only one here. If not you, then who?"

"Paul Norris. Yeah, I know you don't believe me. I don't care. It was him."

"Norris is dead," Dan Bradstreet said.

"See? I told you." Andy fished the Glock from its holster, reversed it in his hand and clubbed the agent in the forehead with the butt end. Dan's head slammed into the oak, and he slumped forward, held up only by the handcuffs.

Andy had promised to call nine-one-one, and he would.

But he needed a good head start first.

And with the blood of his family drying and sticky on his hands, Andy Gray ran for his life.

Excerpted from *30 Days of Night* by Stella Olemaun

I loathe going back to the mayhem of those nights. Too many nightmares since then. Sleeping and waking.

Barrow was overwhelmed so rapidly that Eben and I barely had the chance to process the guilt of not being able to protect its citizens. We were utterly useless in the face of our attackers. They were simply killing machines—swift, tireless, and remorseless in their pursuit of blood, thinking no more of murdering a small child than they did anyone else.

Their strength was incredible, possibly equal only to their viciousness. I saw limbs torn effortlessly from sockets and grown men brought down by what appeared to be children.

For the first few nights we just hid anywhere we could, practically freezing, using the spaces beneath the raised houses as our hidden pathway out of the vampires' sight. I say vampires here, as plain as that, because by the second or third night there simply was no denying what these creatures were.

While running to the aid of the daughter of a woman who taught at Barrow Elementary, I again saw it firsthand.

I was hidden behind stacked barrels of sand alongside the

ruins of the Ikos Bar, looking for food and survivors. I found neither. Instead I encountered the most horrifying scene that will haunt me for the rest of my days: two of them, a man and a woman, stripping helpless eleven-year-old Kylie Grace of her clothes right there in the freezing cold, and then taking turns biting pieces of flesh which they sucked on for blood. Only when Kylie's terrified screams turned to dying whimpers did they bite into a major artery in the neck and drain her. Then they passed her back and forth like a joint, holding a hand over the spurting throat wound, until the whimpers stopped and her body went limp.

But it wasn't over.

When the two vampires were finished, they twisted Kylie's head until the neck snapped and while one held the body, the other pulled her head completely off and tossed it into the snow and moved on, laughing and talking in a language I didn't understand, maybe German.

I cried behind those barrels, not moving for God knows how long, the cold and despair eating away at me.

All around me, near as a few yards and as far as the edge of town, I heard the sounds of murder.

Screams of pleading and screams of pain.

Every once in a while, I would hear gunfire, but it never lasted long, and was usually followed by horrible shrieks as, I assumed, the shooter was disarmed and killed for his blood.

It took some doing, but I gathered my strength and courage and ventured out from the barrels. It was freezing. I crawled beneath the houses for blocks, pausing between buildings to check the streets. If I saw them, I'd change direction and crawl around them.

I had seen crime scenes in my life, but nothing that prepared me for the acres of carnage I witnessed.

There were entire streets painted sickly red with blood, as if a hose had been used to distribute the gore. There were bodies littering my dying town, and in all cases, they were decapitated.

These murderous bastards fed on people, tortured and tormented them, and then after draining them of blood . . . they took their heads.

It would be weeks before I understood why.

When I came across a snow-bank that blocked my path back to Eben, I would edge my way through homes, despite knowing the scenes I might find.

Mostly there were signs of struggle and a vacant home. In one, I found the place completely devoid of life, no signs of violence, food set out on the table, untouched. Had they run and escaped the vampires in time . . . or had they met the same fate as everybody who tried to run?

I made it back to Eben after being gone for hours. He was huddled in the small furnace basement below the sheriff's office—and he wasn't alone.

Worried about me, he had ventured out. He didn't find me, but he located four people hidden beneath cars and brought them back to our meager shelter.

Everyone had the same story, it seemed. They were going about the usual business of preparing for the long period of darkness and cold, reinforcing insulation, clearing the snow from beneath their homes, when all of a sudden they heard sounds of violence. And then, it was like the world went insane.

Sam and Lucy Ikos were there with us. Together they owned and ran the Ikos Bar and Diner. Both were with Eben when I returned, but Lucy was severely injured, a tear down her leg so deep that bone was exposed.

Lucy recounted for us how the vampires had attacked the bar like commandoes on a raid. They had shut down the portable generator, killing all the lights, and blocked the front door. Then, while customers along with Sam and Lucy panicked inside, the bloodsuckers descended from the skylight.

Sam used a shotgun to get his wife and himself free, but the others weren't so lucky. As Sam retreated, carrying Lucy, he heard some of the toughest men he'd ever known cry for their lives before being cut down.

What we didn't know was how Lucy had been injured. Sam suspected she caught herself on a shard of glass or metal when they escaped. Eben and I weren't as sure. The wound was clean except for dirt and threads, but there was an odd pattern, a row of deep grooves. Neither Eben nor I said it, but we were fairly convinced Lucy Ikos had been bitten.

We tended to her injury as best we could and gave her some whiskey to help her sleep.

Eben and I would take turns on watch. There was only one door down into the small cellar and two small windows both high and covered with snow. The door was a hatch hidden under the debris of the destroyed sheriff station. We figured if the invaders came looking it would appear the place had already been ransacked. Eben would clear a peephole-sized opening in the window and watch the streets at bug's-eye level for hour after hour.

That night, after I'd returned, Eben and I hunkered near the small window while the others slept.

"I saw Kylie Grace killed while I was out," I told him.

Eben looked at me and bit his lip. "Jesus."

"There's nothing we can do, honey," I said. "Staying alive and keeping as many folks safe as we can . . . it's the best we can do."

Eben looked at me. "Do you really believe that, Stella?" he asked.

I stared into my husband's eyes, searching for the fear that I felt inside, what I had seen in them before, but it wasn't there. Eben wasn't afraid of anything. All I saw was the frustration, like a little kid, strong as he might be, being pinned by a larger bully.

Finally, I responded, a bit ashamed, but only because it was the truth. "Yes . . . yes, I do."

That night Lucy Ikos died in her husband's arms.

Her soft, kind face suddenly lost all sense of who she had been and her tough, hard-working hands curled into fists. I went to Sam's side and tried to console him, but my true intent was to get him away from her body in case there were any surprises.

As I gently guided Sam away from the body, I saw Lucy's fists uncurl and saw Eben reach for an axe resting on hooks against the back wall near the second window. Sam noticed what was happening and began to sob, but he didn't try to stop Eben.

It was incredible to me how much we had already come to accept what only a few days before would have been impossible for us to even imagine.

I gathered Sam and the other survivors in a corner away from where Eben stood, waiting.

As Eben readied the axe and Sam hid his face in his hands, Lucy's eyelids flew open and her eyes were no longer hers. They were almost entirely white, with pinpoint pupils that immediately fell on Eben.

The axe fell and Lucy's head parted from her body before she could make a sound, or give away our position to the other vampires.

14

Andy Gray was so screwed.

The Bureau didn't like people shooting their agents, even if only in the hand and leg. Especially if said people had already assaulted a superior and disobeyed direct orders.

They would be after him, in a big way. They would be pissed. They would spare no expense or effort to run him down.

Maybe worse than all that, he needed to visit the Sacramento field office before he left town. It was crazy. But he had to find out what the Bureau knew, and there was no better way to do it.

He had rifled through Dan Bradstreet's pockets for car keys. Since he was in there, he also took Dan's cell phone. Out in front of the house and halfway down the block he spotted the agent's car, a silver Ford Crown Victoria. Keys for his own Camry were already in his pocket, and he got Monica's set from her purse. No telling if someone on the block hadn't already called the police after hearing Andy fire his gun. There was no way this would all end well, but he didn't have time to try to cover up the murders of Monica and the girls, or to figure out a way to prove his own innocence. The best he could do was to slow everyone down, make sure Dan couldn't holler in a report until he'd had time to get away.

The moon was rising by the time he reached the local field office. The Bureau was open 24/7, of course, but only a skeleton crew worked at night. Andy parked Dan's Crown Vic in his own usual slot near the west edge of the parking lot, under a spreading oak that offered shade against the merciless sun of Sacramento's hot summers. He had taken a few minutes at home to groom himself and put on a clean suit. He'd also loaded a couple of guns and several boxes of ammunition into the Crown Vic's deep trunk, and tossed in an overnight bag with clean underwear, some changes of clothes, and basic toiletries.

He had hit rock bottom. Drunk for days, smoking like a fiend, ignoring his family. That was all bad enough.

Sleeping through their murder was worse.

Paul Norris had been inside his house. Knew that Andy was ignoring the warning implicit in Angelica Foster's death. Maybe he couldn't bring himself to kill Andy. They'd been close friends, and maybe the trajectory of evil that Paul was on had not yet reached the stage where he could murder a friend.

Killing Monica, Lisa, and Sara, though . . . Andy had, until Paul's disappearance, been a dedicated husband and father. A little too wrapped up in his work, probably, like millions of other American men. But he had loved Monica and their girls. Part of him had looked forward to the day he could retire from the Bureau to spend time with Monica. Travel, maybe. Buy an RV and see America without looking through the prism of law enforcement, not seeing everyone as a potential victim or crook. The girls would be grown by then, of course, maybe with families of their own. Grandchildren.

Andy bit down on his lower lip. He needed to stay cool now, didn't want to start tearing up again, let the grief overwhelm him. There would be plenty of time later for mourning . . . although hopefully not from within the confines of a jail cell.

He checked himself in the rearview. He could use a shower, he decided. There were some streaks of blood in his hair. *No one will look that closely at me . . . I hope.*

His goals were shifting. At first, it had been about finding Paul. Now that priority had slipped a notch or two. He had to figure out what had happened to his partner, and perhaps more important, he had to drag the truth about the vampires into the light.

And then he had to kill Paul Norris.

The glass front door was locked after 6:00 P.M. Andy walked up to it, knowing he was on camera. He held up his ID toward the camera and smiled. In less than a minute, the silhouette of Earl Pombro approached the door, becoming more distinct as he neared the glass. Gray hair, gray uniform, handgun holstered at his side. He nodded to Andy and opened up.

"Working late?"

"That's right, Earl. I've spent so much time in Los Angeles lately I have some catching up to do at my desk." Earl wouldn't know that Andy had been suspended unless an alert had been issued. That would happen as soon as Dan Bradstreet got in touch with ADIC Flores, so Andy had to be out of here before then. "Everything okay with you?" Andy asked conversationally.

Earl took a moment to contemplate the question, mashing his lips together as if trying to squash something between them. "Yeah, I think so," he said after Andy had already started past him. "My wife's finally getting off that low-carb kick, thank God."

"Just keep an eye on the cholesterol and eat your veggies," Andy tossed back over his shoulder. A minute later he was riding the elevator to his third-floor office.

The place looked unfamiliar when he first walked in. Moonlight shone in through the big windows. His computer squatted in its usual spot, his telephone, an old-fashioned wooden pencil cup with pens and pencils and a six-inch ruler sticking up out of it. He had spent a lot of time away, however, and had been through so much in recent days that this was like some remnant of another life, or a set from a movie he'd seen many times.

He clicked on the overhead light, dispelling the shadows, and breathed easier.

He hadn't really thought Paul would be waiting for

him inside here. Anything was possible, though. Or so it appeared. The more he learned, the more he understood that nothing could be ruled out. The world was filled with so many mysteries, the *Weekly World News* was probably more accurate than *The New York Times.*

Lowering himself into his desk chair, he booted up the computer. It was an old PC running a version of Windows that had long since become obsolete to the rest of the world. The Bureau was engaged in a major technological reinvention of itself, post-9/11. Progress had not reached Sacramento yet; the laptop he'd bought for himself two years earlier was far more advanced than the desktop unit here at the office. And while Washington had been spending millions, they had apparently spent it on the wrong equipment, resulting in a miniscandal because of their inability to meet the needs of the new face of intelligence gathering.

The computer was networked locally, though, and from here Andy could tap into the California archives. He found it a bit absurd that he couldn't get into Washington's system, or that of other states. If a bank robber turned up in Fresno, for instance, and he suspected a connection to a series of robberies in Philly, he'd have to call the Philadelphia office on the phone or send an email to request their records, instead of being able to bring them up right on his desk. That was something the Bureau was planning to change, when they got around to it.

He was a bit surprised to find that his security password still worked. Pretty unbelievable, actually. Something else that would be revoked when Dan Bradstreet woke up and managed to free himself from the cuffs. Andy smiled. He was into the California records. Now he just had to figure out how to find what he was looking for.

He tried searching the word "vampire."

Nothing. What he expected.

But if vampires had been around for centuries—even for decades—the Bureau must have had some previous encounters with them. Those encounters would be in the records somewhere. Search "bloodsucker"? "Dracula"? "Fangs"?

Finally, he settled on the word "blood."

Millions of results. Of course.

He added the words "empty," "drained," and "bite."

Jackpot. The system only returned twenty-two records containing all four words.

He read each one, word for word. Stopped after the third to stretch, rub his eyes, fetch a cup of water from the kitchen. He was dehydrated, head dully aching, stomach still queasy, grief welling up again. Miraculously, he had started to feel hungry, which he took as a good sign.

No time to eat. He went back to the computer, kept reading.

Slowly, little by little, a pattern started to emerge. Like one of those big pictures made up of hundreds or thousands of tiny images, all put together in a certain way. Up close, you can see the little images, but when you step back far enough the overall picture becomes clear.

Andy had a few of the little pictures now, but not the big one. Not yet.

He jotted down some names that cropped up more than once. Fredrik. Charles Wildmon Taylor. Brewster. Henrietta Lowrey. Vicente. Marilyn Corle.

A few locations appeared multiple times, too. Andy noted those: Broussard, Louisiana. Chamblee, Georgia. Barrow, Alaska. Tirgu Mures, Romania. Andresy, France. Rosario, Argentina.

The Bureau had looked into strange killings on numerous occasions during its brief lifespan. Fourteen of the files he read were unhelpful, just cases where the words he had searched had happened to show up. But the rest of them all seemed to tie together.

The word "vampire" was studiously avoided but the implication was obvious. Victims found with neck wounds. Drained of blood. Attacks happened at night. No living witnesses.

On a couple of occasions the bodies had disappeared several days later, vanishing from churches or funeral homes. In one case an interred body was gone, the grave apparently dug out from below.

In each of these cases, some superior at the Bureau had felt it necessary to remind the investigating agents to keep their findings quiet.

Two of the cases were different from the rest, and Andy read and reread them with interest, then printed them out. In these particular cases, agents had interrogated suspected murderers, sixteen years apart. The killers had decapitated their victims—both people to whom they had no personal connection whatsoever. Both killers had insisted that their victims were killers themselves—again, the word "vampire" didn't show up in the reports; the word "monster" was used. In the more recent report, from seven years before, the killer had claimed that this victim was just the latest in a string of nine, all of whom had been serial murderers who needed to have their heads cut off in order to save more innocent lives.

More significantly, he claimed to be part of an organized effort.

Some kind of antivampire militia? Andy scoured the reports but he couldn't find anything more about it.

There was another phrase that turned up, though.

"Operation Red-Blooded."

No definition, no elaboration.

When Andy tried to search the phrase he got a warning screen that referred him to Washington. Apparently whatever Operation Red-Blooded was, it was classified at the highest levels.

Andy glanced at the clock on his computer. Ten-fifteen. Dan Bradstreet would have to wake up pretty soon. If he couldn't free himself, he could start yelling.

Someone would come and help him—Andy's was a friendly neighborhood, the kind of place where people knew each other, threw block parties and held multi-family yard sales.

One-fifteen in DC. That was good. Andy called over, worked his way up until he was on the phone with a Special Agent Yolanda Friese.

"I'm working on a case out here and I've come up against something called Operation Red-Blooded," he told her. "Apparently it's classified beyond my level, but I want to make sure I don't step on anyone's investigation or blow anyone's cover. If you could let me know the basics of it so I know what to keep away from, I'd appreciate it."

"I don't know any such operation," Yolanda Friese said. "But let me look it up, see what I can find out."

"I'd appreciate that," Andy said. He waited on the line while she tapped on a keyboard. She made surprised noises while she did.

"I . . . I'm afraid I can't tell you much," she said. "Most of it's even classified above my level. But . . ." She chuckled. ". . . it looks like it's an appellation for a secret organization of . . . vampire hunters."

Andy forced a laugh. "That's got to be a joke, right?"

Yolanda hesitated. "The Bureau isn't known for its sense of humor," she said. "Or for an overactive imagination. I'm just telling you what I can—a group of vampire hunters and vampires. I'm just guessing now, but I would assume that the Bureau was trying to determine if vampires were real—you know, like those Air Force studies of UFOs? They probably classified the operation because we'd be a laughingstock if the public ever found out."

"A laughingstock," Andy repeated. "That's for sure. There anything else you can tell me?"

"That's it," Yolanda said. "I don't know what you're working on there, but if it points to Operation Red-Blooded, you'd probably better close the books on it and move onto something real."

"I'll do that," Andy promised. "And don't worry, I'll keep this whole nonsense on the QT." He hung up the phone.

A secret society? Comprising both vampires and vampire hunters? And the Bureau had known about the whole thing for years, but kept it hushed up?

Andy stared at the phone like it was a rattlesnake that might lunge at any moment. It was almost unbelievable.

Except that it wasn't. Of course the Bureau would cover it up. That's what they did. They put away the approved bad guys of the moment—Italian Mafioso, drug kingpin, terrorist. The rest they kept tabs on, but quietly. How many people in their fifties now had FBI files from the 1960s, when they were in college, because they attended a demonstration or an antiwar concert? How many had bothered to use the Freedom of Information Act to find out? The Bureau had tendrils stretching all across the country, but most of what they learned they would never take to court or reveal to the rest of the world.

Now, it seemed, vampires fit into that category as well.

Andy looked at the clock again. Ten thirty-six. He had to get out of here. Before he shut down, he tried one more thing—a little trick that a friendly MIS tech had shown him before getting canned. A back channel through the files to see who else had been accessing them recently.

Only one name showed up.

Paul Norris.

Andy grabbed for the phone again. *Sally!* He had just remembered—during his drunken stupor, Monica had said that Sally kept calling. Was she worried about Paul? Afraid? Maybe he'd been hanging around the house, upsetting the girls—*Nicole thought she saw him on a rooftop.*

Maybe it was too late—maybe Paul had killed his own family, as well as Andy's.

He dialed Sally's number. The phone rang once, twice, a third time. Then a click and Sally's voice.

"Hello?"

Andy's mouth was suddenly Sahara-dry. He didn't know what to say. Didn't know what he could say that would make sense, or help her at all. Warn her to be careful? Pointless—if Paul wanted to kill her, how was she supposed to save herself?

He hung up.

His gaze flicked over the notes he had made. He knew that time was short, that Dan Bradstreet would surely be conscious by now. He needed to be on the move before he was caught in here.

He recognized none of the names he had written down. And only one of the places had turned up before in this case.

Barrow, Alaska.

It was central to everything, somehow. Linked all the way around. He couldn't go there now—for one thing, since this had all started with the Olemaun case, if he were hunting himself that would be one of the first places he would look.

But he expected he would wind up there one of these days.

15

HE COULDN'T HAVE SAID what alerted him.

Andy went to the window of his office and looked down toward the parking lot. Everything seemed normal out there. Not many cars, but a few, including the Crown Vic he had stolen. No police cars or anything, but then, that would come later. First, he would be held right here in the building, and questioned. The cops would only be brought in later.

Still, something felt strange. Just nerves? Some hypersensitivity? Or maybe he was just freaked by the whole situation.

Either way, Andy knew he had to get out of here, now. He scooped up the files he had printed and hurried toward the staircase. Before he opened the door, he changed his mind. Anything out of the ordinary would tip off Pombro, if he hadn't already been alerted. He went to the elevator and jammed his finger on the button, then waited anxiously for the doors to slide open. He drummed his fingers on the file folders that he carried in his arms, having forgotten to bring in a briefcase to take them out in.

Finally, the elevator came. Empty. Andy stepped in.

He started to feel relieved—two flights down, a few steps to the door, a hurried good night to Earl Pombro and he was gone, safe.

At the ground floor the doors skated open and Andy emerged, back straight, smile pasted to his face, eyes straight ahead.

Earl was on the phone. He glanced up at Andy and looked away, but then his head swung back like it was on a swivel. Sweat dotted his forehead and upper lip.

Andy picked up the pace. "Night, Earl," he said as he passed the guard's station.

Earl said something quiet into the mouthpiece and hung up the phone.

Andy was almost to the door. Reflected in the glass he saw Earl rising, his mouth working, right hand dropping to his holster. "Mr. Gray," the guard managed.

Andy shoved through the door and broke into a run. As it swung shut behind him he knew he didn't have to worry about being shot in the back, at least not for a few seconds. The glass used throughout the building was bulletproof—intended to protect the people inside, but in this case it served double duty.

By the time Earl reached the door and came out, Andy was sliding into the driver's seat of Dan Bradstreet's sedan.

He gunned the engine and saw Earl pivot toward him, weapon clutched in both hands. The big oak blocked his shot, though, and the guard had to hurry down the front walk for a better angle. While he did that, Andy backed out of the parking place, slammed the car into drive, and peeled out.

If Earl ever got off a shot, Andy didn't hear it.

But he was a full-on fugitive now. No getting around that fact. Which meant he had to be smart, or he would be dead.

Hector Flores dropped the phone into its cradle with a curse. Though bilingual, he always preferred to curse in English. Its harsh, guttural sounds made the expletives much more convincing than in Spanish.

And right now, he felt every syllable of it. It had been one heinously fucked-up day.

He had assigned Dan Bradstreet to keep an eye on Andy Gray. Dan had done so, to an extent. But somehow he had missed the moment when Andy slaughtered his own family. Then he had let Andy get the drop on him. Andy had cuffed him to a tree and taken his weapon and his car.

All in all, a less than stellar performance.

Just to put a capper on everything, Andy had then waltzed into his own office and accessed classified files. The only guy Hector had been able to raise in Sacramento had been a security guard who, if Hector had any pull at all, would be enjoying his retirement by the end of the week. The guard had just called Hector back to tell him that Andy had driven away from the parking lot at top speed.

Hector picked up the phone again. Dan had told

him that Andy took his cell phone, along with his weapon and car keys. On the off chance that he still had it, Hector dialed the number. It rang several times, and then he heard Andy's voice.

"This must be ADIC Flores."

"That's right, Andrew. And since you're answering this phone, you know we have a pretty big problem here."

"I know we do, *Hector,*" Andy said. *He sounds weary,* Flores thought, *but not panicked or angry.* "And I know what you think, but I didn't hurt my own family. I wouldn't."

"I don't know what to think, Andy." Noncommittal. *Don't try to trap him into anything. Let him reveal himself.*

"Just think that I was right, before. What I told you about Paul."

"Andy, you've got to realize how absurd that is. Vampires are not something the FBI worries about, or something that I personally believe in."

"As for the first part, Hector, if you don't think the Bureau worries about vampires, take a closer look. Dig into Operation Red-Blooded a little and tell me that again." His voice rose here as emotion swelled in him. "And whether you personally believe is not the issue. My wife, my daughters—their bodies were *drained* of blood, Hector. Where did it go? Who would do that except one of those things?"

"Look, Andy, you're in a bad period," Hector told him. He tried to sound fatherly, reassuring. "You need help. Why don't you come in so we can work all this out?"

Andy huffed something that might have been a laugh. "I must be losing service, Hector," he said. "I'm not hearing you right."

"Andy, come on. You know how this has to go down. Either you come in and we talk about it, figure out a way to solve things that works for everyone, or else you're a fugitive. And you've been with the Bureau long enough to know there's no escaping us. Not just us, but, hell, Andy, we've got three dead bodies. The locals are going to want in on this. The state police too. If you don't come in, there's every chance that you're going to get hurt. I'd rather see you wind up in one piece."

There was a long moment of silence, as if Andy was considering his suggestion. But it went on too long. Hector spoke Andy's name a couple of times. Then a dial tone hummed in his ear.

Andy had either passed out of range, or hung up.

Which meant that Hector had to suffer the indignity of putting out an APB for an agent who was, even if only temporarily at that point, assigned to his office. If it was just Andy running amuck and screaming about vampires, it wouldn't be such a big deal. He could keep it in the family, have Andy quietly dealt with. But as he'd told Andy, there were three bodies, including two little girls, at his home, and Dan Bradstreet swore that no one went in or out except Andy Gray. The locals would demand to be involved. The press might even pick it up, although he would cite national security as much as he could to keep that from happening. The media had become pretty compliant about that sort of thing.

Hector blew out a sigh and reached for the phone again.

Andy knew he'd have to dump Dan's Crown Vic before too long. The license plate and car description were probably being broadcast to every law enforcement agency within five hundred miles by now.

He was barreling out of Sacramento, headed northeast on Interstate 80 toward Reno. Knowing that his bank accounts would be tracked but that it would surprise no one that he was still in town now, he had swung by an ATM near the on-ramp for Interstate 5, heading south, to give the impression that he was headed for Stockton or LA. There he withdrew the maximum three hundred dollars the machine would give him. If the bank was open he'd have gone in to withdraw everything, but he didn't want to hang around town until ten in the morning. He had pitched Dan's cell phone out the window near the ATM, then doubled back to the 80.

Instead of relaxing as Sacramento fell behind him and Nevada neared, he became more and more anxious. His palms were wet against the steering wheel and he kept wiping them on his pants. His hands quaked like a Parkinson's victim's.

Every mile that slipped under his wheels seemed to reiterate just how much trouble he was in.

If they caught him, Hector Flores would make sure he stood trial for the murder of his family. With an FBI agent watching the outside of the house, and plenty of evidence that Andy had touched all the victims—not to mention all the drinking, the assault on a superior, the erratic behavior—the case would be a slam dunk.

He longed for someone to call, someone he could confess his fears to.

But there was no one.

With Paul changed, the Bureau chasing him, and Monica and the girls gone, his support system had fallen apart.

He was as alone in the world as it was possible for a man to be.

Gripping the wheel to keep his hands from trembling, he found he could taste the booze on his tongue, a ghost memory that made the craving return with a vengeance. Just a swig to swish around in his mouth, to feel the flavor and the burn against his cheeks, he didn't even need to swallow . . .

He caught himself scanning the highway ahead for a gas station that would have a mini-mart with liquor and smokes—the craving for nicotine was almost as bad as that for booze—and slapped his hand hard against the wheel. That kind of thinking wouldn't help. It would only wind up with him drunk in some motel, which the Bureau would have surrounded by the end of the day. Staying sober was the only way to stay smart.

Not staying smart would get him dead.

The eastern horizon was gray by the time he parked in a structure behind Harrah's. He hiked across a bridge into the casino, then out the nearest door. Two blocks away, practically still in the shadow of Harrah's, he stepped inside a small print shop, Nat's Reno Redi-Print.

Natan Cebulski looked up from a computer monitor behind the counter and offered Andy a phony smile. He was a little man with dark hair badly combed over a bald spot, an impressive beak of a nose, and little black pearls of eyes that looked like they'd been taken from a much smaller head. "Special Agent Gray," he said, rising from the computer. "This is a surprise. I've been keeping my nose clean."

"Save it," Andy said, raising a hand to cut off the torrent of lies that would issue from the man's mouth. "I need you to do something for me."

One eyebrow climbed up Nat's forehead like a sidewinding caterpillar. "You?" On a counter behind him, a coffee pot sat on its warmer, filling the whole shop with its tarry stink. Nat had always been an early morning guy, hitting the sack by eight-thirty and opening the shop at five-thirty. His bad coffee fueled him through the days.

Andy knew that Natan Cebulski made fake documents in his shop for a variety of criminals. He let the man continue to operate because sometimes, in a pinch, Nat could discreetly point him toward a vanished felon, in exchange for Andy's discretion. Now that Andy needed to disappear himself, he was glad he had let Nat slide.

"That's right," Andy said. He crossed his arms over his chest. He would not elaborate further, and Nat knew better than to ask. "Use the name Andrew Hertz. My photo and stats. I need driver's license, passport, a Visa card, and Bureau identification. Give me an address in LA or San Diego."

"You want me to fake an FBI ID?"

"Don't act like it's the first time you've ever done it, Nat."

"Some things I try not to mess around with."

Andy dropped his existing identification on the counter. "Work with these."

Nat scooped them up into one hand. "Come back tomorrow, about this time," he said.

"Wrong," Andy said. "I'm in a hurry here. You have two hours."

Nat gave him a panicked look. "Andy, I got other jobs, other commitments, you know? I can't just drop everything and—"

"Sure you can. In fact, that's what your plan was all along. Drop the rest and get this done."

"I got these wedding invitations due, Andy. The mother'll—"

"This is Reno," Andy interrupted again. "Nobody uses wedding invitations here."

Nat blinked and wiped sweat from his brow. "Andy, I appreciate that you're in a hurry, really. You've made that abundantly clear. But I do quality workmanship here, you know that. You want the best, you can't rush it. Sure, I could get it done that fast, but you want it to pass muster, I need a little time on it."

"Nat," Andy replied calmly. "You're here instead of in jail because I was willing to look the other way a few times. Now I need you to do this for me, and I don't have time to stick around Reno waiting for it. You can have three hours, but that's all. After that, either I take my documents and I'm in the wind, or you're on your way to a ten-year stretch at Nellis."

Nat blinked again, nodded. *Just play hardball with the guy and you'll get what you want.* Andy glanced at his watch. "I'll be back at nine-thirty."

Nat nodded again, already bending back to the computer to get to work.

Outside, the sun had cleared the horizon. He blinked, feeling a momentary sense of panic because he couldn't see anything, and didn't know who might be out there, watching for him, waiting with guns drawn for him to emerge. He turned back toward the shadowed doorway and let his eyes acclimate to the light.

This is what it'll be like. For God knows how long, maybe forever. Always expecting the worst, fearing every cop, every authority figure.

This is what the guys I've put away felt like before I caught them.

Maybe worse, he realized that the best days of his life were undeniably over. No matter what happened from here, it would never be as good as it had been. He had never loved Monica and the girls the way he should have, but he'd loved them the way he could, with every intention of making it right at some indeterminate point in the future.

Well, the future was here.

And now they were gone.

He shook his head. The street was clear. Reno was barely awake, just a couple of cars moving blocks away. Andy hurried back to the casino. Hiding out there was far from ideal, but at least they were used to transients; an unfamiliar face at seven in the morning wouldn't make anybody ask questions, like it might in other places.

Inside, tired-looking gamblers worked banks of slots and video poker machines. A single craps table was in use, and two people each sat at two blackjack tables while bored dealers flipped cards their way. Andy worked his way down the staggered aisles to a restaurant, found a booth and ordered breakfast. He ate slowly, reading a newspaper someone had left on the next table. When he had killed forty-five minutes, he left a small tip and went back into the casino proper. Fed a twenty into a free video poker machine and played that for almost an hour, winning and losing and inhaling smoke from the gamblers around him.

The smoke made him want to bum a cigarette, buy a pack of Camels.

Drink.

It would be so easy to buy a bottle, get a room.

He resisted the temptation, fed another ten into the machine.

When that was gone, he got up from the game and went back outside. The sun was even higher now, and hotter. He took off his jacket, carried it over his shoulder, and walked the perimeter of the parking structure. He was watching for Feds, eyeing every car to make sure it didn't contain an injured and irate Dan Bradstreet or anyone else who might try to make a move on him.

He saw two drunks sleeping off their nights in their own cars, one of whom appeared to live in his. He saw one couple in a preorgasmic state. One man talking on a cell phone and a young woman pounding out something on a laptop. A couple of cars left while he walked, a few more pulled in. A blue Nissan Maxima with Oregon plates drove in and a middle-aged couple climbed out, dragged suitcases from the trunk, and started the hike toward Harrah's.

No cops, no Feds.

He went back downstairs and around the block. Across the street from Nat's place was a pawnshop. Watching the woman with the laptop had reminded him that he would need one, would need some way to keep up with the world at large. He went into the shop, dropped Nat's name, and got a reasonable deal on an HP with Wi-Fi. He wrote a check for it on his own account, and made the check for ten thousand dollars over the amount. The proprietor did a double take, but Andy told him to call Nat if he had any questions. The guy grumbled and went into the back room, came back with the cash.

Andy stuffed it into his front pants pocket. This would get harder and harder, and he needed to clear as much from his account as he possibly could, today. It didn't matter much that he would have given away the fact that he'd stopped in Reno; Dan's car would be discovered soon enough anyway.

But from here, he needed to disappear completely.

He went back to Nat's at nine thirty-five. The documents were ready of course, and Andy's practiced eye didn't spot any problems. Andy thanked the nervous Nat ("Pleasure doing business with you . . . and stay out of trouble, you hear?") and walked back to the casino again. At a cashier's cage he smiled, produced his new ID, including the FBI card, and bought thirty thousand dollars' worth of chips with his old debit card. The cashier questioned the contradictory names, but he calmly explained that FBI agents customarily used two or more identities, and encouraged her to run the card. She did, and his account was still open. The amount approved, she handed over the chips.

Carrying the tray to a blackjack table, Andy played a few hands, losing every time but one. After twenty minutes he excused himself, tossed a couple of five dollar chips to the dealer, and took the tray to a different cashier. When he walked out of the casino he still had more than thirty-nine grand in his pockets.

Back to the parking structure. The dark blue Maxima was still in the same spot. From the luggage the couple had hauled inside, it looked as if they were staying a few days. They might come out later that day to drive to dinner or someplace else, but then again they might not emerge from Harrah's until they were ready to drive home to Oregon.

He hoped to have a few days before the car was reported stolen, but he'd take whatever he could get. He went upstairs and got Dan Bradstreet's car, drove it down a level and pulled into an empty slot conveniently next to the Maxima. Using a handy toolkit from Dan's car, he jimmied open the Maxima and got it started. Popping the trunk, he transferred all the weapons and other stuff he had stowed in the Crown Vic. He closed and locked Dan's car, then drove out of the structure in the Maxima.

Got to keep moving.

16

ANDY GRAY HAD DISAPPEARED.

Paul Norris had plenty of other things on his mind and didn't want to spend his entire life—well, unlife, or afterlife, whatever—keeping tabs on his former *compadre* and partner. All he had wanted was for Andy to lay off the vampire research, and although Andy had failed to heed the first message he'd sent, he was pretty sure this latest one was loud and crystal clear.

Chicken-scrawny Monica had turned out to be far more delicious than he had imagined.

He would have liked to have known where Andy was, but he had other things to get to. He felt, more than ever, an urgency to find out just what the living world knew about vampires. He knew now that the Bureau had put more effort into investigating them than they were willing to admit. Presumably they weren't alone in that. But did they share their information with other law enforcement or government agencies? Unlikely—the Bureau tended to play their cards close to the vest.

After passing the daylight hours in a Sacramento motel with the heavy curtains drawn, Paul drove south through the night, stopping shortly before dawn at a roadside motel in Buttonwillow. He roused a sleepy desk clerk and checked into a room for the day. The room was small and smelled like mildew, but the shades worked. He would sleep a few hours, watch some TV. He would rather have covered more ground, but the sun could still kill him. *There's got to be some way around this handicap.* Again, he regretted the disappearance—the probable destruction—of the vampire who had turned him. He would happily have continued doing her bidding if he also had the benefit of her experience, the lessons she could teach. As it was, he had to make it all up as he went, had to guess at what survival strategies would prove to be effective.

One wrong guess might be his last.

So far, the changes he'd experienced had been mostly positive. Yes, his movements were constricted a little by having to avoid sunlight. And it had taken a while to be completely comfortable with the idea that serial murder would become his regular routine.

Now, just weeks later, he craved blood even when he wasn't especially hungry. It was more than just sustenance, it was an addiction. He craved it like he had craved booze and sex during his life. Even the desk clerk, a middle-aged guy with a grizzled chin and greasy hair and a gut the size of a Pontiac, had that rich, red drug running through his veins. Paul greatly preferred feeding on women—his libido wasn't what it had been, but that didn't mean he didn't get a sexual charge from them—but he might just have to do the desk clerk before he left.

If nothing else, he could help himself to the cash drawer after he ate.

In life, Paul Norris had never been a guy who could simply exist day to day. He was the same way now. He needed a goal, a plan, something to work toward. Before, that had always been bedding the next hot number or putting away the next bad guy.

His goals had changed.

He wanted to find other vampires, make contacts, find out what vampire society and hierarchy were like. Maybe make himself a big deal among the undead—that could be fun.

Just as important, or more so, was learning how to help his new species protect itself from outsiders, from do-gooders like Stella Olemaun and Andy Gray.

Best thing was, if he did the latter it would no doubt help him accomplish the former. When he brought to the vampire bigwigs the complete scoop on what the mortal world knew, and some ideas on how to defuse that knowledge, they'd have to welcome him into the fold.

They wouldn't have any choice.

That was just the way Paul liked it.

Carol Hino tossed three aspirins into her mouth and swallowed them with a slug of black coffee. *Breakfast of champions.*

She sat at her kitchen table, a retro deal of stainless and red Naugahyde, and turned the cup slowly between her hands. She had pulled on a silk bathrobe and dragged a brush through her short black hair a few times, but that was the extent of the grooming she had been able to do before turning to caffeine and painkillers.

In her bedroom, a guy slept naked between her sheets. She had known his name last night, at least briefly, but she could not for the life of her remember it now. Parting her robe a little, she could see the hickey he had left on her right breast, just above the nipple, and she recalled a fleeting moment of panic when he had clamped his mouth down on her.

He had sucked, but had not drawn blood, and she had eventually relaxed.

"This isn't you, Carol," she said out loud. She let the coffee mug roll to a stop. She had been behaving strangely, breaking her own rules, ever since the call from that FBI agent. What was his name? Something Gray.

Something Gray had taken the carefully composed construct that was her life, post–Stella Olemaun, and kicked the foundation out from under it. The whole experience of working with Stella on *30 Days of Night* had been a nightmare, and literally a source of nightmares. Once she realized that Stella was absolutely serious about the story she was telling, Carol's world had shifted. She was a Sarah Lawrence grad, smart and educated and ambitious. She was, at twenty-seven, a full editor at a big New York publishing house. Several of her books had hit the *Times* list, and a couple had won fairly major awards. She was accomplished as all hell, and if she was a bit emotionally brittle, maybe a little cold, that was okay. One thing at a time, and career came first.

Then she had found out that vampires were real, and that shot a huge gaping hole in her worldview. If that was the case—and she could hardly deny it—then which of the many other offbeat ideas she had discounted her entire life might be every bit as true? ESP? Werewolves? Ghosts?

She found herself questioning everything.

She experimented with a dozen different churches, read philosophy books deep into the night. Finally, with the passing of time, she made a kind of peace with herself. She retreated into the womb of rationality as she had always perceived it, with that single deviation. And she rarely allowed herself to think about that.

Her resolve was only eggshell thick, as it turned out. And when Gray—Andrew Gray, that was it—came into her life asking questions, she realized just how farcical her retreat had been. Not thinking about the world's mysteries didn't make them go away. She had been hiding her head, nothing more, like a scared child pulling the sheets up to keep the monsters at bay.

Once that realization overtook her with the force of a hurtling freight train, she was bowled over. Ass over teakettle, and though the metaphor had never made much sense to her, she knew what it felt like. This time, instead of seeking shelter in familiar intellectual harbors, she had surprised herself by venturing, instead, into uncharted waters.

Bare feet shuffled, and then the man from her bedroom appeared in the kitchen doorway. He had put on boxers—striped: red, gray, white—but that was all. He was well built, muscular, solid. His face, now that she saw it in morning light and sober, was not particularly handsome. A small nose, large liquid eyes, lips too thick by half for such a lean face, a chin that barely carried its own weight. His brown hair was curly, matted where he'd been sleeping on it.

"Hey," he said.

"Hey yourself. I made coffee, you want some?"

"Sure," he said. "Got cream?"

She never used it. "There's some milk in the fridge. I don't know how old it is."

Before he poured himself a cup he bent over and kissed her cheek, more like it was expected of him than because he wanted to do it. Maybe it was; Carol didn't know what the current mating rituals were. His face smelled like her: musky, pungent.

He opened the refrigerator—*what the hell is his name?*—and took out a half-gallon carton. Turned it around to find the expiration date. "Yesterday," he said with a shrug. He poured some coffee into a green ceramic mug, added a dollop of the milk, stirred the cup by jostling it from side to side.

"I'm not big on breakfast," Carol admitted. "So I hope you're not hungry."

"I'm fine," he said. He raised the mug toward her. "This is good."

He peered over the top of the mug as he drank, taking in the retro kitchen. The cabinets were midcentury pine, accessorized with stainless steel diner-style accoutrements: sugar dispenser, napkin holder, toaster. The microwave and coffee maker were modern, but everything else spoke of a bygone era that Carol had not personally lived through. "Nice place, uhhh . . ." he said.

Carol smiled. "Look, I don't remember your name either. I've been racking my brain but it just won't come. I'm Carol, not that it matters because when you finish your coffee, you're going."

He smiled, too, and she recalled why she had been drawn to him in the bar the night before. His smile was at once disarming and cocky, full of self-confidence but with a kind of boyish charm. Somehow it made the disparate elements of his face work together in a way they didn't otherwise.

"In that case, I'm Jake."

He had not been Jake the night before, she was sure. She hadn't noticed, or hadn't cared about, the gold band on his left hand the night before, either. Neither fact especially disturbed her. "Wife mind when you don't come home?"

"There's an understanding," Jake said. Or whoever.

"Fine," Carol said quickly. She didn't want him to

bother elaborating. Whether it was a lie or the truth, just listening to it would be more work than she wanted to give it. "Listen, Jake, I have to get to work, so you need to get dressed and get moving."

He downed the rest of his coffee. "Okay."

Her silk robe gapped open as she rose, and she caught him checking out her breast. The hickey was bright red. "If it means anything, I had a good time," she said. She made no move to close the robe. *Let him stare.*

"Me too."

"So what are you waiting for?"

She stared down at the mark again as he came for her, erect . . . and decided that, fuck it, she was calling in late again. Maybe she wouldn't go in to work at all today.

Maybe never again.

Who cares, anyway?

Jake's hands all over her.

It was that moment that Carol Hino felt the cold embrace of despair and briefly longed for the days when ignorance was bliss.

Before she knew the truth.

It was also that moment she wished she'd never heard of motherfucking Stella Olemaun.

17

THE MONTHS AND THE MILES slipped away, passing beneath the wheels of one stolen vehicle after another.

In Pocatello, Andy bought a car at a used car lot. But it cost him too much of his precious cash, especially when he had to pay extra to get the guy to sell it to him without registering or licensing it. He kept it for a couple of months, until its engine seized up outside Birmingham. After that, he went back to stealing them.

He tried to stick to cities, where an unfamiliar face wasn't an object of curiosity. A week, maybe two, in each place.

At first, he wouldn't stay for more than a night or two. Salt Lake City, Pocatello, Butte, Billings. It didn't take him long to figure out that he would run out of cities at that rate. Anyway, he didn't see anyone paying him any attention. At a truck stop outside Casper, he had a minor panic attack when a couple of state troopers came into Hardee's and sat down at the booth next to his, but they ignored Andy, cracked jokes with the girls at the counter, and didn't follow when he left.

Gradually, he began to calm down, and he started sleeping a little better in his succession of cheap rooms. A week each in Denver, Colorado Springs, Albuquerque. Two weeks in Austin. One in Dallas and one in Houston. In New Orleans, he stayed for almost three. Then Jackson, Memphis, Birmingham, Atlanta. Parts of the country he had never seen before.

He didn't spend time touring around, though. Almost every night, he plugged his laptop into the phone jack and went online. There were the bloodsucker chatrooms, which he quickly discovered were populated by wannabes and Goth teens looking for a new way to scare Mom and Dad. But he lurked anyway, hoping to pick up some stray bits of information. In every city, he haunted libraries and used bookstores, seeking out books he hadn't seen before. He started reading obituaries and estate sale notices, trying to find government employees whose families might unload documents that would further his search.

Bit by tiny bit, he put together new information.

Three days before Christmas, at a church rummage sale in Little Rock, he found a notebook in which a man wrote about an experience he had survived. Most of the spiral-bound notebook was a mundane account of an average life spent working, paying bills, tending the yard, and going to church. But toward the back, the man described an early morning visitor to the grocery store he ran. *"He was thin as a twig,"* the man wrote.

"His hair was windblown and his skin was as pale as Momma's china. When I asked could I help him, he faced me and I could see his teeth, long and pointed and dripping blood. He had been gnawing on fresh beef in the butcher case.

"I turned and ran. At first I thought he was following me, but then I saw a reflection in the shop's doors as I ran out and he was still back there in the butcher section, shoving his face into some of my most expensive cuts.

"I went straight to church, where I felt the cross and the power of the Lord would protect me. Prayed for an hour, and then I went back to the shop, my knees trembling all the way. The door stood open but the inside was empty. The butcher case was a mess, blood everywhere and bits of meat. The odd man was gone, though, and never come back while I was there."

Andy added the notebook to the soft-side suitcase he carried everywhere, containing the accounts he deemed most likely to be true. This one was strange—could vampires live on animal blood? Maybe it had been a new one, like Paul when he had subsisted on vermin.

Most encounters he learned of were nonsense. But there were a few, spread out in space and time, which rang true. Several had been posted to online bulletin boards dedicated to Stella Olemaun's book, and he found the percentage of obviously bogus ones to real encounters was lower there.

Of course, he assumed, there would have been many more accounts if more of the victims survived.

* * *

Christmas.

He couldn't dodge it altogether. Radios and Muzak systems bombarded him with holiday music. TV was awash in commercials and station breaks and programming celebrating the season.

From Little Rock, Andy landed in Tulsa, where people seemed to go out of their way to be cheerful and wish him a Merry Christmas. And a Happy New Year, many threw in.

Somehow, he didn't expect to find much happiness there. He missed Monica, Sara, and Lisa fiercely. Christmas morning he sat inside a bland motel room, unable to get comfortable on the too soft mattress or the too stiff, upright desk chair. He shook his head at his own stupidity. *A grown man should be able to be alone.* He had never liked it, as long as he could remember. As a kid he always had a radio by his bed, with an FM station turned down low so only he could hear it, hoping that the music would chase away the loneliness and the nightmares. When he went to college and lived in a dorm, he used an earplug so he wouldn't annoy his roommate.

After the Academy, Andy was a young single man. He threw himself into the job, not dating much. Every night that he was home and alone, he put music on the stereo or turned on the TV. When he met Monica Schwann—and, more to the point, discovered that she truly liked him and enjoyed his company—he was thrilled. Not because she was the most beautiful creature he'd ever met, or the brightest or most fun to be around—that particular honor had always gone to Paul Norris. But she was someone who would be there through the long hours of darkness. When she slept curled next to him, he didn't need to have the electronics going.

He wasn't sure, in those early days, if he was in love. He thought he was, but he didn't think he'd ever been in love in the past, and didn't have much grounds for comparison. He didn't hear violins or harp music. Flowers were just as colorful as they'd ever been, but he felt no compulsion to sniff or pick them.

Two years later, when Paul Norris met Sally Winston, it had been like two kindred souls spotting each other in a sea of blandness. They were both vigorous, sexual people. Their attraction was incendiary, so much so that others standing nearby were at risk of being burned. Watching from a safe distance, Andy couldn't help feeling envy. He had never had that heat with anyone.

By that time he was convinced that he did love Monica, and that love grew month by month, year by year, until he came to believe that if there was such a thing as soulmates, they were it. He still didn't like being by himself, especially at night, but that was only a problem when he was away from home on a case.

He had never had psychoanalysis and didn't think he wanted to sit on some shrink's leather couch and talk about the various ways in which he was not altogether well. There were too many, he feared, and he didn't want to find out there were more than he thought. On those occasions when he did examine his own psyche, he figured it might have stemmed from being the only child of parents who were cold and distant; parents who acted, most of the time, as if even one kid was too many. His father's death—instigated, just to complicate the issue, by himself—and the resulting rift between him and his mother just added to the brew, he expected. Alone problems feeding into feelings of abandonment. But he didn't want to blame his folks for his own shortcomings. If it came to that, there was enough material there to spread the blame far and wide.

This is getting me nowhere. Instead of stewing in it, he went for a walk, zipping up the cheap coat he had bought against a stiff, chill wind off the Arkansas River. The leaden sky turned the river pewter.

Andy picked up a pebble and threw it sidearm toward the water, skipping it three times. Not satisfied with that effort, he watched the concentric circles spread from the skip points, and when they dissipated enough he tried another. Twelve rocks later, he was sweating in his jacket. He peeled it off and started in on another batch of stones, one after another after another. Now he was spreading circles across the width of the river. No longer trying to skip them, he arced them high and dropped them in, working on placement, trying to make the rings inscribe patterns on the surface.

A couple walking hand in hand stopped to watch him for a minute, bemused by his single-minded, almost frantic determination. He spared only the briefest glance for them and returned to his efforts.

Twenty minutes later, he dropped onto a bench. Sweat stained the armpits of his shirt, ran down his temples and neck. His ribs and right shoulder were beginning to throb and he knew they'd ache later. But he felt better than he had in days. Working out his increasing frustration, his stored anger, in pointless physicality had been a tonic.

He would try to keep that in mind, try to exercise more and brood less, while he remained on the road and on the hunt.

Via one of the *30 Days of Night* boards, Andy found an ex-cop in Cape Girardeau, Missouri. After trading emails for a couple of weeks, the guy agreed to talk to him face-to-face. They met in a dark, quiet bar called Henry's Alibi Room.

Pete Cookson looked like he hadn't been away from the bar in a very long time. Andy couldn't quite tell if there was a cushion on his stool, or if the pole was just inserted directly into his ass. He swiveled around, but never stood while Andy was there.

When Andy came in, there were about thirty seconds of pleasantries, and then Cookson gave him a gloomy, alcoholic's sigh. "Might as well get done what you came here to do," he said.

"You want to move to a booth or something?" Andy asked.

"Here's fine." Pete Cookson was a big guy, a beefy high school football hero type, but his bulk had turned to fat. His blond hair was still cropped short, and his eyes still had the suspicious gaze of a longtime cop. But his chin had merged with his bull neck, and his shoulders sloped down toward a gut that bulged over his belt. He had no lap left, just stomach and knees. He cocked his cannonball of a head toward the skinny bartender. "Gus won't pay any mind."

"Gus?" Andy asked. "What happened to Henry?"

"Died," Pete said. He didn't elaborate. Gus wandered over, looked expectantly at them. Pete just nodded, but Gus seemed to know what that meant.

"Coke," Andy said. The booze smelled inviting, but he'd been dry for more than half a year now and wanted to keep it that way. Gus raised a single eyebrow, as if to say, *What the hell's a teetotaler doing spending time with Pete Cookson?*

The two men sat silently while Gus fetched the drinks. What he put in front of Pete looked like a glass—the same size as Andy's soda—full of vodka. Pete tilted his head back and took a big swallow, then swiveled to face Andy.

"I posted on that message board because I didn't want to talk about it to anyone," he began. "But I just couldn't keep my mouth shut about it, either."

"Why don't you pretend I never read the post and

just tell me what happened?" Andy suggested. Afraid of spooking the ex-cop, he had not told Pete that he was with the Bureau. Pete hadn't asked why he wanted to know about it, but Andy had tried to impress upon him, via email, that it was very important to him. He figured Pete had just held it all in for too long and was busting to spill it.

Pete nodded slowly, took a smaller sip of his drink. His breath reminded Andy of a doctor's office. "I was heading home one night after a late shift. Spent eight hours in a squad car, and then another forty minutes to home, since my wife and I lived out of town."

"This was here in Cape Girardeau?"

"Yeah," Pete answered. "But I'd inherited a small farm from my dad, and we wanted to raise the kids out there. We only ever had the one, James, after my dad. He was about six then—this is all four years ago, now. So I was driving home, but had only just left the station a couple minutes before. I thought I saw a sudden movement out of the corner of my eye, down a narrow side street. I wasn't sure what I had seen, but if you know anything about cops you know we operate on instinct as much as anything else.

"I braked to a stop and got out of the car. Left the door open so it wouldn't slam shut, pulled the keys so the car wouldn't ding at me. Walked back to the corner. I had changed into street clothes but my service weapon was still in a holster on my hip, so I drew it."

He took a bigger drink, put the glass down hard on

the scarred wooden bar. "When I reached the corner I put my face close to the wall and looked down, showing just one eye and my weapon. What I saw there was what had caught my eye in the first place—a man and a woman struggling. Except now I had a better look, come to find out the woman was the aggressor. She had this guy—not some little twerp, either, but a good-sized fella—up against a wall. He was swinging at her, landing some good shots, but she had her hands against his shoulders, pressing him back, and she was leaning in toward him. I couldn't tell if it was rough sex got a little out of hand, or what.

"Either way, I figured it didn't belong on the streets. I stepped out from behind the corner, took a firing stance, aiming my weapon at the woman, and announced myself. Told them both to stop what they were doing and lay flat on the ground with their hands above their heads.

"Instead of obeying, she picked the man up—hoisted him right up over her head like a weightlifter pressing an easy free weight. I probably should have opened fire right then, but I was too surprised by what I was seeing to do anything. Surprised and wishing I had backup. She held him there for a few seconds—like she was showing off—and then she *threw* him at me.

"Now, I was standing probably thirty, forty feet away. Even so, I had to dodge the guy's body when it flew at me. Of course, I lost my bead on the woman when I did. But I tried to keep her in sight and just heard the man scrape pavement behind me.

"I called to the woman and told her again to get down on her fucking face and surrender. I don't mind saying, I was pretty freaked out by this point. I didn't know if she was cranked up on PCP or what. She heard me but again refused to surrender. Instead, she came toward me with her hands out and her mouth open. Now I could see that her fingers looked more like some kind of freaky-ass claws. I shouted again, but she just hissed at me and kept coming. There was blood on her chin, I remember being surprised by that."

Pete dry-swallowed, his liquor glass standing forgotten on the bar. His voice was husky and low and Andy could tell he felt uncomfortable talking about this experience. "At this point I didn't want to waste time or ammunition with a warning shot. I aimed my weapon at her midsection and squeezed off two."

"And what happened?"

"Nothing at all. I know I hit her. She was close enough, and coming closer, and there's no doubt in my mind that the bullets didn't miss. But they also didn't do anything. I fired three more. They slowed her a little, but that was all.

"Next thing I knew she was on me. One of those claws raked my chest, ripped my shirt—I could show you the scars."

"That's okay," Andy said. "What next?"

"She bowled me right over. I got off one more shot, just as she plowed into me, and it hit her in the neck. She rolled off me, screaming this terrible, high-pitched wail. With one of her arms she swatted me again, knocking my head against the pavement. I guess I blacked out for a few minutes.

"When I was able to stand up again, she was gone. I went to check on the guy, to see what kind of shape he was in. He wasn't very good—he had suffered pavement burns and scraped a bunch of the skin off his arms and face. He was weak and I thought maybe suffering from shock. He tried to talk, but he was just babbling, not making any sense. I questioned him, tried to find out about his attacker. He just kept complaining about his neck, and touching it, and finally I looked at it, wiped some of his blood away, and saw a jagged rip in his throat.

"Right then I ran to the car and called for a wagon to come and get him. Blood ran from the wound—not spurting, she hadn't cut the jugular or anything, but it kept coming. It was almost like she wanted a slow leak and not a flood.

"While we waited for the ambulance, I could see him fading, but I didn't know what I could do for him. I tried to apply pressure to the neck wound, but didn't want to crush his windpipe or anything. Couldn't tourniquet it. Anyway, there were all those other wounds, and God knew what kinds of internal injuries, from being thrown so far.

"He died while we waited. I could hear the siren getting closer, and I was talking to him, trying to keep him conscious, keep him with me. It was no good, though. By the time they showed up, and then a squad car right behind, he was gone."

"That must have been tough," Andy said.

"Yeah. But while I was waiting, and then after in the middle of all the activity, describing what had gone down, being interrogated by internal affairs, by my own fellow officers . . . all I kept thinking about was . . . vampires. I didn't want to say the word, or even think it to myself. But how else was I going to explain what had happened? I mean, this isn't the goddamn movies, you know? You probably think I'm fuckin' nuts, just like they did. But I saw what I saw. Nothing can change that. And I put half a dozen slugs into her without phasing her. She had blood on her face like I had surprised her when she was drinking.

"I took a couple of days' leave, and all I could do was sit and think about it. The more I did the more convinced I got. Tina got pissed off because I wouldn't pay her any attention. After my leave I went back to work and told the chief everything. I used the word vampire and explained why I thought that.

"He sat and listened to everything that I had to say. I thought I was getting through to him, but when I was done he gave me the card of a psychiatrist who had a contract with the department. He said I could come back to work once the shrink had cleared me for duty. I could tell by the way he said it that he didn't really think I would be cleared. I asked him flat out, and he said I was probably best off choosing a different career. I handed over my badge and gun, on the spot.

"Well, you can probably guess the rest of it. I couldn't find work, started drinking too much. Tina left me and took James, and finally I sold the farm and got a little place in town. To this day, I couldn't tell you what I saw for sure, but to this day I'm convinced that it really was a . . . I mean, what else would do those things? The more I studied up on 'em, the more I felt convinced that I was right."

He stopped talking, drained his glass, and waved it at Gus. The bartender nodded and brought him another. Pete looked back at Andy, and his skin was sallow, almost gray. "I'm still living on what I got from the farm, but it won't last me much longer. I suppose as long as I can pay my rent and my bar bill I'll be okay, but after that?

"They say suicide is a sin. I'm starting to think it's the only reasonable option."

18

HECTOR FLORES'S MAJOR PASSION, besides the Bureau, was restoring classic cars. He enjoyed removing the wear and tear of the years, stripping them down to their original basic selves, and then caressing and guiding them to new glory. Currently he was working on a 1967 Mustang that had been parked on the street, a few blocks from the ocean, for several years. It had been repainted to a canary yellow—an abomination against the laws of man and God, Hector decided—and the time in the sun and salt air had faded the paint to a kind of sickly pale color, like a lemon squeezed out and left to dry.

Just now he was fighting rust and had run out of naval jelly. So he made a run to his local Pep Boys for a few new cans. The spring day was bright and sunny and he drove his '73 Trans Am—fire engine red, the one car he had restored that he couldn't bring himself to sell—with the radio blaring classic rock tunes as loud as he could stand.

When he worked on the cars, he tried to put Bureau business out of his mind. He was not always successful, and today was one of the bad ones. He'd been looking into Operation Red-Blooded since hearing about it from Andy Gray. He hadn't made much progress—the Bureau was nothing if not adept at keeping secrets. But Hector had put in a lot of years and done favors for a lot of people. He was a political guy, a player in the halls of power, and he knew what levers to pull, but even so he kept finding himself shut out.

He had learned enough to know, however, that the Bureau did not, after all, discount the existence of vampires. To the contrary, it had expended a lot of person-hours and resources studying them. And possibly more keeping that fact quiet.

Coming out of the store carrying a plastic bag full of the rust remover in small cans, he saw a familiar figure walking toward him. Even on his day off, wearing a Hawaiian shirt and khakis, Dan Bradstreet looked overly businesslike. His posture was rigidly erect, his casual pants had a crease in them, his shoes were polished. He smiled at Hector as he approached. "This is a surprise," he said.

"Just needed to get rid of some rust on the Mustang I'm restoring," Hector told him. The two men shook hands. "What brings you here?"

Dan blinked in the sunlight, shielded his eyes with his hand, the one that Andy Gray nearly shot off. *Brilliant surgeon. Hell of a job,* Hector thought. "I don't do my own mechanical work, but I need a new steering wheel cover. One of those leather ones, I was thinking.

But if they're too hard to put on, then maybe rubber. Do you have one?"

"Always," Hector said. He wanted to protect the steering wheels in his cars from soil or the oils on his hands, so he invariably kept them covered. "The leather kind. There's nothing to it."

"Can I see?" Dan asked.

Hector was a little surprised that Dan was so worried about being able to put on a steering wheel cover. He was generally a very capable guy. But Hector was always happy to show off his cars, and talk about them, so he led Dan to the Trans Am.

"That's a beauty," Dan said as they approached it.

"Thanks," Hector said. He unlocked the door and leaned in to toss the cans of naval jelly onto the floor on the passenger side. Dan's shadow fell across him, and he heard a familiar but unexpected sound. He froze.

"Dan, what the fuck?" He didn't know what was going on, why Dan had pulled a gun on him, but he was still sure he could defuse the situation. "Is there a problem?"

Dan didn't answer, but he leaned forward more—Hector could almost feel the agent close behind him. He was trapped by the car's interior—no room to maneuver. Dan had the position and he had the weapon—Hector's was holstered at the small of his back, under a light windbreaker, but he couldn't even make a move for it without Dan knowing.

"Dan, talk to me," he said, desperation growing in him.

Dan stayed silent for a long moment. Finally, he spoke. "I'm sorry, Hector. I like you. But you should have kept your nose out of things that don't concern you."

Sweat beaded on Hector's temples while he struggled to find an appropriate response. Nothing came to him.

A double tap, back of the skull. Two loud reports in a busy parking lot, with engines revving and car doors slamming. Dan casually straightened, replacing the small .22 in his hip holster, covered by the long tails of the Hawaiian shirt, and returned to his car. A new silver Crown Vic replaced the one Andy Gray had stolen. Most people wouldn't give it, or him, a second look.

He was genuinely sorry to have to take out his boss. Hector Flores had done a lot for him at the Bureau. Trouble was, Hector believed that he was Dan's ultimate boss, and that just wasn't the case. Operation Red-Blooded had assigned Dan to Los Angeles in the first place, and it was that op's chief to whom Dan really reported.

That superior had heard too many stories about Hector poking around the operation. Subtle warnings hadn't chased him away. And everyone knew that Hector Flores was a tenacious bastard. He wasn't likely to give up, and he was getting closer all the time.

So it had fallen to Dan to take care of the situation. As he pulled out of the parking lot, he saw that a passerby had finally noticed something odd about the Trans Am. Dan drove away, relieved that it was over.

Taken care of.

Andy stayed a few more days in Cape Girardeau. He convinced Pete Cookson to tell him where the sighting had taken place, and even though there was little chance of it being repeated, he staked out the narrow street for a couple of nights, sitting in the most recent stolen car.

When that proved fruitless, he dropped in on Albert Kennan, the police chief, the next morning. This time, he showed his phony Andrew Hertz Bureau ID. After a few minutes of chewing the fat, Andy closed the door to the chief's office and sat down in a visitor's chair. Kennan went to his own desk and sat, regarding Andy thoughtfully. He was an older guy, probably a lifelong cop, Andy guessed, with thick white hair and leathered skin. His uniform was blue and light gray and his Sam Browne belt creaked when he took his seat.

"I don't want to take up too much of your time, Chief Kennan," Andy said. "But I'm following a lead on an important case—let's just say it has national security ramifications and leave it at that—and it's brought me to you."

The police chief gave Andy a steady smile. "Well, what is it I can do for you?"

"You had an incident here in town, a few years back," Andy said. "A woman apparently attacked a male victim. An off-duty officer interceded, but was unable to save the victim. The attacker, although allegedly shot several times, escaped."

A nod that gave nothing away. "I have a vague recollection of the incident."

"I'd like to see the file, please."

A long pause. Chief Kennan put his big hands, palms down, on the desk. His rugged jaw tightened. The natural, relaxed ease he had demonstrated until this point was gone. "I'll see if I can put my finger on it."

He rose and left the room without another word. Andy sat and waited, looking at photos on the wall of Chief Kennan with local dignitaries and even the Attorney General of the United States: a man who, in Andy's view, confused patriotism with religion, feared naked bodies and calico cats, and had done absolutely nothing to further the advance of law enforcement. Fortunately, as far as Andy was concerned, the man was resigning soon, or being forced out. A few minutes later, the chief returned. His hands were empty.

"I'm sorry, Mr. Hertz," he said. He didn't sound sorry at all. "We had a flood here, a couple years back. You might have heard about it. Had some water get into the building here, and some of the files got ruined. We were in the process of scanning everything in and saving it digitally, but that was one of the files that hadn't yet been transferred. I'm afraid it's completely gone."

"I see." Andy stood. He could insist on searching the files himself, but he didn't think it was going to get him anywhere. Chief Kennan had been gone just long enough to take the file and hide it somewhere else, if he was that concerned about keeping it out of sight. Or he could have destroyed it long ago. Or it could really have been a victim of flood damage, as he claimed. "Well, thanks for your help anyway," he said. He let himself out of the office and the building, hoping that no one had run the stolen Buick Rendezvous's plates while he was inside.

Back in the car, he considered going to the hospital to see if he could find medical records or a coroner's report on the victim. But without a name or a precise date, that would be a long, involved process, and he wasn't sure what benefit he could get from it. Yes, it seemed evident that a vampire attack had happened here. They probably happened all over the place—it was just finding the right person to talk about it that was a problem. This particular attack had been officially covered up, as usually seemed to be the case, and that probably happened all the time, too.

He decided he had learned as much about this case as he was likely to, and digging up more wouldn't help him unless it would lead him to the vampire herself. Instead, he went and stood in the biting cold at the bank of the Mississippi, watching the broad watery avenue. It came from the north in a mighty sweep and flowed south, bisecting the country. Did these creatures come from the north, too? Were Barrow and places like it, lands where the darkness lasted for weeks at a time, the original breeding grounds for them?

He had tried to imagine a reason that sunlight would kill them and hadn't been able to. Maybe it was an evolutionary thing, the result of their birth in the dark places. If he'd lived, Dr. Saxon at UCLA might have been able to shed some light. Or Angelica Foster, if she had been able to continue her researches.

For the first time in months, he remembered the email Angelica had sent him. She had written that Saxon's odd message had appeared on some kind of Internet message board. If that was the case, he reasoned, it might still be there. There might even be replies or other comments, and it was even possible that there were more scientists out there working on the question, even now. Andy had been focused on law enforcement issues and the vampire "community" as a whole, but he hadn't been paying attention to the science.

As urgent as getting back online was, he had been in Cape Girardeau too long, especially since he had now attracted the attention of the authorities. He rushed to his car and headed north, following the course of the great river. At the far edge of Springfield, Illinois, he checked into an inexpensive tourist motel and plugged in his laptop.

It only took a few minutes to find the original message board where Angelica had located Dr. Saxon's exchange about the "Immortal Cell." The discussion had died there. Andy was convinced it was not a final death, however, any more than a vampire's "death" was final. The issue was too unique, too troubling to be ignored by people with curious scientific minds.

It must have been continued, even if only in private emails and conversations and lab work.

He jotted down the screen names of the people who had been involved in the original thread, and the name of Felicia Reisner of the University of Wisconsin, the researcher whose original paper had been the catalyst. Another half hour of digging turned up contact information for some of them. Unplugging the laptop, he started making phone calls.

Most of the people he reached couldn't help him. They were biologists or chemists or grad students who checked the boards on occasion but hadn't paid much attention to that thread or even remembered it all this time later.

He couldn't track down Felicia Reisner until evening. By that time he had started to worry about the motel phone bill he was running up, with the surcharges they added to every call. He had tried not to skip out on motel bills—stealing cars was bad enough, but at least insurance would repay his victims. Andy was a lifelong law enforcement officer and he understood the problem with that justification—the more insurance companies paid out, the more costs they passed along to their customers. They were for-profit businesses, after all. But although it was an obvious justification, he had to live with it, since there was no other way to get around undetected.

He caught Felicia Reisner as she was sitting down to dinner with her family. She sounded distracted, a little rushed, and not at all interested in talking to him. He stressed the FBI angle, national security, and could practically hear her bristle. "Why don't you just yank my library and bookstore records?" she asked. "Tap my phone, while you're at it."

Andy could hear her husband in the background imploring her to calm down. "Ms. Reisner," Andy said, "I'm not trying to harass you or investigate you in any way, believe me. I'm only interested in some of the ramifications of an article you published called 'The Immortal Cell.' I'm specifically interested in any discussion you may have had with Dr. Amos Saxon of UCLA about it. Dr. Saxon, you may or may not know, was murdered. I'm trying to find out why, and by whom, and I think it has to do with some thoughts he had about these matters."

Momentary silence, then: "We live in a strange world, if scholars are being killed because of their research," Felicia Reisner responded. "But then, it's not like Socrates wasn't forced to drink the hemlock Kool-Aid, so I suppose I shouldn't be surprised." She let out a long sigh. "There really is nothing new under the sun, is there?" When Andy didn't reply, she went on. "Very well, I have some free time tomorrow between eleven and noon. My office is in the Biochemistry Addition. Anyone on campus can point you to it."

Andy agreed, and hung up. He crossed to the window, pulled back the curtain. In the glow from the parking lot lights he could see snow flurries.

Madison, he thought glumly. *Great.* He had been hoping to head south again, to escape the worst of winter.

Instead, he would be driving into the thick of it. And if he had to be in Madison in the morning, he'd be leaving right away.

He hadn't unpacked anything from his suitcases yet, hadn't even slept since arriving in Springfield. He stretched out on top of the bed to grab a couple of hours before skipping on the bill and hitting the road.

INTERLUDE

THE GOOD NEWS was that Stella Olemaun was dead.

The bad news—well, there were bucketloads of that.

She was dead, but she—and her husband, Eben, former Sheriff of Barrow, Alaska—had been turned themselves. Just like Paul.

Paul Norris didn't pretend to understand their transformation.

But he was damn sure pissed off by it.

He had gone to Barrow for the dark, 'cause all roads, it seemed, led to Barrow. Arriving there, he had met up with many other vampires, the first ones he'd been able to locate since being changed himself. He had immediately felt a kinship with these creatures, these night dwellers. They came in every race and size and type, but what they had in common was stronger than any differences.

They were defined, now, by their hunger.

And at once, they accepted Paul as one of their own. Upon learning of his background with the Bureau, they were quick to listen to his advice on strategy and tactics. They were preparing for another assault on the town, which was armed and fortified against them in a way it hadn't been three years earlier, during the first siege of Barrow.

The residents knew what to expect, this time. Or they thought they did.

But they didn't expect Paul Norris. They failed to anticipate the rage that had built up in the vampire community against them for surviving and rebuilding, and against Stella Olemaun for writing her motherfucking book. With Paul's guidance and help, the vampires attacked.

No, scratch that. The vampires went to fucking *war.*

The people fought back—some courageously, others less so. The vampires, however, evaded their defenses, made it inside the fences and razor wire. Victory began to seem assured.

And just when the sweetest prize of all—the young son of the town's new Sheriff—was within Paul's grasp, Stella and Eben appeared.

And they proceeded to kick the unliving shit out of Paul Norris.

Norris retreated to Prudhoe Bay, where he planned to wait out the rest of the winter in a nest a few of the other survivors of this second siege had developed there. He healed quickly, now that he was undead, but he still had aches and pains left over from the beating he'd suffered at the hands of the Olemauns.

What they hadn't done was kill him. He would probably never know why. He was dumped outside the house where he had found the boy. His head was torn mostly off, but not completely. Most of the bones in his body were broken, most of his internal organs ruptured. He was sure he had looked dead, but there was a spark of life left in him.

And then, some dumbass yokel, a hunter/trapper named John Ikos, had found him and dragged him to a remote cabin outside town. Ikos was curious, as it turned out, or he fancied himself some kind of hero.

He ended up being just someone who made a very bad mistake.

When Paul came around again, inside Ikos's primitive den, the hunter said that he had planned to cut him up and send the pieces to scientists and law enforcement agencies.

Like the Olemauns, John Ikos had believed Norris was dead.

He fooled them all.

Norris kept Ikos talking while he regained his strength. Finally, the man turned a shotgun on him. Paul returned fire, blowing out the hunter's kneecap. After all he'd been through, shotgun pellets hurt like hell, but they weren't anywhere near life threatening.

Paul walked away from John Ikos. The guy didn't know it, but he had probably saved Paul. If he'd remained in town, either the Olemauns or someone else would have realized they'd left the job undone and finished him off. By taking him away, Ikos had enabled him to survive . . . to heal.

Still . . . Norris meant what he said when he declared that he'd had it with this crazy fuck-ass town.

Paul rose with a wince from the low couch he had been sitting on. Still healing, apparently. A familiar smell had piqued his interest, and from the next room he could hear happy sounds. This nest, inside a big commercial space that had once been a grocery store, housed six vampires, four females and one other male. The cavernous main space was used for lounging and sleeping, but there was also a warren of back rooms that had been used for offices, storerooms, staff kitchen, and the like.

Paul walked down the wide, carpeted corridor into the tile-floored kitchen. Inside, Samantha and Clea feasted on a teenaged girl, still wearing the cheerleading outfit they'd found her in.

Paul grinned at the sight.

"Got enough for one more?" he asked.

Samantha was just leaning forward to clamp her mouth over an open neck wound, but she paused long enough to say, "Get your own." Clea, however, returned his smile and jerked her head, beckoning him. "I can share."

Paul joined her at the side of the nearly lifeless girl, enjoying the press of Clea's body against his. The softness of her substantial bosom against his arm, the firmness of her thigh. He hadn't had a woman since being changed—not a willing one—and suddenly he realized he missed it.

First things first, though. Clea's face was slick with the teen's blood. The girl smelled fresh, vibrant, full of life—at least, until she had run into Clea and Samantha. With a nod of approval from Clea, Paul bent his head to the wound, bumping into Samantha as he did. A pumping heart fired rich, hot blood into his waiting mouth, and he swallowed it down greedily.

Times like this, he could not begin to remember why he had ever liked being human.

19

"VAMPIRES?"

The way Felicia Reisner repeated the word, as if a sneer could be made audible, left no doubt as to her feelings about the subject. "I'm sorry, Mr. Hertz, on the phone I mistook you for a serious person."

He shifted uncomfortably in his seat. Her office was modern and spacious, with blond wood bookcases and desk, but her dark leather guest chairs were cold and uninviting. "The saying is 'serious as a heart attack,' " Andy said. "But in this case, it's more like 'serious as the intentional murder of a university professor and two police officers, and the torching of his home.' "

She had started to pick up a file folder on her desk, as if wanting him to simply slink away, but now she put it down. "Again, I'm very sorry to hear about Dr. Saxon's death. I didn't know about the police officers. And you'll forgive me for not being up on my jurisdictional affairs, but how is any of that FBI business?"

"It relates to a case I'm working on," Andy said. The answer came easily to him now. "It all ties together. I know that Dr. Saxon was intrigued by your 'Immortal Cell' theory, and I know that he thought it could apply to work he was doing to prove the existence of vampires in the world."

That word again. She stiffened when she heard it. She was tall and slender, pretty, with chin-length auburn hair and cinnamon eyes. Her features were neatly arranged, as if someone had put together a composite of the most generally pleasing Caucasian features, but her complexion was just dark enough to suggest some mixing of races in her background. "I'm afraid I just don't see how."

"College professors are supposed to be open-minded," he said. "So try for a minute. Everybody knows a little something about fictional vampires, so use them as a point of reference if you need to. They live virtually forever, as long as they have the right sustenance. They heal rapidly. Killing them is very hard—decapitation or sunlight are the only sure ways. Couldn't they be living examples of your theory?"

"I always thought it took a stake through the heart, or a silver bullet."

"The silver bullet is for werewolves, and the stake, we believe, is fictional," Andy said. "Work with me here, please, Dr. Reisner."

Felicia Reisner tapped her fingernails—brownish red, nicely manicured—on the smooth surface of her desk. They matched her angora sweater almost exactly. "I'm trying to, Mr. Hertz," she replied. "It's just . . . I don't like to see science abused in the service of the absurd."

"If it was true—if I was telling you the truth—then

you could be instrumental in saving a lot of lives," Andy pressed. "But put that aside for the moment and focus on the theoretical. Could the cells you describe do that?"

"We're all just collections of cellular material," Felicia said. "So theoretically, if someone's cellular structure was composed of these cells instead of normal human cells, then yes, possibly." She stopped, chewed on her lower lip for a second. "Yes. Someone could become immortal. Or near enough. As long as . . ."

"As long as what?"

"You know about the seven-year rule? That our bodily cells are essentially replaced, about every seven years?"

"I've heard it," he said. "That explains why some people grow out of, or into, allergies and the like?"

"That's right," she said. "I was going to say, the person would not only have to have an abundance of the immortal cells, but also would have to replace those with the same type."

"Could that happen? I recognize that we're moving into the even more hypothetical realm, Dr. Reisner, and I assure you that this is for my own information only. It won't get back to anyone."

"Well . . . of course it could. I wouldn't have hypothesized the existence of these cells if I hadn't seen evidence of them. Never in the kinds of quantities you're talking about. But they do exist. I've studied them. I have samples."

Andy stood up and walked to the window, looked out at blowing snow. The campus was already carpeted in white, students and staff moving about heavily bundled against the cold. Walking to her building, Andy had seen posters for a Valentine's dance, reminding him that February was half over. So much time gone by already, and he had barely begun to scratch the surface of this whole vampire deal.

"Could they be spread, from one person to another? Like a virus?"

"There is much that we know about how the human body works, Mr. Hertz. The strides we've made, just in the past few decades, are enormous. Sequencing human DNA—do you have any idea what that would have meant to people fifty years ago? If they could even comprehend it?"

"I'm afraid that's not really my area of expertise, Dr. Reisner. I read about it, but I don't really know what it means."

"It's not important to this discussion," she said. "Just an example. The point is, over these past few decades, even while we've made incredible leaps in our understanding, we've also learned that there is still so much that we don't know. Ebola took us by surprise. Avian flu. Hell, AIDS. We're only just now getting a handle on that—treatment, not cure. The way it was able to mutate, to keep itself ahead of the drugs we were throwing at it. We can't even beat cancer yet, and we've known about that forever, practically. The point, Mr.

Hertz, is that I don't know if those cells could spread like a virus. I would suspect not—that isn't typically how cells reproduce. But I haven't yet been able to determine how these particular cells do reproduce. So the answer has to be a qualified maybe."

Andy turned away from the window. Felicia had swiveled in her leather desk chair and sat looking at him. The irritation she had expressed earlier was gone. "Can I ask you to play along a little more, Dr. Reisner?"

She smiled. Nice, even white teeth. Andy appreciated that all the more after having seen what vampires' mouths looked like. "What the hell, I've come this far."

"If we accept that there are vampires—that your immortal cells somehow play a role in helping them live indefinitely, as long as they are fed—then what other elements come into play? Is there anything else specifically that they need to survive? How can we use this knowledge to find and eliminate them?"

Felicia opened her mouth to answer, but then she stopped. "Can we get out of here?" she asked. "I mean—I have colleagues in this building, students. I'd hate for someone to overhear this conversation and get the wrong idea. There's a coffee shop not far away, and I don't know about you but I could use a hot drink."

Andy agreed. She pulled a hooded cloth overcoat from a closet and a few minutes later they were tromping across campus, hands jammed into their pockets. She had snugged her hood up but she walked with her face to the sky, apparently enjoying the sensation of snowflakes falling on it. "You know it's still safe to catch them on your tongue, Mr. Hertz? Not much acid snow problem. Not yet, anyway. Give that one a few more years."

"I haven't done it in a long time," he said.

"Try it. It's never too late to recapture childhood pleasures."

He did as she said, tilting his head skyward and sticking his tongue out. The snowflakes tickled, melting fast and turning into minute drops of water. He laughed, then caught himself laughing, surprised.

It had been a very long time since he'd done that, too.

The coffee shop smelled wonderful—coffees and teas and cinnamon, which reminded Andy of Felicia's oddly light brown eyes, and caramel and other scents he couldn't even isolate all joining together to create a kind of olfactory feast. The place wasn't large but its mismatched vintage tables were tucked into small crannies, so they felt private. Andy had ordered house blend coffee, and Felicia was brewing herbal tea in a small blue ceramic pot with pictures of butterflies glazed on it. Sonny Rollins blew a tenor sax on hidden speakers, softly enough that people could have conversations but loud enough to be listened to if that's what one wanted to do.

She fiddled with the tea bag's paper tag while she waited for it to steep. "I've been thinking about your question," she said after a while.

"And?"

"I don't want to answer it." His face must have registered his disappointment, because she backtracked immediately. "I mean, not in exactly the way you asked it. I'm not sure it's the right question, or at least it's only part of it."

"Which means what, exactly?" Andy asked. He sipped his coffee. Even with cream and sugar in it, it was still too hot to drink. Which, given that he was still freezing from the walk, was a good thing.

Felicia poured a little of her tea into her mug, checked it, then filled the mug. "Okay, if we assume the existence of vampires—which is a huge assumption, and one that I'm not ready to make yet—then there are several things that have to be true. I'm not speaking strictly as a biochemist anymore, but I guess as a . . . as a concerned citizen, let's say."

"I'm all ears," Andy said.

"We're proceeding from the initial assumption, then," she declared again. "There are vampires. They possess an abundance of immortal cells, making themselves virtually immortal. Very hard to destroy, as you said, and with incredible recuperative abilities. And somehow, they can reproduce, turning other people into vampires. If these things are all true, then there are certain things they need."

"Such as?"

"There's got to be some sort of society," she answered. "These . . . beings can't exist in a vacuum. They must look out for themselves, and each other, in some way. There must be some kind of hierarchy, some structure to their society. Even if they're, I don't know, let's say extrahuman, they were human once. They may have abandoned most of their old ways but they couldn't completely divest themselves. Even animals form family units, packs, and so on, and these beings are far more intellectually developed than animals."

"I'm with you," Andy said. "So there's some kind of pecking order."

"Exactly. They wouldn't be able to survive without some kind of rules, some internal structure. Then they've got to have at least some rudimentary sciences, so they know what they are, how they stay alive. Even if they're not exactly intellectual heavyweights, or if they're mostly bound by tradition, they must have some questions. How do they find out the answers? Have they infiltrated colleges, commercial labs?"

"You would know that better than me." Andy drank some of his coffee, which had cooled sufficiently by this point. It was good. Or he thought it was. But maybe it was sitting here with an attractive woman, having a real conversation, that he was enjoying.

"Every school has its 'vampires,' " Felicia said. "In the most metaphorical sense, of course. Students who sleep the day away and only put in their lab hours late at night, when no one else is around. Every now and then you even hear of students who live in the lab buildings or classroom buildings, showering in the athletic department, brushing their teeth in public restrooms. Sometimes they're excellent students, even geniuses, but they either have never learned to adequately provide for themselves, or they're too wrapped up in study and research to get a job and pay rent or dorm fees. I've never heard of any who have crossed the line into criminal behavior, beyond trespassing and some petty theft. Certainly no bloodsucking or anything like that."

"That's part of the problem," Andy told her. "We don't hear about it. If a body turns up completely drained of blood, the first thing everyone thinks is vampire. The second thing they think is that they'll be ridiculed if they admit what the first thing was. So excuses are invented. Questions aren't asked, or if they are the answers are lies. Cover-ups, because nobody wants to be the first to sound like a lunatic. Americans don't like to be wrong, but we like to be laughed at even less."

Felicia nodded, bringing her mug to her perfectly formed lips. When she drank, she lowered her long lashes over her eyes, as if she took a sensual pleasure in the act. "I can see that," she said, putting the mug down again. "Which means that you, Mr. Hertz, have a big problem in front of you. How do you prove that vampires exist if everyone who might be able to supply the evidence is afraid to do so?"

"Call me Andy," he said. "And I never said I was trying to prove the existence of vampires."

She laughed, and he found himself joining her. "I'm

not stupid, Andy. If I was you wouldn't even be asking me about these things."

Andy raised his coffee cup as if to toast her. "Point taken. You are definitely not stupid."

"So are you going to tell me why? I mean, I get why you would want to. I guess I mean how you found out about them in the first place. And, if I can be frank, I'm sensing that this is kind of a solo crusade on your part."

"What makes you say that?"

She let her gaze roam over him for a moment. "Maybe it's just too much TV, but don't you guys usually come in pairs? And wearing suits that don't look like they've spent a little too much time at the Goodwill? Maybe it's your personal sense of style, and I'm all in favor of that. But I don't think so, and I'm generally a pretty good reader of people. So just who are you, Andy Hertz?"

Andy stalled by taking a big drink of coffee. When he had swallowed it down, he said, "How many questions was that? Do you have the rest of the day?"

She laughed again and glanced at her watch. "I don't," she said. "In fact, I need to run, and now all I've had for lunch is a cup of tea. If my stomach growls during my lecture, I'm blaming you."

"I'll take the fall."

"But I still want answers," she said. "Dinner tomorrow?"

He hadn't given any thought to staying in Madison. Since it was still snowing, though, the roads would likely be treacherous, if they were open at all.

And he couldn't deny that he enjoyed talking to her. It had been so long since he'd had anything but the most basic human interactions, usually across a counter and involving the exchange of cash, that this had come as an unexpected treat.

"Sure," he said. "Dinner sounds good."

"Should I pick you up at your hotel? Where are you staying?"

"I don't know yet," he admitted. "Maybe we can meet at your office and go from there."

"Seven," she said. She stood, but gestured for him to keep his seat. "Stay, finish your coffee," she said. "I have to dash. It was nice meeting you, Andy. Or whoever you are."

He watched her walk away with determined, long-legged strides. At one point, she tilted her head up toward the falling snow, and he laughed out loud.

20

DINNER TONIGHT WITH FELICIA. Andy wasn't sure how to feel about it; she was certainly the closest company he'd been keeping since this whole mess began, despite the circumstances.

Andy tried to work, placing a few more calls and sending some emails to other people who had been part of the "Immortal Cell" thread online. But his thoughts kept straying. Monica, the girls. Paul and Sally—especially Sally, the last woman he'd made love with.

Not that he expected Felicia Reisner to tumble into his arms. Or his bed. He wouldn't kick her out, as the saying went, but hello?—she was married. Also attractive, successful. And he looked like thrift shop discards.

That part, he could fix. He went to the Westgate mall and used some of his dwindling cash to buy a new pair of pants and a dark blue sweater. Trying on the pants, he noticed that his shoes looked like he'd been dragging them behind the car on his cross-country peregrinations. It'd use up even more of his reserves but the pants would look ridiculous paired with such pathetic footwear.

When he showed up at her office, he wore the winter

coat he had bought when the weather had first started to turn cold, with the new sweater under it. His dark pants had a sharp crease and he was aware that, at a glance, she'd know he had gone shopping.

But when he pushed open her door, her attention was fixed on the screen of her computer. She didn't even glance toward him. "I'm sorry," she said, "office hours are over."

"Felicia," Andy said, swallowing back disappointment. "It's me, Andy. We were supposed to have dinner?"

She swiveled in her chair, and when she saw him her face brightened noticeably. "Oh, God, Andy, I'm so sorry. I've been just immersed in this stuff since late afternoon, and I completely forgot." Her cheeks crimsoned. "God, that makes me sound like a real bitch, doesn't it? I'm sorry. I'm just easily distracted, I guess. I really did remember when I left the house, and told Pearce I wouldn't be home for dinner."

"That's your husband?"

"Yes. Pearce." She turned back to her screen. "Just two minutes, okay?"

Andy leaned against the doorway and watched her finish whatever she was doing. She was wearing an oversized brown sweater today, somehow both baggy and clingy at the same time. Faded blue jeans over her long legs, tucked into UGG boots. She tilted her head toward the screen as she read, her straight hair falling forward and blocking most of her profile.

It was longer than two minutes, but not by much. Felicia snapped up straight and closed the document on her screen, then shut the computer down. She tossed Andy a wide smile, went to her closet, and emerged with coat and purse. "Ready to go?"

"Do we know where we're going?" he asked. "I guess I should have asked that yesterday, so I could have made a reservation."

"Don't worry about it," she said as she snapped off the overhead lights. He led the way out the office door and she followed, locking it behind her. "I've got a place we'll be able to get right into."

On his budget, Andy had eaten at Denny's many times since going on the run—it was often a welcome respite from fast food places, and usually easy to find from the highway. But he had never seen anyone take as much delight in the menu as Felicia did. She spent ten minutes poring over it, trying to decide between breakfast and dinner, finally settling on a Grand Slam, which she pronounced her all-time favorite.

"Don't get me wrong," she said after they had ordered. "It isn't that I don't like good food, too. I just have this craving sometimes, and I've learned it's often a good idea to listen to my cravings."

"I've learned that mine are some of my worst enemies," Andy replied. "But I can deal with them, it seems."

The waitress brought Felicia a glass of lemonade and poured coffee into Andy's waiting mug. When she left,

Felicia gazed at Andy. "So," she said, her tone suddenly more serious than it had been all evening. She kept her voice low, though there were no occupied tables immediately around them. "I've been giving a lot of thought to your questions, but before I get into that, I have a few of my own."

"Fair enough," Andy said. "I'll answer whatever I can."

"That would be a good start," Felicia said. "You never did answer the biggies from yesterday. Who are you, and why are you so obsessed with vampires?"

Andy fiddled with his silverware for a minute, thinking over what he could risk telling her. "My name really is Andy," he said. "But I'm not with the Bureau anymore, because they didn't want me digging into this. And I couldn't leave it alone."

"Why not?" she asked. "You're not crazy, are you? Because if you're some kind of lunatic, then—"

"I'm pretty sure I'm entirely sane," Andy interrupted. "Or at least as sane as anyone, these days. And the reason it's so important to me is that my best friend became a vampire, and he murdered my wife and our two daughters."

Felicia's dark face turned white. She reached up and tugged on her lower lip for a moment before speaking. "God," she said at last. "I am so sorry, Andy. That's just . . ."

He nodded. "It's pretty unbearable. And believe me, I know how psycho it sounds. I'll be able to prove it, someday, but for now the best I can do is ask you to trust me."

"You haven't given me any reason not to so far."

"I try to be honest," Andy said. "When I can. This is too important for me to lie about, and I really hope you can help me prove the truth."

Felicia drank some lemonade while the waitress dropped off their salads. When the woman was gone, she continued. "About that," she said. "I think maybe I can."

This was the news Andy was hoping for, but instead of being excited he found that he was anxious. What if she built his hopes up for nothing? What if she had something else entirely in mind, or only wanted to prove that vampires couldn't exist? Once, that would have been good enough for him, but no longer.

"Okay," he said flatly.

"I think I know a way to run some experiments on the so-called immortal cells," she explained, "to see if they can be transmitted from one body to another the way you described. It wouldn't be absolute proof, but it would move us in the right direction."

Not quite as convincing as he had wished for, but better than nothing, he decided.

"Here's the downside," she went on. "I have plenty of other work on my plate these days. Research, teaching, a couple of other projects I'm right in the middle of. So I will do this, Andy, and I'll do it for free, on my own time. No one at the university will know anything about it—you'll have to trust me on that, but the truth is that if I let anyone know what I was doing I'd be thrown out on my ass within the hour. But with all this other stuff going on, and the need for secrecy, it's going to take time."

"How much time?"

"I don't know. Months at best. Hopefully not years."

"Years?"

Felicia laughed. "You look so mortified," she said. "And I understand why, Andy, really, I'm not making fun of you or anything. I know it's very important work, and I'll push it along as fast as I possibly can. That's the best I can promise. Okay?"

It wasn't like he had any other biochemists who just happened to already be studying in the right area standing in line to help him. He nodded. "Sure, I get it," he said. "Anything you can do, I appreciate, Felicia."

The waitress showed up with their dinner orders, so conversation ceased again. After she had left the table, Felicia said, "Okay, let's focus on fine cuisine and getting acquainted," she said, "and leave the rest for later."

After dinner and triple chocolate cake for dessert—with Felicia paying for it all—he drove her back to the faculty parking lot where she had left her car. Both of them got out of his and stood together in the brittle night, clouds of steam surrounding them and then dissipating as they breathed.

He wanted that human contact, that connection, to step close, wrap his arms around her, and he almost couldn't bear the imagined sensations—the warmth of her body, the swell of her curves against him, the scent of her slightly fruity perfume. . . .

Stop. Focus—remember why you're here, why you need her.

And at the heart of it all, Andy thought he didn't need to experience intimacy with her as long as he could hear her laugh once in a while. That human contact would do wonders for his waning sanity. "I'm gonna go out on a limb here. I have to tell you, it's been a long time since I've met a woman as fascinating as you. I think I've kind of put a part of me in a box, and—"

"Not literally, I hope."

"A metaphorical box," he clarified. "When this whole thing is over, maybe I'll be able to get back to the rest of my life. And I'm deeply grateful for anything you can do to help me finish it."

"You flatter me." She smiled, leaned in and gave him an unexpected peck on the cheek. "Don't worry," she said. "We'll get to the truth, Andy, whatever it is."

Paul had learned to love the hunt.

On these long nights, it was especially fun. People in Barrow knew enough to stay inside after the sun shrank away from the coming dark, but in the other towns, although word had spread, they didn't quite get the concept. Four in the afternoon was still afternoon to them, even though it was full dark by four-thirty.

They stayed out; running errands, drinking in bars, visiting friends.

Paul didn't care why they were on the streets, just that he could find them there.

Like chickens wandering around the yard even though the fox was about.

He could see better in the darkness than he ever had in daylight. The grain on the leather of a man's shoes at a hundred feet? No problem. The glint of gold in a woman's molars while she talked on her cell phone, six blocks down. The cerulean blue of a distant child's eyes.

Crystal clear.

Clearer, because crystal could become fogged, smudged.

Paul Norris felt like a raptor, a falcon circling the meadow, zeroing in on a cottontail or a ground squirrel.

This night, he followed behind a woman in a black pea coat, red stocking cap, brown ski pants, and black boots. She had emerged from a bar, unsteady on her feet. Strawlike wisps of hair sticking out from under the cap. Skinny. Drinking more than her body weight could bear, and from the whiff he had of her—rancid sweat at forty yards—he got the idea that she had other habits as well.

That was good. He liked the druggies, the tweakers. An extra rush when he drained the veins, swallowed the crimson cocktail.

When he was a dozen paces behind her he scuffed his feet, allowing her to hear his approach. Fear made the heart pound faster, the blood rush through the veins. *Shaken, not stirred.* She turned and he smiled, open-mouthed, showing her his needle teeth, flicking his tongue at her. At first she hesitated, stared, but when he passed an illuminated shop window and the light from the neon fell on him, she bit back a scream.

Turning, she started to run.

Perfect.

Paul let her have a good lead—too easy and the fun would be diminished.

When she was a block away, he started to run.

He could hear her footfalls echoing on the quiet street, even when she had turned a corner. He increased his speed. At the corner, he put on an extra burst so if she was looking back—which he guessed she would be—he would almost seem to be flying.

It worked. This time she did scream.

He charged toward her, inhaling the odor of her sweat—liquor, stale cigarettes, sex and, he was now convinced, crack cocaine.

Just the way he liked them. Paul could still drink, but the thin fluids of alcoholic beverages were bitter and felt pointless. He greatly preferred to indulge this way—secondhand, but much more pleasurable.

The chase began to bore him. The woman ran ahead, but she was clumsy and slow. He decided to end it, and caught up to her with six long strides. She started to cry out again. He cut her scream short, driving a fist into the back of her head and slamming her into a wall. Before she could even recover, he twined his fingers in her hair and yanked her head back, exposing her throat.

Tears filled her eyes, rolled down smudged, dirty cheeks.

Paul Norris smiled. Raked fingernails as hard as bone and sharp as stilettos across the tender flesh. Bent forward, mouth open, to receive the reward.

A motion caught his eye as he drank, and he looked up to see Clea watching, arms folded under her breasts, a malevolent grin on her face. He withdrew his face, pressed his hand against the wound to staunch the flow of blood. "Like some?" he asked.

"You know me, a woman of great appetites," Clea said.

"That's what I like about you." He nodded toward his victim, and Clea moved in, pressed her open mouth to the wound. Paul slid his fingers away slowly, and she sucked the blood from them before releasing them.

When both had taken their fill, Paul and Clea locked eyes. He felt the effects of the drugs in the woman's body running through his own, heightening his senses. In Clea's liquid eyes he could see the same. Attraction had been growing between the two, playful flirtation taking place on a regular basis. Since the change, he had not felt much in the way of sexual desire, but now it was back with a vengeance.

Clea licked blood from her lower lip, eyeing him all the while.

Paul glanced around once, but the street remained

empty. He moved into Clea, wrapping his arms around her back, pulling her close. Their lips mashed together. He shoved his tongue between hers, letting her teeth shred the tender flesh. She gasped at the taste of his blood and bucked against him, pushing her own tongue into his mouth for the same treatment. Closing her legs around his, she ground against his thigh, grabbing at his crotch and belt with her hands.

He pushed her back against the wall, and they tripped over the lifeless body of the woman from whom they had just fed. Laughing, they both went down on the cold sidewalk beside her. Tearing clothes and skin with teeth and claws, bleeding onto the ground and one another, Clea opened herself to him. Both knew that as long as their heads were not threatened, any wounds would heal, and the blood that slicked their skin and filled their mouths just added to the heat of the moment. Paul pushed into her, biting and ripping hungrily—neck, shoulder, arm, breasts. Clea did the same to him. Reaching behind him, she dug her claws into the small of his back, and when she pushed them down through the skin, finding his spine, he exploded inside her.

Spent, they lay tangled together for the next twenty minutes or so, recuperating enough to return to the nest.

Walking back, still tasting her and smelling his own scent on her, Paul knew that he had found yet another benefit to his new status.

21

As she had warned, Felicia's regular work got in the way of her research. To keep out of her way, Andy went back to traveling. To get away from winter, he headed south: Nashville, Huntsville, Birmingham, Montgomery, Tallahassee, Jacksonville. In Orlando, he stayed several weeks, secure in the knowledge that with all the tourists in town he wouldn't stand out. After that, he kept going, down to Miami and then Key West.

Here he slowed down again. Plenty of other snowbirds were here to escape the cold, so he fit in. He spent the days walking on the beach, listening to the keening cries of the gulls and swatting at sand fleas and mosquitoes. He kept in touch with Felicia by phone every few days, but tried not to pressure her too much. Between calls he found himself longing for the sound of her voice, the cheerful ring of her laugh. He realized he was becoming obsessed, but he had been that way ever since Paul's transformation—obsessed with vampires, with proving their existence. The murder of his family only fed into that obsession even more, focusing it, spurring him to leave behind everything else he had ever been or wanted to do.

Now that he was making some progress—or at least felt like he was, since he finally had an ally and something resembling a plan—the days seemed to drag by. He wanted to be moving forward but had to wait on Felicia's availability. He still tried to do more research, but was learning that he had explored most of the avenues open to him. The Internet was full of poseurs and wannabes, but no genuine vampires had turned up, and he had very limited success finding people who had encountered them and survived—or who were willing to discuss it.

Key West was probably the worst place in the country to look. The sun rose early, seeming to burst out of the ocean all at once, and then hung in the sky. In the evenings, after it had set, its glow still seemed to wash the town, glinting off the beach sand and the western waves. Any vampire hunting in this place would have to make the hours of darkness count.

After a few weeks of it, Andy was ready to rip his hair out.

Anyway, he reasoned, the summer was coming on fast and early and with it the humidity and, almost unbelievably, even more insect life. To get away from both he drove north again, still changing cars every few cities, staying in cheap motels, keeping to himself. He headed almost straight toward Madison, spent a couple of days there having meals with Felicia and being reminded that she had made precious little progress.

Driving west, he tried not to dwell on it, but what

had seemed so promising at the end of winter was turning, as summer roared on, into one disappointment after another.

He stopped in Davenport, Des Moines, Sioux City, Omaha, Lincoln. The land was flat on every side, but the sky was enormous overhead, blue as cornflowers. On the Fourth of July, Andy was in Wyoming, sitting in the stands at the Ten Sleep Rodeo, watching cowboys and cowgirls put their animals through the paces, get thrown in the dust, and walk out of the arena, maybe limping a little, but acknowledging genuine waves of applause from the crowd.

By the time the sun dropped behind the hills, Andy was sunburned, stuffed on popcorn and hot dogs and Cokes. He stretched but kept his seat, because the fireworks show came next. Andy, once a very patriotic guy, had become dissociated from his country and the people around him. Here in this group of strangers, he saw flags and smiles and handshakes, yellow ribbons on pickup trucks, men and women who were pleased and proud of their sheer Americanness. He couldn't completely submerge himself in the spirit of the day—there were too many things he knew that they didn't, about the American intelligence community and how it worked, how administrations used what the spies gave them—and of course the fact that there were real monsters roaming in the land of the free, home of the brave.

He tried, though, and every now and then for a few moments—watching explosions of color in the black sky, or listening to the heartfelt laughter of his neighbors, or watching a cowboy pick up his hat from the dirt, slap off the dust, and wave it to the roaring crowd—he managed.

Carol Hino had been fired from Kingston House back in May.

Too many absences, too many mornings when she dragged herself in just before noon, too many publishing meetings when she admitted that she had not read, and did not care about, whatever manuscript was under discussion.

She was too smart not to know that she was blowing it. She just couldn't bring herself to change. Whenever her boss spoke to her, she wanted to shake him. *You're going to die,* she wanted to say. *If the terrorists don't get you, the vampires will. You live in New York, you survived 9/11, but you could go outside tomorrow night to walk the dog or pick up some Chinese and get knifed by some crackhead punk . . . or sliced open for dinner by some bloodsucker.*

She kept her mouth shut but lost her job.

She had some savings, and she made a little money on the side by selling stories to tabloid papers. She tried to tell a little of the truth in the sensationalistic tales, hoping to warn anyone who could tease out the nuggets of reality from inside the absurdist wrapping.

By August, she had lost her nice apartment on the Upper West Side. She moved into a walk-up near the Village with a roommate she found online, a vegan animal groomer who smelled like sandalwood incense and listened to blues late into the night. Carol didn't mind—she was not often home before morning anyway. She was staying out later and later, frequenting bars, after-hours clubs, whatever. Anyplace there were people, booze, drugs, and the possibility of danger. Something about the fragility of life pushed her to seek the edge, the extremes. She wouldn't take a subway if she could walk and would skip the street if there was a back alley that could get her there.

The same way she had known when she was putting her job in jeopardy, she knew she was risking her life every night. Sleeping with strangers, going into unsafe neighborhoods, lurking in the darkness—each time, she put her life into the hands of uncertain fate.

Only the proximity of death made her feel alive.

Carol was convinced that Stella Olemaun was dead. Probably Donald Gross, too, by now.

The vampires were determined not to let the world know about their presence. And the government, for some fucking reason of its own, seemed just as anxious to keep their secret.

She walked down Eighth, wishing there was some way she could blow it wide open, regretted having let the company cave in when they labeled *30 Days of Night* fiction. But now, there was nothing she could do. Stupid pieces in tabloids written for the ignorant and the stoned wouldn't help.

It was almost midnight, and the few tourists who accidentally strayed this way had gone back to their hotels. Men leaned against buildings holding paper bags with bottles inside. A couple of whores came around the corner, strutted their wares for the passing traffic, then hurried out of sight as a cop car hovered into view. When it passed, a guy in a tank top and loose shorts with boxers peeking above the waistband whistled at her and grabbed his crotch.

Carol stopped in her tracks, walked back to where he was, and moved his hand out of the way. She leaned close, massaging his genitals and breathing in the boozy stew of his breath. When he opened his mouth and started breathing heavily, growing hard beneath the shorts, she laughed in his face and released him. With an extra wiggle of her hips, she walked away.

Would he follow her? Pull a gun and shoot? Curse her for being born? Any of them would be acceptable—another match against the darkness.

A way to be reminded that she yet lived.

She glanced back at the guy, still staring at her with rage in his eyes, as she stepped off the curb at the corner. A rush of air, a horn blast, and then an impact she didn't even feel until she was sailing, spinning, slamming into the pavement.

Everything was detached from everything else. Voices shouting, horns and sirens blaring, but none of it had obvious sources that she could determine. The horny guy's alcoholic breath filled her nose again, but faces loomed in and out of her field of view, and none of them looked like his. She was cold even though it was a hot, muggy night in New York. She had been sweating earlier, but now it was her hair that was wet, she guessed with blood, only when she tried to reach up and feel it with her fingers her arms refused to move. She knew she was sprawled on her back in the street, but she couldn't feel its rough surface or the day's heat radiating up from the blacktop.

A taxi door slammed. It sounded like thunder. A guy stalked toward her from the cab's direction, his shirt open over a sweat-ringed gray tee, his hair long and held back with something, maybe a rubber band. Weird details swam into her consciousness—the gold tooth in the front of his mouth glinting in the headlights as he bent over her, the scar below his left eye, the way he sniffed while he swore over and over again.

She laughed, or thought she did, although she could no longer hear her own voice. Even the cabbie's voice had blended into a general roar, like the noise she heard as a kid, putting seashells to her ear. The guy looked confused, so she thought maybe she really had laughed.

"You're not even a vampire," she tried to explain. "Not even the fucking undead. Just some guy."

The cabbie said more, but she couldn't hear it.

Found she didn't care.

A lot of that going around.

On the street in the city she had loved, Carol Hino watched as every light in Manhattan blinked out, one by one, leaving her enveloped in the rich, pure blackness she had sought all along.

Dan Bradstreet had never really liked New York.

Compared to Los Angeles, it was physically intimidating. The buildings went up instead of out, the streets felt narrow, confining. The traffic was insane—in LA, a freeway could jam up for hours, but at least you could tell where the lanes were. Dan had never driven in New York and never would. Cars, especially cabs, darted from one lane to the next with no warning or apparent reason. The place was filthy and smelled bad and the people always seemed to be in a hurry to get someplace.

He preferred to keep out of the city altogether, and when he was there he preferred riding in a limo, or at least a Town Car, to a cab. Subway was always his last resort.

But now he was in a cab, riding from uptown to the Battery. It was after ten at night, but the streets were still crowded. The city had been suffering a heat wave, and the air stayed humid all night long. The people he saw through the windows were wearing as little as they could get away with legally, and sometimes less.

Dan made a show of looking at the cab driver's badge, posted on the window between sections. Guy had long brown hair pulled back in a pony tail, a scraggly beard, bad teeth. His name, according to the sign, was Shane Amthorp. After perusing the sign, Dan leaned back in the seat.

"Didn't I see you in the paper?" he asked.

"Probably did," Shane answered. "If you read the *Post.*"

"Who doesn't? What did they call you? Something weird."

"The vampire hack," Shane reported with a laugh.

"Why?" Dan asked. He knew the answer to the question before he asked it—the answer, at least, that he expected to hear. Shane Amthorp didn't disappoint.

"I hit this lady," he explained. "She was some kinda nut, I guess, stepped right off the curb in front of me as I was turning a corner. I mean, *right* in front—there was no way I coulda missed her. All the witnesses agreed to that, and the cops didn't even charge me."

"Wow, that must have been scary," Dan said. He kind of enjoyed playing the wide-eyed innocent.

"Yeah," Shane said. He met Dan's gaze in the rearview mirror, then looked forward long enough to shoot through the narrow opening between a delivery van and another cab. "Kinda thing happens sometimes. Part of the game is all. I mean, I feel bad about it, y'know? Lady was alive, then she hit my cab, then she was dead. Not something I take lightly, I mean, shit, I had nightmares for like three nights after it. But I don't blame myself, either."

He stopped talking to pay attention to his driving for a minute. Dan couldn't figure out how he did it—controlling a two-ton beast through what seemed like lethal streets, while apparently letting his thoughts wander. Dan was convinced that if he were at the wheel he'd be white knuckling it the whole way and too terrified to speak a word.

When Shane had visibly relaxed a little, Dan asked, "But what about the name? How did that make you a vampire?"

"The lady didn't die right away," Shane replied. "I got outta the cab and went over to see how she was, and she looked at me, kinda bleary-eyed, and said something about me being a vampire. A bunch of other people were gathered around her, and one of 'em said something about it to the reporter when she showed up looking for a story. See, I drive at night and sleep during the day, so the reporter thought the whole vampire thing was an angle she could use. That's all there is to it—I mean, I don't drink nobody's blood or nothing."

Dan studied the man in the mirror closely. His teeth were normal—one gold one in front, and the rest crooked and yellowed, but not vampiric. His hands on the wheel were scabbed and dirty but not clawed. *Good, then. I won't have to kill this one.*

So much of his working life revolved around quieting people who learned too much about the undead, he was relieved to find someone who was genuinely in the dark about it—oblivious to vampires and apparently happy to remain that way. Dan asked a couple of other probing questions, just to make sure, but he'd pretty much already made up his mind.

Which meant he got to head back to LA—a blessing, after the rathole that was New York—and focus once again on trying to find Andy Gray.

There were three Bureau employees at the Crime Center in Clarksburg, West Virginia, who were employed almost full-time watching for any sign of him, tracking credit card and bank accounts, checking to see if his fingerprints turned up anywhere, looking for any sign of a name that might be an alias of his.

So far, nothing. The guy had managed to drop off the planet. He was probably dead, Dan reasoned, victim of one of the vampires he was chasing. Maybe Paul Norris himself. Otherwise, some trace of him would have turned up.

"You want to talk vampires," Shane piped up, "take a look at those mooks down in Washington. They fed their whole administration on the blood of three thousand dead New Yorkers—my sister was in Tower Two—and we still don't have all the dough we was promised. They lied to us about the air quality and soaked up the approval ratings. Then they kept it going on the blood of American GIs and God knows how many innocent Iraqis. You ask me, *those* are the real vampires."

A cabbie with an opinion. How unexpectedly charming.

Maybe he should kill the guy after all, just on general principle.

He turned his mind back to the disappearance of Andrew Gray. Without a body, without confirmation, Dan had to keep looking. As did the drones down in West

VA. At some point he would get the okay to close the file, but that point had not yet been reached.

Whatever. He cashed their checks, he'd do what he was told. Beat the hell out of slinging hash.

Or driving a cab, for that matter.

Excerpted from *30 Days of Night* by Stella Olemaun

Eben and I did our best to find survivors and keep them safe. Hiding had become the safest option. Food soon became almost as large an issue as the murderers ruling the streets of Barrow. We would work as a team, Eben and I, crawling beneath the houses.

When Eben found an untouched stash of canned foods in a storage unit behind Sam Ikos's diner, we had no choice but to venture out once again. They were active again, the vampires, after a perceived period of downtime; we could hear them moving outside around the clock searching homes for survivors. Sometimes, thankfully we heard nothing, but all too often the sounds of the vampires searching were followed by the screams of people we knew begging for their lives.

But each time we went out into the cold night, we learned a little more about their behavior, their tendencies and hopefully, someday, a weakness. The first few times we ventured out, we varied our path and found that the vampires did not adjust their patrol paths. No matter how we varied, they did not adapt, which Eben took to mean they were creatures of habit and tended to walk the same ground over and over, varying only for a new victim in town.

Eben commented that maybe the killer returning to the scene of the crime originated from the vampire legend. I told him flat out, I thought that was probably not the case.

The times we had to lurk about the streets of Barrow put our patience and nerves to the test. Move. Stop. Look. Listen. Repeat.

There were several close calls with the vampires, and during those times we put our heads together regarding everything we knew about them from the movies.

Nothing worked. Bullets, knives, wooden stakes. I even fashioned a cross from two pieces of wood, and the goddamned thing just laughed. "You've gotta be fucking kidding me," it said as it came for me.

Eben put a bullet in its shoulder to slow it down and we ran like hell. It tried to follow but we managed to escape. Next time, we might not be so lucky.

We learned quickly that the extreme cold seemed to affect their sense of smell. Out of everything, it seemed like the only advantage we had. That, and if we lived long enough, see what would happen when the sun finally came up in a few weeks.

That alone made perfect sense as to why they were here—somehow they had figured out how to use the month of darkness in this local environment against us, literally creating a vampire's paradise on earth.

* * *

The days were turning into weeks. I found myself losing hope.

I was going to die here, as food for monsters.

The entire town had been transformed. Without heat and electricity, the roads and buildings froze over like a long abandoned village. The vampires, it seemed, intended to stay and feast for the full winter darkness.

We weren't without our victories, though. Eben and Sam's brother, the trapper John Ikos, and several other men had managed to trap one of the invaders and decapitate it—giving us our first clue that these hideous creatures were incredibly durable, but not indestructible.

Problem was three men died killing one of them. That meant we couldn't really fight back—we simply did not have the numbers.

Luckily, as we were tormented by starvation, cold, and fear, it seemed the vampires themselves were not without their own problems.

As we stayed hidden and quiet, the vampires were out in the open and extremely vocal. Many of them talked in languages I recognized and did not understand, but most spoke English.

Evidently, the idea of attacking Barrow was the idea of the bald, pierced vampire in leather, the one who we had personally seen exact some of the most vicious attacks. We heard him barking orders, and by all accounts he was running the show, ordering bodies decapitated and having families rounded up and paraded before him before they were slaughtered.

It was when a strange new vampire arrived that the entire nightmare turned on its head.

I can only assume what happened by what we could piece together from spying and listening from our hiding places. After so many days of occupation, Eben and I had our crawling routes down to a science, moving with relative ease without being detected by the blood hunters.

From the cellar, we witnessed the arrival of this odd new invader to the sound of applause. He was different than the others, also bald, but with disfigured, almost pointed ears and white skin that shined like porcelain. He was dressed in a fine suit with a red, silk-lined coat. When he strolled into town, past the blood-spattered ruins of Ikos Diner, he had two women on his arms, like some sort of undead visiting dignitary, and we could see by the reaction of the others—if they were feeding or even midkill, they froze in his presence—that this observation was not so far off track.

Words were being exchanged and it was clear, without hearing what was actually said, that these were vampires of different ages or beliefs. Eben and I allowed our curiosity to get the best of us and we crawled close to the vampires gathered near the center of town among bodies and red-stained snow.

Confirming our suspicions, the attack on Barrow seemed to be the younger bald vampire's brainchild. He spoke deferentially to his elder, speaking of his own ingenuity for *discovering* Barrow and its thirty days of night and what a wonderful feeding ground it made for their kind. He ranted that humans were cattle and food for the immortals—it should be humans who hid in shadows, not them.

The elder vampire was quiet at first . . . and then suddenly erupted, enraged. *"You fucking arrogant idiot!"*

The younger vampire was struck with such force at first I thought the elder had taken off his face, but still, he lived, on his knees, bleeding like a fountain from his nose and mouth.

I remember peering over at Eben and seeing a look I hadn't seen in a long time. It seemed almost like hope.

"Holy shit! Did you see that?" I whispered.

Eben just nodded, but he couldn't keep his eyes off the action in the streets. "Yeah . . . yeah I saw it," he said.

My instincts were right—the younger vampire was a brash, arrogant killer who had little regard for what the elder new arrival said or thought. The others seemed split. Some backed away from them. Some fled the scene entirely.

And then I heard the exchange, clear as a bell, through the steady hiss of the harsh freezing wind.

The elder was angry not just because of the killing—humans were food, and that was completely acceptable—but to attack an entire town in such a way that would possibly attract attention was insanity. The elder repeated a number of times that the greatest tool at their disposal was that humans did not truly believe in them, and massacres like this one could raise unnecessary suspicion.

He stood over the younger vampire, berating him.

"I had hopes of arriving in time to stop you. I can see looking around me that I arrived too late. . . . The damage is done."

The wounded younger vampire seemed confused.

The elder was really pissed off. He was going on and on about how many hundreds, thousands, of centuries it took to become a myth, and to be integrated with the world—"to make the humans no longer believe we exist," he said. Now, everything was in jeopardy, as the attack on Barrow would be suspect if the word got out. "Suspicion and fear are the seeds of our extiction . . . again we will be the hunted!" he raved.

I listened to every word. I heard the fear in the vampire's voice. I don't think at the time I could have done anything with the information, being in full-on survival mode, but I tucked the rant in the back of my mind.

Not only could they be killed, but they were also capable of being afraid.

But also, when we listened to the vampires arguing, it was then that we realized how little we meant. We *were* just food to them. And now in the wake of the deaths of just about everybody I knew and loved, I saw what the lead vampire meant . . . the greatest power of the vampire is that no one believes in them.

The brash, young vampire got to his feet. "Who . . . do . . . you . . . think . . . you . . . are?!" he sputtered, shaking with rage, lunging for the elder. "I'll kill you! I'll—"

Eben and I were not prepared for what came next.

The elder caught the young one by the throat. "You will do nothing," he said. "You will die."

With that, the elder took the other by the shoulders and tore him completely in half—with his bare hands. The body shredded liked cooked meat, one side taking ribcage while the other mostly flesh and dislocated bone from sockets.

The young invader's head rolled, still living, into the snow, towards where Eben and I hid beneath the house nestled in the blood-soaked snowdrifts.

The head glared at the elder, still sputtering with rage, almost as if in denial of what had just happened to the rest of its body. "Kill . . . phhh . . . kill . . . y-you . . ."

I suddenly felt unsafe, like we would be discovered. This elder vampire seemed to possess a strength that eclipsed the others and I feared he would sniff us out despite the cold and constantly falling snow.

I tugged at Eben who was glued to the scene. "Eben, we should go," I said.

Eben looked at me blankly, and then as if drawn by the action, we both turned as the elder looked down at the young vampire's head hissing now empty threats in the snow. Then the elder stomped down, smashing and obliterating it for all time.

And just like that, the leader of the massacre of Barrow was dead.

I felt a sudden elation. Was it over? Would the vampires leave Barrow now?

It wouldn't be long until even the smallest hopes were dashed.

22

IN MID-OCTOBER, Andy was in Boise, Idaho.

Having discovered that he liked observing rivers, he'd found a motel a couple of blocks from the Boise River and spent his mornings walking its banks, watching the water and the traffic on it, letting the crisp air wake him up. Afternoons he spent trying to unravel the bloodsucker business, with ever-dwindling luck.

Andy called Felicia every few days from the road, torn between wanting to talk to her—to anyone, really, but especially her—and not wanting to be a pest.

But this morning, when he checked in with her, she asked him to rush back to Madison.

She didn't want to tell him why on the phone, just said that she'd had a breakthrough and needed him there.

He threw his belongings into frayed, worn luggage and checked out immediately. The latest stolen car was a white Nissan Altima, taken from a motel parking lot in Pueblo, plates switched almost immediately for a pair from Tennessee. Within thirty minutes of hanging up the motel phone he was on I-84 headed east.

It would be a couple of days of hard driving before

he was in Madison. He would rather have flown, but didn't dare test the Andy Hertz credentials that far.

Besides, taking a commercial flight would mean giving up the hardware he was hauling around in the trunk, leaving him even more defenseless than he already was.

Not that he'd seen any vampires to kill with the armament he kept. It had been so long since he'd actually encountered one, he was half inclined to think the whole thing had been a bad dream, an alcohol-fueled hallucination.

But Monica and the girls were dead.

That was no dream.

And he hadn't been drinking yet when he had seen Paul.

No, they were out there. As hard to find as four leaf clovers, not much more substantial than whispers in the wind.

That was what he had to deal with, what he had to change.

They couldn't remain just rumors, stories told to frighten the masses. They had to be shown as the real, solid, malevolent beings they were.

Far more dangerous than terrorists or gangsters, more deserving of the full attentions of law enforcement and the military.

If Andy had any sanity left, he was convinced, it was this quest that had preserved it. This mission, this obsession.

When he had accomplished his goal, then he could relax. Or simply fade away.

Retire. Die. Serve out the prison term that no doubt awaited him for all his crimes.

But not yet.

He pressed down on the accelerator and raced toward the east and the single worst mistake of his life.

In her office, Felicia sat Andy down and showed him charts and graphs and equations, none of which meant anything to him. He was utterly exhausted from the drive, wired on caffeine and the wake-up pills they sold at truck stops, jittery. He couldn't focus on what she was trying to say.

"Cut to the chase, Felicia," he snapped. "What's the verdict?"

She blew out a sigh, smiled patiently. She wore a red V-neck blouse, hinting at cleavage it didn't quite display, black pants, red sneakers. "You were right, Andy. What I called the 'Immortal Cell' *can* be passed from one person to another via an exchange of bodily fluids."

Andy had believed it to be true for so long he had a hard time wrapping his head around the idea that maybe he had been wrong. "So a vampire drinking blood from a victim—"

"Two-way exchange," Felicia interrupted. "Vamp drinks the blood, but contributes saliva to the victim. My guess is, if the vampire kills the victim, then it's too late and the cells don't take hold. But if the victim is only partially drained and allowed to live, the new cells—courtesy of the vampire—move in, rapidly replacing the existing ones. As well as granting near immortality, they also change the individual's biochemistry, with the effects you've described. Physical changes that help satisfy the new hunger for human blood. Rapid healing. Extreme photosensitivity."

"So this is the proof we need to go public?" Andy asked, still trying to keep up. Felicia was clearly excited by her discovery, but he thought he sensed some hesitation in her as well.

She shook her head. "Not yet," she said. "This is still theoretical."

"But you said—"

"I said the transfer works the way we thought. The way *you* thought. And I've been able to demonstrate repeatedly that the immortal cells can crowd out the existing cellular structure. But for the rest of it, the vampire part . . . well, there's only one way to prove that."

"What's that?" Andy asked. "That's the part that's important. Without that . . ." He let the sentence die, disappointment racking his spirit. The long, fast drive, the encouragement he'd felt just moments ago. Being shot down yet again just wasn't fair.

Life's a bitch, and then you die. He must have seen that bumper sticker a hundred times since going on the run.

"What do we have to do?" he asked, more subdued now. The weariness was flooding over him.

"Simple. We need a vampire," Felicia said. "We can't prove that the vampiric traits take over unless we can experiment with real vampiric cells."

"But . . . sorry, I'm not following. I mean, if we have a vampire we don't need the rest of it," he said dejectedly. "So this gains us nothing."

"We don't need the *whole* vampire," she corrected. "We just need some cellular matter from one. Blood, saliva, tissue—any of that. How can we get that?"

Andy put his elbows on her desk, leaned his face into his palms. "We're right back where we've always been," he complained. He had never even told her about the vampire's jawbone he had so momentarily possessed.

"I don't buy that for a second, Andy. We have definite scientific proof—evidence that the scientific community can't ignore—of an important aspect of our theory."

"It's not a theory, Felicia, it's a fact. And if we can't prove it, people are going to keep dying."

"We *can* prove it, Andy. There's got to be a way to get some vampire tissue. Once we have that, the rest is easy."

Easy?

Disheartened, Andy checked into a motel, different from the others he had stayed in on his trips to Madison. *All we need is a vampire. Jesus. That's like saying I'd be a rich man, if I only had a million bucks.*

He turned the TV on to some inane daytime talk show, flopped down on the bed, and fell asleep.

When he woke up it was late, after eleven. Looking at himself in the mirror, he decided he looked like death—pale, drawn, unshaven, hair matted from the long drive and the long nap. He needed a shower, but he was too hungry. He stripped out of the clothes he'd slept in, pulled on clean ones, and went to the car. Having never stayed at this motel, he didn't know what the neighborhood was like, what food he might be able to find. But he needed something.

Two blocks from the motel, he suddenly had the answer.

Streetwalkers paraded up and down the block, passing in and out of the circles of illumination cast by streetlights. Cars slowed, circled, occasionally stopping. With just a few words at the curb, the hookers willingly climbed into the vehicles of strangers and drove away.

Prostitutes were often favorite victims of serial killers. They were society's forgotten women—cut off from family and friends, ignored by law enforcement unless they were being rounded up in some sort of sweep. When they disappeared, no one knew about it except their fellow streetwalkers. They were hesitant to file police reports because it would mean revealing what they had been doing out on the streets, and the cops weren't inclined to listen to them anyway.

He needed a vampire. Vampires hunted at night.

When you wanted to hunt a hunter, you needed bait.

Oh God . . . what am I thinking?

Andy drove a few blocks farther, found some fast food, thought about it some more, then came back. Sat in his car under the shadows of low-hanging trees and ate it, watching the ballet of the hookers. They strutted. When a car slowed, they approached the passenger-side window. A quick conversation, and then they slid inside or they twirled away and returned to the sidewalk. When a police car cruised past they melted into the shadows, returning as soon as it was gone.

Andy himself nearly took off about half a dozen times.

Nuts. This is just nuts.

But in the end, he knew it might be insane enough to work.

After a couple of hours, a man appeared on the sidewalk. He was African-American, tall and well dressed in a suit that fit like it was tailor-made. A neat goatee, close-trimmed hair. He didn't look like Andy's idea of a stereotypical pimp. As soon as he walked around the corner, four of the women gravitated to him. He laughed with them, touched them affectionately. Andy could barely see the exchange of money, but at some point each of the women handed him something. Wads of bills, Andy guessed. They disappeared into the pockets of the suit without ruining the line.

Smooth, Andy thought.

He reached up and clicked off the dome light, then slipped quietly from the car.

Staying back in the shadows, away from the lights of

passing cars and the glow of the streetlights, he kept the pimp in sight as the man finished his collections and headed back around the corner he had come from.

This street was residential, and the man went straight to a small bungalow halfway down the block. The yard was hemmed by a metal fence with a swinging gate, and inside the fence, grass and weeds had been allowed to grow wild, some almost waist high on the guy. Lights blazed inside, but the streetlight nearest the house was burned out—*or shot out,* Andy speculated, if the pimp was trying to maintain some secrecy about his movements. The man walked up a couple of steps to the door and went in.

Andy hurried back to the Altima, popped the trunk, and brought out the Remington 12-gauge. He already wore the Glock in a holster at his hip, underneath a light windbreaker.

He held the Remington close to his leg and walked stiffly back to the house.

Beyond the moral implications of what he was about to do, the old anxiety started to bubble up in him, as it had every time he'd had to rush a house as an FBI agent. But in those days there were always several of them, all armed, all wearing blue windbreakers with the yellow FBI emblazoned across the back, and everyone knew what they were doing, it was clockwork.

This time, he was solo.

The gate squeaked when he pushed it open, but he left it ajar and rushed up the steps.

At the top, he tried the doorknob. It didn't turn.

He'd been hoping the pimp was confident enough to leave it unlocked, but it looked like he'd have to do things the noisy way.

The bungalow was at least fifty years old, and the door didn't look reinforced. Andy reared back and kicked just above the knob, putting all his weight into it. The jamb shattered and the door flew open, and from inside he heard a startled voice cry out in alarm.

But Andy went in, shotgun leveled, and shouted, "Freeze! FBI!"

"The fuck?"

The voice didn't sound as terrified as Andy had hoped. More annoyed, as if a telemarketer or door-to-door salesman had interrupted his dinner.

Andy swung around a corner into a small living room, lit only by a standing lamp with a stained and faded shade, near the window. The pimp he had seen earlier sat under it in an easy chair. He'd taken off his suit jacket and loosened his tie, but still wore a long-sleeved maroon shirt that looked like silk. The room smelled like years of tobacco and dope had settled into all its surfaces.

On the arm of the chair were two small stacks of cash.

"The fuck does the FBI want with me?" he asked. He glanced behind Andy, as if looking for the other agents who should be back there in the event of a real federal raid. Then he scrutinized Andy carefully. He kept his hands flat on the armrests, careful not to knock over the money but also not to make any sudden moves that might make Andy's trigger finger twitch.

Easy does it, Andy. Stay frosty.

"I don't care about your business," Andy said. "You just go ahead and do whatever it is you do. Thing is, I need to borrow two of your girls."

The man smiled. "You're welcome to 'em, you got the price," he said. "Don't need a gat for that."

Andy shook his head. "You don't understand, I'm not talking about a temporary loan," he clarified. "I need them for an extended time. Maybe even forever."

"Oh really. Your boss know you're threatening my livelihood?" the man asked.

"I don't care which two," Andy continued. "Give me your two worst earners. They don't have to be beauties, and the worse off the better, probably."

The pimp dared to raise his hand to his chin, scratched at the goatee. "You going into competition with me, you'd want prime goods. So what's your game, bro?"

"How about none of your motherfucking business," Andy replied. "I'll keep them off your turf, away from the others. What I want is for you not to ask questions, just to accept that this is the way it is and let it go. I can bring the heat down on you hard if I want." He hefted the shotgun as a reminder. "And I'm the one with this."

"This time."

"Look, I don't want to be a big problem for you, but I can be. Just give me what I want and I'm out of here."

The guy kept his gaze leveled on Andy, as if he could read something there. "You bother me," he finally said. "I can't quite figure out what you're all about, and I'm usually good at that. Throws me."

"I don't want a relationship. Just two ladies you're maybe looking to turn loose anyway."

"Well, that's just it. I'm loyal to my ladies, and they stay loyal to me."

Andy tried not to let his frustration get the better of him. "I'm sure they appreciate you," he said, tightening his finger on the trigger. "But I'm not negotiating, here. If you're dead, they're *all* mine, right?"

"Okay, okay," the guy said, raising his hands. "Don't get all hinky on me, all right? I got a couple you can have, it means that much to you. You can take Angel and Raven. Save me the trouble of . . . retiring them." He flashed a mouthful of white teeth at Andy.

Not bloodsucker teeth, but a predator's teeth all the same.

"Those are their real names, huh?"

"You'll learn their real names when you meet them," the guy answered. "You'll need to know 'em to bail 'em out when they get picked up. You do know how this business works, right?"

"It doesn't seem too complicated."

The guy laughed. "Then I got my MBA for nothing, I guess."

"When can I meet them?" Andy asked. "I don't have all night."

"You *are* an impatient little bastard," the pimp said, gesturing toward the phone. It stood on a small table in the corner. In contrast to the exterior appearance of the house, the inside was neat, if not especially sterile. "You promise not to shoot me, I'll page them."

"Be my guest," Andy said. Keeping the shotgun pointed at the pimp, he took a seat on an old cloth sofa and settled down to wait.

May God forgive me for what I'm about to do, Andy thought.

Somehow, Andy didn't think his prayers would be enough. They certainly hadn't been helping much these days, anyway.

23

"YOU DID *WHAT?!*"

Andy had never expected to see Felicia so furious.

Oh, that's bullshit, the voice in his head piped up. *How did you think she would react? How would any sane person react?*

They were back in her office. After meeting Angel and Raven and explaining what was expected of them (saying it was a matter of national security, of all things) he had gone back to the motel to sleep for a few hours, then come during Felicia's office hours.

Andy had just finished filling Felicia in on the plan.

And the part about meeting Angel and Raven.

And the part about what was expected of them.

And Felicia just exploded.

"Give me one good reason why I shouldn't throw you out on your ass or call the cops. I'm serious, Andy!"

"You were the one who said we needed a vampire," Andy said calmly, hoping she would mellow out. "They're not so easy to come by, especially when you're looking for them."

"But Andy . . . have you lost your mind?! These women are *human beings,*" Felicia stressed. She looked horrified. "Not *bait*. You *cannot* do this."

"They wouldn't work as bait if they weren't human," Andy countered. "The truth is . . ." Felicia's face started to cloud over again, so he hurried to explain. "Look . . . this is hard for me, too, okay? But *I'm* at the end of my rope here. Okay, you want the truth? Fine. They're both crackheads. Angel is also HIV positive. They live hard—"

"—and they'll die even worse. This is a very, very bad idea, Andy."

"Look, Felicia, I . . ."

"I'm not doing this, Andy."

"Shut up a minute, all right?!" Andy raised his voice and started talking fast. "Listen to me . . . it's not like we have a lot of choices here. This may or may not work, but it's a shot I have to take. These women can stay outside all night long, trying to attract a vampire. If they turn a few tricks on the side—which I'm sure they will, given what I'm paying them—then they can keep all the money, which is a better deal than they had before. They even think they're doing something in the name of national security, which in a way, they are. If they see a vampire, and I've told them what to look for, then they hit the panic button on their phones and call me. I'll be in the neighborhood at all times. I show up, waste the bloodsucker, and we have our tissue sample. At that point the ladies are on their own, no worse off than they were before."

"And we all live happily ever after, the end?" Felicia replied, going heavy on the sarcasm.

"Who knows? Hell, at least my way they're not sharing half their income with a pimp, they're not being forced to whore themselves. I don't have much cash left but what I'm paying them will cover their bills for a while."

Felicia squeezed her temples in exasperation. "Oh my God . . . I can't believe I'm saying this . . . you . . . *swear* you'll be close enough to protect them if they do attract a vampire?"

"Of course. That's the whole idea. It doesn't do us any good if I'm not right there."

"I want to meet them," Felicia said firmly. "*Tonight.* I want to see where you've got them stashed, and make sure I feel okay about their conditions."

"Felicia, I—"

"Sorry, that's non-negotiable, Andy. If you want me to stay on board."

He remembered saying almost the same thing to their pimp, the night before. He had meant it then, and it appeared that she did now. "Fine," he said. "I'll take you to them tonight, introduce you."

Felicia nodded, her face still troubled.

She wasn't taking this well.

It was an incredibly stupid idea, a Hail Mary long shot of a plan. Anyone who went along with it willingly had to be some kind of dangerous lunatic.

Which, fortunately, defined him.

Five nights passed.

Crawled by.

His internal clock already haywire, Andy took to sleeping during the day so he could be awake at night, when the women were out.

He had assigned them a corner far from the usual hooker stroll, a few blocks from East Washington, outside a shoe repair shop that closed at seven.

He had checked into a nearby motel, and the corner was not far from an apartment he rented for the two. They took turns going out, so that most of the time one was on the street and the other was safe at home.

Every now and then Andy would check the corner and find no one there, which meant whoever was on duty was actually turning a trick. He hoped.

But there had been no sign of any vampires. When it came down to it, Andy didn't know if there were even any vampires in the state of Wisconsin. This was, of course, the drawback of his plan—the women might never attract one. *Like throwing breadcrumbs out for absent pigeons.* Felicia had tried to point that out in the first place, but he had ignored her, unable to come up with any better options.

They needed something, though. Some way to let the bloodsuckers know the women were out there.

Finally, he hit on another idea, which in hindsight turned out to be an even greater lapse in judgment than using human bait.

He wrote a classified ad.

30 Days of Night? I know it's true, and I want to join the fun.

He added the intersection he had picked. Using the fake Andy Hertz Visa card, he placed the ad in major newspapers around the country. He was sure most people would have no idea what it meant.

But the vampires would.

Dan Bradstreet looked at the ad in the *Los Angeles Times,* which had been brought to his attention via an encrypted email from Clarksburg. There was no indication whatsoever that Andy Gray had anything to do with it.

But Dan gnawed on his lower lip as he read the line over and over.

A simple message and a street corner in Wisconsin. Could be just about anyone.

There was no denying the obvious connection, though. *30 Days of Night* being the title of Stella Olemaun's book about her experience in Barrow. Andy's partner Paul had been turned while the two of them were investigating Olemaun. In itself, that was no proof. But it was enough to raise Dan's hackles. Andy Gray had vanished from the planet more than a year ago, and if this wasn't much of a lead it was still better than any others he'd seen.

He had an overnight bag with changes of clothes and toiletries in the trunk of his car, so he could leave town at a moment's notice. He picked up the phone to round up a ticket on the next flight to Madison.

* * *

Two more weeks. And still, nothing.

Short of making an appeal for vampires on one of the network morning news shows, Andy was stumped. One more dead end in a seemingly infinite chain of them.

Despite the national security angle, which admittedly only went so far, Angel and Raven were getting bored with the whole thing.

They were turning tricks, doing drugs, and generally little better off than they had been before, except that they were keeping more of their money. But they seemed lonely, too, without the company of their pimp and the rest of his string. When Andy or Felicia dropped in, they were chatty, almost clingy. Not wanting to become too attached to them, Andy made a point of keeping his visits short and businesslike.

Just keep them at arm's length. Keep your eye on the ball and maybe we'll all get out of this alive.

Times like this, he felt like nothing more than a dirty cop.

Dan Bradstreet sat in the van with the local SWAT guys and his own Bureau assault team. A second van, similarly mixed, was parked at the far corner. The building was across the street and partially down the block. Lights on in some units, not in others.

None in the one he believed Andy Gray was in.

His people had been busy canvassing the area around the intersection mentioned in the newspaper ad. They had shown pictures of Andy—Bureau portraits, and computer-altered ones: Andy with a beard, with long hair, with a mustache—all around the neighborhood. Finally, someone had recognized him and pointed them to this place.

Dan hadn't been able to confirm that Andy was inside, but even if he wasn't, there might be some way to determine where he was.

Dan watched a monitor that showed a black-and-white image of the building's façade. Madison cops had been busy clearing out the surrounding buildings, in case this went bad. A couple of minutes before, he'd received an all-clear transmission from them. Since then they'd watched the building to make sure that no one else went in or out.

"Let's get it done," he said when there was no activity.

He pulled on the Fritz-style Kevlar helmet. He already wore a Kevlar vest underneath a blue jacket with the traditional yellow FBI emblazoned across the back in letters big enough to be seen from a chopper. He would carry a Benelli Super 90 12-gauge, his service Glock .22, and he had four flash-bang grenades clipped to his belt. Other members of the assault team would go in with HK G36 5.56mm assault rifles, while snipers had taken up positions on nearby rooftops, their Remington 700 sniper rifles trained on the door and window of Andy's unit. They were all in contact via their Motorola throat mikes.

The motherfucker would be walking out in cuffs, or he wouldn't be walking at all.

At his command, both tactical teams swarmed out of their vans and started toward the target unit. Dan was glad that his long hunt would soon be over—a little anxious, as always, about what waited behind the door, but drawing comfort from the camaraderie of arms, the tromp of boots on pavement, the easy, efficient movement of men and women who were well trained and disciplined.

This was what they were here for.

24

When he left the motel and got to his car, Andy discovered that he had left his phone in it. He checked for messages, just in case. Nothing.

Still, he decided he should drive by the corner, see how the ladies were doing. His knees were wobbly, his mouth dry. Virtually exhausted. He was glad it was still dark out, glad no one would be able to see his face.

But when he drove past the corner, neither woman was on duty. *Probably out turning a trick,* he thought. *Dammit.*

Any time he came around and didn't see them, however, he couldn't help worrying. What if something had happened? What if someone—vampire or not—had attacked one of them and she hadn't had a chance to call for him? Or if she had called, and he had somehow missed it?

He made one more loop around the block, and then drove to the apartment the women shared. Maybe whichever one wasn't on the street had heard from the other.

Lights burned inside, which eased his fears a bit. Parking, he hurried up to the door and knocked.

The door, unlatched, swung open.

From inside, the cloying stink of blood, of death.

Urine and feces and raw meat.

Andy swallowed a gulp of fresh air, drew his weapon, went in. Kicked the door shut behind.

Angel and Raven were both here.

Both dead.

The savagery made his stomach turn.

Angel had been, once upon a time, a cute young African-American woman with an upturned nose and a friendly smile. By the time Andy met her, he had to look deep beneath the ravages of disease, drugs, and hard living to see those things, but they were still there for the careful observer.

Now, her face was unrecognizable as anything human.

She looked like she had been worked over with a meat tenderizer. The flesh was pulpy, torn away in strips to reveal cracked and broken bone beneath. He found her sprawled on the living room floor, in front of a wooden coffee table, with a pool of blood soaking the carpet beneath her and fat, sated flies crawling over her body. Underneath one of her legs, twisted awkwardly around her, the bones no doubt shattered, he spotted a snapped-off chair leg with bits of skin and muscle, bone and hair adhered to it, which must have been what was used on her.

Numb, Andy continued toward the darkened bedroom, praying that Raven was out on the streets somewhere, or with a trick. Before he even reached the door he knew that wasn't the case.

The stench from in there was as bad as in the living room.

When he flipped on the lights he knew why.

Raven was Asian-American, sporting hair as black as her namesake's feathers, light skin, and a tight body, narrow-waisted, with tiny breasts and great legs that she usually showed off in a miniskirt.

She wouldn't be showing anything off anymore.

Her body was crumpled next to the bed, with a thick pool of blood around her neck. But her head sat on top of the pillow, staring open-eyed at the doorway.

On the wall behind her head, accusatory, scrawled in blood, was Andy Gray's folly laid bare:

HOW STUPID DO YOU THINK WE ARE?

Bile filled his throat and mouth, burning. He spat on the carpet.

Andy had done this. *All my fault.* The two women had been hookers, addicts. But they had also been *human,* alive, and nobody deserved to have their last moments on Earth be so horrible, so degrading, so terrifying.

In hindsight, part of Andy's plan had worked perfectly—they had been bait, and they had attracted vampires. Only these vampires had understood that the women were a trap. Instead of feasting, they had let Andy know just how awful his plan really was.

Was it Paul? he briefly wondered through his horror. No way to tell for sure, not without spending way too much time here, looking for fingerprints or DNA evidence. But he guessed not—after this much time, he suspected that Paul would have hung around, waited to have a face-to-face conversation with Andy instead of just sending another telegram in blood.

The anger began a slow boil in his veins.

He would have to live with Angel's and Raven's murders on his soul . . . but like Paul, though, whatever bloodsucker had done this didn't understand Andy Gray. These murders, like those of his family, would backfire. Rather than scaring him off, this would just triple his resolve.

He would expose these abominations of nature, he would come up with the proof he needed, evidence that couldn't be denied by the press, the public, and a government that preferred to sweep unpleasant truths into dark corners.

He took a long last look at Raven's severed head, to steel himself for what lay ahead, and noticed something white clutched in her lips.

Forced himself closer.

A business card, it looked like.

He leaned over the head, attempting to read it without touching it. And his blood turned to ice.

The card was Felicia's.

Dan Bradstreet stood in the middle of the motel room, turning his whole body to take it in at a sweep because his bullet-resistant visor and the edges of his helmet obstructed the view at the corners of his eyes.

Andy Gray wasn't here. But he had been, and it looked like he would be back. His clothes still hung in the closet, his suitcases stood empty at the back of it. Toiletries in the bathroom, personal effects on the dresser and nightstand. The desk clerk had said that he had been renting the room for more than a month, and had paid in advance through the end of November.

Dan couldn't deny his disappointment. He had wanted Andy here, now, had hoped to finish this tonight, one way or another. Already, some of his men were working on hanging a replacement door and swapping out the room number. Others would wait here to take Andy into custody when he came back.

No telling when that'll be, though. Maybe later tonight, maybe tomorrow. Maybe next week. From the looks of things, Andy was just out for the evening, and would be back right away.

But underestimating him hadn't worked so far, and Dan didn't want to count on it now. He needed to get back on the street, keep looking.

He had started for the door when Sergeant Washington, his liaison with the Madison team, walked in. Dark skin, short hair, a little smile on his mustached face. "Special Agent Bradstreet," he began, "you're going to want to hear about this."

* * *

Felicia's cell phone went right to voice mail.

Same with home and office phones. He left urgent messages on both, how everything had gone horribly, horribly wrong. Steering with one hand, he kept scrolling between the three numbers on his cell, punching the TALK button, then END when voice mail picked up again.

He didn't know where she or her husband Pearce were. Out maybe? Goddammit!

The streets weren't crowded at this hour, but a fall rain had started, making the streets slick and treacherous. Andy's attention was divided, and he kept the accelerator close to the floor, screaming around corners, fishtailing onto the straightaways. He expected to hear sirens at any moment, but he couldn't slow down. Just had to get away.

He brought up her home number again, running a stop sign, jammed his finger down on it.

A voice answered. Finally. Male. Mature. "Hello?"

"Is Felicia there?"

"No, who—?"

"Pearce, right? Felicia—"

"Is this Andy Gray? Felicia's mentioned you were—"

Pearce couldn't seem to understand the urgency, and Andy couldn't take time to explain it. "Where is she?"

"I dropped her at her office, she said she had some stuff to—"

"Call her if you can. Keep calling her. Tell her to get out of there, to go someplace safe and public. Then she should call me and tell me where she is. I'm on my way over now."

"What is this all—?"

"Just tell her, Pearce, it's important." Andy disconnected, tried her office again. No answer. He did a fast U-turn, swerved, narrowly missing an SUV parked at the curb. Correcting, he shot into the other lane, pulled back into his. This time, he did sideswipe a parked car, scraping, shooting sparks. Kept going.

Oh God. Felicia . . .

The place was a slaughterhouse.

A neighbor had called it in. Looking out a window, she had seen a guy running from the apartment with a piece in his hand. He had left the door open behind him. She'd been too afraid to actually go look inside, but she'd called the building manager and he had taken a peek.

Dan's team had had to step over the guy's vomit to get inside. The manager still looked green. But he had positively identified Andy's photo—said he didn't live in the building but had rented the unit and came around all the time. He suspected the women were prostitutes, but they never brought clients here, so he couldn't do anything about it. The witness had also recognized Andy's picture as the guy she had seen running away.

One thing that didn't play was that neither of the corpses had bullet wounds. No one had heard any shots.

These looked like vampire attacks.

Why would Andy have killed them this way? Dan couldn't figure out the message on the wall, either.

Whatever. They were getting closer, that was the main thing.

And Andy, it seemed, had gone from nuisance to full-on homicidal. Even if he hadn't killed his family—and that was still up for discussion—he would go down for these two.

Plus for fucking up my hand. Can't forget about that.

Dan smiled. Easier for him. Now when Andy was killed while trying to escape, the story would be that much easier to sell.

And—*sloppy, Andy*—he had left a card telling them where he was headed next. Or else where he'd just been.

Either way, there would be cops on the scene within a few minutes.

All the way to campus, Andy had been terrified at what he might find there.

Various scenarios, from awful to worse, flitting through his head. He tried to convince himself that Felicia would be in her office, working hard, too preoccupied to answer the phone.

He hadn't been able to make himself believe that one.

None of the nightmare possibilities he had considered were as bad as what he found.

Because she wasn't dead.

He had burst into the office with his shotgun in hand to find her sitting in her desk chair, slumped over her keyboard. The place didn't stink like the apartment had.

Maybe she had simply fallen asleep at the computer. *Just let her be okay,* he thought.

"Felicia!" he called, crossing toward her. She didn't respond.

He reached her, grabbed her shoulder to rouse her.

She flopped back in the chair. Muscles loose, lifeless. Andy's heart slammed in his throat. Too late.

But then her eyelids fluttered. Those cinnamon eyes almost focused on him, just for a second, then closed again. Alive!

So pale, though. Skin like fine china, not her usual dusky hue.

And then he noticed the tear at her throat. Clean, bloodless, ripped flesh, like hastily torn paper.

He forced himself to part the wound. Not a drop of blood. She had been drained. And yet, she lived.

Terror welled up in him like a rising tide. His mind almost went blank as he tried to remember what conclusion they had reached in their numerous conversations.

If a vampire killed a person, that person was just dead. But if a vampire drained a victim and left him or her alive . . .

Oh no.

If it was true, he couldn't let her live. But if it wasn't, she needed medical attention. Now.

She shifted slightly in the chair, and he thought he heard her moan. Didn't know what it meant. Was she coming around? Slipping into vampirism? How could he tell?

Answer: he couldn't.

He reached the only conclusion he could. Swallowed hard, biting back the pain.

Medical attention couldn't save her now, not if she'd been left virtually bloodless. It was amazing that she still had any consciousness at all.

And letting her join the undead, as a vampire, really wasn't an option.

Hands shaking, eyes filling with liquid, he raised the shotgun.

Nothing lives without a head.

"I'm sorry, Felicia," he whispered, aiming the weapon. It suddenly weighed a ton. "I'm so sorry."

25

As Andy pulled out of the campus parking lot, he saw what looked like campus security moving through the shadows toward the Biochemistry Addition, where Felicia's office was. He fought panic and drove away at a leisurely pace, not wanting to attract attention.

When he was two blocks away, he floored it.

A trail of bodies bobbed in his wake. A first-year criminal justice student—hell, an avid *Law and Order* watcher—could connect him to all of them.

He needed to get away from Madison. This time, for a change, he even knew where he should go.

Figuring that whoever was on his trail probably hadn't found out about the cell phone Felicia had obtained for him yet, he dialed Northwest Airlines.

There was a flight leaving Madison at six-fifty in the morning. He would have to change planes in Minneapolis/St. Paul, and then again in Anchorage.

He glanced at his watch. That would leave him sitting around the airport for almost three hours before they boarded. No good. He was safer on the road right now. Leave his things behind in the motel room, buy new ones on the way.

He ended the call. Instead of going to the airport, he headed out of town on I-94. He would drive to Minneapolis and catch the Anchorage flight from there.

Once in Alaska, he would make separate arrangements for getting to Barrow.

Barrow.

He had no idea if there were answers to be found there. But he had run out of other ideas.

As morning came, the sky stayed a flat pewter. The rain of the night before turned into snow—first flurries, then a steady, driving downfall. Andy didn't mind—focusing on the road helped him push the fresh, awful memories and the crushing guilt from the forefront of his mind. The highway grew slick and dangerous, and cars started pulling over to the shoulder to wait for better weather, or snowplows. Andy even saw semitrucks waiting it out.

He kept going.

The wheels of the stolen car slipped and slid on the icy asphalt. His arms and shoulders ached, his eyes burned with exhaustion. He rolled the window down a little, cranked the radio up, to help keep him alert. A few times, he thought he was done for, convinced he would fly off the highway, or skid into oncoming vehicles. He gave consideration to pulling over, joining the other vehicles idling beside the road.

Death, he decided, would be better than not trying.

He kept on.

* * *

Once in Anchorage, Andy left the airport and took a cab into town. Where he was going, he would need special clothes.

He found an outdoor outfitter and paid cash for a parka, silk long johns, boots, heavy lined gloves, a ski mask. He stuffed it all into a new nylon backpack that he could carry on a plane along with his existing overnight bag and checked into a motel.

He stalked the floor of his room. The TV was on to distract him, but it didn't help much. His mind kept spinning around what he'd learned, like clothes in a drum dryer.

Images of Monica nailed to the fence pushed into his consciousness.

His girls, drained of life.

Angel and Raven torn to pieces.

Felicia, her eyes fluttering open as the cold steel of the shotgun barrel touched her chin.

When he'd been on the airplanes, on the move, he could almost outrun the ghosts for a while. Not now, stuck in one place, afraid to venture out into the snowy darkness.

When it became obvious that he wasn't going to fall asleep, he went down to the night clerk at the front desk. The guy sold him a couple of sleeping pills for five bucks; then asked him if he wanted a companion. Andy wasn't sure if he was offering himself, or a female hooker. He turned the guy down without asking for elaboration.

Anyone he came into contact with might become a target.

Back in his room, he took the pills and sat on the bed, fidgeting and twitching until sleep overtook him.

Andy cracked his eyes open, the nightstand clock announcing it was already ten. He got up, looked out the window. The sun was just starting to edge over the horizon.

He showered quickly, brewing coffee on the little in-room coffee maker while he did so. When he got out he downed a cup and dressed in the warm clothes he'd picked up. A vending machine down the hall had a roll of minidonuts and a bag of peanuts. He carried them back to the room, ate them with another cup of the weak brew.

So much for eating right.

But he'd slept too long for a real breakfast—his flight left at eleven-twenty. The flight had been full, but he'd flashed his Bureau ID at the ticket counter and someone had been bumped in his favor. When he was finished with the makeshift meal, he brushed his teeth, checked out, and caught a cab to the airport.

When he got to Fairbanks, he changed to yet another plane. This one was small, an eighteen-seater. Only one seat on his side of the aisle, two across from him. Six rows. Six of the seats were empty, and the flight attendant, who was on the far side of forty and skinny as a heroin addict, asked a couple of people to change seats so the plane would be "adequately balanced." Andy's fellow passengers were all dressed pretty much like him, ready for the weather when they landed. As if to accommodate people in snow gear, the temperature on board stayed frigid.

During the flight, Andy pretended to read a three-month-old copy of *Newsweek* he found in his seat pocket while he thought about what had brought him to this place.

Maybe he should have stayed in Sacramento, so long ago, and cooperated with authorities to solve his family's murder.

What if they'd been killed by someone other than Paul? Andy had put a lot of bad guys behind bars—some of them might have gotten out, or ordered a hit from jail. He shook his head. It was Paul. *Had* to have been Paul. No sense even considering alternatives. He was just as sure that the vampire or vampires who had killed Angel, Raven, and Felicia hadn't been Paul.

Ehhhhhhhhhhh, the voice in his head buzzed loudly. *Sorry Andy, I didn't catch that. Who killed them again? I mean, really?*

Shut up, he told it.

He probably should have stayed sane and sober down in LA. Attacking ADIC Flores had been a big mistake. If he had just done what he was told, he could have served his time and retired with a reasonable pension. His family would be intact. Paul would have had no reason to target them. Felicia would never have heard his name, Pearce wouldn't be a widower, and the deaths of Angel and Raven wouldn't be haunting him night and day.

But maybe he was overthinking the whole thing.

After all, had Paul really needed a reason? Was it a reaction to Andy's obsession with his case, or something he had planned all along?

Maybe Andy had misread him from the start. Maybe he had already turned squarely toward the side of evil. He would have known that taking Andy's wife and kids would cause Andy far more pain. Andy Gray, big FBI agent, was supposed to be able to protect the helpless. Now he had to live knowing that he had failed those closest to him and caused the murder of innocents. Death would have been merciful by comparison.

So what's stopping you?

The thought was banished as quickly as it had come. The release it promised might be sweet, but Andy had two things he had to accomplish before he could allow himself to taste it.

One, he needed to expose the vampires to the rest of the world.

And two, Paul Norris had to die.

Or die again.

Andy closed the magazine, and was about to put it back in the seat pocket when the guy across the aisle spoke up. "Can I see that?"

Andy glanced at him. Fiftyish, heavyset. A working-man's face, lined and creased from the elements. Small blue eyes, short dark hair, an open, uncomplicated expression. "It's a couple months old."

"Better than nothing," the man said. "Which is the other alternative—I got a few Westerns in my suitcase, but it's checked."

Andy passed the magazine over. "Be my guest."

Andy had a book in his suitcase, too, one he kept with him always, but he wasn't about to start reading *30 Days of Night.* Especially on an airplane headed to Barrow, Alaska.

He closed his eyes, still a little thick-headed from the pills he'd taken the night before. He found himself craving a cigarette, which he hadn't had since waking up on that tragic morning. He would not give in to that urge, he promised himself. If it would not help him find the evidence he needed, or Paul, there was no reason to do it.

He felt the pressure in his ears when the plane started its steep descent into Barrow. He yawned, plugged his nose and blew, trying to equalize things. The pilot's voice crackled over the speakers but Andy couldn't understand what he was saying. Sounded like the traditional coming-in-for-a-landing notice. The flight attendant made a hurried hike past the rows of seats, looking at passengers' laps, and then buckled herself into her own seat in back.

The angle of the plane seemed too steep to Andy, but he knew nothing about Barrow's airport. Maybe they had to go in over mountains or something.

He looked out the window, but it was still dark. A few lights, widely spaced, rushed past the plane. Then he heard the engine sounds change, turning into a high-pitched whine, and they bumped against the runway. Caught air again. Andy looked out, saw low buildings floodlit in the darkness whipping past. The plane landed again, hard. Andy could feel the braking, the shudder as the small craft tried to stop. Another hard bump and Andy's tray table bounced out of its restraint, slapping him on the knee.

As he pushed it back into place, the plane started to skid sideways. Andy looked at the guy across from him, panicked. The guy stifled a yawn and flipped another page of *Newsweek*. Andy peered out the window instead, saw the blue runway marker lights coming closer, closer.

Finally, the plane stopped.

One wing hung off the edge of the runway.

The pilot's voice returned. *"Sorry about that, folks. Little ice on the runway. Welcome to the Wiley Post-Will Rogers Memorial Airport here in Barrow. It'll be a short hike to the terminal, so watch your step at the bottom of the stairs, and thank you for flying with us today."*

Andy looked around at the other passengers, but they must have been old Alaska hands. The close call had not disturbed them in the least.

Andy waited his turn and stepped off the plane into an icy wind. He zipped up the parka, wrestled gloves from the pockets, and snugged them on before trying to descend the airplane stairs to the runway. He had visions of slipping on ice, trying to catch himself on the railing, and leaving the skin of his palms on the frozen metal. His breath steamed.

On the ground, he waited uncomfortably while luggage was retrieved from the hold. When he had his overnight bag and backpack he followed the other passengers to the terminal building, a corrugated steel structure that looked temporary. Floodlights lit its façade. Andy checked his watch just to make sure, but it really was two in the afternoon. A thick layer of cloud filled the sky, blocking out any sunlight that might have filtered in. It might as well have been nighttime.

The inside of the terminal wasn't much more impressive than the outside. A few rows of plastic chairs, a board showing arrival and departure times, a Coke machine, a cracked Formica ticket counter. On the wall behind the counter was a paper turkey wearing a pilgrim hat. As with the plane, the inside air temperature was kept cold so people in heavy winter clothing wouldn't be too warm.

Andy stepped out the front door onto a lighted walkway, looking for a cab. There weren't any, or any sign of rental cars. Or shuttles, for that matter. A couple of trucks idled at the curb, and Andy spotted the guy to whom he'd given the magazine on the plane getting into one. "Hey!" he started to call, but the man had already closed the door and the truck lurched into motion.

Andy turned around. A couple of people were still filtering out of the airport. "I need to get into Barrow," Andy said to no one in particular. "Anyone give me a lift?"

A short man stopped and looked out at Andy from beneath a fur-trimmed hood. He was a fireplug of a guy, not much more than five feet tall, but solid looking, with a fighter's broken nose, a couple of chipped teeth in front, and squinty eyes that looked like they'd seen it all and then some. He gave Andy a strange smile, appraising and accepting all at once.

"I'm going that way."

"I'd really appreciate a ride," Andy said. "I was kind of expecting there'd be taxis."

"You came in the summertime, there would be," the man said. "First trip?"

Andy nodded. By the time Stella Olemaun had come to the Bureau's attention, she had already left Barrow. The events described in her book had already been investigated and the reports—whitewashed, Andy was convinced—had been filed, so he and Paul hadn't bothered to come up.

Their interest was in what Stella would do next, not in whatever had happened to her here.

"Strange time of year to come here," the man said. "But your business, not mine. I'm parked just over here."

He led Andy across a gravel parking lot to an old Ford pickup. "Name's Sam," he said as they walked. He offered a hand. When Andy shook it he could feel the hard calluses. "Sam Lorre."

"Andy Hertz," Andy said. The phony name had become easier to remember than the one he'd been born with.

"Pleased to meet you, Andy." They reached the truck and Sam Lorre tossed his own backpack into the back. It was loaded, Andy realized, with spools of razor wire, glinting wickedly in the glow from the parking lot's bright lamps.

"Doing some fence work?" Andy asked.

"Just tryin' to finish fixin' what all got wrecked, last time it went dark," Sam said.

Andy put his bags in the back, cautiously avoiding the wire. As he climbed up into the cab, he thought about what the man had said, and looked at the sky again.

It wasn't just cloudy.

It was dark.

He looked at his watch, at the little date window he usually paid no attention to. The paper turkey inside should have tipped him off.

November 28.

"How long since it got dark?" he asked, settling into the seat.

Sam cranked the key, tossed him that odd smile again. "Ten days," he said. "Usually they stop flying by now. Little more traffic this year—more out than in, but some of each. I just dropped off my wife and kid for the last flight out—won't have them stay for the dark anymore."

He didn't offer to elaborate, and Andy didn't ask him to. They were already on the road, outside the airport grounds, going fifty down a graded gravel track. Sam handled the wheel with practiced efficiency. As he drove he dialed up the heater, and air blew into Andy's face, cold at first but warming fast.

The airport was only a few minutes outside town. Before long, Andy could see bright lights reflecting off the layer of cloud cover. Then they topped a low rise and he could see the lights themselves, like brilliant stadium lighting, on poles all around the town, aimed down toward its perimeter. The light made a kind of moat around the town, containing a high barbed wire fence instead of a castle wall.

Inside the fence, Andy could see more gravel roads—nothing paved—that looked freshly cleared of snow. Snow piled up in huge drifts against the stilt legs of elevated houses, high on the walls of those buildings that remained at street level. Pitched roofs were caked with it.

Andy had been to plenty of cold places—Madison had been no picnic—but he'd also lived in California for a long time. He couldn't quite imagine why anyone would choose to live someplace like this.

More than that, he couldn't imagine why anyone would be crazy enough to stay after what went down here a couple of years ago.

Excerpted from *30 Days of Night* by Stella Olemaun

After seeing the young leader of the invaders of Barrow easily dispatched by the elder, dapper vampire, Eben and I mistakenly took it as a sign of hope. But the truth was the elder, with his smooth bald head and pointed ears, had much worse plans for us.

He addressed the remaining vampires, those that hadn't fled, with a ferocity that sent a chill down my spine.

"This is what we're going to do," he hissed. "First we are going to gather the dead and place them inside their dwellings. I want you to find any and all survivors. I want them killed. Feed on them if you like, or just kill them. I don't care, just *don't* turn them."

I wanted to get out of there, get back to the others and warn them that a sweep was coming, but Eben would not budge. He stayed lying in the snow, his eyes wide and his breath hard. He could not take his eyes off the gore of the young vampire's shattered body, his smashed head.

I pulled at my husband, but he shrugged me off. Something was growing in his mind, a plan of escape, something he would not or could not vocalize except for, "Maybe . . . there is a way."

I didn't know what he meant and I didn't care. We had already discovered that vampires could be destroyed, but our numbers were small and weak. We didn't stand a chance fighting them. Now with the new leader, I felt a fear like nothing before.

I had the sudden urge to gather all the survivors and run, scatter into the frozen forests and hills, and pray that some of us made it out alive.

As the vampire spoke, my fears only got worse.

He raised his arms into the air, and I saw his long cruel fingers coated with the blood of one of his own, as he rallied the undead.

He was planning to sever the pipeline, flood Barrow in oil, and set the whole town on fire, burning everything in it to the ground. No survivors, no problems.

I pulled Eben away finally when he saw that I was near tears. We had to move and the echo of the vampire's orders only solidified the notion:

"By this time tomorrow, I want this town erased from the map!"

We had a meager gathering of survivors in the basement hold, fifteen starving, freezing residents of Barrow, including poor Derek Ott, who had escaped an attack, but not without getting bitten on his arm. Derek was fading fast and we were certain that he would wind up like Lucy Ikos and all the others.

We just didn't have the heart to do what was necessary before he turned. We were still human down there, after all.

Eben's mood had dramatically changed. He insisted that running was the worst thing we could do. "They have us outnumbered," he said, "If we run, they'll get all of us."

I became frustrated. He was telling us what we couldn't do, but he had yet to suggest any alternative, and I let him know.

Instead of fighting me, Eben sat down and placed his head in his hands. Everybody in the shelter seemed to notice and it felt like the last wisps of hope fell away as Eben looked up and spoke.

"I can't paint a pretty picture for these folks anymore, hon," he said addressing me as if knowing what I was thinking. "Those things are tearing the entire town apart. We can't fight. We can't run. The only thing that's done any damage was—"

Eben didn't get to finish his sentence.

Derek Ott had turned.

He was leaping at me and shrieking so loud the *others* were certain to hear. His appearance had changed so abruptly and completely none of us even had time to scream.

Just a few moments ago, he was a teenage boy with shoulder-length hair and a touch of healing acne, but the *thing* lunging at me looked anything but human.

All I could do was watch those needlelike fangs growing from his gums, larger as he neared me.

Until Eben stepped in with an old whaling spear and impaled the screaming vampire in midair and slammed him to the floor hard.

"Stella," Eben yelled. "Axe!"

In a single motion I reached for the axe lying on a crate, grabbed it, and slammed it down on the Ott boy's neck as hard as I could. I felt the resistance of his flesh and bone and then the hardness of the concrete as a spark flew and his head rolled away.

We all fell silent and listened. The streets above us were quiet, but what we did hear was just as bone-chilling; in the distance we heard the screams of other survivors who had managed to hide being dragged from their hiding places; we heard children crying and parents begging for their safety.

I ran to the window to see if I could see what was happening outside, but all I could see was fire and smoke everywhere. I could hear the screams of people, but the vampires were nowhere in my line of vision.

And then the strangest sight of all.

A helicopter approached from the south, moving toward us fast, and I understood where the invaders' attention had been diverted.

I stupidly allowed hope to rise in me when I saw the vehicle coming toward town, but just as quickly it was dashed as I saw dark figures leaping through the air and clinging to the helicopter like leeches.

Someone had come to save us, but even they were no match for the vampires.

The helicopter, overwhelmed with weight, near as I could see, crashed to the ground and exploded as the insectlike attackers scattered joyfully from the flames.

Now it's really over, I thought. They would go house to house. It was only a matter of time until they found us. Even with our few weapons, we couldn't fight long. Soon, they would have us and Barrow would be gone, devoured by the evil that stalked our streets.

It was then that I saw Eben digging through the medical kit and retrieving the syringe. I don't know what I thought at first, but he didn't wait long to make his intentions clear.

He stood over the Ott boy's body where blood was pouring from the severed neck like a free-flowing fountain.

"Eben?"

He looked at me with an expression I'd never seen, so sad and yet determined. "There's no other way."

Eben was insane, had to be, but really I was pleading because I knew what he intended and what it meant. "Please, there's got to be another way," I said crying.

Outside, explosions, cries mixed cruelly with laughter.

Eben regarded the sounds. "If there is, we haven't found it," he said calmly, "and time is running out . . . fast."

Panic was rising in me as I watched Eben kneel down and use the syringe to extract blood from the neck of the Ott boy.

Eben gestured toward a couple of the male survivors, I don't remember who, to hold me back, but I fought them all—"Get OFF me!"—and they backed away.

I pleaded with Eben. "You don't know if it will work! It's crazy! It's someone else's blood! I don't want you to. We'll make it. We'll get out together. All of us."

But Eben didn't argue back.

Instead he settled this fight the way he always did when we fought, when each of us had had our say, with a loving smile and a soft stroke against my cheek with the back of his gentle hand.

"I love you, Stella."

I just stood there helpless, knowing he would not stop even if I pleaded, even if I physically tackled him, or tried to restrain him. I knew my dear Eben well enough to know when he set his mind to something, right or wrong, risky or not, his mind was set.

It was so hard to watch. Suddenly all sound, from outside and in, disappeared as Eben injected himself with the vampire blood and instantly reacted as he drained the tube into his arm.

Eben threw his head back, clenching his teeth tight to hold a scream I could only imagine he wanted to release.

He was in burning agony but I stood there frozen like the rest, not knowing what to expect, not knowing if in the next few moments I would have to actually kill my own husband as we had Lucy Ikos and Derek Ott.

I watched, sobbing, as his face drained white and his eyes transformed to white orbs with black pinholes and veins shot up his neck and hands like snakes running beneath his skin.

And then he collapsed on the floor and silence fell over the room except for my own gasp and continued sobbing.

My Eben was dead.

But only for a moment.

As he lay there, his body twitched and his hands began to curl as if reaching for new life, but he never started to breathe.

He was back, but not alive.

My husband, Sheriff Eben Olemaun, was now . . . undead.

Everyone backed away as Eben crawled back to his knees. Even then, I could see he moved different than the man I had married. He more . . . glided to his knees and then turned to us looking from survivor to survivor with his new eyes, and then finally came to rest on me.

I whispered, "Say something. Talk to me, Eben."

He smiled and I saw his teeth had changed. They were not rows of razors like the Ott boy, but more refined . . . like the fangs of legend.

And then he spoke. "I can smell your blood, Stella. I can see your veins . . . all of them . . . pulsing."

His voice sent a chill and I stepped toward him as I saw one of the men, Stephen Adler, reach for the axe. I looked at Stephen and shook my head.

Eben reacted to me reaching for him and crawled away, almost desperate. "No, keep away from me!"

He stood and looked around. He looked at his hands and then again at the frightened survivors in the shelter. "I won't hurt any of you."

His words sounded choked back like he was defying something trying to take hold of him, and then he gave me one last glance and bounded out of the shelter like a ghoul from a graveyard.

What followed I did not see much of. We waited in the shelter for most of what I can only imagine was Eben fighting for his life. We heard screams and hollers of anger.

Finally when I could wait no longer, I took what weapons we had and joined my husband on the streets of Barrow. To my amazement, everybody in the shelter did the same. When I walked out into the final days of winter darkness, on the blood-soaked streets of our beloved town, I was not alone.

And our group was not alone either—other survivors who had remained hidden like us were emerging to see the fight on top of the world, between Eben Olemaun and the vampire leader.

On one side stood the remaining vampires, but rapidly, more and more people emerged, humans—carrying everything from guns to makeshift spears.

But the focus was on the two figures tearing each other to pieces in the center of town. Eben was not doing as well as we had prayed. He was bloody and weak and by the looks of it, the bald vampire was merely toying with my brave husband.

Sensing the coming loss, the other vampires began to turn their attention to those of us who had come out. I yelled for everybody to band together in a tight group just in case they decided to attack.

I don't know if Eben saw what was happening or simply figured out how to control his newfound skills, but he shocked the hell out of everyone when he got a punch in that not only knocked the vampire leader to the snowy ground, but also drew blood from his nose.

He wiped the blood from his face and began to shake with rage. Eben braced himself for a brutal attack and both vampires and humans alike held our collective breath waiting for the explosion.

It came, but not how any of us could have imagined. The vampire charged Eben, so fast that all I saw was a blur of black streaking toward my husband, who remained poised and focused, eyes narrowed and fists clenched.

As the blur was about to hit him, instead of dodging, Eben greeted the charge with a punch to the head that not only made contact with the vampire, *but went right through*—the most glorious explosion of blood I have ever had the pleasure of witnessing.

His body slid in the ice, headless, and came to a slow halt right at the remaining invaders' feet.

Eben stepped forward, his arm coated red, his new fangs bared in an angry smirk, and he addressed the invaders.

"Get . . . out . . . of . . . my . . . town."

But the invaders, those murdering bastards, had already begun to flee for their undead lives.

I instinctively ran to Eben and hugged him, and he returned the embrace, but there was now a strange coldness juxtaposed with the warmest smile he had ever delivered.

"Should I go after them?" he asked, referring to the fleeing invaders.

"They won't come back," I said, still holding him. "Besides the sun will be coming—"

Oh God. Yes, that was true, right?

Eben's plan worked. He had saved Barrow, but at what cost? He was one of *them* now, fully in control of himself for the time being. But one of them nonetheless.

Now, the sun was his enemy as it was theirs.

Much later, certain authorities would say one hundred and fifty-nine residents of Barrow, Alaska, lost their lives in a pipeline fire that nearly destroyed the town. Others say it was a chemical spill.

Don't believe anyone who tries to sell you that line of bullshit.

I was there.

When the sun came back up, out of the four hundred sixty-two people caught in Barrow when the sun went down, only nineteen of us were there to see it.

The most horrible thing of it all was that it had been twenty at first.

It is difficult for me to recount our final moments together.

After we helped clear the fires and restore some semblance of order and comfort, the survivors became uncomfortable with Eben's presence. After what we'd all been through, it was understandable.

Eben and I walked just outside of Barrow to the hillside where we would always watch the sun disappear, but this time we sat on the other side waiting for its return.

It was Eben's idea. I wanted him to leave, but he was as stubborn in his ways as I was.

The sky changed from smoky black, gradually to brown and, as the sunrise came closer and closer, this golden shaded tint of ashy grey.

Eben held me close and tried his best to explain how he felt. His voice was hollow, odd. "It's getting hard to fight, Stella. I forget sometimes . . . who I was . . . and I feel this pain."

"You could hide," I said. "Live . . . like they do. You could—"

Eben smiled gently and shook his head. "Shhh, that's not what I meant."

He placed his hand on mine. Even through the thick gloves I wore, I could feel his icy touch.

He looked me right in the eyes. "I could live forever, sure, but I don't want to breathe another second"—he paused—"if I can't remember what it feels like to love you."

By then, the sun had crept over the horizon.

It was too soon. I didn't want to let go.

I closed my eyes and in my hand I felt Eben grow soft until I could feel nothing in my grip. Slowly I opened my eyes and looked beside me, where my husband, my partner, my best friend had sat only a moment before.

Now it was only his clothing and some ashes blowing in the warming wind.

26

THE GRAVEL ROAD ran up to a huge, fortified gate.

Multiple layers of chicken wire with boards attached for strength and stability.

Six feet of razor wire at the top made the entire construction eighteen feet tall.

Blinding lights shone down at the gate, where a dozen men and women in heavy parkas held shotguns and automatic rifles.

Sam Lorre slowed the truck and cruised to a stop outside the gate. Behind this one, there was a second gate, protected with armored gun turrets on tall watchtowers. The guards in the towers swept the truck with searchlights. There seemed to be two different types. When Andy asked, Sam told him the second ones were special UV lights, but he didn't elaborate.

"Hey, Sam," one of the guards at ground level said. She smiled at Sam, who seemed known to all of them. "You got it?"

"It's in the back," Sam said. "Everything we need to reinforce the fences."

A few of the guards had wandered over to Andy's side of the truck. As if at some signal Andy didn't catch, the one talking to Sam asked, "Who's the passenger?"

"Picked him up at the airport after I dropped off Candy and Bob," Sam replied.

One of the guards on Andy's side tapped on his window with the barrel of a Mossberg 12-gauge. "Mind stepping out, sir?" he asked politely.

Andy had no reason to antagonize them, even though it grated on him to be treated like a criminal—like he had treated so many other people, he realized—with no grounds whatsoever. "Sure," he said, opening his door slowly. He climbed down with his hands visible. "I have ID," he said. The guard with the shotgun nodded and Andy fished his ID wallet out of a pocket, held it up. "Andy Hertz," Andy said. "FBI."

"That's just fine, sir," the guard said. He lowered the shotgun—there were at least seven others pointed at him, Andy figured—and drew a small Maglite from somewhere. "Open your mouth, please?"

Andy complied, surprised that identifying himself as an FBI agent had generated no reaction whatsoever. The guard shone the light in his mouth for a few seconds.

"Thank you," he said. "Now let me take a look at your eyes."

Andy understood. They didn't care who he was—as long as he was not a vampire.

A moment later, the guard shut off the light. "He's clean!" he called. "Welcome to Barrow, Mr. Hertz."

"Thanks," Andy said. "It's a . . . pleasure to be here."

He went to the back of Sam's truck, retrieved his backpack and overnight bag. Passing the open driver's side window, he stuck his hand in, shook Sam's. "Thanks for the lift, Sam," he said. "I guess I can walk from here."

"Any time, pal," Sam answered. "You plan on staying, just be careful, okay?"

"Don't worry," Andy said. "That's my middle name."

"Not according to your ID!" the guard who had inspected him shouted. Andy laughed and nodded. He hadn't thought the guy had even looked at the ID. *Guess they don't take chances around here.*

"Welcome to Barrow," a couple of the others said. Andy acknowledged their greetings and walked into town.

Inside, beyond the glare of the searchlights and the stadium-style light banks, the town was well lit but quiet. Andy walked for several blocks past buildings that looked abandoned: boarded up, padlocked, chained. The sidewalks were narrow, the streets graded gravel frosted with snow. After the blast furnace heat of the truck, the cold air tore at his exposed cheeks and nose like the claws of an airborne wolverine.

The first person he encountered inside the town surprised him, rounding a corner almost silently. He wore a heavy snow parka, like most of the others, with the hood snugged up and his long black beard sticking out. Over his shoulder was a Remington pump-action. He gave Andy a hard-eyed stare, then nodded once. "Evening," he said. His tone was cool.

Andy wondered how one could tell, in the dark. "Hi," he replied.

The man hurried past him without another word.

Two blocks farther on, Andy saw a neon sign that said HOTEL glowing through the gloom. He went toward it, passing a couple of other men who stood in the street beside an idling SUV. Everyone was armed, it seemed. Rifles or shotguns. Andy's Glock, which he'd been allowed to carry on the airplanes only because of his FBI credentials, seemed tiny and inadequate by comparison.

At the Northern Lights Hotel, he had no trouble getting a room. The desk clerk seemed surprised and maybe a little overjoyed to have another guest. "Quiet this time of year," he said. He was thin and dark, probably part Eskimo, Andy guessed. "Summer, you didn't have a reservation you'd be sleeping on the street. Everyone likes to come and see the midnight sun, the northern lights. But this time of year, most of the hotels just close down. I stay open because there are always a handful, like you."

"I'm glad you did," Andy said. "I didn't really have a plan, just came on the spur of the moment."

"Hope you know what you're in for," the clerk said.

"I think I have a good idea." He signed his fake name on the register and the clerk gave him the key to Room 210. Andy rode the tiny elevator up one flight and found his room, where he dumped his bags on the floor and turned up the heat against the chill that seemed to have leaked in through the walls. He stripped off his coat, went into the bathroom, ran hot water onto a washcloth, and draped it over his face. He was weary from traveling, but he couldn't sleep yet. He had to get his bearings here. Right now, he was exposed, unprotected. If Paul showed up, he'd only have the Glock, and he'd be history. The hot, damp cloth was refreshing, but after a few seconds he took it away and threw it into the rust-stained tub. It felt too much like relaxing.

And he hadn't come to Barrow to relax.

As he started for the door, however, his knees felt like rubber. He dropped onto the bed, heard the springs squeal under his weight.

Maybe he did need some decompression time after the long journey. He pawed the TV remote off the nightstand and clicked on the set. Satellite reception, which only made sense. He spent a few minutes thumbing through the channels, looking for anything appealing enough to leave on while he tried to grab a few minutes of shut-eye. Finally, he settled on a *Seinfeld* rerun, watched through it and a second episode before he could rouse himself again.

He forced himself to his feet and tugged on the heavy clothing, aware that, since it looked like he'd be staying awhile, he would need more. There was already snow on the ground, but he knew it would get even colder.

Torn between putting the ski mask over his face and worrying that it might give strangers the wrong idea, Andy compromised by stuffing it into the zippered side pocket of his parka. If he got uncomfortable enough he could put it on later. He zipped up the coat, donned the gloves, and went back out into the chill night.

By his reckoning it was early evening now, but the sky looked just like it had earlier—dark and cloudy, with the bright lights rimming the town reflected. He guessed he had better get used to it.

The streets hadn't changed much, either. Still a few people walking about, alone or in pairs. Most carried rifles or shotguns, and Andy even spotted a couple of automatic rifles in the mix.

Barrow looked more like a war zone than a sleepy Alaska town.

A few minutes of wandering brought him to the sheriff's station, a good-sized trailer with a foundation of concrete blocks. The windows were barred, the door reinforced with iron straps.

Remembering what had happened to Stella and Eben Olemaun, though, Andy decided it wasn't surprising that a new sheriff might want more secure digs.

A young man stood outside the office. Like everyone else, he wore a hooded parka. Below it, though, his khaki pants had a heavy black stripe. A uniform, then.

"Sheriff?" Andy asked as he approached.

The man turned to him. A square face with a strong jaw and piercing blue eyes. Short blond hair showed under the hood. "Yes," he said. His eyes widened a little as he regarded Andy, registering surprise. "You're a visitor here."

It was a statement, not a question. Andy answered anyway. "Just got off the plane."

"Then you won't be leaving again," the Sheriff said.

"That's what I hear. Hope I didn't make a mistake."

"I'm a relative newcomer myself," the Sheriff said. "But I love it here. Wouldn't think of leaving now."

"Even with all the troubles?" Andy asked.

The Sheriff shrugged, a motion barely observable under the heavy coat. "We get troublemakers time to time, just like any other place. They see we're a little different—ready for pretty near anything they could bring. They turn around and go home."

Andy nodded. This guy was playing his cards close to his vest, but not outright lying. Andy knew he'd do the same if their circumstances were reversed. "My name's Andy Hertz," he said, sticking out his hand. "FBI. I've closed the file now, but I spent a bit of time checking out your predecessor. Or his wife, anyway, the deputy. Stella Olemaun."

The Sheriff kept his face steady but his head ticked up just a little, as if re-thinking the measure he'd taken of Andy at first. He touched Andy's gloved hand with his own. "Then you're not just here doing the tourist thing."

"Not entirely. Stella and her book piqued my interest. I wanted to see where it all happened. How it happened."

"My name's Kitka, Agent Hertz. Brian Kitka. As for what happened, if you read Stella's book, you know as well as anyone, pretty near. At least, you know what happened the first time."

"The first time?" Andy echoed. "You mean . . ."

Brian Kitka nodded, eyes growing steely. "They came back. Been a while now, but I don't see the folks up here ever really letting their guards down again."

Andy had seen oblique postings on message boards about a second attack, but hadn't believed them.

Of course, nothing had ever hit the mainstream news sources. He'd been out of the Bureau loop by then—not that he had ever been in it, when it came to vampires. Without any kind of confirmation, he had assumed the second invasion was imaginary or fictional, Internet rumor. "When was that?"

Brian thought for a moment. "Two thousand four," he said.

"So, three years between the first wave and the second," Andy said. "And this year?"

"Nothing," Brian replied. "Quiet as church on Tuesday morning. So far."

"But even so," Andy pointed out. "I saw the fences, the light towers."

"We try to keep it all in good repair," Brian said. "We had that stuff last year. They came anyway. A Barrow year plays hell with infrastructure, and no one wants to take a chance, so each year we rebuild almost from scratch."

Andy tried to get the timeline straight in his own head. "You weren't here the first time," he surmised. "When Eben was Sheriff."

"I came later, just in time for the oh-four attack," Brian said.

"And you stayed."

"Gets in your blood, I guess," Brian said. "My son Marcus likes it, too. Doing real well in school."

Andy was impressed with the man and a little stunned.

Brian Kitka had lived through one vampire attack on his town and admitted that another one could come at any time. The long night had set in. How could Kitka be so composed, so casual?

And all along I thought I was the one who lost his mind.

"That's . . . that's good to hear," Andy said, with a quaver in his voice.

"You're cold," the Sheriff said. "Let's step inside."

"Thanks." Brian was right. Even with the cold weather gear, the Arctic air was getting to him. "Guess I never got over my thin California blood."

"Well, it's not much inside," Brian assured him. "We like to spend our taxpayer money on town defenses, not on fancy digs for me. But the space heaters work real good."

Andy followed the Sheriff inside, wondering if the folksy thing was real or just an act. The last down-home, regular Joe Lawman he'd met, back in Missouri, had turned out to be as hard as iron.

He was barely through the door when he heard a female voice, grating as a squeaking gate hinge. "New meat?"

"Donna, this is Special Agent Hertz with the FBI," Brian Kitka said. "That's Donna Sikorski, my deputy."

The woman who waddled out from behind a desk was almost as wide as she was tall. She stuck a pudgy hand out toward Andy, but when he took it, her grip was crushing. She may not have met Bureau height/weight requirements but that didn't make her soft. "FBI, huh? Don't see many Feds up here. The ones who do come don't usually get out of Anchorage."

"I'm on special assignment," Andy lied. "Actually, tell you the truth, I'm here on my own time, not the Bureau's."

"That's good," Donna said. "That means we don't have to be nice to you, buy you dinner, shit like that."

Brian laughed. "Donna's got a problem being honest," he said. "We can never get her to say what she really thinks."

Donna looked Eskimo: broad, flat face, dark skin, black hair tied in a bun. She smiled but Andy couldn't tell if it was genuine or not. "John complains about that too," she said.

"Who's John?"

"John Ikos," Brian explained. "Trapper, lives southeast of town a bit. Her boyfriend."

Andy thought that maybe she blushed a little. "John's not my boyfriend," she retorted. "You call your right fist your girlfriend? Because I know you haven't dated since you moved here."

"All right, all right," Brian amended. "John Ikos is a trapper Donna sleeps with from time to time. Helps take the edge off. You should see her when she's snippy."

"I'm not sure I'd survive it," Andy said.

"Survival is what we're all about," Donna said. "Way John puts it is, 'Survival is job one.' Just like that old car commercial."

"He's pretty much responsible for helping the town survive the last attack," Brian said. "I mean, we all pitched in. He got shot up bad, but John Ikos took out more than his share. Donna's just about the only one in town who likes him, and vice versa, but—"

"You hear me say I like him?" Donna interrupted.

"—but everyone *respects* him," Brian continued, ignoring her. "Hate to think where we'd be if we hadn't had him."

"Sounds like quite a guy."

"He's all right," Donna said. "You want some coffee, Fed?"

He had started to warm up inside, but still felt the chill in his bones. "Coffee would be great."

She went to a coffee pot sitting on top of a metal filing cabinet, poured some black sludge into a Styrofoam cup. "Something in it? Cream, sugar, booze?"

"Go for the booze," Brian said. "Nothing else is going to cut the taste."

"John likes my coffee," Donna protested. Even as she did, though, she took a bottle from the top drawer of the cabinet and splashed some whiskey into the cup.

"John eats woodrat," Brian countered. "And I've never heard of him burying any of his sled dogs, but he's always getting new ones."

Andy was hesitant to drink the whiskey. Not a great idea to go down *that* road again. But he wanted these people to trust him, and if he came off as some kind of teetotaler—even though that's what he had been, since Monica's death—he was afraid they'd close up. He took the cup from Donna, sipped from it. "What does he trap?"

"Whatever he can," Brian said. "I'm glad he's out there—he's kind of an early warning system for us. Anything comes across his turf, he knows about it, and that includes . . . well, you know. Them."

Andy took another sip. Stuff was foul. "Sounds like a good guy to have around."

"Got that right," Donna said. She had squeezed back behind her desk and busied herself with some kind of paperwork. "More ways than one."

"Only for you, Donna," Brian said. "But yes, John Ikos is a blessing in many ways. I'm no Eben Olemaun, I'm afraid—or Stella, for that matter. I need all the help I can get."

"The Olemauns sound like remarkable people."

"They are," Donna said.

Andy noted the present tense she used, with some surprise, but decided not to ask about it.

It sounded like the guy he really wanted to meet was John Ikos. He probably knew as much about the bloodsuckers as anyone else, and maybe he would be more willing to talk about them. At the very least, he was probably the kind of backwoods Gomer who Andy could trick into revealing something.

He stayed long enough to be polite and downed as much of Donna's brew as he could stomach. They talked about the Olemauns a while longer, then Brian and Donna started giving him tips on dealing with the cold and the extended darkness.

That part, he was pretty sure he could handle. He had been living with the darkness of his own soul for some time now.

When he was able, he excused himself. He had teased from them a general sense of how to find John Ikos, and he wanted to get busy looking for him right away.

After all, it wasn't going to get any lighter outside.

Thirty minutes after Special Agent Hertz left the office, Brian Kitka's paperwork was interrupted. "Something you should see," Donna said. She was walking toward him with a piece of paper in her hand. He had a vague recollection of having heard the fax machine, but he had ignored it.

"What is it?"

"Your garden variety general law enforcement bulletin," she replied. "Some guy already wanted for murdering his wife and two daughters just killed three more people. A college professor and two hookers."

"What's it got to do with us?" Brian asked.

Donna handed over the sheet.

A photograph on it clearly showed the face of the man who had introduced himself as Andy Hertz.

According to the bulletin, he really was FBI, but his name was Andrew Gray.

By the time he finished scanning the page, Donna was back at her desk, typing something on her computer's keyboard. "That FBI guy look to you like someone who would kill his family?" Brian asked. "Or maybe like someone looking for his family's killer?"

"That guy?" Donna didn't look away from her screen. "He's no killer."

Brian nodded. *Same thing I thought.*

He crumpled the fax, leaned over his desk, and fired a perfect swish into Donna's wastebasket.

"Two points," he said. "Puts me up by what, twelve? Fourteen?"

"Bite me, Kitka," Donna said. She didn't even stop typing. "You know you cheat like a motherfucker."

"No I don't."

"And," she added, turning around this time to shoot him a malicious grin, "you lie like a pig."

27

I LIE TO EVERYONE *I* MEET.

Andy trudged across snow packed as hard as concrete, heading to where he hoped John Ikos lived.

He hadn't wanted to come right out and ask, so he was only vaguely sure where he was going. Besides which, his head was still buzzing a bit from the first taste of alcohol he'd had in a couple of years.

When was the last time I was completely honest with another human being?

Who knew? Without exception, he had been lying to everyone. There were random truths mixed in among the falsehoods, of course. More, with Felicia, whom he had largely trusted. But he had been playing a role for a long time, and he knew as well as anyone that one couldn't risk going undercover indefinitely without becoming, to one degree or another, the part that he played.

Where Andy Gray left off and Andy Hertz began was a blurry line at best.

Also blurry was the line of low hills facing him. The endless night wasn't pitch black—maybe it would get that way, but it wasn't there yet. Instead, it was like the sky just at the end of dusk—hazy, hard to make out any kind of detail, especially in the distance where everything blended together. Andy knew he would find the trapper somewhere in those hills. But which hill? He hadn't counted on there being so many.

He turned around to make sure he could find his way back to town, if necessary. No problem there. The lights sent a glow up into the sky that illuminated the undersides of high, thin clouds. But when he turned back it was even harder to distinguish anything in the dimness ahead. The cold seeped under his hood, into his gloves. Another cup of Donna's horrible coffee sounded good just now.

But he had set himself a goal, so he slogged on. The only sound was the brittle snow crunching under his boots. In spite of the ski mask, his nose was too frozen to smell anything. He was beginning to accept how stupid he had been to come out this way, only hours in the region, exhausted from his ordeal in Madison, and subsequent flight from there. *Another item to add to the ever-growing list of idiotic things I've done lately.* He should have waited, acclimated himself to the weather and conditions, before setting out across country on his own. Being stubborn, pushing himself too hard, could wind up getting him lost out here.

Hypothermia, freezing to death.

At least he'd heard that you went numb before you died and didn't really feel much at the end.

Some comfort in that.

Another fifteen minutes or so passed, and he started to genuinely worry. His mind was wandering, his focus going. His legs moved stiffly, robot-like, but they kept him headed forward. To where, he didn't know.

He watched the red light on the snow for several seconds before he figured out what it was. Finally, it clicked.

A laser sight.

The beam played about him, then landed on his feet.

He froze, watching it work its way up.

When it reached his stomach, Andy broke his paralysis, hurled himself to his left and flattened in the snow.

"Don't shoot!" he shouted as loud as he could. "I'm looking for John Ikos! Kitka sent me!" Another lie.

He struggled to his feet with his hands in the air. "Don't shoot!" he repeated. "I'm a friend of Brian Kitka and Donna Sikorski!"

A dour voice sounded across the snow. "Come forward," it said. "Keep your hands where I can see 'em, and stop when I tell you to, or you won't live to make a second mistake."

Andy obeyed the voice. As he walked, he kept checking his chest. The red dot from the laser sight was centered there, steady. Guy was good.

The voice stopped him about ten yards from the base of a hill. Peering through the gloom, Andy could barely see a structure, largely concealed by snow drifts, built up against the hill. A horizontal slit window faced him, making the thing look more like some kind of military bunker than a trapper's cabin. He couldn't see the man inside, or the gun, but he knew both were there.

"Hold it!" the man commanded. Andy stopped.

"Let's see your hands."

Andy held them up.

"Those are gloves," the man said. "I said your hands."

Andy understood. Vampires had clawed fingers. This guy was taking no chances. He was hesitant to comply because it was so cold, and he didn't want to lose any fingers to frostbite. But for a few seconds, he could do it. He tugged off the heavy gloves, raised his bare hands.

A spotlight blazed from the slit window. Blinding.

"Okay," the man said. "Put your gloves back on and show me your teeth."

Andy fumbled with the gloves, but got them on. Rolled up his face mask to his upper lip, shut his eyes and opened his mouth. He could feel the spotlight on his face. Then it clicked off and he was back in the cold and dark.

"All right," the man said. "Keep your hands up and keep coming."

Andy obeyed, and a door opened in the bunker, spilling light out onto the snow. Then a silhouette appeared in the doorway. A tall man, lean, wearing a fur-trimmed parka. Weapon in his hands—the odd-looking steel Barrett M82A, complete with bipod—but at ease now, no longer pointed at Andy. Andy was glad he hadn't fired it—just one of those .50 BMG rounds would have torn him apart.

"John Ikos?"

"That's me," the trapper replied. "Who's asking?"

"My name is Andy Hertz," Andy lied. "I'm with the FBI."

"Uh-huh." John Ikos paused for a moment, stood in his doorway staring at him. Andy had the impression the trapper was going to order him away. Instead, he nodded gravely. "Well, I won't hold it against you, I guess. But I want to see your gun before you take another step."

Andy didn't bother to deny carrying one. Awkward with the gloves on, he worked it free from its holster and held it by the butt. John came a couple of steps forward, limping slightly, and put out a hand. "Give it over," he said. "You can have it back when we're done here. Which won't be very long, so don't think you're staying for a meal."

Remembering what Brian Kitka had claimed about the man's eating habits, Andy didn't think that would be a problem.

He put the Glock in John's hand. "I'm getting the idea Feds aren't very popular up here," he said.

"Are they anywhere?"

"Maybe not so much, now that you mention it," Andy admitted. "But some places less so than others."

"Come on inside." John Ikos led the way. The front section was indeed bunkerlike. The wall was concrete block, and below the slit were weapons, ammunition, binoculars, a spotting scope, night vision goggles, all arranged neatly. Looked like it all got plenty of use.

A second door, steel clad, opened into the main cabin. This was a more traditional trapper's cabin. A woodstove burned in one corner, heating the main room nicely and scenting the air with wood smoke. Pots and pans hung on the wall between that and an open fireplace, where a large kettle hung over glowing coals. A wooden cabinet held a basin that Andy figured was the extent of the indoor plumbing. He couldn't quite imagine using an outhouse in the Arctic's brutal winters, but he was pretty sure there was no other option here.

John Ikos nodded toward a table and chairs made from local woods, rough hewn and unpolished. A propane lantern glowed on the table. "Sit," he said. Andy did, and John sat across from him, putting the Glock on the tabletop and holding the rifle on his lap. "You probably think I'm one of those Waco, Ruby Ridge survivalist nutcases."

"I don't know about that," Andy said. "I just know Brian and Donna said you're the one to see about vampires."

"Well, I'm not," John continued, ignoring Andy's comment. "Far as I'm concerned, those people got what they deserved. I got nothing against the law, or federal agents in general. I'm just a careful guy is all. I protect what's mine, and I sure as hell take no chances with the F-B-fucking-I."

"Why's that?"

"Met another one a while back. You noticed the limp?"

"I did."

"He's the bastard did it to me. My own fault, of course. Let my guard down that time." In the lantern's light, John Ikos's eyes looked deep and sorrowful, his face lined with age and concerns. His teeth were bad, his nose had been broken, and a latticework of scars ran up from his right cheek to the corner of his eye.

"What happened?" Andy asked. The trapper seemed to want to talk about it. Get him going, gradually shift over to what Andy wanted to discuss. Classic interrogation technique.

"It was after we'd fought off the last attack," he said. He seemed confident that Andy would know what attack he meant. "I found one of 'em in the snow, and had this bright idea, which turns out weren't such a bright idea."

A lot of that going around, it seems, Andy thought.

John said: "I'd bring the body back here, check it out, then slice and dice it and send pieces to scientists and laboratories to study. They could figure out what makes 'em tick, and how to get rid of 'em."

"I've tried to do the same," Andy said.

"Only thing is, this one wasn't as dead as I thought," John went on. "Came to after I got him here. I should have known better—his head was barely hangin' on, but it was still attached. But I'd been up for days, fighting, I was beat and not thinking clearly. I got it home, sat down, and fell right asleep in my chair.

"When I come around, he was sittin' up lookin' at me. Holding my shotgun. Said he owed me, for savin' his worthless life. He was some kinda self-hating bastard, that was for sure. Complaining about how complicated it was to be undead, how much there was to figure out. I'd've happily finished him off but he wasn't having any of that.

"But then he surprised me. Maybe because he owed me, like he said. I never knew. But he passed me over the pump-action. I tried to use it, but he'd taken the shells out. Time I got new ones loaded in he had drawn his own piece and shot me in the leg. Blew out most of my kneecap. I shot him too, but him shootin' me spoiled my aim and I missed his head. Both of us wounded, he starts laughing. Shows me his FBI ID, then takes off. Like the whole damn thing is some kind of joke that he got and I didn't."

"You just let him go?" Andy asked.

"Nothing else I could do," John answered. "I thought I was gonna pass out from the pain and blood loss. Eventually managed to get a tourniquet on it, stop the bleeding, and a couple days later made it into town so a doctor could take a look. That fucking bloodsucker was long gone, of course. Swore he'd never come back to Barrow, so that was something.

"I went looking for him after I'd healed up a bit. On his ID there was an address in Los Angeles, California, so I went there." John chuckled softly. "What a place that is, I tell you. See more freaks in a day than in a whole lifetime up here. And worse—not just individual bloodsuckers but whole gangs of 'em."

"Gangs?" Andy repeated. He had never heard of any during his time there. But he hadn't been back to California since Monica's death.

"That's right. Roaming, killing . . . organized, like drug gangs or whatever. Scary shit. Scarier than one lone motherfucker with a federal ID."

Andy hadn't dared to hope the trapper was talking about Paul Norris, but it almost had to be. "What was his name?"

"I'll never forget that," John said. "Norris. P. Norris. P for prick, you ask me."

Icy needles stabbed Andy's heart.

Holy shit.

"P . . . for P-Paul," Andy stammered. "He was my partner, before . . . before he got turned."

John Ikos's deep eyes burned into him. "You looking to kill him?"

Andy could only nod.

John laughed dryly. "Well hell, man, why didn't you say so? You want a drink?"

He leaned the rifle up against the table and went to the cabinet underneath the washbasin, coming back with a jug and two metal cups. He filled them both, set one in front of Andy. Andy was afraid of what was in it—not even out of a bottle with a brand name on it, but a ceramic jug—but he'd turned a corner with John Ikos and didn't want to lose the ground he had made. He smiled, took a sip. Choked it down. "Wow," he managed. "That's strong stuff."

"Make it myself," John said. "They won't sell hooch in town because it makes people homicidal or some such, during the dark. I whip up a batch every summer. Saves good all winter long."

"I bet," Andy said, wheezing a little. "So you were here for both attacks, right?"

"Damn straight," John replied. He helped himself to a long swallow from his cup. "Took out a goodly number of the bloodsucking bastards, I do say so myself."

Andy raised his cup in a toast. "Here's to that," he said. They touched cups, then Andy took a tiny sip while the trapper finished off his own. He refilled his cup from the jug, which he'd conveniently brought to the table.

"I've spent most of my life killin' things," John said. "Animals and such. I'm no stranger to death, and in my more philosophical moments—which you might see, six or seven cups from now, you stick around—I find a kind of beauty in it. But these things—there's nothin' beautiful about them. They are just machines of death, goin' through life like a thresher through a wheat field at harvest. Raw, ugly, brutal. That one, Norris, tried to say he was like me because he eats what he kills, same as I do. But it's *not* the same. I don't see those animals as useless chunks of meat that happen to be breathing until I get my sights on 'em. I see their value for what they are, and when I'm not trying to fill my larder, I'm happy to watch 'em running wild and free.

"To those monsters, though, we're all just lunch. Some of us are today's lunch, some of us are in storage till tomorrow. But we're all lunch and good for nothing else."

"These attacks," Andy began. "Fighting them off must be more like a war than a hunting trip."

"Exactly," John said. "I've done that, too. The Gulf. Hottest place I've ever had the displeasure of being, I can tell you that. This was just like that—about strategy and overwhelming force and mass casualties. Sometimes about collateral damage and acceptable losses, too. This last time, though?" He smiled—an act that looked oddly out of place on his grim visage—and stopped his cup just short of his lip. "This last time, we had help."

"What kind of help?"

"Don't expect you'll believe me," the trapper said. "But you've come this far so maybe you will anyway. Me, I'm not so sure about any of it."

"What happened?" Andy asked.

"I really don't know," John said. "You've maybe even heard of 'em. Eben and Stella Olemaun?"

Heard of? Stella was ultimately the reason he was here at all. But she had last been seen in LA, right around the time that Paul had been changed. "They were here?" Andy asked, perplexed.

"In a way," John Ikos said. "Some of us saw 'em, Kitka and Donna and me and a few others. They showed up and just tore through the vampires like they was old toilet paper or something. Then they told us they'd be here, watching over Barrow. Then they were gone."

Andy touched the rim of his cup. "You sure you hadn't been hitting this stuff too much?"

"I know how it sounds," John answered. "Sounds nuts. I'd think so, too, I didn't see it. And if there hadn't been other witnesses I'd most likely doubt my own eyes."

Andy didn't quite know how to take this story. It sounded like a crock, the kind of tale people told each other to help make the long winters go a little faster. *Guardian angels?* Andy had quit believing in them before he gave up on Santa Claus.

But the trapper didn't seem like the fanciful type, and he looked dead serious.

Andy decided not to press him on it.

"You just here to kill Norris?" John asked him after a few quiet minutes. "Or you got something else in mind?"

"I don't even know where Paul is, to be honest," Andy replied. "I'd love to find him and kill him. But my first priority is to find out whatever I can about the vampires—get real proof of their existence, that nobody can ignore. Once they're exposed, then I can worry about Norris."

John Ikos nodded. "Makes sense," he said. "Tell you what, you want the goods, you got to talk to a fellow in town, name of Harlow."

"Who is he?"

"Chris Harlow. That's not his real name, but it's what he goes by. He's the writer worked on Stella's book with her."

"Gross?" Andy asked, drawing the name from the recesses of his memory. Carol Hino had mentioned him. *"Donald Gross?"*

"I think that's his real name, yeah."

"He lives *here?* In *Barrow?"* One astonishment after another.

"I think he knows we'll protect him," John said. "He's got a lot of information about them in his head—oh, they'd *love* to see him dead."

"Can I talk to him?"

"I expect that's up to him. It'd be worth a shot, at least."

"How do I find him?"

John described an unmarked trailer in the center of town and told him how to find it. "He values his privacy, like most of us," he warned. "But if you tell him what you're after he'll most likely be happy to help." He finished off his second cup of moonshine and rose from his seat. Andy's first still sat unfinished on the table. He raised it, drained off the last, put it down, and stood. "Thanks for the drink, John," he said. "And the conversation."

"My pleasure," John Ikos said. "I like what you're doing here, Andy. I can help, you just let me know." He extended his hand, and Andy took it. His grip was firm, offering what seemed like genuine friendship. If he was interpreting it correctly, that was an offer Andy was happy to accept.

"I appreciate that," Andy said.

John opened the door into the bunker, then crossed and did the same for the exterior door. "One more thing," he said. "Just keep your sights on the simple fact that I forgot once."

"What's that?"

"Nothing lives without a head."

Andy stopped short, his thoughts flitting briefly on Felicia's cruel fate. "That's something Paul Norris told me once. And Stella wrote that in her book—or Donald Gross did, I guess. I've . . . I've had to keep it in mind."

"Good advice," John said. "You hang onto that, you'll stay alive. You can put that in the bank."

28

Andy couldn't have said if it was the booze or the friendly company, but when he left the trapper's cabin he didn't feel as cold or as lost as before.

The five miles back to town seemed shorter than the hike out, and of course the town's lights shone like a beacon so he didn't have to worry about finding his way.

The hard part about living above the Arctic Circle, he could see, would be getting his own internal clock set right.

By his watch, it was well after midnight now, but there were more people out on the main streets than there had been before. Since the sun didn't determine people's schedules, they were left to do it for themselves, sleeping when they were tired and going out when they weren't. Shops were open, people were chatting and laughing. Even though he wasn't part of it, Andy got the impression that Barrow was a real community, in a way the big cities he had spent most of the past couple of years in could never be. As if to reinforce his separateness, John's directions sent him down narrow side streets instead of the bright, busy avenues.

John's description was accurate, so a short while later he found what had to be Donald Gross's trailer.

It sat by itself on a block that had been burned out. Scorched foundation walls marked the limits of where buildings had once stood. The trailer itself was at least thirty years old, Andy guessed. It had been white with dark brown trim, but the brown had faded and the white muddied, so the two colors almost blended now. The windows were screened and curtained, but there were lights on inside.

Andy knocked at the door.

From somewhere inside, he heard a rush of movement—doors closing, hurried footsteps, frantic activity. Over the rest of it, Andy thought he could hear someone having energetic, passionate sex. That stopped suddenly, but the other sounds continued a little longer. He was reminded of a kid hiding dirty magazines from his mom, or a dope dealer running to flush the evidence.

He waited, wondering if Donald Gross actually thought he was being subtle.

Finally, the trailer's front door opened, though a screen still separated him from the writer. "Yeah?" the man said.

"My name's Andy Hertz," Andy told him. "John Ikos sent me over to see you. I'm with the FBI."

"Jesus," the man said. "I haven't done anything."

Looking at him, Andy doubted the truth of that statement. He didn't know how old Donald Gross was, but the man he was looking at seemed to be in his sixties. His hair was long and stringy, matted, and faded to an unhealthy yellowish white. Which pretty much matched his skin, except that the hair lacked the large blotches of melanin that marred his cheeks. His hooded eyes were filmy and bloodshot, surrounded by a relief map of a face. His teeth, when he opened his mouth, were blackened and rotting. He didn't stand still, but shifted his weight from foot to foot while he waited for Andy to say something.

Great. A tweaker, Andy thought. *Meth or crank or some such. No wonder it took him a while to get to the door.*

"I know," Andy said finally. "I'm not here on official business, don't worry. I'm actually off the payroll for now." *Right. For now.* "I'm trying to learn about vampires, and I'd like to talk to you about Stella Olemaun and *30 Days of Night.*"

The man behind the screen blinked and ran his fingers through his scraggly hair. "I don't . . . I don't know what you're talking about."

"You're Donald Gross, right?"

The man smiled nervously. He wore a stained sweatshirt with a plaid flannel shirt open over it, and filthy gray sweatpants. "Nope. You got the wrong guy. My name is Chris Harlow."

"Look, I know who you are, Mr. Gross," Andy said. "I just want to talk. You can check out my fingernails and my teeth if it'll make you feel better. Hand me a crucifix, whatever."

"That religious shit doesn't work, man. I got crucifixes and Stars of David and I can light candles to seven different saints, because I figure, what the fuck, you know? Just in case. But the truth is they don't care about that stuff, that's just all fictional nonsense."

"Can I come in, Mr. Gross? Because I've got to tell you, it's not exactly warm and toasty out here, and we've established that you are Donald Gross and I don't care what you've got going on in here. I just need to learn what you can tell me about the vampires."

Donald's head bobbed and he fumbled with the screen door lock. "Sure, sure, sorry," he said. "Come on in, I guess. Just, you know, don't mind the mess and whatever."

As Andy climbed the little metal steps into the door, the smell of ammonia almost knocked him back outside. He considered asking Donald to open a window, but then decided that would just ratchet up the man's paranoia again. When he was in, he saw what Donald was worried about him seeing: the arrangement of hot plates, batteries, beakers, propane, and chemicals that indicated a homegrown meth lab.

No surprise that the writer had stopped checking in with his editors. From the looks of him, his drug habit was nothing new.

In the front section of the trailer was a little dining table with a bench-style seat. Donald shoved a stack of papers off onto the floor and invited Andy to sit. Andy did, putting his gloves and ski mask on the table, but

Donald stayed on his feet, bobbing and weaving like a punch-drunk fighter. He leaned down and picked up an envelope from the pile he had just tossed aside. "You want vampires?" he asked. "Look at this. It's a preapproved credit card solicitation. They want me to consolidate my other credit cards onto this one card at a low introductory rate. Isn't that great? Then after six months the rate shoots up to twenty percent or something." He started to laugh, a bit manically, Andy thought. "And you know what's really beautiful? I mean, look at me! Do I look like I have any fucking money to you?"

Andy didn't respond. From the looks of it he wouldn't have to say much of anything. "But the thing is," Donald rambled on, "they do this all the time. They make credit cards easy for poor people to get. Then they hit them with offers to consolidate their payments. Eventually the poor suckers are paying most of whatever they make in interest to banks and credit card companies, and when they can't pay any more then the banks just garnish their paycheck, if they have one, before the people even see it."

He stopped pacing and talking at the same time, looked at Andy. "Sorry," he said. "I get too much time to think up here and nothing to do with what I come up with. I read the news off the Internet and it just pisses me off."

"I know the feeling," Andy said, finally able to get a

word in. "But you didn't move here to get away from the *corporate* bloodsuckers. What are you doing here in Barrow?"

Donald eyeballed Andy like he was looking at an insane person. "This is the safest place in the world, man," he said. "These people have fought them off more times than anybody. They know, man. They know what they're doing and how to beat them."

"By 'them,' you mean . . . ?"

"Vampires, man! The bloodsucking undead."

"Just making sure," Andy said. "So you feel safe here?"

"Safer than anywhere else. I don't know if I'd say safe, but safe*r*."

"Even though they've attacked here twice."

"That's right," Donald said. "Because they're everywhere else, too, you know? Only everywhere else, they have free rein. Here, they can't even get in anymore."

"Did you know about them before the Kingston House hooked you up with Stella?" Andy asked.

Donald turned his gaze toward the ceiling, as if Stella's name were written up there somewhere. With his left hand he reached under his sweatshirt and scratched his protruding gut. "No, I guess not. I mean, not that they were really real."

"How did you know she wasn't just making the whole thing up?" Andy asked him. "I mean, I know from personal experience that it takes a lot to convince someone of something like that, when he's been told his whole life that it's nothing but superstitious nonsense. How did Stella persuade you?"

Donald stopped his perpetual motion for a moment. "She just spoke the truth, man."

His eyes grew clearer as he spoke.

"You know, when you hear the truth and you just know, you can just see that it's true, like it's wrapped in a golden light or some shit." He paused, shook his head as if to chase away unseen insects, and went on. "And also, she brought me up here, man, showed me some shit you wouldn't believe."

Which was what Andy had been driving at in the first place.

He figured the guy was—had been, anyway—a professional writer who, according to Carol Hino, could write just about anything. So he probably could have told Stella's story even if he didn't believe.

But he was clearly a believer now, so something had to have swayed him.

"Like what?" Andy pressed. "What did she show you?"

Donald wrapped his arms around himself in a bear hug. "Oh, so much, so much. Not just her, but since I've been here I've been kind of collecting, I guess. Saving it all."

"Can you show it to me?"

Andy didn't know why, but Donald suddenly looked terrified.

He gestured toward a dark doorway, which Andy assumed was the trailer's bedroom. "It's in there, man. I keep it all in there."

Andy had to fight not to shrug. "But can I see it?"

A furtive smile. "Sure, hold on, I'll get it out." He went into the other room, turned on a light. *Addicts,* Andy thought, shaking his head sadly. *Guy was probably half smart once.*

When Donald emerged, he was carrying a skull. He set it down with a thump on the little table.

It looked, for the most part, like any other human skull.

Except for the teeth.

Andy had seen Paul's new dental work up close, and the jawbone he'd found at Amos Saxon's house, and these teeth reminded him of those.

Sharp fangs surrounded by rows of tiny razor teeth, like a shark in miniature.

No human ever had a mouth like that.

"Where . . . where did you get this?" Andy asked with barely concealed awe. If it was real and not some masterpiece of sculpting, it would go a long way toward convincing doubters. There might even be marrow with DNA material that could be extracted.

"Ikos gave it to me," Donald said. "When Stella and I were working on the book. He said he wanted me to have it."

"What else do you have?" Andy asked, his excitement building.

"Right back." Donald went into the other room

again, came out with a wooden box. The box was carved on top and scalloped on the edges, detailed with brass hinges and hasp.

Donald put it on the table beside the skull. "Open it."

Andy did. Inside he found red velvet lining, and nestled in that a small plastic bottle. It could have been a NyQuil bottle. Seemed strange to find something so mundane in such an elaborate container. "What is it?" he asked.

Donald picked the bottle up, shook it, held it up to the overhead light. Andy tried to see through the green plastic. Some dark liquid. "It's blood," Donald said. "From one of them."

"That's vampire blood?!"

The Holy Grail. If only he'd had it when Felicia had been alive to do something with it. Hell, if he'd known about it he would never have come up with that stupid plan to trap a vampire, and Felicia, Angel, and Raven would all be alive.

"That's right," Donald said. "I got it myself, during the last attack. Somebody blew one's head off, right outside. I grabbed a bottle and rinsed it and ran out and filled it up."

"That's incredible," Andy said, unable to help himself. He'd tried to play it cool with this guy, but the things he was seeing were just astounding. If he could get these to scientists . . .

"You want to see the real goods?" Donald asked.

Why do you think I'm here? Andy thought. "Definitely."

Donald went into the bedroom one more time, returning with a DVD. "You like movies?"

"Sure," Andy said, hoping the writer wasn't planning to show him one of the dozens of versions of *Dracula,* or something worse. Donald went to a little TV/DVD combo unit and ejected a disk—the porn that had been playing before, Andy guessed—replacing it with the one he carried.

"I got this from Stella," he said. "She never even saw it until after we wrote the book, when she was on tour. She burned a copy for me and mailed it to me, for safekeeping, she said. I guess she met this woman whose son shot the video, while she was in LA."

Andy remembered a woman that Stella befriended while she was there for the UCLA gig, a lifetime ago. Woman turned up dead, he remembered. *What was her name again?*

Donald started the disk, and Andy watched, spellbound. First static, then a couple of seconds of black screen. But then an image filled the screen. Dark rectangles, structures. The screen flared where some of them were on fire. A male voice, terrified, could barely be heard over the chop of a propeller. This was taken from a helicopter, then. *"The place is torn apart,"* he thought the voice was saying. *"There's blood everywhere."*

Andy went closer to the little TV, wishing it had a bigger screen, better definition. The copter was drifting lower, more detail coming into view, but it was still hard to make out on this little set. He was pretty sure he was seeing bodies in the snow, haloed in crimson. Then a struggle, someone trying to get away from a stronger someone. The strong one whipped the other around, finally slamming the weaker one on the ground.

Finally, a sudden ripping motion. Blood fountained toward the copter from a ravaged throat. The stronger one bent toward the blood, and then his bulk blocked the camera's view.

"He's feeding," Donald said. "See that?"

"Yeah," Andy said in a hushed voice. He was trying to make out the pilot's words, but they were slurred, inaudible over the helicopter's roar. But that's what it had looked like to him, too.

He's feeding.

Suddenly there was a loud *whump* and the image jerked crazily.

"What's happening?" Andy asked.

"Just keep watching."

The camera bounced around as it dropped toward the earth. The helicopter must have been under attack, Andy guessed. Maybe someone down below had shot out the tail rotor. It spun as it fell; just watching it was making Andy seasick. He could see more flaming buildings, more dark figures moving about the town, more blood in the snow. Lots more blood.

He heard a loud scream. The pilot? Then another

voice, deep and confident, with maybe a trace of European inflection although it was hard to be sure over the copter's noise, said, *"Where do you think you're going?"*

The pilot shrieked something back, but his words were unclear, muddied by terror. The camera continued its dizzying fall, but then, almost as if the pilot had somehow regained control—of himself, of his equipment—it panned up, away from the ground and toward the front of the helicopter. Now the dark sky whipped around and around behind the windshield.

But something else blocked part of the sky. Andy had to look away, blink, and look back, because he just couldn't believe what he was seeing.

And there it was.

A vampire—bald, bat-eared, wearing a dark suit and a red tie—clung to the windshield of the spiraling aircraft. Blood spewing from his open mouth, spattering the glass and blowing away in the furious wind. His clawed fingers digging through the glass, until finally it shattered in his grip and he lunged inside.

The screen went black again, and Donald Gross ejected the disk.

Andy sat staring at the TV.

Sure, the whole thing could have been special effects, CGI.

He didn't think it had.

Something about the vampire on the helicopter, clinging, almost calm, like what he was doing was no big deal.

Like he knew he'd survive it.

His eyes, wide and feral. His clutching hands reaching in for the pilot.

"God, that poor guy," Andy said. He shivered even though it was warm inside the trailer.

"Gotta figure the impact killed him, so they didn't," Donald pointed out.

"That's probably true," Andy said. "But . . . my God . . . that was . . . awful."

"That's why I wanted to show it to you," Donald said. He seemed more subdued now, as if the drugs were wearing off. Or kicking in.

"Have you shown it to anyone else?"

"Are you crazy?" Donald asked. "Do you know what they'd do to me?"

"But they can't get to you here."

Donald leaned against the kitchen counter, all the manic energy sapped out of him. "I know. But everyone here knows about them, so they don't need to be convinced. We don't get many strangers here, and I don't talk to the ones who do come. I wouldn't have talked to you if John hadn't sent you."

Judith Ali. That was the name of the woman Stella had met in Los Angeles. "Do they know who the pilot was?"

"I don't think so," Donald said. "Doubt if there was enough left of him to identify. But where his chopper came down?"

"What about it?" Andy asked.

"Where we're sitting now," Donald said. "Used to be some stores right here, but the chopper exploded, took them all out. Lot was vacant until I moved onto it."

"Urban renewal," Andy remarked. "But I still don't understand why you didn't take this stuff out of Barrow, show it to the rest of the world. That's what Stella was trying to do, right?"

"And look what happened to her. They want to stay a secret, man. They have to. And they'll do anything to make sure. It's the perfect cover, right? We don't exist, so don't waste your time looking for us. We're the boogeyman, the thing your big brother told you about to scare you on the family camping trip. But we're not real, oh no. You'd just be wasting your time."

"I've run across some of that, too," Andy admitted.

"It's their best defense, and they know it. So if anyone tries to prove they're real, then look out, man, because you've just painted a huge fucking Day-Glo target on your ass. Ever see that movie, *The Usual Suspects?*"

Andy nodded. "What about it?"

"You remember what Kevin Spacey said in that? 'The greatest trick the devil ever pulled was convincing the world he didn't exist.' I think about that every day, man."

A chill settled over Andy, one not from the Arctic deep-freeze of Barrow.

"That's why I live up here," Donald Gross continued. "It ain't for the weather, or the money, or the chicks. I just want to keep out of the crosshairs."

Andy understood. He was already working on a way he could get the writer's proof back down to civilization, while keeping Donald Gross's name out of it. He would take all the heat. He was fine with that.

He was about to say so when the whole world caved in.

29

ACTUALLY, it didn't so much cave in as explode, Andy decided in the fraction of a second before he saw what did it.

The far wall of the trailer, on the other side of the little kitchen area, just seemed to rip off of its own accord. He knew that meth labs sometimes detonated and wondered if that's what was happening here, that somehow his brain was unable to process the fireball and the noise and was just observing the effects.

But Paul Norris was standing where the wall had been, blood running from his hands where he'd cut them tearing the trailer apart, a smirky scowl on his ugly face.

"Hey, partner!" Paul yelled. "Thanks for leading me right to him!"

It took Andy a few seconds to react.

The booze he'd had that night, the fact that he still hadn't slept, maybe the outright terror at facing Paul again after all this time, slowed him down. But he reached for his Glock. "I didn't lead you anywhere," he said. "I haven't seen you in ages."

Paul laughed, and it was an unpleasant sound, just as

bad as it had always been. Paul's laughter had always been utterly without joy and usually directed at some other poor unfortunate. "That's true," he said as he climbed inside. The damaged trailer shifted under his weight. "But you've been flashing Bureau ID all over Alaska. Did you really think I wouldn't hear about it? And know it was you?"

He came closer.

Donald Gross was behind Andy now, terrified wet sobs bubbling up from his throat. "You two have had quite the bonding session in here, haven't you?" he continued. "Believe me, Andy, I also wanted to come in and get reacquainted a long time ago, but I wanted to hear what old Donald had on us first. Not a bad collection for a washed-up junkie."

"Please . . ." Donald said.

"Just leave him alone, Paul," Andy said. "This is between you and me."

Paul made a sad face. "Oh, that's right, I'm a bad friend, boo fucking hoo. Don't you get it, Andy? It's never been personal between us. It's just that I'm trying to keep a secret and you keep nibbling around the edges of it, sort of like a scared rabbit in a vegetable garden."

"Maybe not as scared as you'd like to think," Andy said, hoping the show of bravado would disguise the panic he was feeling.

From behind, a new stench overpowered the ammonia. Donald had soiled himself.

Andy knew he'd only get one chance, and he had to take it in the next second or two or it would be too late. He had to get Paul's head off, which he couldn't do with the Glock alone. But if he could get Paul outside, then maybe he could use a shard of aluminum from the trailer's torn skin to finish the job.

He aimed and squeezed the trigger in the same motion.

But Paul was faster.

He covered the remaining space between them and slapped Andy's gun hand up. The shot tore through the trailer's roof. Before Andy could react, Paul punched him twice, first in the stomach and then, as he doubled over from the blow, in the chin.

Andy spun away from the second shot, into the kitchen, his flailing arms knocking over the meth paraphernalia and the little TV.

He collapsed against the counter and felt it all falling on top of him as consciousness slipped away.

Paul didn't even spare a glance for his old friend.

Andy was down, finished.

The threat, absurdly enough, was from the emaciated man blubbering in front of him with the stained pants. This was the man who could expose him, expose all his kind.

He had been Stella Olemaun's ally, her sounding board. He knew as much as she did, and he had the "collection" to prove it.

He looked pathetic—he *was* pathetic—but he required Paul Norris's attention, immediate and undivided.

The writer made no attempt to escape. His feet were probably cemented in place by his own bodily fluids. From deep in his throat he made a kind of gasping, hitching sound. If he was trying to beg for mercy, he was doing a poor job of it. Tears ran down his sunken cheeks and snot bubbled at his nostrils. Sickened by the sight of him—but hoping some of his drugs were still in his veins—Paul charged forward through the detritus of his life and grabbed the back of his scrawny neck. With his other hand, he hooked his clawed fingernails into the man's throat and tore, shredding skin and artery.

Blood jetted from the gash, splashing Paul's clothing and skin. He thrilled to the metallic scent, the hot liquid stream, pulsing in time with Donald Gross's failing heart. The sensation was almost sexual, and as always at the beginning of a meal, Paul's senses were alive, tingling with expectation. His delight was enhanced by the fact that Gross still lived, his eyes wide with horror, his lip quivering, his arms and legs jerking and kicking as Paul held him still.

Paul lowered him to the floor of the trailer, almost as gently as if he were a lover. The blood sprayed into Paul's face now, getting in his eyes, up his nose, dripping down between his lips.

Paul ran his tongue over his lips, tasting it, and laughed softly.

The writer tried to jerk out of his grip, even in the last moments of his life too afraid to accept his fate. He knew what was coming, though, and that was enough to satisfy Paul.

He lowered his face to the wound, opened his mouth, fixed his lips around it. His sharp teeth bit and tore at the mangled flesh as the blood rushed into his mouth. He swallowed quickly, not wanting to waste any more of the precious fluid than he already had.

He had done this enough times, knew at what point the world was darkening for his prey, closing off like shutters over a window.

Norris could feel the life slipping away from Donald Gross, so he stopped once, clamping his hand over the severed artery to staunch the flow, and put his eyes close to the writer's.

"Now, was helping the Olemaun bitch write her book worth all this?" he asked.

Unable to speak, the only response Gross made was a terrified fluttering of the eyelids.

It was good enough for Paul. He released the artery and drank deep.

When he was finished feasting, he looked around for dessert.

But Andy had taken off while Norris was enjoying the writer.

Always clever, old Andy, especially when it came to running away.

A pair of gloves and a ski mask sat on the dining

table, he noted—if they belonged to Andy, in Alaska only a short while, he would be regretting their absence soon enough.

Alone in the trailer, he chuckled. He should go after Andy, but he had already been here an awfully long time.

After his near destruction at the hands of the deceased Stella Olemaun, he had vowed never to return to Barrow. Next time she got to him, John Ikos might not be around to drag him to safety. At any rate, he wouldn't be as careless as he had been before.

And even though Andy was probably on his way to call for reinforcements, Paul had more important business right here.

Finally killing Donald Gross was a plus, but it didn't address the issue of his collection of vampire evidence. The proof could speak far louder in the writer's absence than Gross could without the goods.

Beside the TV, he found the DVD with the footage of the first Barrow attack. He had already destroyed one of these, the one he took from Judith Ali, way back when all this had started. He hadn't known, at the time, that she had already given a copy to Stella Olemaun, or that Olemaun had had time to burn a copy for Gross. But she'd had a whole crew working for her then, so any one of them could have done it.

The footage was damning, no doubt about that.

This disk had been around for a couple of years without getting more widely disseminated, though. He suspected that this was the last copy out there (beyond the Internet issues that he'd heard some others of his kind were dealing with)—Stella Olemaun's own copy was long since lost or destroyed. He held it between finger and thumb and squeezed, bending it in half. Then he bent it back the other way, repeated it a couple more times, and finally snapped it in half along the stress line he'd made.

The skull was next. He dashed it to the trailer's floor and ground it under his feet until it was dust.

In Donald Gross's bedroom he found folder after folder of news clippings, letters, and the like, which he brought back to the kitchen. If there was anything a meth head had plenty of, it was flammable liquids. He dumped some onto the pile of paper.

Just before he dropped a match, he saw the wooden box. Didn't Gross claim that it contained vampire blood? Well, that wouldn't do.

He shook the match out and retrieved the box from where it had slid, behind the kitchen counter. Unhooked the little brass hasp.

Empty.

He sniffed the velvet lining. Faint traces of blood.

Andy, Andy, Andy.

Double-checking to make sure he had taken care of everything else, Paul struck another wooden match and tossed it on the saturated pile. It caught with a *whoosh* and flames shot up, licking at the trailer's ceiling.

He had originally caught up with Andy outside

town, between there and the trapper's cabin. Andy, not knowing he was being followed, had left perfectly clear footprints. Paul had walked in Andy's path, not leaving one of his own.

On the way out, however, Andy had been smart enough to walk in the same prints. Paul followed suit, knowing at some point Andy would veer away. He moved fast, sure that the fire in the trailer would turn out the townsfolk even if Andy hadn't raised a general alarm.

Surprisingly, he never saw Andy's footsteps diverge from his earlier path. Andy took the same route, down quiet side streets, to the edge of town and through a small gate. As he had earlier, Paul avoided the gate and the tower bank of UV lights. He rushed to the center point of this section of fence, where the lights of the two corner towers met on their regular sweeps. But after they met, there was a moment when both lights were sweeping in the other direction, and chances were that the eyes of the guards directing them were doing the same. Paul waited for that moment, took a running leap, and sailed over the fence. Same way he had come in. He wondered when they'd plug that hole.

Safely on the far side, Norris breathed a sigh of relief and located the tracks again. Now that he was out of town and not in danger of being spotted, he moved faster. Finally, a mile or so from the fence, Andy stepped away from the existing tracks and set off toward a forested patch of wilderness.

You fucking idiot. You think you can outrun me? Out here? At least in town you had a slim chance of survival.

He stalked on, ever faster, following the prints in the crusted snow.

Even with his eyesight, far better since he had changed—as the rest of him was, in virtually every way—he was almost on top of Andy before he saw him. The dusky light was hard to penetrate and Andy had gone to his knees just below a rise. Paul literally smelled him before he saw him, sweat and blood and fear rising off the snow like steam.

When he topped the low hill he saw Andy down below, turned away from him, kneeling down. He thought maybe his old friend had tripped and, in his exhaustion, was having a hard time getting up.

He could fix that.

Not so Andy would be getting up, but so he'd never have to worry about doing so again.

He moved closer, silent as falling snow.

And then he stopped cold.

The snow in front of Andy was splotched red with blood.

Below his right hand was a plastic bottle, empty. The kind cold medicine came in.

Traces of blood adhered to its insides.

Beside that, a Swiss Army knife, blade open and bloody.

Paul recognized the knife. He should. He had given it to Andy, years before.

And Andy had read Stella's book, goddammit. He knew what Eben Olemaun had done, how he had defeated Vicente, driven off the first invasion.

"Andy," he said, projecting boldness he didn't entirely feel. "You don't know what you've done."

Paul's voice, so close behind, chilled Andy more than all of Alaska's ice and snow.

He had intended for the vampire to follow him, of course. Was he really ready for it, though? Past time to figure that out.

"I think I have a pretty good idea," he said. His voice cracked a little, but he mostly kept it under control. *Just play it cool. Let him be Paul.*

"I've been playing you like a violin, Andy. Like what's his name, Perlman, with his favorite Stradivarius. All along, you didn't know who was plucking your strings . . . but it was me."

"Bullshit, Paul," Andy said. Getting his feet under him, he struggled upright. "You lost track of me, you haven't known where I was for years. You just told me you found me again after I got to Alaska."

"Sure, I wasn't on you every day," Paul said. Andy had always known when he was bluffing. "But I've been one step ahead of you all the way."

More truth to that, but Paul was still just blustering. Andy drew strength from that certainty.

"You don't honestly think this is going to work?"

"It worked for Eben Olemaun," Andy reminded him.

"And I have a hunch against tougher vampires than you."

"Bring it, then, baby. Show me what you got."

"That's not like you, Paul." Andy started to turn, slowly, blood still running off his left wrist. "You were never a fighter. You would never put yourself on the line if there was an easier way out." Fat drops of blood rolled off his fingertips, plopping into the snow.

"Sure you're not getting us confused, buddy?" Paul asked. He couldn't seem to take his eyes off Andy's bloody arm. "You did always want to be me, after all."

Andy shook his head. "No, you just always thought that. There were times you almost had me convinced. But I've been away from you long enough to figure myself out—figure both of us out, I guess. And the truth is I have no interest in being anything like you. You've never earned a thing in your life, just taken what's been handed to you. Just took whatever came along like it was owed to you. News flash, pal. The world owes you jack, except for the pain you've inflicted on it."

Paul's laughter was genuine, but without a trace of warmth. "Ouch. You wound me, old friend."

Andy's patience had run out. Besides, he needed to get this done with. "You killed my family, didn't you?"

"You fucked my wife."

The perfect Paul Norris response.

"You killed my family!" Andy repeated. Louder this time, almost shouting. Had he really been friends with this guy? Yeah, if he hadn't been he wouldn't be so pissed now. *"Didn't you?!"*

"Yes," Paul answered. "Yes, I did."

Not remorseful at all. Boastful, even.

Which was good. Made the rest of this easier.

"That's what I wanted to know," Andy said.

Paul Norris didn't get it.

Andy Gray should be cowering in terror.

He had mixed the vampire blood with his own, but he hadn't changed yet. Until he did, he was helpless against Paul's strength.

Instead, Andy was advancing toward him.

Not in any hurry, but steadily, step by purposeful step. Andy's eyes ticked to the left, as if he was glancing over Paul's shoulder. Maybe if they hadn't both been through the Academy together, he'd have fallen for that.

Unless . . .

The blood had stopped flowing from Andy's wrist.

No wound there.

Just leftover traces of blood drying on his arm.

He hadn't cut himself at all. Just poured some of that blood on his arm.

Ah, fuck me!

Paul started to turn . . .

When Paul figured it out, Andy knew it from his face.

Paul had changed—hell, who didn't? But not so much that Andy couldn't gauge his reactions. The flaring of his nostrils, the minute widening of his eyes. Oh, did his old friend *hate* to be tricked.

Paul started to turn around, to see what was behind him that Andy was looking at. As he did, Andy spotted the red laser dot sliding across Paul's cheek.

The impact came first, then the boom of the weapon, crackling across the snowy landscape, echoing like thunder.

But the impact . . .

Paul Norris's head *exploded* off his neck and collapsed like a punctured balloon, all at once.

Andy's face was spattered with blood and brain and a tooth hit his left cheek just below his eye.

The deflated bulk of Paul's head, flat on one side like a blown tire, spun half a dozen times before it plowed into the snow.

Paul's body remained upright, hands raised sternum high, swiveling his hips, looking for all the world like a surprised man searching for something he'd misplaced.

Which isn't too far from the truth, Andy thought.

Norris actually took two steps toward his own head before his knees buckled. They hit the snow and he stayed there, his arms flung out behind him now as if for balance. Blood burbled up from his open neck. He stayed upright until Andy stalked over to him and booted him in the chest, at which point he teetered backward. His knees slid out from under him and his headless corpse collapsed, all the residual life gone.

Let the dead be dead.

Just in case, Andy checked on the head, half expecting that it would still be alive, snapping and snarling and complaining about the injustice done to it.

It was, thankfully, silent, half blown away, the tattered flesh of Paul's homely face revealing bone and part of that vampiric jaw.

Andy kicked snow at it, smiling at his own juvenile response. He went back to the corpse and hoisted it by the collar. Paul seemed almost weightless, but Andy figured it was his own elation more than the absence of a few pounds of head that made the difference. He didn't have the little bottle of vampire blood anymore, but he had something better.

A whole vampire, or most of one.

Paul's death didn't make up for the loss of Monica, Sara, and Lisa. It couldn't begin to. But it was a step on the right road, at last. And with Paul's body in hand he could make progress toward getting past Felicia, Angel, and Raven's deaths as well.

The only way to justify those was to do what he had promised Felicia—drag the existence of these bloodsucking shitbags kicking and screaming into the light of day.

He hauled Norris's body toward John Ikos's bunker, only realizing as it started to grow heavy that he had misjudged the distance. Good thing John was a hell of a shot, because he had left him far more yardage than anticipated.

The trapper himself stood in his doorway, limned by yellow light from behind him. When he got close enough, Andy could see the beginnings of a smile on his bearded face. He dropped the headless body to the ground at John's feet.

"Nice work," John Ikos said.

"Nice shooting. Sorry about the distance."

"Not a problem."

"I'm just glad you saw us."

"Guess you haven't been here long enough to know," John said. "Nothing gets by me."

"I'm getting that impression. I sort of figured it out earlier, so . . ." Andy inclined his head toward the body on the ground. "Would have been safer if we'd discussed it before, maybe, but I had a hunch it'd work out."

John squatted over the body, flipped it over onto its back. "This the guy? Norris? Hard to tell without a head."

"That's him. Not enough left of the head to carry."

"The scavengers will appreciate the gift," John said.

"They're welcome to it," Andy replied. He laughed. "As long as it doesn't turn them into some weird vampire scavengers."

John actually considered it for a moment. "Seems unlikely."

Both men stood in the cold and the dark, though

Andy kept glancing toward the east, as if the sun would be coming up any time. It wouldn't, not for weeks and weeks.

"So," John said, breaking the silence. "You going to stick around, now it's all over?"

A shrug. "I missed the last flight out, so it looks like I'll be here for a while. But who says it's over?" He reached into one of his parka's oversized pockets and pulled out the DVD he had liberated from Donald Gross's place. *Hope the porn disk that Paul no doubt destroyed wasn't a rental, or borrowed from someone,* he thought. "I'm just getting started."

"Well, ain't that a bitch?" John Ikos broke into laughter. It sounded awkward, and Andy figured it was rare for him. He didn't care. He hadn't been laughing himself much, not for a long, long time. Awkward it may have been, but he remembered that, back in the distant past, he had liked it.

He joined in. Chuckling at first, but then he felt it building in him, and he threw his head back and let it out.

There in the cold and dark of the world's longest night, his fingers and face numb and brittle feeling, his best friend and his worst enemy dead at his feet and the man who had killed him standing at his side, Andy Gray roared.

Roared in exhaustion.

In grief.

In triumph.

ABOUT THE AUTHORS

STEVE NILES is one of the writers responsible for bringing horror comics back to prominence, and was recently named by *Fangoria* magazine as one of its "13 rising talents who promise to keep us terrified for the next 25 years." Among his works are *30 Days of Night, Dark Days, 30 Days of Night: Return to Barrow, 30 Days of Night: Bloodsucker Tales, Criminal Macabre, Wake the Dead, Freaks of the Heartland, Hyde, Alistair Arcane,* and *Fused. 30 Days of Night, Criminal Macabre, Wake the Dead, Hyde,* and *Alistair Arcane* are currently in development as major motion pictures. Niles got his start in the industry when he formed his own publishing company called Arcane Comix, where he published, edited, and adapted several comics and anthologies for Eclipse Comics. His adaptations include works by Clive Barker, Richard Matheson, and Harlan Ellison. He also recently formed Creep Entertainment with Rob Zombie, as well as the film production company Raw Entertainment with Tom Jane. Niles resides in Los Angeles with his wife Nikki and their three black cats. No word on just what is buried in the crawlspace, though. Visit his official site at www.steveniles.com

JEFF MARIOTTE is the author of more than thirty novels, including several set in the universes of *Buffy the Vampire Slayer* and *Angel, Charmed, Las Vegas, Conan, Star Trek,* and *Andromeda,* the original horror novel *The Slab,* and Stoker Award–nominated teen horror series *Witch Season,* as well as more comic books than he has time to count, some of which have been nominated for Bram Stoker and International Horror Guild awards. With his wife Maryelizabeth Hart and partner Terry Gilman, he co-owns Mysterious Galaxy, a bookstore specializing in science fiction, fantasy, mystery, and horror. He lives on the Flying M Ranch in southeastern Arizona with his family and pets, in a home filled with books, music, toys, and other examples of American pop culture. More information than you would ever want to know about him is at www.jeffmariotte.com.